The Urbana Free Library

To renew materials call
217-367-4057

A COLD DAY IN HELL

Ken Rand

Copyright © 2009 by Ken Rand

All Rights Reserved.

Cover Images:
"Sunset in Saguaro National Park" (2005), Shizao; "Welcome To Vegas" (2005) by David Vasquez; "Graveyard under Snow" by Caspar David Friedrich (1826).

Cover Design Copyright © 2009 by Vera Nazarian

ISBN-13: 978-1-934648-89-6
ISBN-10: 1-934648-89-2

FIRST EDITION
Trade Hardcover

February 1, 2009

A Publication of
Norilana Books
P. O. Box 2188
Winnetka, CA 91396
www.norilana.com

Printed in the United States of America

A Cold Day
In Hell

Norilana Books

www.norilana.com

Other Books by Ken Rand

Novels

The Paradox Stone
Phoenix
Golems of Laramie County
Fairy BrewHaHa at the Lucky Nickel Saloon
Dadgum Martians Invade the Lucky Nickel Saloon!
Pax Dakota

Collections

Tales of the Lucky Nickel Saloon
Through Wyoming Eyes
Bad News from Orbit
Soul Taster: Four Dark Tales
Where Angels Fear
The Gods Perspire

Nonfiction

The 10% Solution: Self-Editing for the Modern Writer
From Idea to Story in 90 Seconds: A Writer's Primer
Human Visions: the Talebones Interviews
The Editor Is IN
Kaleidoscopes Made Semi-Easy
In Their Own Words: The Port Chicago Letters
Dan Colchico: In Defense of Port Chicago
Port Chicago Isn't There AnymoreBut We Still Call It Home

A COLD DAY IN HELL

A Novel

Ken Rand

Dog

Dog sighed and upped the chances against a steak breakfast from Hell to one in ten.

The girl rent-a-cop had snuck out a bundle of frozen t-bones Wednesday, three nights ago, or Thursday morning, actually, and set them by Hell's back door for Teresa Santiago to grab and share with Dog and other Las Vegas streeties. She didn't do it again last night as Dog had hoped she would. He'd waited all night for it to happen—Teresa was busy, so she wasn't there to do the grabbing. The duty fell to him, but it didn't happen.

Somewhere between two and four a.m. he gave up waiting for the girl rent-a-cop to be charitable again and started plotting to go into Hell to do it himself.

Damn, but those steaks were good. Dog, Teresa, and a couple other streeties had commandeered a dry swimming pool behind a house under construction in the new Cascade Hills subdivision between Laramie and Memphis Street. They'd organized a few two-by-fours for firewood, and other essentials, and set to breakfast. Nobody around.

Somebody had screwed up—bank or lawyer or contractor, who gave a rat's ass—and work on the subdivision had stopped weeks earlier. Fifty or so houses semi-built, abandoned, right in the middle of Las Vegas, more or less. It was hot, even at 8 a.m. or so, when the feast began. A hot day, nobody out, except gypsies, tramps, and thieves having themselves a clandestine breakfast barbecue in a swimming pool in an abandoned housing development on t-bone steaks stolen from Hell. Damn good t-bone steaks.

Dog's stomach growled again and he re-upped the odds to one in twenty against. She wasn't going to do it tonight either.

To hell with the girl guard, Dog thought, but not bitterly. He understood. Nice of her to help, but it wasn't right to expect she'd do it again. Maybe she got cold feet, figured even as she did it how stupid it was to steal stuff from the place she was supposed to guard—then giving the stuff to unreliable riffraff such as Teresa Santiago, and Dog, and their comrades. The girl had been dumb for a minute, but she smartened up quick enough. At least she hadn't gotten caught, or fired. Dog had seen her go to work hours ago, after sundown, when he began his vigil by the big trash bin outside Hell.

Hadn't Teresa said the guard had a kid? Real bummer if she'd gotten canned.

Damn Teresa Santiago anyhow, probably got the girl all excited, chatting her up. She did that a lot, Santiago did—getting people excited. She was good at raising a crowd for a protest rally, playing to the cameras and reporters, pissing off the State, but sometimes she got carried away. Working up that little guard into stealing—

Ah, well. Done is done. Dog shook his head, exasperated, but he couldn't stay pissed at Teresa Santiago. Not for long.

So, it wasn't going to happen again—thirty to one against. Unless . . .

Unless Dog went into Hell and got them himself.

If that doe-eyed little girl-cop who looked like a high school cheerleader and weighed ninety pounds if she had a Volkswagen in her purse could summon up the guts to steal steaks to give to the homeless—at considerable risk and no benefit to herself and her youngun's security—then he could damn well summon up the same guts. Which, as if on cue, growled again. He wished he had some Tumeze.

If he got busted—well, bummer, but now and then, a guy has to roll the dice.

Dog reviewed the possibilities. B&E, theft, vandalism. He wouldn't get out of jail till Monday morning, soonest. Not a pleasant prospect. Weighed against . . .

On Dallas Street—across the Hell back parking lot, toward the west, sixty or seventy yards away or so—a cruiser stopped, bubble-gum lights flashing blue and red against the pink adobe wall of the Foxtrot Triple-X Bookstore on the far side of the street. Dog scootched back farther into the trash bin shadow at Hell's backside and watched the pigs roust Booger from his sleep hidey in the recessed doorway of Cantrell and Son's DDS walkup above the bookstore.

Mostly toothless, alcoholic, inoffensive Booger took the rousting with his usual smiling, bleary-eyed stoicism. One pig was Dennis the Menace, a good enough cop, but still a cop. The other was new and Dog didn't recognize him. The new one held Booger's raggedy coat collar with one hand and smacked his bald dome with the other hand like he was dusting it off. Whack, whack, whack. Not hard, but slow, deliberate and persistent, as if he were swatting a puppy who'd gone potty on the sofa. Not angry, but annoyed. Dog could see sweat spray off Booger's dome with each pop the pig gave him, even at this distance, a glistening shower in the red and blue flashing circus light.

Dog heard their voices, but not what they said. Booger's blubbery, nervous giggle floated to Dog over the super-heated night air, interrupted like a hiccup by the pig's leisurely, meaty smacks to his dome, and Dog remembered why Booger didn't have any teeth. He suddenly felt angry—an old, familiar feeling, like a toothache.

His stomach growled again. Fifty to one or more against a steak breakfast delivered, but who gave a shit? Dog resolved to snatch some steaks from Hell just as soon as the pig finished dusting poor old Booger's bronze scalp and hauled him off. He'd save a juicy slab for Booger, somehow.

Dennis the Menace sighed, rescued Booger from his partner's recreational bum-thumping, and put Booger in the cruiser's back seat. The pigs drove off, Dennis shaking his head and chiding his partner, the younger, stupider, piggier pig.

Dog waited a few minutes, then came out from behind the trash bin. He looked around.

The parking lot behind Hell had ten or fifteen cars in it though it had a capacity of maybe a couple hundred. It was Saturday night—Sunday morning, actually, but that didn't mean anything in Las Vegas. The place was always humming, any time, any day. It never slept. The cars were parked on the far side, closer to Dallas Street. Maybe spill-over patrons of the Sunset Bistro, half a block up from the Foxtrot, around the corner. It was better lit there, toward the west side, and the Strip four blocks beyond. That part of the lot was finished, yellow lines freshly painted, and not littered with mounds of dirt, construction equipment, lumber stacks, plywood, and rebar, cardboard and wooden boxes stacked on pallets, and the detritus that accumulated near any building under construction, as the casino part of the Hell restaurant-hotel-casino still was.

Dog watched the occasional boisterous couple heading to or from a car. A drunk pissed in the same dark doorway Booger had been rousted from a minute earlier. Now and then in the past few hours, somebody or two, drunk or sober, would take a shortcut through gaps in the inadequate, tottery, chain link fence around the building stuff and the industrial trash bin where Dog crouched.

Hell's backside parking lot was too damn busy, though not as busy as the Strip, and Dog didn't see his chances for a break to improve. A hundred to one against the girl delivering, and like odds of getting away with do-it-yourself take-out. Damn.

Dog's stomach growled. Again.

Do it or don't, risk it or not. Dawn would come soon, and he was down to decision time.

If he wrote it off, he could get a good spot in line for breakfast at Jesus' Bread Basket over on Nashville. Dog hadn't eaten anything notable since steak breakfast the day before yesterday. He'd gotten tangled with a bunch of drifters later that day who had a gallon of Ripple, and there'd been a fight and he'd ended up passed out, or unconscious, he didn't remember which and when he woke up, he was on the other side of town. Then he'd been sick, and—something else, he didn't remember what, exactly. Anyway, he hadn't eaten in a long time.

Now, if he stayed, waited. . . .

It was hot—damn hot—where he squatted in the dumpster's shadow maybe a hundred feet away from the back door to Hell. Late August in Las Vegas and the days were so hot people thought twice about picking up a silver dollar in the street, afraid they'd get second degree burns on their fingers.

The nights were little better. The desert air sizzled with leftover heat stored in the sticky asphalt streets like a griddle during the day, and exhaled at night, a brimstone belch.

Dog's cotton shirt stuck to him, a sweat-sodden second skin. He tugged at his collar, the leather studded band around his skinny neck chafing from the sweat. He thought, and not for the first time in the past month, about taking it off. He didn't, even if nobody watched him now.

"If I'm not me," he often said, "who am I? And if I'm somebody else, why do I look like me?" Dog was, to friends and enemies, the irrepressible, hairy, skinny little rabble-rousing prankster commie wino who wore a dog collar all the time. Some said he slept in it. Why disillusion his fans?

He also said, "Never let them see you sweat."

Inside Hell, it was cool, maybe. Air conditioned, maybe.

Or maybe not, since they'd closed Hell's restaurant late that morning, before lunch, just a couple hours after it had

opened for its first business day. Dog had watched from across
the street by the Foxtrot as city and maybe county or even state
people converged in official-looking trucks and vans and cars
and walked in and out through the back door, talking and
pointing, shaking their heads, making notes on their little
computers and clipboards, talking to God-only-knew-who on
their cell phones about God-only-knew-what. Something about
dirt in the food, he'd overheard once when he'd ventured nearer,
and a crack in the wall, and foundations settling and—anyway,
they closed the restaurant a couple hours after it had opened.
They'd shooed everybody out and put a yellow Keep Out tape
across the door.

Left the back door wide open, with an itty-bitty tape strip
strung across it.

Which puzzled Dog for a little while. He'd caught
enough engineers and health-inspector type's jabber before they
shooed him away to realize Hell's kitchen might have some
structural problem. So, the back door was sticky, wouldn't open
or close right, he'd seen. For safety's sake, they had to leave the
door open. It was an emergency exit.

The flimsy plastic yellow Keep Out tape was supposed to
keep people from going in.

Stupid, Dog thought, but who understood the Suits?

Would they shut down air conditioning with no
customers? AC just for the security staff? With the back door
open? Nah.

It would still be cooler inside Hell compared to the
mostly empty backside parking lot. Maybe.

Dog thought about the barbecue breakfast the day before
yesterday, about his rumbly gut, about Booger, about the odds
against getting away with stealing steaks from Hell. He thought
about how hot it was and he thought about the Hell restaurant
walk-in freezer, where the steaks would be lined up on tall wire
racks, waiting for him to snatch, cook, and eat. That freezer was
maybe fifty or sixty feet from where he stood now in the Hell

casino-restaurant-hotel backside parking lot, sweating. He walked over and touched the warm cinder block wall, thinking maybe it was *right here*, on the other side of the wall, maybe inches away. All that coolness. He pictured a frosty February morning in Wyoming he remembered well and thought of often.

Dog craved the cold—*real* cold—on his sweaty, hairy skin, wanted to feel icicles in his beard and mustache. It would feel good—like home. He wanted that coolness.

He wanted revenge against the pigs who'd abused Booger. Stealing steaks, a symbolic "fuck the State" gesture, would do.

He wanted breakfast.

He wanted steaks for breakfast. Hell steaks.

Dog looked around the lot and the street again. Nobody around. He felt ready. He'd walk in and out like he owned the place, and if somebody saw him and looked like they were going to stop him, he'd just turn invisible. All homeless people had to do was reach a hand out as if about to ask for spare change and they turned invisible. Picking your nose made you invisible too.

If the catcher was a rent-a-cop—"Oh, wow, sorry, man. This isn't the Seven-Eleven? Hey, like, I got to take a leak really bad—" If the catcher was a real cop, Dog's stupidity act would be the same but he'd be more alert, wary. He'd try to get in public, quick, among witnesses, but he'd be prepared to take whatever lumps might be his due if he couldn't. Most pigs were okay but some were—pigs. Luck of the draw.

Gut rumble.

Dog wiped sweat from his forehead on his cotton shirtsleeve and took a breath like a diver ready to jump off the high board. Then he took a step toward Hell's restaurant back door.

He stopped.

He'd forgotten about the black van.

A light just above and to one side of the back door was bright enough so the door and surrounding sixty or eighty feet could be seen by the occasional cruiser on Dallas Street, and anybody else who cared to look. The van was parked in an incongruous pool of darkness, a gap in the light on the far side, to the south, opposite from the trash bin side. The van was black. Invisible.

The van belonged to Mark Trane Enterprises, the outfit that owned Hell. Richly decked out, tinted-windowed, TV antennaed, all the trimmings. Black, extra long and sleek, like a sluggish cat. A fat cat. In the past few months, Dog had seen some foxy-looking woman executive get into or out of it a couple times.

He usually saw it parked where it sat now, facing out, butt-end to the wall. It was there the night before, when he'd waited in the trash bin shadow for the girl guard to cough up more steaks. Nobody had gone near it, and it hadn't moved. Ditto all afternoon today, while the official types had walked by it and around it, to and from the back door.

Maybe that's why Dog forgot it tonight, until now. He'd become used to it there, like the rebar piles, lumber stacks, and supply pallets here and there in the semi-finished Hell backside parking lot.

And he was distracted—tired, hungry, angry. Hot.

It wasn't important. Dog saw Rolls, Beemers, Caddies, and stretch limos and the like everyday. This was Las Vegas.

He now thought, standing at the edge of the pool of back door light, ready to dive in, what if somebody sat behind those tinted windows—tonight? Dog had ducked away during the night to piss against the restaurant wall behind the trash bin. If somebody had gotten into the van, they might have done so then. What if, as he walked by now, somebody in the van jumped out, grabbed him, and hauled his sorry ass off to jail? Not a pleasant prospect.

Dog retreated behind the trash bin to take a leak. Zipping up, he was a step from heading to Jesus' Bread Basket, getting in line for breakfast, when he heard a siren squeal a few blocks away, and he recalled Booger's missing teeth.

Then, on a sudden breeze, he caught the tantalizing tang of steaks cooking somewhere, maybe the Sunset Bistro, overriding the smell of his own piss.

"Fuck it."

Dog bunched his fists, and looked for a suitable rock. He found one, picked it up, and strolled—swaggering, like he owned the place—across the pool of glare to the van. On the passenger side, he scrawled his sig with the rock. A downward stroke, then two broad, graceful loops side by side, a reverse twist, and a jaunty tail trailing off rasped into the gleaming black paint.

He tossed the rock away, not caring if he hit a parked car across the lot, but he didn't look, and strutted—King of the Road—to the door.

It wouldn't do, he decided, to break the flimsy Keep Out tape strung across the door. Dog figured he could come and go all night with armloads of steaks and whatever else he fancied stealing from Hell and nobody would notice, but if he broke the yellow tape, a dozen cops would see it in a second. That's just the way luck worked, Dog thought, as he bent under the tape and entered Hell.

He took two steps inside and waited for his eyes to adjust to the dark. A light bulb winked, as if ready to go out, above a doorway down the corridor a hundred feet to his left—the dumpster was behind the wall over there. The other way down the hall—fifty feet to the right—Dog made out a faint, ghost-gray outline. The walk-in freezer door.

Breath held, he listened. Silence, except for the dim shush of traffic outside, and an occasional horn honking. Inside Hell, nobody around.

It was cool. Dog smiled, and he shivered. He'd been sweating all day and all night, his skin and his cotton shirt and his jeans were damp with sweat, and he loved the sudden chill. He had goose bumps. Felt like home.

Dog headed down the hall, away from the dim bulb *that* way and toward what looked like the freezer door, *that* way. Ahead—blackness, except for the rectangle ghost-door. He stepped gingerly to avoid tripping on anything hidden on the black concrete floor or barking his shins on a box. To his right, against the restaurant kitchen back wall, beyond which the black van was parked, he passed rows of dark shapes. He touched and saw the dim outlines of boxes and shrink-wrapped cases of canned goods on shelves and on pallets. He held his right hand out, touching the dark stacks as he passed, stepping gingerly.

His eyes had adjusted well enough by the time he reached the walk-in freezer door to make out the big chrome door handle at waist level. He touched it, felt metal coolness, and held his breath to listen again, looking back over his shoulder. A mechanical hum came from the freezer, but he heard nothing else.

How often did the security guards come this way?

He opened the door.

White light shot from the freezer, and an Arctic-cold cloud billowed out, a frozen version of the heat waves that mushroomed up from the streets outside in the day. The freezer machinery hum erupted too from the opened door, seemed to explode in Dog's ears, and he shut the door, heart in his throat. He stood, breath held, listening, sweating.

Eyes even more adjusted to the dark now, Dog looked around. To the right of the freezer door as he faced it, equipment lay jumbled on the floor and in the corner formed by the freezer and the cinder block back wall. Dog made out a footstool and buckets and mops and brooms leaning against each other and the freezer side, like a covey of drunks. Janitorial stuff.

Dog reached for a broom in the gloomy mess and almost tripped over the footstool. He pulled the broom out and hefted it. Wooden handle. Too flimsy, he decided, and put it down. Feeling among the other handles against the wall, he found one and drew it out. A mop. Sturdy metal handle. It would do.

Dog went back to the freezer door, again almost tripping over the footstool, and touched the door handle. A quick glance over his shoulder back down the hallway—nobody around, still—and he jerked the handle back. He stepped inside.

Dog tested the inner handle before closing the door and it worked well enough. This freezer, the size of a delivery van or a large apartment living room, wasn't like a common household refrigerator a person couldn't get out of once inside. People were supposed to get in and out, but Dog didn't trust it. What if the inside door handle decided to malfunction—*tonight?* That's the way luck worked.

The mop handle, jammed in the door crack so it wouldn't close all the way, eased his mind on that score.

The light from the cracked door could be seen in the darkened hallway like a beacon, and the machinery seemed loud. A security guard could come along any time. How ironic, he thought, if the girl rent-a-cop who'd stolen steaks herself from this very freezer the night before last busted him tonight.

He'd have to move fast now, but that was okay. He knew what he wanted and he didn't plan to lollygag.

He scanned the room, breath coming in frozen puffs, as he rubbed his goosebumpy arms. He bypassed rows of cans, bottles, and boxes, and found the meat rack. Above white paper-wrapped bundles in cardboard boxes hung a side of some small critter, butchered—calf, or sheep, or pig, or something. Dog dismissed trying to steal the gutted critter. He didn't know what it was, didn't know if he could carry it—it looked heavy, and would be pretty conspicuous on the street—and besides, he had his mind and palate set on steak. Which he soon found.

Filet mignon. Why not?

There'd be bacon somewhere, but Dog wasn't interested. Bacon would be better for breakfast, more traditional, and easier to share with more streeties than steaks, but he wanted steaks. Stealing steaks said Fuck You much louder. Besides, why not?

He hefted one white paper-wrapped, football-sized lump,

labeled *filet mignon*, and guessed it to be about ten pounds.

The pervasive, loud freezer machinery hum suddenly dropped in pitch and, puzzled, Dog turned to the door.

The mop was gone. The door was closed.

Heart aflutter, Dog went to the door, almost slipping on an icy spot, and set the steak bundle down on the floor. He jerked on the handle with one hand and pushed on the door with the other. The handle worked but the door didn't move. Stuck.

He braced himself against the door, pushed harder with his shoulder.

It wouldn't budge.

He slammed his shoulder against the door again and again, feet slipping on the slick floor, denying him a firm grip. His breath came now in quick gasps, frozen white explosions. His shoulder bruised, his lungs hurt, and his heart hammered.

"Hey!" He pounded the door with his fists. "Heyyyy!" Pounded. "Somebody!" Pounded. "Anybodyyyy!" Pounded.

Nobody around.

Lois Ward

Lois jerked awake as her flashlight rolled from her limp fingers and thumped to the carpeted floor. She sat up, gasping, blinking.

Nobody around.

She'd fallen asleep on duty, sitting in a stiff-backed, armless chair, head cushioned on her arms on a table at a booth. The booth was in the restaurant corner farthest from the dim light on the other side of the door to the kitchen. She could have lain down on the booth's wide seat and stretched out on the cushy, cool plastic. Four foot eleven inches tall. She could have. She refused herself that luxury, knowing that if she'd done so, she would have given in to fatigue and slept for hours. Instead, she'd sat in the hard chair facing the booth, and put her head on her arms on the table, like a kindergartner at naptime. Just for a minute. Just a minute to rest her eyes, then back to rounds, but how long had that minute lasted?

"Doggone it, doggone it," she muttered as she looked at her wristwatch. She couldn't make out Mickey's hands in the dark—a graduation gift from her step-dad back in Rock Springs, two step-dads ago, or three. A sliver of faint light seeped from under and around the kitchen door across the table-and-chair-filled, cavernous room where she now sat, panting and blinking. She couldn't see the flashlight either.

She got down on hands and knees on the carpet and felt around for the flashlight in the aisle and under the table. She found it, bumped her head under the table as she stood, but it didn't hurt much, and flicked it on.

Three o'clock. She'd slept for only a couple minutes.

She sighed. Not late for her half-hourly rounds, much.

Lois pocketed the flashlight, wiped sweat off her forehead with the back of her hand, tucked a loose wisp of straight chocolate brown hair behind her ear, and leaned on the table, feeling dizzy, yellow spots swimming before her eyes. The restaurant was hot, not like it had been the night before, when they had the AC on to cool the place, ready to open for business in the morning. The cool air had felt good then.

Tonight, the air hung still, syrupy, and hot.

The restaurant, and the rest of the complex, had been decorated in a comic nightmare Hell theme. The decorating had been done in a few days, after Trane had decided on the name at the last minute, and done in frantic haste, to meet the projected opening date. The result looked like a cheap Kiwanis Halloween spook house, everything painted red or orange, flames flickering on the black, fake-lava walls. Thumping drumbeats, like Hell Muzak, had played on the sound system. The menu offered Devil's Stew and Satan Salad and Mephisto's Melt. The drinks came with little pitchforks. Witch's Brew. Perdition Punch. Demon Rum.

The restaurant opened that morning, as advertised, but it closed hours later. Joseph Foxworthy, owner of Trustworthy Vigilance Agency, Lois' boss and the company charged with security, had called Lois right away. Something to do with the health department, Joe had said. He didn't elaborate and Lois didn't ask, although she was curious. TVA's contract for night-guarding the restaurant part of Hell ended, Lois had been told earlier, when the restaurant opened. Joe had promised she could continue night-patrolling the casino and hotel parts of the complex for the few days remaining before those parts opened too, and TVA's contract expired entirely, no interruption or cut in pay or hours. So last night was supposed to be her last night in the restaurant.

But Joe had called Lois at her waitress job at Laceby's Ice Creame and Sandwiche Shoppe that afternoon to say the Hell restaurant hadn't opened after all, not entirely, and she needed to continue patrolling it too.

The restaurant still smelled of fresh paint and wet plaster.

Too bad the gig would have to end, she thought. She needed the money. The car was in the shop and Mary needed dental work.

TVA was too small an outfit to handle security at the complex after it opened. That task would go to a different agency, one certified and experienced with casino security, a specialty. Joe—again, Lois had heard—got the Trane gig as a favor from Mr. Trane. Why, she didn't know. Her curiosity had been tweaked when she'd overheard this much and she thought about finding out why the billionaire would trust a small-time operator like Joe with his construction-phase security—just curious—but she hadn't, yet.

If Joe didn't have another gig right after Hell opened for good, as he'd promised—things fell apart, how well she knew, and sometimes Joe promised more than he should—she'd spend her evening hours, after Mary fell asleep, in the TVA office using Joe's computer to look for Steve. If her roommate Annie, who she called "Roommate Annie," was at home to watch Mary while Lois was gone. If the car ran.

But not tonight. Tonight, she was night security guard at the Hell restaurant-casino-hotel, walking the long, dark funhouse hallways between the three parts of the oddly-arranged building, checking doors, checking the stalls in the bathrooms, shining her flashlight here and there, walking, walking, walking. Just the ground floors. The elevators and doors above the hotel lobby were sealed—she checked to make sure. The doors to the casino upstairs—to the money vaults, offices, surveillance peepholes, the crow's nest, and other gambling stuff up there—were locked. She checked anyway. The restaurant had no second story, but it was laid out oddly, with narrow halls, hidden rooms, and awkward angles, and it took a while before she learned the layout. All those doors, in and out, up this way and down that way, including the kitchen, back storage hallway, and the back door behind the restaurant and the casino and hotel back exits on the building's opposite sides. Checked them all, once every half-hour. She'd gotten it down to twenty minutes, which is why she thought she could take a catnap tonight.

Lois got off work at six a.m.; after she saw Mary off to school, she'd nap for one hour, then shower, dress in jeans and a shirt, dab a bit of lipstick on her too-wide lips, dab a bit of makeup on her sort-of crooked and too-freckled nose, pluck at her dark, too-full eyebrows, try to do something with her straight brown hair, give up and pin it back with a barrette, puff out her chest and wish she had one, sigh in resignation—she was doomed to be a twenty-seven-year-old woman with a fourteen-year-old girl's body—and go into the TVA office and use Joe's computer to look for Steve. If Joe wasn't using the computer. If he was, she'd go to the library, wait till it opened, then get on the Internet there, and keep looking. Then she'd report for her six hours of getting underpaid at Laceby's. Then home for another nap, a quick dinner, change into her uniform, and then off to Hell.

So went a typical day in her life.

If the car were in the shop, like now, she'd take the bus, where she could get another quick nap, maybe fifteen minutes. The driver understood, and would wake her at her stop.

Tonight was Saturday—well, Sunday morning—her one day off from waitressing, and Mary would want to go out maybe to the park if it wasn't too hot. Pack a lunch, pickles, Kool-Aid, and peanut butter and jelly sandwiches, and a couple of books.

No air moved through the restaurant except in the kitchen's back hall, the storage area. There, by the opened back door, it was cooler, but not much. It had been a scorcher of a day.

She took a deep breath, and tried to relax, leaning on the table, waiting for the dizzying yellow fireflies to fly away. Her heart raced, but it wasn't fear of getting caught napping that scared her.

She remembered the dream.

Her legs wobbled—she should have packed more than a peanut butter and jelly sandwich and a pickle for her midnight lunch—and she plopped down into the booth. The cushy seat threatened to seduce her and she rose and moved to a hard-backed chair, sitting on its edge, leaning forward, elbows on her knees. Shaking.

Breathe. Relax.

The dream.

Had the falling flashlight jolted her awake, or the dream?

She's seen Steve again. Rather, his body. No—neither. Just his grave.

Maybe.

A glimpse of desert was all she'd seen, all she recalled from the dream.

Lois shivered as she tried to remember the details. The details always faded fast right after the dreams, and Lois had gotten into the habit of trying to grab them as fast as she could. Fingers fumbling, she took out the tape recorder in her breast pocket.

"There was a road, no more than wagon ruts in the dirt, or sand, I think. Yeah, sand. Don't know which way they were going, the ruts, I mean, and I don't remember tire tracks. Just deep ruts, a couple inches deep. There was cactus here and there—that tall kind with the long arms reaching up to the sky and the thorns. What are they called? Joshua trees? Saguaro? I'll have to look it up. Probably help me tell the area. It don't grow all over, I'll bet. And some sand dunes, like, not very high, maybe ten or twenty feet up, with bunches of spiky grass all over the tops, kind of like hair. Don't know the name of the grass either. I'll look that up too. Cactus and grass. And wind. Okay."

She flicked the pause button on the recorder and wiped her brow again, trying to remember the faded dream. In a moment, she continued. "There was—there were these two dunes and there was this dirt mound between them, like the dunes were boobs and you'd tucked a handkerchief between. The dirt was darker than the dunes on either side, the boobs. I feel like it was made of the same dirt as the dunes, but a different color cause it was dug up. It didn't have no grass or weeds on it like the big dunes on each side. The mound was shaped like—like—"

Lois clicked off the recorder. No point in going on. She knew what the thing was shaped like.

A noise grabbed Lois' attention and she froze, listening. An indistinct meaty thump or scrape, as if something semi-soft falling on the concrete floor, back there. From the kitchen.

"Doggone."

Lois stood and remembered the back door, behind the kitchen, left open for safety reasons, Joe had said. An emergency exit. Something to do with why the restaurant had been opened for breakfast then closed up again before lunch, "so you need to pay particular attention to it. It's a gap in security you'll need to cover, got it?"

She got it.

The back door had been taken off its hinges and propped against the wall inside the corridor. A little strip of yellow tape had been stuck across the doorway hole, waist high. The tape said Keep Out.

Just in case somebody couldn't read, Lois was to poke her head out during rounds, flash her flashlight and look around the parking lot. That, and the official tape, should keep burglars away. Otherwise, anybody might sneak in and pee on the wall, or steal some ashtrays, or a case of beans, or a carton of butter. A bundle of steaks from the walk-in freezer might grow legs.

Or somebody stupid, she thought as she headed for the kitchen door, navigating past the salad bar, between dim booths, tables and chairs, might take a bundle of those doggone steaks and put it outside that door for poor people to take. *Maybe that stupid somebody might be me.*

A rash act, inspired by a sudden dose of sympathy for Teresa Santiago and her streeties, after a quick, casual chat with the bag lady on her way to work two nights before. Lois had been angry over her own plight after a bad day at Laceby's and skimpy tips—she was so near homelessness herself with Roommate Annie's baby due soon. When Roommate Annie had her baby and moved back in with her folks in Fresno, Lois and Mary would have to find another "situation." So she'd wanted to do something for the homeless, right then, with all this on her mind and Teresa talking about how poor the street people were, how lucky Lois was to have a job, compared.

Lois had taken the bus to work, and Teresa Santiago was at the bus stop a block away from Hell. "See," Teresa had said, gesturing with big spade-like hands as they stood on the sidewalk, "everybody is the hero in their own movie, the movie in their head. Real life ain't like Hollywood where everybody's pretty, and they have good teeth and hair, you know?"

Lois nodded. She was a few minutes early for work and Teresa fascinated her, so big and bold and brash. She seemed as tough as Lois felt wimpy. Lois couldn't remember how the older woman had gotten onto the topic of—what were they talking about?

"No sir, it ain't. Life is gritty and dirty, and there ain't no commercial breaks for you to run to the bathroom and take a leak or brush your teeth or fix your hair. No sir. The heroes on TV and in the movies, they got a lot at stake—saving the world, saving the girl, beating the devil, getting away with the loot—always a couple million is tens and twenties, or a ton of gold, or a fistful of diamonds. Big stuff at stake."

Lois nodded. Teresa's favorite topic—life and the

movies.

"It ain't like that in the street, no sir. We got to wonder if we're going to find a flat place to sleep, where we don't get robbed or busted, that ain't been peed on in the last few days. We got to wonder where to get breakfast, or a meal *at all* today, or what the hell to do about a cold that keeps on, keeps us from working when there is work available, or where we're going to get the money to get home for Christmas when home is Maine or Ecuador, or how we're going to afford to go to the dentist—"

Lois nodded, remembering Mary needed dental work, and she couldn't afford it, and that she owned a car, even if it was busted, and Teresa didn't.

"—and where to get shoes and—oh, hellfire, you get the picture. Street people, even regular people, even if they got regular jobs, meals, and places to stay—hellfire, *everybody* has something at stake."

Lois nodded and Teresa cocked her head and squinted down at her. "You get me, child? People don't always win, neither. Don't always defuse the bomb the last second, save the girl, solve the crime. Sometimes the bomb blows up, the girl gets killed, and the mystery don't get solved. For little folks, sometimes the zipper breaks, The Man bust our ass, and we never find out who stole our shoes last night. Little things at stake for little people. Little losses and little wins. That's what's at stake."

The idea of snatching steaks from Hell for Teresa and the streeties came to Lois in a flash. She'd smelled them cooking as she'd passed the Sunset Bistro after she got off the bus. Why not? It was her way of giving the doggone System the finger, of venting her anger at a System that could lose a full-grown man in the middle of the night, in the middle of Las Vegas, and not give a doggone what happened to him, or to the wife and child still trying to find him months later. It seemed the right thing to do at the time.

She talked with Teresa a few minutes more before she

told the bag lady what she had in mind. Saint Teresa said "hellfire," and laughed, slapping her knee with a meaty palm, doubled over laughing. Lois left her that way.

She put the steak bundle outside the door for Teresa to take—and instantly regretted it. Stupid.

She'd forgotten about Mr. Trane for a moment. He had been coming around at night now and then, unpredictable, prowling around in the semi-dark like a sleepy-eyed kid looking for a midnight snack. He showed up to chat with Lois at odd hours, God-only-knew-when. What if he'd *seen* her steal those doggone steaks? Stupid, stupid, stupid.

She'd gone fifty steps back inside Hell before she turned around to get that bundle and put it back in the freezer.

It was gone. Nobody around.

She'd been too busy with her day job, and with Mary, and looking for Steve to sweat it much, after, but nobody had said anything. She'd been lucky. Her anxiety about it had eased since, but not entirely.

Now, the doggone back door was wide open.

Lois bumped into a chair and caught it before it fell over. She took her flashlight from her belt and she stood outside the kitchen door, licking her sweat-salty upper lip, breath held, listening. Silence.

She gripped the flashlight like a weapon, as Joe had showed her. She touched the cell phone in her hip holster, just to make sure it was there. "You need any help, you call. No goddamn confrontations. I don't pay you to be a hero. Let the police handle it, got it?"

She got it.

She eased the kitchen door open.

The door gave a timid, mousy squeak. Garlic, bacon, and antiseptic soap scents lingered in the kitchen. Lois stood still in the doorway, getting her bearing, adjusting her eyes to the dim light from above the door at the far side of the kitchen, a hundred and fifty feet away. The flickering bulb that looked like it was about to go out—she should change it, but later—hooded by a crooked, frosted plastic globe, cast sharp shadows across metal tables and ovens, racks of pots and pans, and shelves.

Lois waited, still, as Joe had taught her. A minute, two minutes passed. Not a sound.

She eased the door shut behind her, the door mouse squeaked, and she turned on the flashlight. She probed the gullies and caves of sharp-edged darkness in the kitchen, moving on tiptoes.

Nothing.

She approached the door between the kitchen and the back hallway with the same caution she'd used in approaching the door between the restaurant and the kitchen, tense, flashlight-weapon ready. She listened, ear pressed to the door.

She opened the door. No squeaky mouse this time.

"Mr. Trane?"

To the right, the hallway beyond the door led to the hotel. To the left, it led to the back door, the walk-in freezer, and farther on, to the casino. Along the hallway back wall, supplies were stored on pallets, on racks, and in loose stacks on the floor. Faint traffic sounds came from the street beyond the opened back door fifty feet down the hallway to her left. A siren wailed in the distance. In the hallway, her probing flashlight found nothing.

"Mr. Trane?"

The floor shook, like there was a freight train passing.

It kept on shaking.

Earthquake?

The rumble intensified, an explosion in slow motion. Faint and twitchy with fright, Lois dropped her flashlight on the concrete floor and it winked out. She crouched in the doorway, knees gone rubbery, hands clenched above her head and neck. That's what you're supposed to do in an earthquake, she recalled. Crouch in a doorway, protect your head and forget the flashlight.

"Mr. Trane!"

The gut-wrenching rumbling continued and things fell. In the kitchen, metal utensils rattled and clanged, and in the hallway, supplies shifted, stacks came apart, things large and small, light and heavy, fell off shelves and clattered and banged into the narrow concrete-floored hallway. The whole place *groaned*, as if in agony, and Lois remembered some submarine movie she'd seen. Gritty dust rained. Then the light bulb above her head popped and glass tinkled to the floor in the abrupt darkness.

Above the gut-deep, sinking-submarine rumble and shriek, and the tumult and clatter of supplies falling to the floor a few feet from where she crouched, Lois heard a man scream in pain.

Mark Trane

Mark Trane awoke to intense pain in his gut, again, and reached for the Tumeze package on the bedside table. None left.

"Oh, heww," he muttered. He coughed as he sat up, gripping his pale white abdomen. He fumbled for the switch on the night table lamp and knocked the lamp over. It came on when it hit the edge of the rug that dominated the hardwood floor of the spacious bedroom, casting a stark white spotlight through the darkness.

Wincing, Mark got out of bed and put the lamp back on the table. He looked around the table for his precious antacids. He found none. He tightened the waist cord of his pajama bottoms over his paunch as he padded on bare feet into the bathroom, fumbled for the light switch, and began rummaging through the medicine cabinet above the sink, and the big walk-in bathroom supply closet next to it. He kept his prescription meds there, but the last bottle of little white pills was empty, and the damn things hadn't worked anyway, so he relied on his over-the-counter remedy. He kept a gross-count box of Tumeze in the closet, not because they worked better, but because he owned the company. The box was his main stash, but he found it empty too.

No meds, no Tumeze.

No problem, he told himself. He put Tumeze packages

all over the place, so whenever he needed one or two, wherever he was, he could just reach out.

Mark returned to the bedroom and checked his pants pockets, draped over the cushy sofa at the foot of his gigantic canopied bed. He turned on the light and checked under the sofa cushions. He checked the bedside table again, and the floor under it, and under the bed. Not even dust bunnies. He checked the dresser drawers and the clutter on the dresser.

Nothing.

"Oh, heww." He coughed.

Intense pain and the futile search had brought him awake. The bedside clock said three a.m. in large, square red letters.

Mark sighed. He felt gritty-eyed and groggy. He felt older than fifty-whatever. He wanted to be asleep. He didn't want to leave the comfort of his bed to go to his office down the hall and check his desk drawers there, even if it was only a few feet away. But he had to.

He sat on the bed and tucked his feet into his over-sized fuzzy pink bunny slippers, stood, donned a bathrobe—checked the robe pockets and found nothing—and left his private apartment in the Hell penthouse eight stories above Las Vegas for his office. Just down the hall.

As his search on the desktop, through desk drawers, in an empty trash can, and under sofa cushions and plush chairs in his office continued, Mark grew grimmer. Bum luck, he decided, as he gave up on his office and walked down the stairs to Ripley's office one floor below. Maybe his "right-hand man" was working late. He hoped.

Roberta Ripley was not working late, though her distinctive fragrance—peaches, but a bit minty—lingered in the air in the hallway outside the apartment she'd converted into an office. No light came from under the door, and the door was locked.

No Tumeze, no meds, no Ripley. No luck.

"Oh, heww, heww, heww."

He grimaced at a new stab of pain, scratched at the white mustache that covered his upper lip and much of his cheeks, and pondered what to do next.

Mark Trane was a private man, a self-made billionaire who shunned attention. He avoided business associates, necessary or not, and fans and hangers-on and social climbers. To him, a nod to a vice president was the same as a grunt to a secretary, porter, or bellhop. A loner. He liked it that way. He kept no personal servants or bodyguards to summon at a whim. Nobody named Jeeves stood by in the night to say "At once, m'lord," and to play "Go fetch, Jeeves, there's a good man."

Mark Trane had done for himself all his life, pulling himself up by his own bootstraps. He was born Elwood Trane, the only son of Edwin Trane, a small-time stage magician-clown-actor in Peoria. Eddy the Magical Clown, a semi-clever and sort-of witty but hard-working man, expected to make it into the big time Any Day Now. Elwood's mother, Eddy's wife and former assistant, had fled with a dentist, a former friend of Eddy's just back from Nam, so Eddy pinned his hopes for immortality of Elwood, expecting his son to follow him onto the stage. Edwin Trane fell off a stage at a "sweet sixteen" celebration for a local debutante in 1968 and broke his neck when Elwood was ten. Elwood was left orphaned and penniless.

Although Elwood loved "the roar of the greasepaint, the smell of the crowd," he wasn't a performer, not like his dad. His hands were too big and his arms too long. He was bigger than his classmates and looked twice his age. He was clumsy. Shy.

Speech impediment.

But damn good at business. Damn good.

He'd been in a foster home after his father's death for less than a year before he ran away with a carnival. At eleven, he handled PR, bookings, and the carnival's accounts—the business end. He *owned* Dinwoody's Emporium of Fun two years later.

He owned his own carnival chain by the time he was

fifteen, and became a millionaire before he turned seventeen. At twenty-one, he bought a fleet of paddle wheel steamboats on the Mississippi and made them into floating carnivals. He changed his name to Mark Trane, and got on the cover of *Time* and *Rolling Stone* and *Wired* and *Spooch*, posing in the pilothouse of one of his ships, dressed as an old-time riverboat captain.

A failure at relations, though. He'd married, a fluke.

There had been a daughter, Stacey.

One day, the story went, Stacey disappeared. She was fourteen. Mark looked in characteristic fashion. He bought more carnivals. And circuses. And amusement parks and animal shows and zoos and roadside attractions and daredevil shows and air shows and stock car tracks and festivals and exhibitions and acts and reviews and medicine shows and rock and roll bands and booking agencies. He bought an interest in Walt Disney's amusement parks worldwide. He became a billionaire buying places and businesses where she might show up. He hired detective agencies to search, but he never found her.

So the story goes.

Twenty years, still looking.

His focus on business had long ago become a means to feed his obsession—find Stacey. That, and his wealth, his eccentricity, his shyness, and his speech impediment, all conspired to isolate him: a conspiracy he embraced.

He was not lonely, just alone. He knew and appreciated the difference between loneliness and solitude.

Ripley was as close to him as anybody had ever been. He'd caught her cooking books for a carnival he'd bought fifteen years ago. She was fourteen at the time, but she looked and acted like she was in her mid-twenties. She was as precocious and as cocky as he'd been at that age. He didn't fire her, as he did the rest of the carnival's inept management. He admired her boldness and intelligence as much as he admired her creative bookkeeping. Reminded him of himself. She didn't make fun of his speech impediment, didn't seem to notice it.

In fact, she protected him. With Ripley around, nobody mocked him. She respected him, Mark sensed.

Mutual respect and attraction, intellectual and maybe spiritual, an ideal match.

He made her a deal. As long as the carnival made a profit, Mark got his share, and she insulated his privacy, she could pay herself as she liked.

Ripley gave Mark time, freedom, and privacy. He could play.

In time, Ripley handled more and more of his business and private affairs, and she did so with finesse.

To be sure, his knack for business hadn't faded over the years, but he'd never had a killer instinct, not like Ripley had. To him, business wasn't much of a game, not all that fun. He left that part to Ripley.

He played.

Maybe God played dice. Maybe other rich people played God. All Mark Trane wanted to do was play.

A little boy at heart, which may have explained in part his disinterest in sex, although his spoiled marriage may have contributed to the anomaly, Mark Trane intended to die with more toys—literally—than anybody. He bought toy stores and store chains, and manufacturers, and toy designers, although he refused to put his own name on any toy line suggested to him. He bought playgrounds and playground equipment makers. He had a warehouse in Kansas City where he kept his toys, the largest toy collection in the world, most of them unused, unopened. Most he had never seen, and didn't even know he owned. He seldom visited the warehouse. Ripley hired somebody to buy toys for him, and gave Mark periodic, cursory reports of what he owned. Mark didn't remember his chief toy buyer's name, had never tried to remember.

Then, one day, he told Ripley to set up headquarters in Las Vegas. "I got a wead on Stacey."

"Oh? So you want to—what? Hire another detective?"

"I want to wewocate thewe. Set up headquawtews." He had no particular opinion about or interest in gambling.

"*Move* to Las Vegas?"

"Wight. Acquiwe a hotew, a westauwant, whatevew. Something with an office. Somepwace I can—"

"Got it."

She bought Yellowstone Entertainment Inc.'s bankrupt casino-hotel-restaurant. The place was a white elephant—wrong location, designed by an idiot, and built, or half-built, by a contractor turned fugitive when his fraudulent billing practices were uncovered. The Yellowstone people were fools to let the architect get away with his unworkable design, as they were to hire the contractor-thief, but they knew a good bailout when they saw one. Ripley got the property for a song and the Yellowstone people got out of their financial nightmare, fast.

Mark didn't care that the place was a turkey. He got his headquarters while he looked for Stacey, and he found games to play.

It seemed impossible to open the complex for business, ever, but Ripley said she could do it. She'd done it before, turned an impossible business situation into millions, so he said okay. Might as well let her play too. To her, a tough business challenge was play. To paint stripes on the white elephant and make it jump through hoops would keep her entertained for months.

Mark hired Joe Foxworthy to look for Stacey soon after he arrived in town and occupied his penthouse apartment. He told Ripley to give Joe's Trustworthy Vigilance Agency night guard duty at the construction site as a favor for a past Good Deed that Joe had done for Mark, and to keep Joe close and on the case.

Joe found no sign of Stacey.

Ripley had opened the restaurant—almost. Only for one meal, or part of a meal, rather, but even that was a feat. It looked like the hotel would open in a few weeks. The casino—no way,

Mark thought, could Ripley get it open. Maybe a few slot machines, but not the whole shebang. Ripley was good at manipulating law and lawyers, regulations and regulators, and getting contractors to perform miracles, but not that good.

She'd worked late a lot in the past few days, though, making the restaurant opening happen, meeting the creative business challenge in her usual George Patton, two-gun, gung-ho style, but not tonight.

"Oh, heww, heww, heww."

Here stood the reclusive self-made billionaire, Mark Trane, at three a.m., bleary-eyed, white hair-fringe tousled and mustache askew, in bathrobe and fuzzy pink slippers, in the hallway outside his right-hand man's office. He stood in the dim light, plump tummy killing him, and he didn't have any Tumeze, or any way to get any except calling Ripley to ask her to order some hapless underling out of bed to fetch some from a corner drug store. Which, as independent as he was, Mark would not, simply *would not*, do. He'd go out and do it himself, or . . .

Or the security guards downstairs might have some, or he could send a guard out. That would be okay, since they were likely bored anyway and would welcome a diversion.

Then he remembered the young woman guard, and he smiled. It had been coincidence that, in his nocturnal wanderings in the past couple weeks, he'd found her instead of another guard walking the dark corridors on the ground floor. In fact, he'd never seen any other guard but her.

That didn't bother him. He'd enjoyed those encounters with the young lady—with Lois. She wore a Mickey Mouse watch, like his, and didn't think it odd that a billionaire should have a watch like that, or wear pink bunny slippers. She knew who he was, but she treated him like a real person anyway, not one of the richest people in America, not like a big, clumsy child-man with a quirky sense of humor.

He returned to his office, got his keycard from the desk drawer, and headed for the elevator, thinking about Lois Ward.

He hoped his luck would hold and that he'd bump into her rather than another TVA guard.

He arrived at the ground floor lobby before he realized that he'd forgotten his flashlight, something he'd discovered he'd need after that first venture downstairs a few weeks ago, when he'd first met Lois and decided to call the place Hell.

He'd stubbed his toe on something in the hallway between the hotel and the restaurant and Lois had responded to his howl.

"Are you okay?" she asked.

"Not wiwwy." Mark plopped without dignity to the floor, pulling off his pink slipper to rub his toe. "It huwts."

"Stubbed your toe, huh?" Lois flashed her light on the offending two-by-four scrap, and tossed it aside.

She then knelt and looked at the toe, turning it in the light. "It's just a bruise, Mr. Trane." She knew who he was. He nodded, grimacing, expecting her to make it hurt more. She didn't. "Let me give it a look-see."

The girl guard was tiny, and looked as fragile as a porcelain doll, not like somebody who would carry a gun— which she didn't, Mark noticed with some relief. Kneeling next to him, she seemed even tinier. He must weigh twice what she did, he realized, and wondered that she wasn't intimidated being with such a huge man, alone.

Mark Trane was a big man, yes, but he was also flabby, pale, and innocent-looking. He was a big, partly hairy teddy bear, and everybody knew it on first glance. Still, it must look odd, he thought as he appraised his rescuer. In the hallway of a hotel under construction, in the middle of the night, in the dark, the little guard in her tidy well-pressed official-looking uniform that made her look more Girl Scout than police officer, sat nursing the giant, puffy teddy bear in his bathrobe and fuzzy pink slippers, one on and one off, the injured, bare foot like a long, white paddle.

If the guard felt ill at ease being alone with him, she

didn't let on. Mark decided she was not only unimpressed by his bulk, but she truly wanted to ease his pain. Somebody's mother, even if she didn't look old enough.

Her name tag said LOIS WARD. She wore a Mickey Mouse watch. Like his.

A stab of stomach pain stopped Mark's giggle.

"I got just the thing," she said, pulling something from a pouch or purse at her belt. Mark thought of Batman. "This'll feel cold for a while, but it'll keep the bruising down, ease the pain. Hold still, now."

As if he was the one made of glass, or as if he was a baby, Lois—he'd already started using her first name—tended to his bruised with a salve. It didn't hurt.

"Thank you," he said. "I'm sowwy if I stawtwed you—"

"No problem, Mr. Trane. Truth is, I heard you coming and I was on my way to see if—"

"You know who I am?"

"Sure. Joe, my boss, he talks about you. And I hear about you from your right hand—from Ms. Ripley, too. In the news. I think Ms. Ripley does a good job."

"Oh, she does hew job aww wight. Wikes it. What about you? Do you wike youw job? Wowking so wate and aww. Joe mentioned you have a chiwd? A wittwe giww?"

"Mary. She's ten. I see her in the morning, and before she goes to bed. Sometimes." She shrugged again. "It's okay."

"No, it's heww. Twuewy. I can teww."

Lois laughed. "Yeah, it is. Hell, missing my daughter so much." She hrumphed and changed the subject. "So what are you doing down here? Anything I can help you with?"

"Besides the toe? No, nothing. I'm okay. Weawwy."

Mark knew Lois didn't believe him—he could see it in her big, brown eyes, which glittered in the glow from her flashlight like they had ice chips floating in them—and he was relieved when she pretended to be satisfied with his reply. They talked about other things. They talked about Lois, about night guard duty, about Joe's detective agency. And about Mary.

They talked about wearing good shoes when you walk a lot and about carrying a flashlight when you go out at night.

"Dark as hell—I mean *heck*—in this building, Mr. Trane."

"Caww me Mawk."

They talked about fuzzy pink slippers—Mary had a pair too. Then, as if she remembered an appointment, Lois checked her watch, then dashed away—"My rounds, you know." Mickey Mouse, her watch, like his. She didn't find it at all remarkable.

Before their chat ended, Mark had gotten the name for his hotel-casino-restaurant, something he'd been pondering for months, but more seriously in the last few days.

The next day, after he set Ripley to work on the new name—news releases, sign designers, permits and so on, her bailiwick—he got a flashlight, seeing it as a sign that meant he'd find excuses to go night walking again. He'd looked forward to it.

He'd avoided human contact for years, a latter-day Howard Hughes, but not as much anymore. There was something about Lois Ward. He liked her. Maybe that was all there was too it. It didn't have to be any more complicated than that, did it? Anyway, he wanted to see her again, but not this way, all clenched up and stressed out. His stomach clenched around another stab of pain, and he decided against going back up for the flashlight.

The lobby looked plush, though empty and dim, a movie set waiting for actors to show up. Polished brass railings flanked rich hardwood paneling and ceiling-high mirrors along the walls. The carpet was deep, blood-red. It might be ready for its first customers soon, despite the lingering aroma of fresh paint.

It was hot and Mark remembered the air-conditioning wasn't on on the ground floor except in the restaurant which opened—and closed—that morning. He wiped sweat from his high forehead.

The oddball floor plan had made it so a person couldn't see the lobby from the street. The street-side doors were heavy glass, floor to ceiling. When someone opened those doors, they had to make an abrupt turn down a narrow, short and curved hallway, to reach the lobby. The weird bottleneck, more like the entrance to a funhouse than to a grand hotel—Mark thought it was funny.

In the lobby, tiny sconces spaced wide apart gave off enough light to see the hallway that led toward the restaurant to his right and the casino to his left. The narrow, tunnel-like hallway to the unfinished casino was blocked off from the lobby and the hallway to the street, plugged up with bare plywood, plastic tarps, and wooden sawhorses. Dim light came from down the restaurant hallway.

That's where he'd find Tumeze.

Despite the plush carpet under him, Mark stepped down the long hallway toward the restaurant carefully, running his right hand along the wall to steady himself, and gingerly raising each slippered foot. He remembered the stubbed toe.

Mark made his careful, quiet way toward the restaurant. He found a junction, a bend in the corridor. Turning left, he'd go to the restaurant main floor. The right corridor led to the kitchen back door, and the hallway behind it where they kept the freezer and where they stored equipment and supplies, and where there was a back door to the parking lot.

He reasoned that he might find Tumeze behind the cash register in the restaurant, so he headed that way. He got no more than three steps when he heard a sound coming from the other corridor, the one that led to the kitchen back door.

A scraping sound, as if something dragging on the concrete floor, and a change in the background noise, noises he hadn't noticed till then—a machine hum, the swoosh and honk of traffic outside. Back door must be open, he realized. Feeling clever, he decided the change in the sound happened when somebody had opened the back door. That somebody, he also decided, would be Lois Ward, security guard. Such had been his good luck.

She'd have Tumeze, he decided, and if not, she'd know where to get them. Anyway, Mark would have the pleasure of her company for a while till a solution could be found for his gastric woes.

Smiling, walking with greater confidence, hand no longer guiding him along the wall, he walked toward the back hallway.

He was almost to the door that separated the hotel hallway proper and the kitchen back hallway when he felt a rumble. He thought it was his stomach again.

It was more, bigger. He stood frozen, puzzled as the ground seemed to roll under him, like a boat on the river. The rumble continued, intensified, and his puzzlement turned to horror as it came to him . . .

Earthquake.

Thinking fast, gasping for breath, he raced to the doorway between the hotel and kitchen back hall a few yards ahead of him, remembering you were supposed to get in doorways in an earthquake, to protect yourself from falling objects. He got there, and crouched, hands over his neck, falling dust tickling his scalp, when he heard another sound over the rumbling and his own gasping breath.

A pain-filled scream, a man's voice.

Joseph Foxworthy

Joe hesitated just as he turned onto Dallas Street until the patrol car pulled away from the curb with its cargo of jail-bound bum. He waited another minute, then he parked his battered and rusty brown and tan 1982 Buick two-door sedan on the west side of the street, just up from the Foxtrot Bookstore, facing south. He cranked the tinted driver's side window down another few inches to get more air. The night was blistering, breezeless.

He adjusted his side view mirror to get a good angle on the parking lot and back door of the restaurant across the street. He adjusted the oversized rearview mirror. Then he settled his bulk lower in his seat to watch through the mirrors.

Few cars passed along Dallas between the Foxtrot and Hell, and fewer people strode the sidewalk on that block. Dallas was a side street, almost an alley, two blocks long; not a main drag, like the Strip four blocks west, where the action was. Poorly lit, decrepit, too many winos and druggies. Too much construction going on, and building crap lying around; those obnoxious orange cones and yellow flashing lights, stacks of lumber, rebar, and other stuff all over. Bad location.

He checked his watch. Three a.m.

Nobody around.

Joe absently reached for the crumpled, charred piece of

butcher paper on the seat beside him. The brownish stain could be blood, or not, human or cow or whatever. In the dim yellow light from above the Foxtrot front door a few yards behind him, and the ever-present light that filled the Las Vegas air, he again read the label on the paper.—*sky Packing Co. item#198. T-bone steak. 16 oz. Quantity: 5. Order#61614 Mark Tra—*.

He sighed and his fat ass strained the seat, springs creaking.

"Goddamn it, god*damn*damn it."

Earlier, Joe had phoned Lois Ward, his part-time, temporary night guard at Trane's, telling her the gig was on again tonight. Was she still available? Same hours, same pay, don't know how long. She was, promised to show up on time, and Joe hung up.

Then Devon Coleman had stepped into the office.

Devon, a sometimes employee, had brought the palm-sized paper scrap folded in his small, callused hands. Coleman, a retired cop from Delta, Utah, but not a good one, had moved to Las Vegas to scratch a minor but persistent gambling itch his small hometown did nothing to assuage. He did construction or landscape work, laborer stuff, when the mood hit him, "to keep belly-button and backbone apart" as he put it, and an occasional gig for Joe, when Joe needed him and he felt like working.

"Found this in the gutter over on Laramie," Devon had said, "near that closed-up subdivision, you know? Went over to check if they were back up, hiring. They're still shut down, but I saw me this dollar bill in the gutter, my lucky day, and found this when I got the dollar. It's that Hell guy, ain't it, the one you work for? Trane? Figured you'd want to see it."

"I do not work for Mr. Trane," Joe said, unsmiling but without rancor, as he took the paper and unfolded it. "I'm an independent contractor. Like you."

Devon snorted.

Joe read the label. "Goddamn it." He gave Devon a ten, nodded grim thanks, and sent him away.

Even after handling it all day, the paper still smelled delicious, and Joe tried to remember the last time he'd had a good steak dinner. His stomach growled and he took another Tumeze from his shirt pocket. He'd skipped dinner and had only napped a couple of hours around midnight on the office sofa.

A quick computer search had coughed up a name after Coleman left. Bronsky Packing Company, North Las Vegas. He'd done employee background checks for them, but the latest was more than a year ago. He couldn't fathom how the paper could have gotten onto Laramie.

Possibly, somebody had stolen the steaks that used to be wrapped in the paper, maybe one of Bronksy's drivers. Joe intended to check it out later this morning. It might be worth something for Bronsky to learn one of his drivers was ripping him off, but Joe wouldn't ask for pay. He wouldn't refuse it if offered, but he wouldn't ask for it. No, he'd give over the evidence, drop his card, and let Bronsky or whoever was in charge these days deal with it. Being discreet was always good business. Occasional altruism was also good business. It might translate into another paying gig with the company later.

First, he had to deal with the "what if" that somebody took the steaks from Trane's freezer, instead of from Bronsky's truck. That meant—

That meant maybe construction or one of Trane's people was snatching snacks from him, or somebody from outside had figured out how to get in to raid the fridge, or—worse case scenario—his own employee had stolen the damn thing.

If somebody on the inside were stealing from Trane, Joe would do well to find out who, and soon. Joe could count on a third to a half of his pay any given month to be related to employee theft, or suspected theft, or the prevention thereof. It was such a big problem in Las Vegas. He spent a lot of time doing background checks on new employees, tailing delivery trucks, surveilling parking lots and employee break rooms, staking out delivery entrances and back doors.

After Devon left, after Joe did a quick computer search for the packing company ID, he pulled up a map to check the relationship between Bronsky, Laramie Street, and the casino. He keyed in businesses and residences—his own, Ripley's, and a few others—though he didn't expect the preliminary search to reveal anything. It was just a way to acquaint himself with the territory, a warm up, something that may come in handy later. Lois Ward, he noticed with some annoyance, lived beyond Laramie from the casino. Yeah, he knew that. She rode the bus, mostly.

Puttering done—he's found out as much as he could for now—he pulled an old video camera from storage, something he'd taken in payment for a custody investigation a few years ago in lieu of cash, a charity case. An old, cheap, battered machine, but rugged. His backup. He usually had two or three video cameras—he used them a lot for surveilling—but he was down to just this old beater. His last one was in the shop, and the one before that had been stolen.

He dusted off the relic, put new batteries in, checked it—it would do—and put in a tape, a long one. He drove to Hell through the blistering hot afternoon—the Buick's AC was broke, but thank God for tinted windows—and duct taped the camera to a supply rack top shelf in the hallway behind the kitchen. He'd remembered to bring an AC adapter; there might be a plug nearby, hidden from casual view.

The bureaucrats who'd closed the restaurant before lunch had finished their business and left the scene. Nobody saw Joe duck under the yellow Keep Out tape across the back door, or if they did, nobody gave a damn. Nobody was inside the back hallway to see him climb up a stepladder to secure the camera. Nobody saw him put the ladder up when he left and nobody saw him leave. Or if they did, nobody gave a damn.

He hid all but the lens under a stack of towels. The camera faced down the hallway, westward, toward the back door and the walk-in freezer not far beyond the back door. The flickery bulb above the kitchen door behind the camera provided the only light, but Joe judged it would do. He knew a good shop where he could get the tape enhanced if he needed it. If between three p.m. when he installed the camera, and three a.m., when the tape filled up, if anybody came in the back door, or anybody went into the freezer, they'd be caught on tape.

He promised himself he'd replace that kitchen door light bulb—later. Or get Lois to do it.

Nothing might happen. City officials had since closed the restaurant right after it opened, so nobody would be in there except Lois. He'd warned her about the door being open "for safety reasons," so she'd keep an eye on it when the building emptied of construction workers in the hotel and casino side and she went on duty.

Joe picked up the blank videotape on the seat beside him. Twelve-hour tape. He'd swap it for the full tape in the camera inside Hell in a minute, go back to his office, and watch the tape on fast forward. If he saw nothing useful, he'd wait till three p.m., then he'd refill the camera with the tape he'd just viewed—no need to buy another one—and get on with another project. Meanwhile, he'd spend part of the day seeing what he could find out about Bronksy's drivers.

He'd also hire another night guard. "Goddamn it." It wasn't supposed to be this complicated a gig.

Or maybe a bold and hungry streetie, so many in this neighborhood, had snuck in and done the deed.

He pushed from his mind the thought that his own employee might be stealing from a client. That could get complicated. Trouble. He liked Lois Ward, goddamn it. A nice girl. Naive, sweet, innocent. Nice. Smart too. Reminded him of—somebody.

His brother.

He shook his head, took the tape recorder from his breast pocket. "Call Erroll's doctor after nine. Get the generic name of the new meds he ordered." Outrageous, drug prices these days.

He repocketed the recorder, popped another Tumeze, checked his watch, grabbed up the blank videotape. He checked to make sure the dome light was off, and opened the car door.

Then he stopped.

Across the street, across the parking lot, near Hell's back door, somebody walked, almost trotting, through a pool of light, then disappeared into deep shadow. He couldn't be certain, since it had been a fleeting glimpse, but it looked like the person—a woman, judging by her gait—had just come out through the restaurant back door.

She may have come out a second ago, the instant he stepped from his car, the instant he wasn't watching that back door.

Acting on instinct, Joe got back in the car, reached across the seat for the digital camera in the glove compartment. Then he looked for the woman. She was gone.

So fast?

Then Joe remembered the van. The big black Trane executive van that always parked near the back door. He didn't hear anybody get into the van, and he didn't see the dome light go on. The van didn't move as he stood watching.

He thought of Ripley. Had it been *her* he'd seen?

Maybe.

A good guess. So Ripley worked late. Something to do with the restaurant closing hours after it opened? That couldn't be much fun for somebody in corporate PR, trying to put a positive spin on the problem. Joe wondered what miracle she was trying to conjure. The problem was structural, he'd heard. No way Ripley could put a positive spin on that.

Then it occurred to him—maybe the mystery woman had seen something that would help him in his investigation into the steak stealer. The woman figure would be on the video tail end, her shadowy form walking down the corridor to the door, ducking under the yellow tape—yes, it was still there—and into the night. If, that is, she had in fact come from inside the place.

He'd check the videotape, and call Ripley in the morning. Or the afternoon. After he had another guard on the payroll. He wouldn't tell her about that. Of course.

An odd thought: what if it was Ripley raiding the fridge? Joe shook his head. Nah. Why would she do that? That didn't make sense. She didn't need to.

Joe grunted, and decided to wait for the van to leave before crossing the street and getting the videotape. He checked his watch and changed his mind. Maybe it wasn't Ripley, or maybe whoever it was hadn't been in the restaurant anyway. Or hadn't gone to the van—he didn't hear the door open or see a light.

Maybe it was a hooker.

Or maybe *whatever*, he sighed, exasperated with himself. He crossed the street briskly, checking his pockets. Videotape, tape recorder, digital camera, cell phone, penlight. Cybersleuth. James Bond. But life wasn't the movies.

He found a gap in the chain link fence around the building equipment that fronted the street side of the parking lot and stood between him and a direct path to the back door. He squeezed through the gap, puffing and sweating. He wiped his forehead, caught his breath, and looked around.

Fifty yards away, a woman got out of a white car parked amid the small group of cars at the lot's far north end. Sunset Bistro patrons, most of those cars.

This lone woman—what was a woman doing alone in this neighborhood at this time of night? Hooker? Another one? She didn't leave the lot and cross Dallas Street for the Bistro, or businesses farther along that block. The woman walked across the lot, heels tapping, toward the restaurant back door—no, not the door. She got in the van's passenger side and closed the door. No light came on inside the van, Joe noticed, when she opened the door and closed it. The van started up, and without headlights on, coasted quietly around the corner, toward the hotel front, beyond Joe's sight.

"Goddamn."

The face of the woman Joe had just seen had been hidden in deep shadow as she crossed the parking lot, and when she crossed the glare from the light at the restaurant back door by the black van, she had her back to Joe.

Two women, in the van. And it drove away. "Without lights. What the goddamn hell is going on?"

Joe walked across the lot toward the cars parked at the north end, zeroing in on the one the second woman had left, the woman who'd gotten into the passenger side of the Trane van. Brand new Mercedes sedan, white. Nevada plates. He glanced inside the car, but saw nothing through the tinted windows, a common feature in the Las Vegas oven.

Here, the light was iffy, lots of shadow. He photographed the car from several angles anyway without a flash, which he didn't have, fixing its spot on the lot as best he could against the background. He got close-ups of the license plate for a later check with his contact in the bureau. He took out his tape recorder and talked into it, reading off the time, license plate number, and describing the two women, the car, and what happened in the past couple minutes—or what he *thought* had happened.

Habit. Joe had spent too many hours in a witness chair to screw up such details, and one never knew when such details meant a clean—and profitable—bust. He had a steak thief, maybe, and a job to do, and a client to satisfy.

He had a brother.

Finished at the mystery woman's Mercedes, Joe sauntered toward the restaurant back door. He checked the lot— nobody around—ducked under the yellow tape and stepped into darkness.

He stood still, listening, letting his eyes adjust. He heard nothing but the muted rumble of Las Vegas traffic punctuated with the occasional horn honking and siren blaring, and the more subtle and steady hum of the restaurant walk-in refrigerator down the hallway to his right. A feeble light flickered over a door to his left—*got to replace that*—cast bottomless shadows. Joe eased a few steps down the hallway to his left, waiting until he got farther inside before he turned on his penlight.

He found the metal-frame rack where a stack of towels hid his camera. The stepladder he'd used that afternoon to set up the camera had been moved, but not far. Penlight between his teeth, he set the ladder on the rack and climbed up.

Joe was pleased with himself that he fumbled as little as he did when he took out the tape and replaced it with the blank one in his pocket. He thought of Tom Cruise in *Mission Impossible*, but switched to Sean Connery in the Bond movies. *More my age.*

He had just closed the little lid on the camera, turned it back on, and was about to climb down the ladder when he froze. He thought he heard muffled thumping, as if somebody pounding on a door through a foot of sand or water, or like somebody pounding to get out of a buried coffin. He squinted into the dark down the hallway toward the kitchen door and tried to penetrate the darker beyond, down the hallway toward the hotel. Nothing there. The other way, the hallway to the back door and beyond, past the walk-in freezer and the casino further still. Nothing.

The sound repeated. From the . . .

. . . from the *freezer*?

"What the goddamn hell?"

The noise, so vague, muffled in the traffic sounds beyond the back door, and the lesser noise of the freezer itself, seemed to blend even as Joe listened, into another sound, a rumble that came from nowhere, everywhere. The rumble intensified, a freight train roaring down the hallway like an express down a tunnel.

It grew, and grew. And grew.

"What the goddamn—"

The rumble grew to a roar and the ladder shook, and the

metal rack under the ladder shook. The world came apart and things started falling in the hallway, clattering, with a noise like small arms fire, onto the concrete floor.

Earthquake.

Here he stood on a goddamn stepladder, which now felt as rickety as if it were made of toothpicks. The toothpick ladder cracked, twisted sideways, falling away from him. He fell to the concrete floor. He cried out in pain as he hit, his leg twisted under him with a wet snap. He felt—sensed more than heard— the metal rack coming down at him, groaning as it twisted away from the wall. He held his arm up to ward off the blow and tried to scramble away. His leg hurt like hell and he screamed.

Something big and hard hit his head, and cut off the scream.

As he blacked out, he wondered where Lois was.

Then, nothing.

Roberta Ripley

It was the best orgasm she'd ever had, and Ripley moaned with delight. Sammy moaned too. Never happened like that before, both at the same time. Usually they took turns, took their time, lots of gentle, loving foreplay, but this time, this time . . .

Wow. Just wow.

The pleasure spasms went on and on and Ripley wished they'd never stop. The orgasm receded, but the world continued to move, to vibrate beneath Ripley's sweat-soaked back and butt, like a vibrator bed in a cheap motel.

She lay on the plush, velvety-soft carpet in the back of the van, her sweaty cheek hot against Sammy's sweaty hot inner thigh, the smell of Sammy's sex pungent, sticky pubic hair tickling her chin. The orgasmic tide had ebbed, or changed rather, to a low rumble. Sammy, nestled below Ripley's hiked-up skirt, locked in a lover's leg-lock, groaned as she caressed Ripley's cunt with short, quick, licky-sucky strokes.

The sensation went on and on, and Ripley thought of the old cliché—"did the earth move for you, too?"

Until she realized the earth *was* moving.

She sat up.

"What?" Sammy said. Awkward, tangled in twisted skirt and blouse—she hadn't worn underwear either—Sammy sat up too. How beautiful Sammy is, Ripley mused, hair tangled and sweat-sodden, cheeks and eyes rosy in the dim light leaking in through the tinted windows and from a dashboard light. For that radiance, Ripley was glad the van's air conditioner was broken.

Ripley had called her for the rendezvous to talk, that's all, just talk. She'd intended to drive a mile away to a dark street over by the boarded-up Cascade Hill's Subdivision between Laramie and Memphis, park, and talk, just talk.

When Sammy had climbed in on the van's passenger side, her leg arching up out of her skirt to expose smooth upper thigh, all her plans evaporated like a cup of nickels in a slot machine. They hadn't been together since before Mark announced he was going to call the place Hell. Ripley had been too busy since then with PR—damage control—and finalizing plans. The need for Sammy had built up, and now Ripley couldn't help herself. She unbuttoned her blouse as she drove. So did Sammy.

She never left the lot. She got as far as a spot around the corner, a few hundred feet away, the side where workers parked during the day, empty now. She parked the van and pounced into the back, Sammy right with her in body and spirit.

They dropped onto the carpeted floor and into each other's arms and legs, without word or hesitation, and with the same heat they had experienced in their first time together. Talk later, Ripley had thought as she pulled Sammy's skirt up over her hips and opened her own legs. As their passion mounted in their frantic, thrashing embrace, Ripley forgot what she wanted to talk to Sammy about.

Now she remembered. *The plan. The plane.*

"Wha—?"

"Shh," Ripley held up a slim finger.

The vibration continued, but it changed, she noticed, now that she focused on it, listening, feeling. It was like—

"Eart—earthquake?" Sammy said, swallowing the word.

Or a bomb, or the building collapsing, or—"Or worse."

"What? What could be worse?" Sammy had already

pulled her skirt down over her rounded hips. Ripley hiked her skirt up a tad, enough to get mobile, get to the drivers seat, get away.

If the gut rumble shaking the van like a roller coaster ride was an earthquake—or worse—she had to get away from Hell, farther out into the parking lot, into the open, away from falling walls. The building was coming down.

Not now, please God, not now.

She gritted teeth as she jammed the van into reverse and backed away from the wall, expecting any second to see rubble cascade in front of her, onto the tinted windshield, precursor of the whole Hell's restaurant coming down, and the hotel too.

Ripley jammed on the brakes when she judged she was far enough away from danger, almost to the chain link fence around the parking lot side and back, maybe eighty feet away. Sammy squealed, and Ripley realized her sudden move had dumped Sammy onto her butt in the back just as Sammy had tried to reach the front seat. Ripley ignored her protest, focused on the building.

The restaurant was one story tall, and the eight-story hotel was on the other side of the restaurant, so she was out of immediate danger, but the scene transfixed her—falling dust, intense shaking. She'd been in an earthquake before, downtown Seattle, on the fifth floor of the Bon Marche, shopping. A gift for Sammy. It had scared the shit out of her.

The building *was* shaking. Dust rained down the cinder block wall in miniature waterfall rivulets onto the asphalt where the van had been hidden seconds before.

The building *was* going to collapse. Now. She looked in the rearview mirror at the pastel glow from the Strip to the west. No buildings that she could see were damaged, or had broken glass, or drifting whips of dust. No other buildings were collapsing, like Hell was. *Only Hell is falling. Not an earthquake then. Bomb, or . . .*

In an instant, Ripley assessed the situation, made an

abrupt change of plans, something she did quite well. She'd have to leave sooner. In the van. To the airport. With Sammy. Now.

The money was secure—she'd send for her stuff later. All worked out. Except for Sammy.

It was what she'd wanted to talk to Sammy about.

She decided, and put the van in gear again, started forward.

Suddenly, the shaking stopped, startling Ripley, the world went still, and Ripley jammed on the brakes. The van faced the still-standing Hell and Ripley watched the wall, but it refused to collapse.

She saw Sammy trying to climb into the passenger seat too late as she braked. Sammy slammed into the dashboard this time, squealing in protest. She had been putting on an earring and had lost her balance.

"Sorry, Sammy, honey, I—"

"What the heck's going *on*?" Sammy sounded more irritated than scared or hurt. She plopped into the passenger seat, fumbling with her blouse buttons, and Ripley noticed she'd gotten a button in the wrong hole. "What are you doing? Are you trying to kill me or what?"

"I'm sorry, Sammy."

"Hmph." She made a kissing sound. "I'm okay."

Ripley put the van into gear again, shot forward. She aimed the van toward the Hell restaurant back door, to put it back in its place.

"Sammy, I wanted to talk, but—"

"Yeah." Sammy giggled, high-pitched, nervous. "Hard to talk with your mouth full."

Ripley slid the van butt first into its shadow hidey, and turned off the key. "I have to get back to work, and find out what happened. The press, the police—"

"Yeah, I'd better go too." She was already halfway out the door even as the van stopped. She stumbled and fell—

"Sammy, honey?"

—and rose wobbling back into Ripley's view.

"I'm okay. Call me." Sammy made a kissing sound, then ran across the lot, through the restaurant back door light glare, into the deeper darkness and past the trash bin, and toward her Mercedes, tucking her blouse in the back and patting her hair as she ran, her heels clip-clopping on the pavement like nails pounding into Ripley's heart.

It's not supposed to be like this.

For a moment, Ripley sat in the stifling hot van, fists bunched, frustrated.

They hadn't talked, and Ripley *needed to talk to Sammy.*

Yes, but not now. Now, she wondered what Hell looked like on the *inside*.

How was Mark? Where was he? His apartment was on the eighth floor and he had gone to bed before midnight. He was still there. Ripley had determined that much before she'd called Sammy—just a little snooping—and before she'd gone to the van. He was there, she was sure—or rather, had been there fifteen minutes ago.

Ripley found her cell phone in her purse and tapped Mark's number. Maybe he was up. Maybe he had a phone with him.

Maybe I should go inside and look. She dismissed the idea. Dust like a sulfuric belch from an overstuffed dragon oozed from the back door. *Too dangerous.*

As she waited for him to answer, the smell of Sammy's sweet pussy rose and she grabbed a mint from her purse, popped it into her mouth, and sprayed cologne, peachy, with a hint of mint, liberally over her face, hands, and crotch. Satisfied that she wasn't giving out unwanted pheromones, still waiting for Mark to answer the phone, she put her hand on the key, ready to restart the engine and drive around front to the hotel entrance. There, the police and press and God-only-knew who-all else would show up and she'd have to Take Charge, smile, be pretty, competent, reassuring. Professional. In Control.

Nothing to worry about, folks. Roberta Ripley is In Control. See her flash The Smile? Hear those capital letters? Professionalism and Competence is what you hear. Her all-business face on, no makeup but Larry King had once told her she was pretty enough without, hair a bit mussed but that's because she's working hard. On the job. Competent. Nothing to worry about, folks.

"Ms. Ripley, where's Mr. Trane? Did he get hurt in the explosion? Or killed?"

"First, there was no explosion. Second—" Second, she hadn't the faintest idea. She'd have to wing it, which she did quite well, thank you.

Where is he?

She was ready to turn the key when, from out of Hell's back door, the night guard darted, ripping the silly yellow Keep Out tape from the door frame like a cobweb. The guard—the little girl Joseph had hired, what'shername—looked disheveled.

A fine powder coated the girl's face and uniform. What looked like mustard stains splotched her front from chest to knee, and bloody handprints accented her small breasts.

Ripley froze, one hand on the ignition key, the other holding the phone. It rang and rang. She disconnected and froze.

She can't see me. The tinted windows. She didn't see Samantha leave. She doesn't know I'm here. I'm invisible.

The doll-sized girl rent-a-cop walked a few steps away from the back door to within a dozen steps of the van and looked around, as if looking for a cab, but frantic, her haunted, wide brown eyes desperate.

Looking for an ambulance? Somebody hurt? Mark?

Ripley's heart jammed into her throat where it had been minutes before when she had her orgasm, and then again when she realized Hell was falling. It took all the will she could muster to keep from opening the door and yelling—*What's going on?*

She dropped the phone back into her purse and reached for the door, to open it, to call out, when the dusty girl-cop stopped ten feet from the van's passenger side, stooped and picked up something from the ground that Ripley couldn't see, turned as if in response to somebody—calling for help?—from inside Hell. Then she ran back inside, and Ripley sat there, heart beating wildly.

She thought again for a second about going to the back door, seeing what was wrong—*was it Mark?*—helping, if she could, but at least *finding out*.

She heard sirens and she changed her mind.

She started the van, brought her erratic breathing under control, and rebuttoned her blouse. She checked herself in the rearview mirror. Pretty, if a bit frazzled. It would do.

She checked the night sky toward the Strip. Nothing changed there. Hell had teetered, shattered by some as yet unknown force, but the rest of Las Vegas was business as usual. The curious, idle and professional, would converge on Hell to see what had happened, rubbernecking like people did at a freeway accident.

She sighed, then she drove, not too fast, around the lot, past where she and Sammy had parked minutes ago—it felt like ages—toward the front. And her job.

It took less than a minute to reach the wide, domed curve before the imposing and gaudy Hell hotel front entrance, now littered with glass fragments. By the time she reached it—two cruisers converged, sirens howling, circus lights blazing, and a TV camera truck followed in their wake—Ripley had revised her plans yet again.

Teresa Santiago

Something disturbed Teresa Santiago's sleep and she rolled over on her ample hips and pulled the old, tattered and too-small woolen sweater back over her exposed butt cheek. A few layers of old but not-too-musty cardboard topped with fresh newspaper—last Sunday's *Clark County Chronicle-Progress*—softened the otherwise unyielding asphalt alleyway surface, and the back wall of the Sunset Bistro and a few garbage cans flanked her, providing some privacy. She was used to it. The uncomfortable accommodations hadn't disturbed her slumber. It was hot, so it wasn't a chill that rankled. Something else.

The sweater, a lucky bus station find she'd had for a year or two, made a poor excuse for a blanket, but it was all she needed in the oven-baked night, a token concession to modesty and habit. Still, it was too short. Pull it up to one of her chins, and the used-to-be-white slip over her plump belly was exposed. Tug it down and her neck and shoulders were exposed. Couldn't win. Nothing to do but sleep, and forget it.

It wasn't cold, or rain—*ha!*—or a noisy drunk pausing to take a leak near her hidey in the alley between Eugene and Fresno streets that woke her up, disturbing some dream about the French Revolution—or was it the Bolsheviks? No, it was something else. Some—*vibration.*

Like a vibrator bed in a cheap motel. Stick in fifty cents

and get an instant cheap thrill.

Where's Dog?

Teresa sat up, heart thumping. A truck coming down the alley, right at her, drunk teenagers in daddy's Hummer on a tear, going to crash into the trash cans, a goddamn movie chase scene, yahooing as cans and garbage and a goddamn bag lady fly left and right. Goddamn teenage punks—

Where's Dog? "Dog? Dog, honey, where—"

Teresa remembered where Dog was as she stood up, ready to run, but she saw no truck coming. The almost-mechanical growly sound, a freight train now, continued, but she couldn't see where it came from. The ground continued to tremble and she felt it in her stout legs.

A bomb. Somebody's bombed a casino on the Strip.

From up and down the long, narrow and mostly dark alley, voices rose. Other streeties camped here and there, in and under a trash bin, and in a doorway recess behind the Sunset Bistro, called out. The alley was a haven. The cops knew streeties slept here, but they usually stayed clear. Teresa had seen to it, made a deal. "No trouble from us, you cut a little slack, okay?"

Most voices she heard, fewer than a dozen, were male voices, some cracked, slurred and alcohol-garbled, but one or two women were among those homeless vagrants camped nearby. All of them, it seemed, shouting. "What the hell's going on?" "Help! Somebody trying to rob my stuff!" "Fucking earthquake, you idiot." "Fuckin' A-rabs, that's what."

"Everybody okay?" Teresa's bass tones, a bit gravelly from decades of smoking pot and unfiltered Camels, overrode the general din. "I said, is everybody *okay?*"

The din—some voices seemed verged on panic—tapered down. Muttered responses, grunts, came back to her. Tom-Tom, Little Ricky, Captain Freddy, Teach, the new kid from down South who didn't seem to have a name yet, Mrs. Doran, and Larry and a couple she didn't recognize. *Nobody hurt. Good.*

Lucky.

Teach sidled up to Teresa, gripping her elbow as if to hold herself upright. Her breath smelled of curdled milk and gin. "See here, Teresa—"

"You seen Dog?"

"See—see here, Teresa, I don't mean to frighten you, b-but I think you should know I was sleeping down th-that way—" she pointed over her stick-thin shoulder toward the alley mouth, and Dallas Street beyond, and Hell beyond that, the top of the hotel visible above the Foxtrot, "—and I think that all the r-r-rumbling came from o-over—" The Hell hotel top floor gleamed golden in the eternal glow from the Strip against the purple-black night sky like a stick of radioactive butter. "—by Hell. You can see the d-dust. See?" She pointed again, as if instructing a child.

Others gathered around, listening, not muttering or grumbling, much. Waiting for her to say something, do her Saint Teresa thing.

They're afraid. Me too.

Deep breath. "Dog's okay." *God, I hope.* "Everybody else?"

"We better get moving," Little Ricky said. People were coming from the Bistro, kitchen types in white aprons, a man in a suit. Security, maybe. Sirens howled far away in the neon night. The Man was coming.

"Right," Teresa said. "Let me know if anybody needs help. I'll be—"

"They picked up Booger," Little Ricky said.

"Huh. Did you see who?"

"Dennis the Menace and some new kid. Thumped him a bit." He shrugged. "The new cop did. Not too bad, I think."

"Took him in?"

"I think so. I took off."

"Okay." Dennis the Menace wasn't too bad. Booger would be pretty safe in lock-up. The jailers knew he was under her protection, another deal with The Man. He'd get a good breakfast. Teresa made a mental note to drop by the jail first thing, check on him, after she checked on Dog. "Anybody else?"

"Dog's over-over—" Teach began, pointing again at the silvery-dusty sky.

"I got it." Teresa gave Captain Freddy a bear hug, lifting him off his feet—he shivered with fear, as usual. Somebody passed her a joint and she took a lungful and handed it back. Larry, gravely, silently, offered his paper-wrapped bottle. She knocked back a gulp of bitter-fruity cheap wine, returned the bottle, nodded solemn thanks, and turned to go. "I'll tend to Dog. Y'all scatter." Over her shoulder—"Let me know if anybody needs anything."

Mothering again. Like it had been back before, in college, after the cancer took mom, after her Jeffrey bought it in Nam. And the baby. All those poor, angry, frightened, desperately ignorant, self-deluded druggies and hippies—children, all of them—coming to the door of the little farmhouse in Big Sur she'd inherited, looking for a fix, or salvation, or a place to hide from The Man, or to sleep off the confusion, the fear. So she'd quit school, given it up just a few yards from the home stretch on her economics degree, and tended to the wounded in body, mind, and spirit. It was good work and she was good at it, even if she didn't always win those battles, and it helped heal an ache in her own heart, the loss of mom and Jeffrey. And the baby.

The house burned down and then the police and all that hassle, so she took to the street, joined her charges there. Like them, she lived day to day, tending as she did so to whatever lost and stricken soul stepped, stood, or fell in front of her as best she could. She won some, lost some.

The street eventually led to Las Vegas, and she'd long ago forgotten exactly why. Something to do with helping a teenage girl dry up, get off the street, go home to her family. Or something like that. Anyway, here she was, caring for the fallen, or the about-to-fall, and doing a good job of it. It fit a need in her, filled a hole.

Mutterings of agreement followed as she stalked, fists bunched, broad hips swinging, down the alley toward Dallas Street and Hell. The soundtrack from *Terminator* played in her head, the scene where Arnold rises from the flames and stalks after Linda Hamilton.

Stan Gomez

S tan caught the phone before it clattered to the floor and slipped under the bed, as it sometimes did when he answered it, fumble-fingered, at—"Jesus H, it's three in the goddamn a.m.—"

"So you really didn't get your badge out of a Cracker Jack box," the voice on the phone crooned. Mary Ellen Blake, dispatcher, regular weekend night duty. Good girl. Old enough to remember Cracker Jacks. "I feel safer."

Stan sat up, eyelids pasted shut with crud, mouth full of garlicky cotton. His stomach roiled. Bad pizza. Or whatever. Long night writing reports.

Dispatch never disturbed senior officers unless it was an emergency. Las Vegas itself didn't have a police department. Law enforcement in Clark County was divided into seven district bureaus under the Sheriff's command. The Sheriff's second in command rotated among the bureau commanders, and tonight, Captain Stan Gomez held the short straw. He was top dog for the next week and a half, or until Sheriff Hanson got back from vacation in Pocatello.

"Glad to help," Stan said. "Give."

Stan heard Mary Ellen's smile disappear as she turned all business. "Disturbance on Dallas Street, at the Hell casino. An explosion or something. Patrol units on the way."

"Or something?" Stan tapped on the bedside light, cupped the phone between cheek and shoulder and grabbed his pants.

"Yeah, a bomb. We haven't gotten any calls from a perp, or anything like that. Before or after."

"How long ago? Did you say at Trane's place?" Some people hadn't gotten used to calling the complex "Hell." Stan was one of those. He sat on the edge of the bed, tugging on his pants.

"Three, four minutes ago. And yeah, at Hell, I said. And you're up, so—"

"I get it." To the closet for a shirt. A row of clean white shirts, all the same. "I'm up, I know—and I'm *up*. But I'm not 'up' for it." Tie from the rack, draped over a shoulder. Sit down on the bed again for socks, shoes. "Anybody hurt?"

"No reports."

"Shit, there are people in there." Holster. Check the weapon. *Trane lives on the top floor, and his staff has offices up there. Security people—Joe's people.*

"Suspects?"

"Nothing yet."

The fire department and police would have the upper hand before he arrived, but he had to go anyway; it was his job.

The job. The goddamn job.

"I'll be on my portable." Stan hung up. He didn't bother to turn on a light as he stalked, pulling on his jacket, down the semi-dark hallway, through the kitchen, to the alcove that led to the garage. He grabbed the compact portable radio from its recharge holster on the table by the back door and pocketed it.

He stood at the door, doing a quick inventory, patting himself down, a habit. Wallet, cell phone, tape recorder, weapon, cuffs, spare change, Tumeze—

No car keys. "Shit." On the hook by the kitchen sink.

He retraced his steps, threading his tie as he moved. He got the keys, and returned to the back door.

He hesitated again, hand on the doorknob. He listened to the house behind him, to the low, ever-present hum of the air conditioner. Background noise, the always-running AC blended with the endless hum of traffic on the streets outside. Suburban, yes, Stan's home, more or less. Deadwood Community Estates was a gated community of middle-middle to upper-middle-class homes not too close to the Strip, but not too far away either. High pink stucco walls with a row of cast iron decorative-appearing but sharp spikes along the top, typical Las Vegas faux Spanish décor, kept the noisy world out, as did the surveillance cameras and the 24-hour guard at the gate, and the subtle but constant roving security patrols. It never quite worked. Las Vegas never got quiet, really.

And never quite dark either. Even here, miles away, the Strip's pervasive gigawatt glare, an atomic bomb blast freeze-framed forever at the moment of greatest intensity, invaded through the window above the sink and formed a surreal neon-pinkish trapezoid on the kitchen wall opposite the dining room table. The glow illuminated a framed picture of him and Samantha, the wedding reception shot. Wedding cake on his chin and mustache, not streaked with gray yet, tuxedo tie askew. Longish hair, seventies style. Young. Hip. Her pretty face framed in a white lace headband, a string of pearls curving under her model-slender neck, and dark, wavy hair against bronze cheeks.

Smiles, real ones, both of them. It was an old picture. He was bald now.

The other picture on the wall, hidden in shadow, beside the wedding reception shot of him and Samantha and Jason, a head taller than his parents flanking him, gaunt and awkward in cap and gown. All smiles, all three of them. That too was before.

Light and noise, like a 24-hour movie set. Las Vegas never slept. Sometimes, Stan thought, neither did he—he only dreamed that he slept.

Behind the noise—nothing. Silence. Emptiness.

Samantha isn't home.

His badge could have come from a Cracker Jack box or not, didn't matter. He didn't need to be a detective to know she wasn't home. If she were there, sleeping in what Stan still called the guest room, she would have come out, tugging on her bathrobe, blinking, pouting, muttering about being "woke up from a decent night's sleep at three in the gosh-darned morning, and on a gosh-darned weekend too." If a cockroach farted in the garbage disposal, it woke her up. Usually grumpy, muttering her prissy version of vulgarisms. All she ever did when she was at home was sleep, and when she work up, if he was there, all she ever did was bitch about his noise. Like he was lighting cherry bombs in the bathroom or shooting the neighbor's dog for practice. "Gosh-darned noise all the gosh-darned time." He tried to be quiet. He dreaded it when she woke up, so he tried to be quiet.

She wasn't there. Working late as usual, her job with the city, maybe the Trane thing, the latest in a chain of crises. She'd complained about how Trane's idiotic decision to call his facility "Hell" had given her fits with the media, local and state regulators, the Casino Owners Association, a few church groups up in arms and God-only-knew-who-else. The papers and local TV hadn't been kind. He'd seen her on CNN last week, looking edgy, trying to put a good PR face on, which was her job. Her goddamn job. First amendment issues, moral issues, business issues. Legal problems. "No, Las Vegas isn't going to Hell." "No decision has been finalized." "You'll have to ask Mr. Trane on that." "We see no reason to be apprehensive, blah, blah, blah." Trying to put stripes on a donkey and call it a zebra.

Was she cracking up? Stan wondered. She was tough, yes, but she'd looked frazzled on the tube.

No note on the fridge, nothing on the answering machine, but she'd stopped leaving notes months ago.

Still, he tiptoed to the guest room. The door was ajar, the pervasive nightglow showed the bed empty, still made. She hadn't been home since the night before. Working late, as usual.

Stan sighed. The adrenaline rush that galvanized him with the call from dispatch dissipated a few degrees, replaced with a numb sadness, a too-familiar sensation of loss. As if she were dead.

He went, more slowly this time, into the blast furnace desert night, to his car.

He tried not to think as he drove to Trane's place about Joe, his people in there, night guards. *They're okay. Joe is okay. Trane is okay. Everything's okay.*

Dog. He thought about Dog.

As he drove down Philadelphia Street, air conditioner full blast, past the darkened and barren Cascade Hills subdivision and the wooden skeletons of the partly built homes there, he listened to police radio chatter.

Cops on site. Sergeant Stern in charge, holding the fort. Good cop. Nobody hurt. From the outside, Hell looks partially collapsed. Debris in the parking lot behind the restaurant. Hotel and casino look okay. Broken glass all over the place. No damage anywhere else but at Hell. Nobody inside yet. Fire Department on the scene.

County building inspectors on the way.

"Shit."

Stan listened to the chatter, but he didn't hear. He forced his thoughts from Joe and his people, and Trane and his people, maybe still in there, and he thought about Dog.

Did the son of a bitch finally go bonkers and blow something up? Had his mind games just been a scam?

Dog had played mind games with Metro, the FBI, and ATF in the past few years, since he'd showed up in town. Stan remembered the gun bust at Dog's trailer, when he had a trailer, up in the desert north of town. Lots of cops, fed, state, in on it. Lots of media.

Squirt guns.

The ridicule that followed him after the crates of plastic

squirt guns turned up was, he admitted, somewhat justified. He took the heat for the botched investigation. He'd let himself be suckered in on an elaborate practical joke, Dog's set-up, reinforcement for his hippie "enemy of the state" image. It took him a long time to live it down and advance in the department.

There was more to it. Dog had a plan. He'd redirected local and national media attention from him and the squirt gun bust to the city council, at the time planning to pave a north side vest-pocket park that the homeless favored, no more than a weedy lawn around a duck pond. Dog's shenanigans helped the little people carry the day. Time and CNN had helped celebrate the victory on the tiny, narrow strip of semi-greenery.

What rankled as much as that Dog had embarrassed Stan in particular and the department in general—nothing stuck on the feds' shoes—was that Dog had gotten away with it. No charges. What rankled even more was that Dog had to have had inside help. Somebody inside Metro must have helped set up the gag, and Stan *still* didn't know who'd done it.

Either that, or Dog was an atomic-mutated psychic werewolf, as one supermarket tabloid gushed. Dog got his picture on the cover of *Insider's Daily*, right next to a story about Madonna's heroic fight with bladder cancer.

That was long ago. Fool me once, your fault. Fool me twice—

The last time, eighteen months ago, another embarrassment for Stan and the department—FBI and the Bureau of Alcohol, Tobacco, and Firearms had sat this one out. More squirt guns. Teresa Santiago, angel of the street, had arrived on the scene by then, and joined with Dog as a co-champion of the downtrodden. Together, they beat the city fathers and mothers, playing the media like conga drums. Again, it involved saving a pathetic patch of lawn and a couple flowers from evil bulldozers and the streeties and media rejoiced in another little peoples' victory over big, bad City Hall.

There had been talk of a Movie of the Week with Jim

Carrey as Dog and Regis Philbin as Stan.

God, how they'd enjoyed laughing at Stan. Twice.

"Shit."

So maybe it was a set-up. Embarrass the local fuzz, do it twice, and hit them hard the third time, with the real thing this time. Hard to cry wolf the third time in the box.

"Shit."

On the radio, a call for an ambulance.

Stan turned on his light and siren and hit it.

"Shitshitshitshit."

Samantha Gomez

It was the best orgasm Samantha had ever had, and she cried out, louder than she ever had before, her moan muffled as she pressed her lips against Roberta Ripley's labia, tongue lapping in swift, probing arcs, fingers gouging Bobbie's firm round butt. Bobbie moaned too and their mutual orgasm went on and on and on. Both, at the same time. It had never happened like that before, but this time, this time . . .

Wow. Just wow.

Suddenly, with a sharp gasp, Bobbie sat up, disentangling from Samantha's embrace.

"What?" Samantha sputtered, spitting pubic hair. Bobbie had shot up as if she'd been poked in the ass with a sharp stick. It scared Samantha. Heart hammering, Samantha tried to sit up too. Her skirt had twisted side to front and she bounced and jerked on the van's plush carpet trying to straighten it out.

"Shh." Bobbie raised a wet finger. Samantha froze. In the dim light from the dashboard and the garish city lights that leaked through the van's tinted glass, Samantha marveled at Bobbie's glowing features even as she wondered why Bobbie had interrupted their love making at its climax. Bobbie's full lips parted slightly and she cocked her head, listening. Her upper teeth glowed florescent white in the semi-dark, and the tip of her agile tongue pressed against them. Sweat beaded on her upper lip, her cheeks, and her forehead. Her blonde hair formed a tangled halo around her pale, oval, oh-so-beautiful face. One strand clung to her sweaty cheek, accenting a perfect model's nose. Her blouse hung open, clinging to her round breast, the nipple hard.

So darn sexy.

"What is it, Bobbie?"

The love making had started too fast—they usually took their time, but they didn't seem to have any time lately—and it ended far too abruptly, and they sat up, more or less, still in a twisted tangle of sodden quickly-shed clothes, but the—*the shaking, or vibrating, or whatever*—continued. The van still rocked under Samantha's thighs, still *swayed.*

Earthquake.

As the thought occurred to Samantha, Bobbie moved. She shoved her clothes into a quick semblance of order, ignored her open blouse, and dived into the driver's seat. "Honey, we've got to get away from here," Bobbie said as she started the van.

Samantha reacted slower, sweat-soggy skirt refusing to untangle from around her hips, and she got half to her feet, when the van shot backwards, dumping her against the back of the passenger seat and onto her butt. She cried out in surprise and Bobbie muttered a "sorry," as she slammed on the brakes, sending Samantha again to the floor.

The van then shot forward, turned to the left, and Samantha took advantage of the brief lull that followed to plop into the passenger seat, where she groped with one hand for the shoes she'd dropped there, and buttoned her blouse with the other. Bobbie drove the van back around Hell's side parking lot, to the place where she usually parked it, by the restaurant back door. Samantha had just bent down to adjust one shoe strap over her heel when Bobbie slammed on the brakes again.

"Ouch, gosh-*darn* it," she protested as her head hit the dashboard. She wasn't hurt since the dashboard was made of padded leather trimmed in polished teak but she was annoyed.

Bobbie often fancied herself a stunt driver in a B car-chase movie, though she wasn't that good, but this was ridiculous. *An earthquake. Big deal. So what?* Samantha was from Fresno.

"It stopped," Bobbie said. Samantha, again a beat behind her lover, noticed the sudden silence. Through the van's tinted windshield, a cascade of dust oozed down the side of Hell's kitchen back wall. No bricks had fallen, at least as far as she could see, *but what if the wall* had *come down? We were parked—*

Samantha gulped. They had been within feet of the sidewall of Hell, and if Bobbie hadn't acted so fast, they might have been buried in falling brick, crushed to death.

Not a bad way to go, Samantha thought, remembering the spectacular orgasm. Then—*she saved our lives, moving so fast*—came with a nervous giggle.

But the wall hadn't come down so Bobbie hadn't saved their lives. They'd been lucky. If the wall had collapsed, and if Bobbie had been less alert, had moved slower—

"—better go," Bobbie said as she shot the van back into its hiding place in the dark spot by the back door. "There'll be police here soon and I'll have to—"

"Right. Me too." Samantha thought of Stan. Would he be on duty? If so, he'd be over on the Strip. More important real estate on the Strip.

Then, just as quickly as the thought of Stan came to her, she dismissed it. And him. She opened the door to step out an instant before the van stopped.

Samantha couldn't afford to be seen like this with Bobbie any more than Bobbie could afford their affair being discovered. Samantha's position with the city government made a private life impossible. The news media would boil her in ink and bad lighting if they found out about her and Bobbie. The affair would be over, and their lives would be damaged forever, unlivable.

The rendezvous had been a bad idea, or at least bad

timing, but who expects earthquakes at three in the morning in Las Vegas? Fresno, maybe, but not here.

Still, Bobbie had insisted when she called Samantha at her office out of the blue less than an hour ago. Urgent, her tone had implied. Samantha left the room just off her office where she'd had a daybed put in for when she worked late—most nights lately—and she'd come. In fact, Samantha was ready for the conference, had thought about it for days, trying to get up the courage to call Bobbie.

"Sammy, honey, we need to talk," Bobbie had said.

"Yes, we do," Samantha had responded, relieved Bobbie had taken the initiative. She refused to think about what Bobbie wanted to talk about, and tried as hard not to think about her own agenda. It was all so—difficult. So sad.

When Samantha got into the van, Bobbie's perfume had hit, and the too-long drought in their lovemaking had overcome her resolve to talk, just talk. Bobbie too declined to fight the urge to merge, and they didn't even get out of the parking lot.

Neither had talked much in their first meeting in weeks, since before Trane had announced his decision to call the hotel-casino-restaurant "Hell," and both Bobbie and Samantha had been plunged into a heap of work dealing with the immediate impact of that decision. Bobbie had PR work to do on behalf of Trane Enterprises, and Samantha had PR work to do on behalf of the city. At odds, sometimes, their efforts to manipulate the media and others concerned about Trane's strange—*darned stupid, if you ask me, but nobody ever does*—decision to call the place "Hell."

Now, things would get even more complicated, at least for the next few days. Who knew how long it would take or how complicated this new development would get. Whatever, Samantha knew she'd be in the hot seat. So would Bobbie.

The heat would start even before she got back to her office. She'd left her cell phone in the Mercedes, and it would be ringing when she got back to the car. As she opened the van door, still fumbling with her blouse buttons, resisting an urge to reach over and kiss Bobbie, the grimness of the situation came home to her.

This could ruin everything. She gave Bobbie a wistful look. "Call me," she said, then stumbled as she stepped to the pavement. She went down to one knee—

"Sammy honey?" Bobbie called out, concern in her voice.

"I'm okay." Samantha stood, shakily. Nobody around. "Call me." She blew Bobbie a quick kiss and ran toward her car, and to her office.

And to the job. The goddamn job.

Lois Ward

Lois' breath caught when she heard the scream. It came from the hallway, not behind her in the kitchen she'd just searched. It had to be Mr. Trane, out on another evening stroll. Or one of his employees. Ms. Ripley, maybe. She worked late sometimes.

Or maybe not. A streetie who'd snuck in to steal something or to find a place to sleep? Could be. One of Joe's other guards? She'd never seen one of the other guards who worked the night shift. They worked separate sections of the place, never crossed each others' paths.

The scream became a teeth-gritting groan, and Lois realized she'd been babbling mentally, putting off what she had to do—check it out. Find out who was hurt and do something.

Lois didn't handle blood well, or other people's pain. It was something she'd dreaded Joe might ask about when he hired her, but he didn't. Even when Mary got a minor knee scrape, Lois had a hard time smiling while wiping away the blood and tears. Like the time she'd helped Mark. She'd forced a smile.

A male voice moaned in pain. Hurt real bad. From over *that* way, down the corridor between her kitchen doorframe earthquake shelter and the back door. In the dark hallway, where it looked like part of the ceiling had crashed down and—and maybe hit somebody on the head.

Lois found her flashlight, which she'd dropped when she'd dived for the shelter of the doorframe, a few feet away. Sitting in the doorway, she aimed the light down the hallway, toward the moan. The beam stabbed through a haze of glittering dust, like something seen at the ocean bottom in one of those *National Geographic* TV shows, the search for the Titanic, or Atlantis. The floor was littered with boxes, cans, broken shelves, and—stuff. No fish.

Fifteen or twenty feet away, a waist-high stack of debris, a skeleton of twisted metal shelves, had spilled a dozen gallon-sized bottles from a split cardboard box. One bottle had broken open, splashing a bright yellow paste across the floor and onto the opposite wall. The hallway smelled like mustard, fresh-cut lumber, and fresh concrete.

Beyond that barrier, the far tip of Lois' flashlight beam caught a movement. The moan moved, extended a hand, and pulled down on a towel dangling from another tilted metal shelf just beyond the yellow mess.

"Mr. Trane?" Her voice clogged with dust, and she coughed and sputtered. She tried to stand, found her knees had gone to jelly and she had to use the kitchen doorway wall to pull herself upright hand over hand.

She thought she heard Mr. Trane's timid, reedy voice answer from behind her, from the hotel doorway, away from the debris-filled hall, the opposite direction from where she'd heard the scream and the moan. The moan repeated from behind the debris—*that* way—and she began to move toward it, dreading what she might find. She tiptoed through the yellow mess—a gallon jug of pungent mustard, like a broken ostrich egg, yolk spilled, poor baby, and sharp glass shards upthrust in the mess like bones. She slipped in the narrow space between the toppled shelf and the inner wall, and fell, getting the mustard all over her hands, knees and legs, but luckily not cutting herself on the glass. She wiped sticky hands on her shirt and eased past the debris obstacle course between her and the moan.

Where she found Joe.

"Joe? What are you—"

Her gorge rose to her throat and threatened to add peanut butter lunch brown to her mustard-yellowed uniform as she probed Joe's body with her flashlight beam. He lay on his back, right leg caught under an edge of a twisted shelf. Blood, neon-bright red, matted his scalp and the side of his face. Eyes wide, face twisted in pain.

"Lois—Lois—"

"Don't talk, Joe." She set the flashlight down on the floor, beam facing past Joe's face, and knelt at his side, pushing a loose pile of towels and an assortment of small cardboard boxes aside. She reached shaky fingers toward his bloody scalp, afraid to touch him, uncertain of what to do, but certain something needed to be done. "Tell me what hurts."

"Ha." Sputtering blood and dusty spittle, Joe barked a cough that might also have been a laugh. Between rapid, labored breaths, he repeated it. "Ha. Ha."

"Ha?"

"First you say—don't talk. Then—you say—tell me—"

"Well, all right, darn it, so you ain't hurt bad, but you've got blood all over—"

"Yeah. Banged my noggin on the wall. Superficial. Hurts like hell though. Get one of those towels—"

"Got it." Lois grabbed a towel and raised Joe's head off the floor, cringing as he grimaced, half-recoiling as warm, sticky blood coated her hand. She eased the towel under his neck. In a second, Joe gave a weak nod and smile.

Lois wiped her hands on her shirt front, then shifted the flashlight to get a better look at the head wound, and found the blood—it seemed like gallons—came from a quarter-inch gash at the hairline, top of Joe's forehead, just above the right eye. She grabbed another towel and dabbed at the gash. In a few seconds, the blood flow eased. "Not that bad," she said as much to herself as to Joe.

"Better," Joe managed between gritted teeth. His face, where not blood-coated, was dust-coated. He looked like an extra in a war movie. Dirt, blood, and sweat.

"Hold this to your head," she said, pressing the already blood-soggy towel into Joe's hand. He complied.

"You smell like a hotdog," he grunted. Blood spluttered from his pressed lips.

"You smell like—" Joe had soiled himself. "Where else you hurt?"

"My leg—" Then Joe screamed again. Something shifted, the fallen shelving maybe, with a metallic shriek, fingernails scraped on a chalkboard. It came from below Joe, by his leg.

Lois grabbed the flashlight and pointed it at Joe's right leg. The leg was crushed. Lois saw little blood, but the angle of the leg below the knee—

"Darn it, Joe—"

"What? *What?*"

Lois threw up. The blood all over Joe's face hadn't forced her stomach to rebel, but that leg did the trick. Thoughtfully, she turned just in time to toss her lunch on the other side of Joe's body so he didn't see it.

"Now, *that* stinks," Joe said.

"You got some selective sniffer." Lois sputtered and spat bile. She wiped her chin, smearing it with blood and mustard.

"What?"

"Never mind. We got to do something about that leg." She scooted down to get a closer look.

"Oh, that. Lucky I got two of them, and the left one works good. See?" Joe flexed his left leg at the knee and bit off another scream.

"You got to stop yammering," Lois said. "Stay still, hear?"

Joe nodded, teeth clenched.

Lois didn't look up to see if Joe listened or not. He was

still conscious. A good sign. She studied the metal bar crushing Joe's leg.

She felt like she had to get his leg out, some instinct told her so, though she didn't know much about first aid. Something about shock, she'd seen in a TV show. Besides, it looked so darn awful twisted up. Listening to Joe moan, it was like listening to Mary cry when she was teething. She couldn't stand doing nothing.

Joe groaned again, galvanizing Lois' resolve to get the leg out.

The metal bar, one bent leg of the shelf that had stood along the outer hallway wall until a few minutes ago, didn't look heavy, but it looked as if it had jammed sideways between the two walls of the hallway. Maybe she could pull it aside.

She pushed up on the bar till her arms ached, but it wouldn't budge.

All ninety pounds of me, doing the circus strongman act. Superwoman, I ain't.

Panting, Lois dropped to her knees and changed her mind about moving the bar. She needed help. Somewhere between the kitchen door and where she was now, she'd lost her cell phone. "Darn it."

"What? What?"

"Do you have a phone with you?"

"Yeah, I always bring one—oh damn."

"What? What?"

Joe struggled to sit up. "I *had* a phone." Lois crouched at his side and eased him back down. "In my pocket—when I came in. It must be—must be—"

"I got it." Lois noticed for the first time the rip in Joe's coat. She looked through the tangled debris around them on her hands and knees for the phone. She found his tape recorder and camera nearby and tried to put them into her pants pockets, but she was bent over and it was too awkward so she just stuffed them down her blouse. At one point, flashlight held in one hand, she almost put her other hand down in a pile of broken glass. The debris was too thick and tangled. The phone could be anywhere.

"I can't find the phone," she said.

"You got the camera and tape recorder?"

"Yeah, but—"

"Hold on to 'em. Where's the video?"

"The what?"

Joe shook his head as if to say "Never mind."

"Phone," he gritted. "Back door."

"Yeah, I remember." Lois stood and stepped toward the door, twenty feet away, where a phone hung on the wall next to a fire extinguisher. Beyond the door, traffic hummed, distant sirens wailed. Las Vegas never slept. Help would come, but who knew when. She couldn't wait.

On her second step, she kicked a small object on the floor, plastic. She focused her flashlight on it. Not the phone; a video tape. She picked it up.

"Hang on to that." Joe gasped. "Maybe—important—"

"I got it." Lois stifled her curiosity about the tape—Joe didn't always confide in her—and tucked it down her shirt with the camera and tape recorder. *Why was he here, anyway?*

She found the phone on the wall by the back door. She wiped her sweaty, dirty, bloody, mustardy hands on her pants and picked up the receiver. Dead.

"It's dead, darn it." She hung up.

Behind her in the dark London Blitzed corridor, Joe groaned.

First aid kit.

It was in the kitchen on the wall next to another fire extinguisher by the door where she had crouched when the quake hit. Back past Joe through the dark and the mustard and the glass and the debris obstacle course—back *that* way. *Should've grabbed it before, but—*She took a breath, preparing to go get it.

She heard a siren again and thought she heard a car engine in the parking lot. Help.

"Hang on, Joe," she called over her shoulder as she turned toward the door.

She slipped on something and fell forward, barking one knee on the concrete floor. She rose and hobbled to the door, teeth gritted against the pain. She hesitated, then ripped aside the yellow Keep Out tape and stepped into the bright outdoors.

The night air hit with a cool breeze, and she wondered how it could be hotter inside than outside. How un-Las Vegas-like the sudden coolness felt. But she'd been sweating, exerting herself, stressed, and the air inside Hell had been as dusty as she imagined a coal mine might feel.

There was a car outside the back door, a van, rather. *The* van. Ms. Ripley's company van, the plush executive van she used to commute back and forth to her apartment, or house, or wherever she lived, and to go wherever she went when she went anywhere, which she didn't do often, as far as Lois could tell. Lois had seldom seen it anywhere else but in its darkened spot by the back door of the Hell restaurant, and she'd seldom seen Ms. Ripley getting in or out of it, and she'd never seen anybody else in it.

Of course, there it sat, it its usual place. Like it hadn't moved in days, which maybe it hadn't. Lois sighed. She must have been mistaken.

"Hello?" Voice cracked, desperate, dust-choked. "Anybody?"

Silence, or the Las Vegas version of silence—traffic hymns, the occasional horn tootery, distant sirens, the city murmuring to itself—greeted her.

She stepped farther out into the parking lot, started to call out again.

Nobody around.

Lois fleetingly noticed an odd, intricate gash on the passenger side of the black Trane van ten feet from where she stood. Some kind of graffiti she'd missed when she came to work a few hours ago, and hadn't noticed the last time she'd looked out the back door during rounds, something she'd seen before and vaguely recognized.

Then she saw a glint of light from an object on the pavement by her foot. She bent over and picked it up. An earring? Hers? But she didn't—

Joe moaned again, louder, a higher octave of pain, and Lois heard another voice in there with him, muffled. Lois tucked the earring in her shirt pocket and ran back inside the restaurant.

"—can I do to hewp?" Mark Trane, calling to Joe from the darkness down the hall, beyond the mustard and broken glass.

"Mr. Trane, this is Lois Ward."

"Hewwo, Wois. Awe you okay?"

"Yes. What about you?"

"I'm okay. Joe is huwt."

Joe added a groan, his end of the conversation.

"Don't try to come closer, Mr. Trane. There's glass."

"Okay. I just have swippews. Did you caww an ambuwance?"

"No. The phone doesn't work here. Can you—"

"I'ww go to the hotew wobby and caww fwom thewe, okay?"

"Okay."

Mark Trane

As they talked, Mark saw enough of Lois' face in brief glimpses when the flashlight in her shaky hand happened to arc in the right direction. They were twenty yards apart, but he saw enough to doubt she wasn't hurt, despite what she'd said. Her hair was messy, she looked wild-eyed, and her face was dirty, and her uniform blouse seemed in the iffy, shifting light covered with blood splotches.

"Awe thewe any othew—" He coughed. "Othew guawds in the westauwant?"

The blood looks yellow.

"No," Lois shouted. "Joe said only him and me."

Ripley gone home for the night. Good. Just me, Lois, and Joe. Nobody else.

"Okay, I'ww get hewp now."

He retreated toward the door to the hotel hallway, where he'd sheltered from the earthquake, thinking about yellow blood, and Lois' wild, wide eyes glinting in the darkness as her flashlight passed under her chin. She had the look of a deer caught in headlights. It scared him, as much as the yellow blood, and more than Joe's groans did.

Joe had even tried to be funny while he'd talked with Mark in the dark, which was funny. Joe tried to be funny when he had occasion to talk business with Mark, which didn't happen too often since Ripley handled hiring, but he wasn't ever very funny. Mark laughed anyway. He liked Joe.

Mark found the hotel door in the now not-quite-so dark. The air had filled with floating, glittering dust in the narrow hallway between the kitchen and the hotel. The earthquake had shaken dust loose from the walls and ceiling plaster and it was a bit lighter—not much, but enough—in the hall, and he could proceed faster than he had when he'd come down it a few minutes ago. He saw no toe-stubbing debris as he shuffled along.

He hesitated at the junction between the hotel and restaurant hallways. Lois said Joe said there was nobody in the restaurant, but what if Joe was wrong? What about the casino? What if a streetie snuck in during the night to sleep under a table or under the slot machines? Lois and the other guards were supposed to keep them out but what if one broke in anyhow? And there *were* no other guards, just Lois and Joe, as Joe had said.

Why not? Why was Joe here anyway? Didn't he hire people for this kind of duty? There must have been a mix up, Mark decided, with the restaurant opening that morning then closing, and Joe's contract off then on again. Something like that. Ripley had rehired Joe per Mark's orders so Mark wasn't sure what had happened, why Joe was doing guard duty this night with no other guards in the building. Maybe Joe couldn't get his other people back on such short notice. Nobody's fault, but Joe, short-handed and responsible, had to fill in himself. Good man.

It made more sense than yellow blood.

Mark decided, as he turned down the corridor to the hotel lobby, it was good there'd been a mix up. Lucky. Sometimes things go wrong—and it's good. If there had been other guards—

Mark shuddered to think about people killed in his hotel. He'd lost a tourist on one of his riverboats once—drunken fellow fell overboard and got decapitated by the paddlewheel—

and it had made him super-safety-conscious, but he couldn't watch all his business affairs all the time. He had safety directives written and updated often, and hired safety inspectors—or he'd had Ripley hire them—and he kept them busy, paid them well. He'd been lucky over the years.

Joe hadn't been hurt too bad, it seemed. Neither had Lois. Despite the yellow blood, she looked and sounded okay.

And Ripley was—*Where* is *Ripley?*

He reached for his cell phone in his robe pocket, but he'd forgotten it too, along with his flashlight, when he went downstairs looking for—

His stomach cramped, and he remembered he'd been looking for Tumeze when the earthquake hit. He'd forgotten about the pain since. Now, he remembered.

"Oh, heww, heww, heww."

He turned around and headed to the restaurant, pain and desperation propelling him to a near trot. The light there was dimmer than elsewhere, but his eyes had adjusted. With little effort and no stubbed toes, he found a box of antacids—not Tumeze, but they'd do—tucked in a drawer under the cash register. He grabbed two rolls, put one in his robe pocket, and ripped the other open. He popped two chalky wafers in his mouth as he retraced his steps to the hotel lobby phone. He felt better but not much. He took two more tablets as he walked.

He was down the hallway between the restaurant and hotel lobby when it occurred to him there was a phone in the restaurant, by the cash register where he stood a minute ago.

"Oh, heww, heww, heww," he muttered through chewed Brand X antacid. He was closer to the lobby now so he kept on going.

In the lavish, mirror-lined lobby, so plush that when he'd first seen it, it made him think of Oscar night in Hollywood, he went behind the concierge's desk next to the check-in counter. As he reached for the phone there, it rang.

He picked it up. "Hewwo?"

"Is this—is this—"

"I'm sowwy, whoevew you awe, but—"

"You're Mister Trane, right? Are you all right? This is Miles Doughton from the *Clark County Chronicle-Progress.* Can you tell me what's—"

Mark, flustered, slammed down the receiver and bit back a curse. He took a breath, ready to lift the receiver again to call for help, and the phone rang again.

"Mister Trane, this is—"

Mark disconnected.

"Heww, heww, heww." He punched 911.

A woman's voice, officious and calm, came on the line. Mark told her about Joe and she asked a few questions. Calm, deliberate. Reassuring. Help was on the way.

Mark hung up. The phone rang and he took it off the hook. He took a deep breath and looked around, hearing the tinny but insistent voice on the discarded receiver, and the commotion from out front. The lobby was separated from the front drive by an architecturally stupid long, curved wall of mirrors and brass finishing, so Mark couldn't see what was going on, but he heard. Sirens, police radios blaring, and voices shouting. He thought he heard Ripley's voice above the din, commanding attention as she usual did, but he wasn't sure.

He didn't care. The instant he got off the phone and looked up, his jaw dropped in horror. What he saw in the lobby, not what he heard beyond it, commanded his attention.

Bare walls. Splintered mirror glass shards littered the lobby carpet, from wall to wall, from one end to the other, around the curved hallway, as far as he could see in any direction. The lobby glittered in a million little fragments, a carnival hall of mirrors.

"Oh, heww, heww, heww."

Mark had walked some twenty or thirty feet over that glassy carpet. So focused had he been on getting to the phone, calling for help, that he hadn't noticed.

He looked down at his feet. Dust coated his fuzzy slippers like clown makeup. He would not have been surprised to see yellow blood. He saw none. He wiggled his toes. No pain.

He looked back the way he'd come. Glass fragments, none larger than a foot or so, covered every inch of the carpet.

How had he made it from down the hallway to the desk without slashing himself to ribbons? He didn't recall hearing any crunching glass as he walked over it. Did he not step on any, or did he just not hear it?

Luck? Miracle?

Another unsolved mystery, for another time.

Right now, trapped by the glass, he had a problem.

He picked up the phone. "Hewwo? Mistew Doughton? I have a pwobwem."

Percy Oswald

Percy Oswald squirmed in his bed sheets as his recurrent
dream went into its final act, the part where the man in the
dream—the man who had just levitated the wrecked van so
Percy could pull the unconscious or maybe dead driver out from
under it—disappeared. In the dream, one version or another, the
man sometimes told Percy how to do the levitating act just
before he vanished, but Percy never could remember what he'd
said. Or he couldn't hear him in the steady, drumming rain. Or
he spoke in a foreign language, and Percy tried to keep up while
thumbing through a soggy dictionary that didn't seem to be in
the same language the man spoke. Or the man spoke in a lisp, or
a jet passed overhead drowning the man out, or a bird had
defecated in Percy's ear sideways but he couldn't dig the feces
out before the man disappeared. Or something else.

It was always *something* in the dream. Sometimes he
didn't even get to ask before the man disappeared. Sometimes he
spent the last act of the dream, long after the man had gone,
playing detective, examining the scene by flashlight, or in the
light of dawn, looking for clues in the mud, blood, broken glass,
and mangled metal.

Sometimes he knew—sometimes he even did it, levitate
something, not always the van—but then he'd wake up and
forget how he'd done it. Always something, always different, the

dream.

Always the same, too. The same van on its side, wheels still spinning, the same woman trapped, maybe dead under it, the same man levitating the van so Percy could drag her body out from under it, and the same man then vanishing in the rainy night. No dream was ever quite like it had been, back then, back in October 1967, when it had happened for real.

Percy squirmed, the sheets tightening in a tangle around him, as so often happened, as the dream ended. Theodora nudged him, a pudgy elbow, muttered annoyance, and resumed snoring.

Percy squinted puffy eyes at the bedside clock. The TV was still on, silent, beyond the end of the bed. Three-twenty a.m., blurry red letters told him. Theodora had fallen asleep watching the news again. The remote was on her side of the bed. CNN was doing a live report. He wanted to turn off the annoying flicker-show, but didn't want to disturb Theodora to do it. He sighed and closed his eyes. He wanted to regain the dream.

No use. As usual.

Back then. October, 1967. He'd been driving back to his tiny studio apartment in Concord, California, from a meeting held in the living room of a supposed friend of a supposed friend in nearby West Pittsburg. A group that had been represented to him as good Christians had met to discuss issues involving the Vietnam War and the Navy base, where they shipped ammunition across the Pacific to the boys in the war.

Wrong bunch at that meeting, it turned out.

All through seminary, Percy had pondered the moral questions. Oppose the war, or support the government? Or what? What was a good Christian to do? His peers had become divided as the war escalated. Percy had tried to remain neutral, praying for guidance, and studying, listening, pondering.

There had been a big march on Washington, DC, a few days earlier. It ended up at the Pentagon, where Abbie Hoffman and his crowd planned to rid the place of evil spirits, and levitate it. A prank, designed to gain media attention. A joke, nothing more. Just a joke.

He drove his battered VW to the meeting to study, to learn. He went with no agenda, still undecided even in his last few weeks of school.

A few radical hippies held the floor in that meeting in the basement of a local church. They seemed bent on forcing a peculiar agenda on fellow Christians like himself who thought the meeting was something it wasn't. Inspired by Hoffman's pranks, still in the news, the group wanted to imitate the event here—they wanted to levitate an ammo ship, lift it right out of the Suisun Bay. That somebody might get hurt in such a silly, self-centered prank never seemed to cross anybody's minds, Percy observed. They didn't seem to care. Not Christian.

It was all a game to them. And they smelled bad, many of them, especially the most radical and foul-mouthed. Percy pointed it out; a mistake.

They laughed at him, taunted him. Angered, embarrassed and frustrated, Percy left the meeting early, under a cloud. Literally. It was raining.

He drove through the hills up Bailey Road, a windy, narrow stretch of badly patched, pot-holed and cracked two-lane asphalt that bisected the Navy ammo depot being discussed in volatile terms behind him. The rain obscured his vision. His wipers didn't work worth a darn. The road was wet, slick. It was night. He was angry and tired, coming down with the flu, and, he later decided, maybe the hippies had snuck some LSD into his punch.

He didn't see the van.

He swerved in time—he'd drifted over the median—and the on-coming van went off the road. In his rearview mirror, he saw it smash into the barbed wire fence that lined the road, rise into the air in a wash of flying dirt, fence post and wire, as if to take off, then roll down the road. And roll and roll and roll. Like nothing he'd ever seen in a movie. He heard nothing over the pounding rain and his startled scream. A silent movie.

The van ended up just off the pavement, on its side.

Percy stopped, left his VW in the road—no shoulder lined Bailey Road because the Navy wanted to discourage people stopping for security reasons—and ran back to the crash. He found the woman, legs stuck out from under the van. In a lightning flash, he saw the blood, a lot of it, neon-crimson against the black mud, and knew she must be dead.

He threw up.

He still had his head bent over, retching, when he smelled the bum over the stench of his own puke. He smelled him before he saw him. He looked up. Lightning flashed. There he was. The bum. In the cold, relentless rain, he stood hands on his hips, clothed in black, face hidden in shadow, head cocked as if in question.

The bum reeked. "Well, what the fuck are you going to do, asshole?" Urine, feces, body odor, fetid breath. "Huh, dipshit?"

"I—I—" Percy felt dizzy. The crash, the blood, the rain. The bum's stench. Shock. The onset of the flu—and maybe the acid the hippies had slipped into his punch. Or something. Dizzy.

"Sit there with your thumb up your ass, huh? Jesus H goddamn fucking Christ, dickhead. Lucky to be alive, huh? What about the bitch? Fucking *bas*tard, you. Cocksucking mother*fuck*er—"

The bum reeked and cursed incessantly.

Then, in a lightning flash, Percy saw the bum step back a few paces into the middle of the road, wave at the van like a magician conjuring doves from a hat, cursing all the while, and reeking. The van rose in the air on the end of the invisible magic strands emanating from the bum's fingertips. Six feet into the air, where it hovered.

"Well, get your fucking ass in gear, dickhead," the bum said, magic fingers still pointed at the levitated van, "and pull the bitch out."

Percy did, and found the woman alive. Lots of blood, yes, but alive. It might have seemed a miracle to Percy if he hadn't already seen the van floating in the air. Hands shaking, he tended to her as best he could on the roadside, in the rain and the mud. He wiped blood away and muttered to the unconscious woman. "There, there," he muttered, not knowing what else to do.

"Anybody else hurt, sir?"

The voice came from over Percy's shoulder. Not the bum. A Marine, from the Navy base, outlined in another lightning flash, had appeared on the empty road from out of nowhere. The faceless bum had disappeared, the van lay where it had been moments ago.

What had happened?

Percy told no one about the incident until he met Theodora three years later. By then, he had found his recurrent dream—the incident replayed over and over again in slumberland, a macabre, teasing, surreal event, never too real, or too unreal either. The bum. His odor, his language. His magic. The levitation. The woman, maybe not really dead. Or maybe she was, and—

He'd also found his mission: Find out what happened that night.

In the blanket gully between him and Theodora, Percy found the clipboard with his latest editorial. He picked it up and fumbled for the red-ink pen attached to the clipboard by a cord. He'd been editing the piece when he drifted off to sleep. Now fully awake, he decided to finish.

The fuzzy, flickery light from the TV across the room wasn't enough to read by—CNN had some disaster on, but he couldn't see what without his glasses.

He tapped the bedside light up a notch, checked to see it hadn't disturbed Theodora, who snored on. He pushed another pillow behind his back and sat up, pushed the sleeves of his striped red-and-white flannel pajamas above his elbows, and focused on the editorial.

The piece would run in the next edition of his weekly newspaper, *Christian Conspiracy*, and in a longer version, in his monthly magazine, *Miracle Monitor*.

He read: "The Oswald College of Miracles, on our ranch outside Idaho Falls, has the largest library in the world devoted to the subject of miracles. The Internet has accelerated that growth in recent years. We now have more than half a million volumes, and we're growing daily . . ."

Not one of those books can tell me how to do it . . .

". . . The inviolable law of gravity, for example, seemingly violated by the infrequent occasions of reported levitation, requires intensive investigation, to separate the imagined from the real, the mundane from the extraordinary . . ."

I've tried, Lord, how I've tried. India. That faith healer in Brazil. Peyote, LSD. The tank. If my readers knew . . .

". . . and we've increased our grant fund to help independent scientists explore the subject. No strings are ever attached . . ."

. . . I won't tell my faithful readers about the detective agencies I've also hired over the years, oh no. Scientists or detectives—all a waste. Nobody knows who that bum was . . .

Theodora stirred, a hitch in her snoring, and she rolled over. She fumbled at her bedside. "Still at it?"

"Um."

". . . seems to be no pattern that scientists, confined by the rigors of the Scientific Method, may grasp, which prompts yet more questions . . ."

. . . like why a filthy bum can levitate a two-ton van, and maybe bring a dead woman back to life, and I can't lift a pencil without my arthritis kicking in, or even heal my own warts . . .

"Mind if I watch TV?"

"Um."

". . . can occur to anyone, any time, anywhere, under

any circumstances. Defying classification, clarification, compartmentalization—rationalization—the miracle, whether it be levitation, healing, or any of a hundred more mundane cousins . . ."

Why would that *woman be saved? A prostitute, a doper, died of an overdose three years later. Then somebody like Tommy—If birth is a miracle, is Sudden Death Syndrome the opposite?*

"Oh, dear." Theodora stirred, alarm in her voice. The TV murmured. "Percy?"

"Um?"

". . . even as Job, to rise again and reaffirm our faith that miracles occur, and that despite their insubstantiality, their defiance of reasoned inquiry, there is a reason . . ."

"Percy." She tugged on his sleeve.

"What?" He glanced at her, annoyed. Her gaze, shock and concern, riveted on the TV. He set the editorial aside, grabbed his glasses from the bedside table, and looked.

He knew the woman on the TV, even before her name flashed below her image. "Roberta Ripley, Executive Secretary for Special Affairs, Trane Enterprises," the legend on the screen said.

Ripley. Trane's so-called right-hand man. He'd seen her on TV before, of course, but he'd also seen her—where? When?

"Turn up the volume, dear."

"—injuries with the exception of Mr. Foxworthy," Ripley was saying, "who heads the agency maintaining security for the building. Also his associate, a Ms. Lois Warden, whose injuries are minor. Both have been taken to Clark County General for treatment. There are no—"

Theodora sat up straighter. "Isn't that—"

"Yes."

In the dream—this one, tonight. He'd seen her in the dream. Seen her—and heard her.

Ripley stopped, cupped an ear to hear in indistinct

question from one of the herd of reporters. Behind her, what looked like the front of a hotel.

Hell. Had to be.

Something wrong, yet familiar . . .

"Not a bomb," Ripley said, face angry, an indignant lilt to her tone. "There is evidence that an earthquake . . ."

Percy barked a laugh. He'd not intended to name the casino in the editorial, but . . .

"Earthquake?" he muttered. "I wonder if . . ."

He'd seen it in the dream. The exact spot. The camera lights, the broken glass. He'd seen *Ripley* in the dream, dressed like a bum, in front of the hotel. She was telling him—

—telling him how to do it.

"No," Ripley said, "Mr. Trane, was unhurt. Nobody besides the two security officers—" Another interruption. "No, I left the building *before* the disturbance and was in my car when it occurred. Mr. Trane was inside where he saw Mr. Foxworthy and Ms. Warden. They told Mr. Trane—" She waved away another interruption and plunged on. "Mr. Trane was the *only* one inside. Besides Mr. Foxworthy and Ms. Warder, I mean."

Her, in the dream.

Percy jumped out of bed.

"Dear, what are you—"

He saw it all clearly, at last. At long, long last.

"Get dressed, Theo." He picked up his cell phone and punched a number as he walked to the closet.

". . . only minor damage, and no injuries—except to the two security guards . . ."

"Percy, who are you calling? It's three-thirty . . ."

He hadn't intended to mention Hell in the editorial, but it had been on his mind. The effrontery of Trane calling the place "Hell." Even in Las Vegas, that hellish place, the notion galled.

". . . private doctor, who is out of town at the moment, but is expected to arrive within the hour . . ."

"Hanson, Percy here. How soon can you get the jet

ready?"

He'd intended the editorial to be about how God speaks in mysterious ways, often through messengers disguised as—as bums.

"Percy, where are we going?"

"Good enough," he told Hanson. He clicked off, tossed the phone on to the bed.

He smiled as he pulled off his pajamas. "Signs and omens, Theo, like I said." He pointed to the TV. "This—*thing*—down there has bothered me since Trane gave it that abominable name."

He'd been troubled about Hell since the announcement, but couldn't put his finger on why. Now—*now* it was clear. The earthquake, and the message in the dream, made it clear.

Nobody had been hurt in the earthquake.

Earthquake. Insurance people called such events "an act of God." Nobody hurt.

"Yes, I know." Theo dressed. "So?"

He pulled on his pants. "It's a sign, you see? An earthquake shakes a casino named Hell. Nobody hurt. A sign."

"God has spoken?" Theo's tone wasn't dismissive.

"I've never had a clearer vision, Theo. I had a dream tonight, and now this—"

"All right, but what—"

"We're going to Hell."

Samantha Gomez

Her desk phone buzzed as Samantha stepped off the elevator and headed down the hall toward her office. She'd turned off her cellular while she drove from Hell to city hall. She needed time, even if a few minutes, to think. It hadn't helped.

City hall was modest by Las Vegas standards in size and adornment, and utilitarian to a fault, almost Stalinesque. It had no flashy lights, gaudy ornaments or tacky paint schemes so common to the Las Vegas landscape. A huge parking lot surrounded it, lined with palms and narrow aisles of neat lawn dotted with flowers and shrubs.

Tonight, as most nights, city hall was empty except for security, a few janitors, and the odd late worker or two. Las Vegas never slept, but city hall tried to. It was quiet, now. It won't last, Samantha thought, as her heels tattooed down the tile floor to her tenth-floor office, the phone, and the ceaseless demands of her job.

The job. The gosh-darned job.

An earthquake in Las Vegas. Or a bomb. Please, God, let it be only an earthquake or a bomb.

Hell to pay either way.

Samantha had managed to worry herself into near apoplexy as she drove the ten minutes to her office. She didn't know what was going on back at Hell, and with Bobbie—they hadn't had a chance to talk after all—so she didn't know what to do, not now. She knew there'd be work for her on this earthquake—*or maybe a bomb, or worse*—lots of it, and right now. PR work. Plug leaks, fend off media sharks, keep people happy, keep the money flowing. Hell to pay. She'd just have to put that much-needed, long-overdue talk with Bobbie on hold.

All regular lines were rerouted to her answering machine. It was the special private line reserved for her secretary that buzzed. She popped on the speaker, said "Yes, Donald?" and noticed her reflection in the big window behind her desk, overlooking the Strip. Her hair was a mess, her blouse buttoned crookedly. Luckily, nobody had seen her arrive.

"Ms. Gomez, are you up?"

Donald sounded excited, his mellow tenor hiked up a notch to a squeak. She took off her blouse. "Donald." She forced a smile into her voice. "Are *you?*"

"I was working on my screenplay when I got a call—"

"Yes, and?" She pulled a fresh blouse from a closet just off the alcove where she'd had a daybed installed not long ago for when she worked late. She put it on.

"There's been a disturbance down at the Hell casino, ma'am. I hear that it's a bomb or an earthquake, but I got this call—"

"I know." *Oops. How would I know?* She buttoned up the blouse. She could see Hell from her vantage, among the city lights, six miles *that* way. A cloud of luminescent yellowish haze seemed to hover over it. It looked like pictures she'd seen on TV news, bombings in Baghdad, smoke rising from bombed out building. Cars entered the lot below, in a hurry. Busy night.

"You *know*? How would you—"

"I can see it out my window." *Why am I up at this hour? I always work late, remember? Dedicated. Right.* "What do you hear?" She checked herself in a wall mirror. Fresh blouse tucked into her skirt, but hair a mess.

"I got CNN. Ms. Ripley is outside Hell. Nobody hurt—"

"Thank god." She turned on the TV, found CNN, muted the volume. She brushed her hair as she watched. Bobbie looked beautiful, but disheveled. "Nobody hurt? Are you sure?" She checked in a mirror. She still looked wrong, undone, somehow. Pretty, still, but not as pretty as Bobbie looked under the TV lights. Not as ragged either.

"That's what Ripley says, ma'am. She says it wasn't a bomb, it was an earthquake. No—a *disturbance*, she calls it. Sometimes she says 'earthquake,' too, but I got this call—"

"Yes, and?"

"A gentleman from UNLV, a professor. A Dr. Hawthorne, Frank Hawthorne, ma'am. He says he tried to call you but he got your machine and he remembered that he had my number because we'd consulted with him a few years ago—"

"Yes, I remember Dr. Hawthorne." *Who the heck?* "What department was he in, again?" She did her face. A calming ritual.

"Geology. He was monitoring seismic activity in southern Nevada—that's his job, with the AEC—"

"Yes, and?" Dr. Hawthorne? Sounded familiar.

"He said it wasn't an earthquake, Dr. Hawthorne did. He went on and on about 'P' waves, or 'Q' waves, or whatever. I didn't understand—"

"Not an earthquake?"

"No, ma'am. Subsidence, he says."

Samantha remembered Hawthorne. *That* long ago, first year on the job, doing city PR, they'd found cracks in the wall of a new high rise going up on the Strip. The Buttes. Old West theme. The place had *sunk* a foot. It baffled engineers and inspectors.

Hawthorne came in on the problem, on loan from the University, or from the AEC. Whatever. Turned out the initial ground survey for the Buttes had been faulty. The ground was over a "soft" spot, a sinkhole, unlike its neighbors a few dozen yards away. The building couldn't hold the weight of its proposed 25 floors. The builders had to scale the project back to a dozen floors and alter the whole design from the ground up— the soft ground up—to eliminate most of the weight.

"Subsidence, you say?" She squinted in the mirror. Something still not right.

The media had been quick to remind readers and viewers—and voters—about the folly of "building your house upon the sand." Biblical pomposity or bad joke, never mind. Samantha had worked overtime spinning the incident. The city engineers and building inspectors weren't at fault. They were the best in the world, as they had to be, since they dealt with billion-dollar construction projects every day, and the error was just a fluke, blah, blah, blah. Keep the gamblers happy, keep the money flowing. It was a tough project and Samantha had done well, endearing herself forever to local bureaucrats and investors.

The Butte hotel's investors, out-of-town money, had taken it in the shorts. Somebody had to be sacrificed. They, and some unfortunate middle-grade engineer who made an unfortunate error. Thrown to the wolves. It was a hard lesson, and it had ended any naiveté about her job Samantha might have nurtured so fresh out of college. The real world was hell.

Gosh-darned job.

"Yes, ma'am, like the Buttes. Remember, back when—"

"Yes, I remember." Maybe it was her skirt. She should change her skirt, too. She'd have to open up the phone lines, soon, get in the thick of things, find out what was going on, schmooze with the media. Do the job. "Where's Hawthorne now?"

"He's at the U. He gave me his number—"

"I want you to get him in front of the media, quick." She pulled off her skirt, selected another from the closet, tossed the old one onto the closet floor, shut the closet, and pulled on the new skirt. "We've got to get this subsidence or whatever it is out there, dilute this talk of earthquakes or bombs. You have numbers for CNN, and for the *Chronicle-Progress*? Call up Miles Doughton, see if he—"

"Yes, ma'am, I got it."

"After that, get in here." In the mirror, she looked fresh, energetic, professional. Something was *still* wrong.

Samantha hung up and sat in the big leather chair behind her desk, frowning at the TV against the near wall, twisting the earring on her left ear. Thinking. *Subsidence, or whatever. Good.*

"Not good enough." She found a package of Tumeze in the desk drawer and popped a wafer, chewed.

An earthquake in Las Vegas, or a bomb, spelled economic disaster, but she'd dealt with the like before, most often in "war games," simulations, but sometimes pretty close to the real thing. No problem. She'd dealt with a subsidence-type problem, too. The Buttes. She'd had to. Spin it right, no problem. Keep the customers happy, the money flowing.

If she failed . . .

If she failed, Samantha could kiss her job goodbye, and her shot at mayor.

Hell had been a nightmare since Trane, through Bobbie, had announced his decision to give the place that abominable name. Luckily, Bobbie had tipped off Samantha, given her enough advance notice to get ahead of the curve on it. It had helped, some.

Now this.

Maybe this is a good thing, she mused. Hell was a pain in the patootie, and having it topple—bomb, earthquake, subsidence, or whatever—would help make the problem go away.

Then things would go back to normal.

Samantha sighed, as she opened up her phones. No, things would never get back to normal. That's what she wanted to talk to Bobbie about. *What did* she *want to talk to* me *about*?

Bobbie had been evasive for weeks. When they did get

together, pillow-talk, Samantha got the impression Bobbie was hiding something. Another woman?

Samantha had hired a detective to follow Bobbie to find out. Joseph Foxworthy had reported Bobbie wasn't seeing anybody. She worked late at the Trane complex—this was before Trane had named it "Hell." Then she went to her apartment across town. Foxworthy had worked for Trane—Bobbie hired him for it on Trane's behalf. In fact, he handled hotel security. Reliable, discreet service.

No, that wasn't it. Samantha had had a hunch that tonight, their impromptu meet in the van, was to have been the moment Bobbie had chosen to say what she wanted to say to Samantha.

The phone lines lit up.

Did Bobbie plan to break off their relationship?

No, that wasn't it. If anything, Samantha got the impression that Bobbie wanted their relationship to—what? Escalate? Whatever. She couldn't believe, after those passionate minutes in the van, that Bobbie planned to break up with her.

What had Bobbie wanted to talk to Samantha about?

It was not quite four a.m., and her phone lines were lit up. Media, all of them, no doubt.

Whatever it was with Bobbie, she wouldn't find out soon. There, on the TV, Roberta Ripley regaled the media in front of the damaged Hell hotel, spinning the damage to molehill size, using her famous smile. Same thing Samantha would be doing in a few seconds—and for hours, days, or weeks after.

Subsidence. A sinkhole. Earthquake. Or whatever. Anyway, there'd be an investigation.

She opened the first line, to interrupt her thoughts, not good ones. "City offices, may I help you?"

Bobbie had bought the property for Trane Enterprises under a cloud that the Yellowstone investors created with their illegal activities and shoddy practices. State and fed offices were still trying to indict a few principals in that mess. What if—

"Ms. Gomez? I recognize your voice. This is Miles Doughton of the *Chronicle-Progress.*"

"Yes, Mr., uh, Miles. How may I direct your call?"

Samantha had looked into the Yellowstone affair, made sure nobody got hurt, that the money kept flowing. She hadn't looked as carefully at Trane Enterprises. Trane had come—had sent Bobbie—to save the property, take care of things. Trane Enterprises became the Good Guys. Samantha had been so glad to see Bobbie—living right here in Las Vegas!—she hadn't looked too deeply into what Trane intended to do with the property. Rather, and to the point, what Bobbie intended to do. What if—

"Doughton, Ms. Gomez," the reporter said without rancor. "Miles is my first name. You remember me. Do you have a minute?"

Don't think about "what if," Samantha told herself—*how many times have I told myself that?*

The maybe-next mayor of Las Vegas, with a lot of hard work, and a little bit of luck, stopped thinking negative thoughts and went back to her job.

The gosh-darned job.

"Yes, Mr. Doughton." She smiled at the bank of blinking lights on her phone. "What's on your mind?"

Joe Foxworthy

Joe regained consciousness. Sort of. He felt cotton-headed, like he was going to puke or faint or both. He blinked nine-pound eyelids, couldn't focus. He hurt—somewhere, but he didn't know where. Didn't want to know.

In a moment, he had it. He lay in an ambulance, and Lois sat next to him, holding his hand. The ambulance was moving and a siren wailed far away. No—it was close, the siren. Loud.

Two EMTs sat in the ambulance with him and Lois. He could hear one above his head, at the front of the ambulance, and see the other's back, by his leg, facing away, doing something to the leg. The broken leg. He didn't look closely. Didn't want to.

Woozy.

The siren came from the ambulance he was in. It was for him, the siren, and for his leg. Lucky. It could have been worse.

The ambulance. He was going to a hospital. Broken.

"—all right? Huh?" Lois was saying. She looked between Joe and the EMT Joe couldn't see. He couldn't move his head. There was something up his nose.

"Wha—" His tongue stuck to the roof of his mouth.

"Hang in there, Joe."

Joe nodded. He had a headache, the thing in his nose itched and his left hand stung, like a bee-sting. IV. He couldn't move. Didn't want to.

"Anybody—" He swallowed, licked papery lips, found enough spit to continue. "—body hurt?"

Lois smiled, a look of profound relief crossed her face, and Joe realized she must have been very worried. She looked awful. Hair messy, face dirty, and her uniform—

"Besides you? You said we were the only ones there, right?"

Joe nodded. *That's because I lied about how many people I hired for the job.* A yellow gunk stained her blouse.

"Okay. Good. That's what I told them." She tipped her chin at one of the EMTs, the unseen one, who fiddled with a computer box, clickety-click, and barked numbers and cryptic syllables into a microphone. Cybermedical stuff. He'd seen it on TV.

"Trane?" Joe croaked. Besides the antiseptic medicine smell, and shit—he'd shit his pants—he smelled mustard.

"He's okay. He said there was nobody else in there. So just me, you, and him. Are you sure?"

That's mustard on her shirt.

"Yeah, I'm sure. No other guards but you. And me."

And red handprints on her boobs. Blood. "And Trane."

Lois nodded at the EMT—a woman, Joe noticed. She repeated the information into her microphone.

"You got mustard on your shirt."

"Please try not to talk, sir," the invisible woman EMT said.

Joe nodded. It hurt his head. "Did you get—get—"

"I got it. Your camera, your tape recorder, that video tape you had with you. Couldn't find your phone, but I found mine."

"Take my wallet—" A coolness on his thigh told Joe he didn't have any pants on.

"Please, sir."

"I got it." Lois held up the wallet. "And your keys. Don't talk. I'll—I'll—" She gulped, took a big breath. "I'll go back to the office, store this stuff. Take calls. I'll hold the fort."

Joe nodded. "Erroll, he—"

"Please, sir."

"Erroll?"

Nod. Woozy.

"Do you want me to—what? Call him?"

I want you to find out about those new meds the doctor ordered. And find out about the cost.

"I—I—"

"Please, miss, you have to—"

Lois faded from Joe's view as his lids grew heavier, and he grew woozier. The EMT that told Lois to shut up had pushed her aside and tinkered with the things in Joe's nose. The world turned to cotton, like a dream sequence in a bad horror movie.

Broken leg. Can't work. No insurance. Lois will hold the fort. I can't pay her, maybe not ever. Maybe jail for me when they find out I've been padding my bill to Ripley.

And how the goddamn hell, then, can I help Erroll?

Fade to black.

Teresa Santiago

Teresa waddled her fat butt the block and a half over to the Hell casino, fists bunched. She sweated and cursed a blue streak under her breath. Larry ran his little legs off to keep up with the taller woman. Teresa let him come. It was a free country.

"In the movies," Teresa said to Larry, "the hero gets away from the bomb at the last second, or he disarms it, and he don't get hurt, maybe except for a dab of catsup on his forehead, make it look how lucky he is. It don't matter how big the bomb is, it don't kill him. Like that one movie, where Christian Slater and the girl get away from the nuclear bomb?"

Larry said nothing.

"*Broken Arrow*. That's the one. John Travolta in it, too. Not just men stars, no. Like Xena, or Sigourney Weaver in the *Alien* movies. Woman heroes make good box office these days. It don't matter everybody know they use stunt doubles for those explosion scenes. Audience don't care, long as the star okay.

"Anyway, it don't matter cause it ain't like real life. In real life, the bomb go off, everybody in three blocks dies. You remember 9/11? Seen it on the CNN?"

Larry said nothing.

"Me too. People get fingers blown off every Fourth of July. Folks fall off ladders putting up Christmas tree lights.

Salmonella kills every Easter. Bad eggs. Cigarettes." She coughed. "Don't get me started on cars. Be glad we can't afford the damn things."

Larry trotted alongside the big woman, silent. Larry never said anything. She didn't try to shoo him away. Larry could go anywhere he wanted to. It was a free country.

Where's Dog?

Across the street from Hell, on the Foxtrot Bookstore side of Dallas Street, Teresa stopped, panting and sweating, surveying the scene. Construction equipment and supplies littered the Hell backside parking lot, like a war zone, and Teresa saw signs of an explosion, or something like it. A stack of wooden pallets had toppled over. Bricks and pink dust by the trash bin lay in a pile below a gap in the top of the restaurant wall, like a giant had taken a wheelbarrow-sized bite out of the wall and spat out the debris. A long crack in the wall led from the giant-chewed brick gap to the top of the back door. A pipe scaffold had collapsed by the wall, splashing buckets of pale blue paint onto the pavement. It looked like candy. A cloud of fine dust hung suspended in the breezeless night around the skirt of Hell's backside: it glittered, lit by the streetlights lining the parking lot, and the farther-away, pervasive Las Vegas Strip pinkish-neon glow.

Teresa had never seen the aftermath of a bomb blast before, except on TV and in the movies—she had been away when her farmhouse burned down, and that was long ago—and this didn't look like one of those fake explosions. The damage appeared too—what? General? Light? Unless the bomb had exploded further inside the building, or somewhere else. Or something.

"Hell, I ain't no expert." She shook her head. "Maybe it ain't a bomb. Larry, what do you think?"

Larry shrugged, frowning.

"Yeah, I got you. We'll check it out."

Sirens howled like banshees, some closer than others.

Teresa could see their obscene flashing neon at the far side of the building, out front of Hell, a block away, reflected on the walls and palm trees there. Maybe Dog was out front.

Or maybe not. An ambulance had just pulled into place at the back door of the restaurant, flashing red-red-red. Two EMTs got out of the ambulance and ran toward the back door with medical box-things and a stretcher. At the door, somebody waved them in frantically, and disappeared behind them into the dark. The waver somebody looked like the girl security guard, Lois Ward, the one that stole the steaks for her and Dog and the people two nights before. She wore some kind of scruffy yellow bib with red polka dots on her boobs.

Larry held out a handkerchief to Teresa. She nodded, took the kerchief, wiped sweat off her face and neck. Returned the kerchief. Coughed. Larry tucked it into a back pocket.

More sirens, closer. Two patrol cars entered the back parking lot from around the side of Hell and stopped near the restaurant back door; one of them almost hit the big black luxury van that always parked there. Cops got out of the cruisers and the crisp rap of police radio shoptalk added to the din.

"Let's go," Teresa said, and stalked across the street, Larry on her heels. Midway across, another cruiser nearly ran her down. It parked a half block away, at the end of Dallas, and more cops got out.

The Man was everywhere. Finding Dog might be a task. Larry helped Teresa squeeze through a largish gap in the rickety chain link fence that lined the buckled sidewalk on the Hell side of Dallas, and followed her through. Teresa bunched fists, set her broad jaw, and waddled straight toward the back door. Nobody stopped them. *So far*.

By the time they'd crossed some fifty yards of parking lot to the back door, another half dozen cop cars had converged on the area as well as three or four other official vehicles. Suits and uniforms milled and shouted, radios blared, lights flashed.

Teresa walked up to the doorway and peered into the

dark. She glimpsed a mob of uniforms around a bomb victim on a stretcher on the floor. She couldn't see who it was in the iffy light from a dozen flashlights. Debris littered the hallway.

The uniforms stood as one and hefted the stretcher. A cop came to the doorway. "Clear the way," he said. Larry tucked behind Teresa's skirt.

Teresa cleared and watched as the stretcher passed. She saw the body on the stretcher, enough to know the victim was a man, a big man, alive.

"Not Dog," she said. Larry nodded, frowned, already looking around for Dog.

"Hey, you." It was a familiar greeting to Teresa. She'd been "Hey, you'd" a zillion times, when she wasn't invisible, and always by cops, security guards, store owners, or other official types—suits or uniforms—determined to see she "moves along." Another uniformed cop approached Teresa and Larry. He had one hand on his truncheon in its hip holster.

"Move along," he said. Teresa recognized Officer Watson as he got closer. A young cop, fresh white Hollywood-handsome face accented with a mustache that added maybe a month or two to his age. He looked sixteen with it, maybe fifteen without.

Move along. Hey you, and move along.

Teresa stepped back, raised her hands, hunched her shoulders, bent her head. Smiled, a cowed posture that said "You be The Man."

"Hey, Officer Watson, how the wife and—"

"Look, ma'am, you have to—" Watson stopped as somebody bumped into him, another cop, rushing by. Then somebody called him from behind him and he turned and trotted away, Teresa and the more successfully invisible Larry forgotten.

"We got to find out if anybody else in there," Teresa said to Larry. He nodded, looking around the chaos, eyes wide. More people and cars had arrived. The lot was getting crowded.

Teresa tried to attract the attention of another cop, this one next to his car, talking on his radio.

"S'cuse me—"

The cop frowned, annoyed. He gave a dismissive hand gesture, and turned away, cupping his ear to the two-way on his shoulder. She'd interrupted, and she got ignored.

She turned to try the ambulance driver a few feet away, but as she did so, the driver got back into the ambulance and slammed the door. The ambulance siren blared, and it took off.

"This is a pain in the ass," she muttered. She stood, fists anchored on her hips, looking around at the gathering chaos. They stood fifty feet or so away from the back door.

At last: "We're going in," she said, and started again toward the door. She got two steps from it before another cop stepped in her way.

"S'cuse me, ma'am—"

"Outta my goddamn way, you little—" Teresa's size and momentum intimidated the littler cop, and she backed up into the door jamb, where she got pinned between Teresa's mobile bulk and a big fireman coming out of the building.

"Clear this doorway, officer—" the fireman said.

And: "Ma'am, sir, you got to clear—" the woman cop said.

And: "Anybody else in there?" Teresa said.

"Ma'am, you have to—"

"*Where the goddamn hell is Dog? What have you done with him?*"

For a moment, it seemed to Teresa as if everybody and everything stopped at once, even the sirens and radios paused, and people turned to stare at her. Annoyed. Puzzled and curious too, some of them seemed, but mostly annoyed.

Get some answers now, goddamn it.

Teresa caught the eye of one fireman wearing one of those funny firefighter helmets and a huge yellow jacket, standing a few feet away with a radio in hand. He looked mildly curious at Teresa rather than annoyed.

As Teresa walked to him, ready to speak, the sudden, impossible, incongruous silent pause ended—Teresa decided she'd imagined it—the noise resumed at full volume, and somebody babbled unintelligible on the man's radio. He looked away from Teresa and she turned invisible. The cop and the fireman she'd yelled at disappeared too.

She lost her moment. If there had been one.

"What?" the firefighter yelled into his radio. He put a hand over his other ear to cut out the noise. Teresa stood inches away. He didn't seem to care, or notice.

"Yeah, nobody inside. All clear. We questioned the last people out. They said they were the, uh, last people out. Sir."

Pause.

"What?" Then: "Yeah, we're looking anyway, but there's a lot of debris and glass. Some areas partially blocked. Uh—"

Pause.

"*Partially blocked*, I said. *Part*—"

Pause.

"Yes, sir. Of *course*, sir. Structural integrity looks good. Uh, so far. We haven't gotten in all the way yet. Uh—"

Pause. The man looked pained, frustrated.

"Well, what do you want to do first? Check for people or check for the structural—"

Pause. He rolled his eyes.

"Yes, sir. What? I mean, *no*, sir. Don't want to risk that, no, *sir*."

Pause.

"Well, it looks like the electricity didn't go down, and it checks out, sir. Should we cut it off, do you think? Sir."

Pause.

"No, sir, I said the *electricity*—Okay. Yeah, I got it—"

Pause.

"No—I mean, *yes*, sir. I'll get right on it. *Sir*."

The man turned off the radio and blew a heavy sigh.

"S'cuse me, sir," Teresa said. Futile, but she had to try.

Sure enough: "Hey, Pete." The firefighter waved to another firefighter chatting with another man in a suit near the door. Pete came over.

"Pete, you checked for people, right?"

"Yeah." He stood close to the man and yelled into his ear. "We talked to those two rent-a-cops and there's Mr. Trane and his secretary—"

"Did you check, go inside, look around?"

"Well—"

"Goddamn it, I got Hard Ass on the line, I got to pee and—"

"We checked, all right?"

"Good. Now I got to talk to the fire marshal about the electricity. Still on?"

"How the hell should I know?"

"Well, it better be. Go figure, but Hard Ass wants it left on. Where can a lady take a leak around here?"

"There's a porta-potty that way." He pointed.

Teresa sighed and stepped out of the woman's way as she stalked by, a lady with a full bladder.

"No dice, Larry," Teresa muttered. Again, she surveyed the scene. Busy officials in uniforms and suits. The Man looking busy. Too busy even to arrest her for getting in the way. *Lot of ways a bum gets invisible, but not as many ways to get visible, when you want to. Damn.*

She heard a familiar voice. "Who's in charge here?"

Captain Gomez. *He*'d talk to her, if only because he knew she and Dog were close and he wanted to bust Dog's ass.

She spotted him in the crowd toward the door. "Come on, Larry." She waved her arm up high.

"Captain Gomez," she yelled. "Mr. Gomez."

The man looked around. He spotted Teresa and turned to face her, hands on his hips, belligerent. "Santiago. What the hell are *you* doing here? What do you know about this?"

"I just got here." She puffed, coughed. "Looking for Dog."

"No shit."

"You mean you don't know where—"

"I thought he hung out with you."

"Well, yeah, but—"

"He's not with you now?" Gomez seemed to notice Larry, hiding behind Teresa, for the first time. "If your buddy Dog is involved—" He pointed to the restaurant behind them.

"No, goddamn it. He didn't have nothing to do with—with—"

"If you or your—*people*—are hiding him—"

"Ain't nobody hiding Dog, I don't know where—"

Gomez suddenly seemed to realize what Teresa was saying and his demeanor changed. "Shitshitshitshit. You mean, you think—" He pointed again at the restaurant.

"Well, I don't know, dammit. I ain't been in there."

"Look, Santiago, we'll find your friend, wherever he's hiding. And when we do—"

"He ain't hiding."

"I thought you said you didn't know where he was?"

"I—I—"

"Yeah, right." He turned away. "I'll let you know," he said over his shoulder as he stalked away, his mind already elsewhere. She'd been dismissed.

She stood, flabbergasted, as Gomez dived back into the official fray. *"I'll let you know," The Man says. Yeah, right. Call me on my cell phone.*

She sighed. "We'll put the word out, Larry." Larry nodded.

As she walked away, shoulders slumped, she heard Gomez raise his voice. "All right, who's in charge here?"

Four, maybe five voices answered him. The chatter got lost in noise as she walked away, back across Dallas.

Where's Dog? Dammit, where the hell is that man?

Stan Gomez

As far as Stan could remember protocol, Clark County Disaster and Emergency Relief Services Coordinating Supervisor Darrell Hemingway would have been in charge of the mess if he'd been there. A competent man, a commander-type, loud and abrasive, Hemingway was. If he'd been there, Stan would have spotted him in the center of things, shouting orders, Getting Things Done. Instead, Stan found chaos. Hemingway wasn't there, and nobody, it seemed, knew what to do.

"Shitshitshitshit."

Stan learned from one of Hemingway's lieutenants that he was up in Carson City with the state legislature. Budget talks.

The lieutenant, named Bates, was one of four voices who'd responded when Stan yelled into the crowd of officials, police and rescue officers, suits, and God-only-knew-who-else, to find out who was in charge. Sergeant Hanson also answered. Hanson looked harried and wild-eyed, like a freshman cop in his first riot. Twitchy. A good man, Hanson, near twenty years, but this was too much on his nerves. Stan relieved him with a nod and he relaxed.

Dick Delgado also seemed to be in charge. Delgado had been named Acting City Fire Chief last week, Stan had read in the *Chronicle Progress*, after ex-Chief LaMar Frankowski left town suddenly for parts unknown, an under-aged stripper named

Candy Graham in his lap. Until Stan brought it to his attention, Delgado didn't know Hanson was on the scene. Busy. He too seemed relieved to hand Stan the gavel.

Some weasel from some state agency in a suit, wire-rimmed glasses, and a hard hat, who hadn't a clue, who yelled a lot, who everybody ignored, also claimed to be in charge. Stan ignored him too, and forgot his name and the agency he represented.

He'd read—skimmed, since he'd been busy at the time, as usual, and the thing had been in two three-inch thick binders—parts of the Southern Nevada Regional Intergovernmental Agency Executive Emergency Coordinated Response and Relief Policies and Procedures Manual when it hit his desk three years ago. He'd missed a few interdepartmental meetings and disaster training seminars. Busy. The job.

It looked as if nobody else had read it either.

It also looked as if Stan was, like it or not, In Charge.

When that had been determined in a hasty, fragmented, convoluted, confused conversation among the other Chief Honcho types, as much implied as stated, Stan sighed and looked around. A few faces turned toward him, like expectant puppies, all with "tell-us-what-to-do, oh fearless leader" looks.

The job. The goddamn job.

"You absolutely sure you searched—"

"Yep, yep." Delgado nodded. "My men been in there up and down, up and down. All clear. Yep."

"Have *you* been in there?"

"Oh, yep, yep." Nods again, like one of those ceramic dogs you see in the back window of a low rider. Nod, nod, nod. "Yep, yep, yep. My men have been in there, all over."

"No, I mean *you*, personally. Have *you* been in there?"

"Me?"

"Yes, you. Who else do you—" Stan sighed. "Never mind."

He turned and found a young fireman—firewoman.

Right. You're supposed to call them "firefighters." Right. Her
name tag read "Smith." "Uh, Smith, right?"

"Yes, sir." She straightened slumped shoulders, almost
stood at attention.

"You been inside?"

"Yes sir, I just got back out. There's a lot of debris—"

"Yeah, right. I want to go inside, have a look around."

"Sir?"

"Show me."

Smith gave a quizzical glance at Delgado, her boss.
Delgado nodded a few times, and Smith followed Stan to Hell's
back door.

"Watch your step, sir," she said, voice lowered and a bit
echoy as they entered the dark hallway.

"Somebody said the electricity was still on."

"It is, sir. Imagine that." She handed Stan her flashlight.
"I guess there wasn't any light back here, in this hallway, I
mean, when the quake hit."

"Uh-huh." Nobody else inside now, it seemed. Stan
moved in, turned his light toward the mess to his left, toward the
kitchen, and the hotel farther on. A collapsed metal shelf had
spilled stuff across the hallway, blocking it. A yellow substance
smeared across the floor and part of the wall. Stan couldn't see
much.

He turned his light to the right. More debris. Glittery dust
filled the light beam as it stabbed through the darkness, and Stan
recalled a nature show he'd seen on the Discovery Channel,
where they sent cameras down to explore the Titanic.

Shelves lined the outside hallway wall, to his right,
stacks of restaurant supplies and equipment, food containers,
cleaning equipment, and so on. The casino proper was down that
hallway. Stan started toward it. Smith followed, breath echoing
off the close, cave-like walls.

Stan hadn't gotten more than a dozen steps down the
cluttered hallway when he found a pond of swimming pool blue

sludge, with several white gallon plastic jugs afloat in it, many of them split open. Some kind of liquid cleaner.

Stan started to tiptoe through the blue detergent when he lost his balance.

"Careful, sir," Smith said. She reached to steady him and they both fell.

Stan got up to his knees. "Shit," he muttered. He'd dropped the flashlight in the liquid and fumbled to pick it up. Sticky.

He turned it back on and probed further down the hallway, as far as he could see. At the farthest reach of his light, maybe fifty of sixty feet down the hallway, he made out what looked like the door to a walk-in freezer. Between him and the ghost-white door, clutter, debris. More crap.

Beyond, Stan saw nothing.

He listened. Heard nothing but the muffled chaos beyond the door, twenty or thirty feet behind him, and Smith's breathing.

"So, Smith," he said at last, "you've been down this way?"

"Yes, sir. I mean, no sir, not me, personal. But our guys have. All the way to the casino, I hear."

"Did you *find* anything?"

"No, sir. Nobody inside. Right now, just me and you in Hell, sir. Except for the ones maybe out front, by the hotel entrance, still looking, maybe. I don't know what they're—"

Stan turned to Smith and faced her. She must have seen his scowl in the dim light from the back door behind her, because she paused, took a breath, and her eyes widened. Apprehensive.

"If you haven't been down this hallway—*personal*—how do you know that it's clear?"

Smith took a deep breath, to gather herself. "Because, *sir*," Stan heard the hint of anger in her voice, "I've been told. Our men are good—and the women, I mean. Too. If they say they checked, then they checked. *I* trust them." The challenge in her eyes prompted Stan to realize how tired he was.

He sighed. "Sorry, Smith. We're all tired."

"S'okay, sir. Best check with Delgado on your question. He's supervisor—I mean, *you* are now, but I mean, we report to him, us fire department people. So if anybody knows—"

"Yep, yep, yep," Stan said, bobbing his head, and Smith stifled a laugh.

Still, he hesitated. He flashed his light down the corridor toward the casino again, and started to take another step that way, past the liquid detergent pond, when the soap-slick flashlight slipped from his hand and clattered to the floor.

"Shit."

"I got it, sir," Smith said. She retrieved the light and they made their way over, around, and through boxes, cartons, spilled bottles, cans, shelves, and assorted debris toward the back door of Hell and out into the light.

Stan lost track of time as he conferred in the parking lot with officials and experts. He questioned and commanded, as needed. Things calmed down. No fatalities. Two injuries, though, to Joe Foxworthy and one of his employees, but not serious. They'd been taken to the hospital.

Trane had been inside but was unhurt, Stan heard.

Nobody else inside. Property damage isolated, minimal, outside the casino complex itself. Building inspectors closed off the site. More yellow tape sprouted in the area like cobwebs.

Stan got a call from Ripley on his cell phone. She praised him for doing a good job—*How the hell does she know?*—and promised, on behalf of Trane Enterprises, and Mr. Trane himself, full cooperation with the appropriate authorities and blah, blah, blah. Stan learned she had been in front of the building talking with reporters after the bomb—no, *disturbance*—and he wondered where she was now. He got the impression she talked to cameras when she talked to him on the phone.

Stan thought about calling Samantha. No; she was busy. So was he. As usual.

Not a bomb.

His own people, and the fire folk, determined a bomb didn't cause the damage. Some experts from the university talked shop—scientific mumbo-jumbo—about subsidence, about sinkholes, and ground survey errors. Sounded to Stan like trouble, but trouble for another bureaucrat, not his department. No bomb.

Lucky me.

Yet, Stan felt disappointed. Like Santiago had earlier, he wondered where Dog was. Something like this, Dog would be on hand, making some kind of street theater out of it. He asked a few cops. Nobody had seen him, but they'd keep a look out.

The sun had come up. It was going to be another scorcher of a day. Stan yawned and checked his watch. Six-fifteen. The crowd of cops and firefighters and officials had dissipated, a little.

Had he really hoped to find Dog had bombed Hell? So he could bust him? Had Dog so pissed him off that he hoped he could bust the scruffy little son-of-a-bitch on some really big charge, and make it stick? Was his personal vendetta against the smart-ass rabble-rouser hippie asshole punk so intense that he felt—

"Yep, yep, yep."

Mark Trane

A burly rescuer carried Mark out of the broken-glass filled hotel lobby on his back. The news herd in front of Hell assaulted the long-famous rescuee and instantly famous rescuer with a glare of lights, a flurry of clicking, whirring cameras, a forest of jostling microphones and unintelligible shouted questions.

Ripley, disheveled but pretty, arrived on the scene in time to divert media attention and get her boss into an ambulance and spirited away. They didn't have time to talk.

Mark watched Ripley through the rear window of the ambulance as it drove off. He watched with satisfaction and admiration as Ripley instantly Took Over. Impromptu news conference in front of the shattered hotel, Ripley at the center of things. The Smile. Roberta Ripley, Trane's right hand man. Charismatic. In Charge.

As they sped—but not too fast, and sirenless—toward a nearby hospital, Trane prevailed on the paramedics to give him some antacid. It wasn't Tumeze but it helped, at least for now. They administered oxygen for his breathing, too, but found nothing else wrong with him.

With no reason to hospitalize him, the ambulance turned around in the street at Mark's insistence and dropped him off at The Buttes on the Strip. Mark took a suite, compliments of the management, who'd heard about his bad luck.

Most hotel and casino owners in Las Vegas were pissed that Trane would call his place Hell. Bad PR, especially now when everybody in the gaming and hotel industry was trying so hard to cultivate a family-friendly image. Bad for business.

Owners had huddled in secret to decide what to do. They discussed and dismissed lawsuits, boycotts, muscle, and other notions. They tried to pressure Ripley. Maybe it was another of Trane's notorious practical jokes and he'll yell "Just kidding!" next Monday. "Say it ain't so. Please?" She danced her best diplomatic dance, spun them around, smiled, and left them in the air. Absent real information, and since it was still early in the game, the consensus became "wait and see."

No owner or investor spoke aloud in support of Trane's eccentricity, or against their colleagues' opposition to it, but a few quietly liked the idea, for a variety of perverse reasons. Somebody in The Buttes management thought it was funny.

Besides, it wouldn't be charitable to tell a homeless billionaire they had no room at the inn. Bad for business.

In his suite, alone at last, Trane called Ripley, told her where he was.

"I'm on my way," she said. Mark could hear reporters yell in the background as she hung up.

He ordered breakfast for two.

He phoned the hospital and tried to talk to Joe. A clerk or nurse or somebody told him that Joseph Foxworthy was under sedation and couldn't talk right now, but she took a message and promised to pass it along to his doctor. The clerk said the hospital had not admitted any "Lois Warder" recently, nor did she have any "Louise Warden" on staff, if that's what the caller actually meant, but maybe Patient Information had that information. She transferred the call to a recorded message before Mark could speak and he hung up.

He showered.

Minutes later, as he dried his sparse hair with a towel, a

knock came at his door, and the hotel's assistant manager stood with a suit of clothes over his arm like he was a wine steward offering a bottle of pricey vintage. He had a carton of Tumeze.

The suit fit. Of course. Ripley's doing, and the Tumeze? All hotels kept files on high-profile customers—whales, they called them—but Trane had only stayed at The Buttes once, and how would the management know about his stomach problem? Another minor mystery for another time.

As a waiter brought their breakfast minutes later, Ripley arrived. She had her cell phone in her ear, setting up a meeting with the building contractor.

She broke the connection as she sat, turned off the phone, dropped it into a purse, and gulped a glass of iced tomato juice. She pulled a slice of green pepper from her omelet and chewed with gusto. Mark wondered how her stomach stood the assault.

"Joe and Wowis awe okay," he said. "I guess. I twied to caww, but I didn't tawk to them. I got the wunawound." He stirred a fried potato with his fork. It looked a bit too spicy.

She nodded, and spoke around a slice of toast, soaked in strawberry preserves. "I talked to a doctor on my way over here. Foxworthy broke his leg, and Ward didn't get hurt at all. Nobody else inside except you. We got lucky."

Mark shook his head, amazed. He couldn't get through at the hospital, but even as busy as she was, Ripley had.

"No othew guawds? How come?" Greenish flecks dotted the potatoes, lightly fried.

"Change of shift? The others on break?" Ripley shrugged, chewed. "We'll ask Joe. Remember, his contract ended yesterday, then you asked me to call him back after—"

"Wight." He scraped some greenish spicy stuff—oregano?—off a thumb-sized potato fragment. "What do we do now?"

"First, it wasn't a bomb. The media got all over that, but I stopped it." She gulped a glass of milk and licked a thin, white mustache from her upper lip. "Not an earthquake, either. I found out this professor from the University thinks it was subsidence, or a sinkhole."

"Wike they have in Fwowida." He broke the potato fragment in half with his fork.

"And in Pennsylvania." She poured pepper on her omelet. "Places where the ground gets saturated. There was a hotel on the strip a few years back that sank a foot, did you know that?"

"Wiwwy?" He put the potato fragment on his tongue.

"An engineer blew the report." She scooped up gobs of omelet and spoke with her mouth full. "It can happen here."

"So, that's it, then? Somebody did the wepowt wwong?" He chewed the potato. Not too spicy.

Ripley ate vigorously for a moment. Then she looked long at Mark, hard-eyed, nails tapped clickety-clickety-click, and he girded for The Bad News.

It wasn't so bad.

"You knew this was a white elephant."

"I toyed with cawwing it that."

"We may have inherited more than just a lousy location and a flawed architectural design."

"Bad engineewing?"

"What you mean is—" Ripley sighed deeply and pursed her pert lips, stabbing more omelet. "—maybe bad construction."

"Hm." He took another piece of potato on the end of his fork. "Ouw contwactow wipping us off, do you think? I heawd you scheduwe a meeting."

"A real possibility. I'm really sorry, Mark. We were in a hurry and I may have—that is, I may have *not* checked into his business as thoroughly as—"

Mark waved a hand dismissively. "Don't wowwy, Wipwey. You know I didn't expect to make a pwofit hewe." He chewed the potato thoughtfully.

"Big loss. Don't know how much yet, but big." She

chewed. "You may never open."

"Again, that's okay with me. I just wanted a pwace to set up an office to wook for my daughtew, and—you know." He didn't need to say: "to pway." She knew.

He looked around the room as Ripley ate. "This wooks wike a good enough pwace. Pwenty of woom. You couwd set up in the suite next doow. I'ww need to get some fiwes fwom Heww—"

"Building inspectors have closed it. Nobody in until they can get a full structural assessment. Worried about somebody getting hurt, walls falling. But."

"But?" He took another delicate bite of potato.

Ripley waved a hand, dismissive. "I'll see to it."

"We'ww need a new computew hewe, and a—"

"I got it." She gave him The Smile. She ate.

Mark knew it would be taken care of. He didn't have to worry about that anymore. He smiled, relieved.

On to the central issue, then, his primary focus.

"About Joe." Another bite, a bit bigger. "Did you weawn when he'ww wecovew, get back to wowk?"

"I got the impression they were going to let him go home in a couple of days, but he won't be getting around, walking, I mean, for a couple of weeks."

"He couwd wowk out of his office, then? Get his empwowees to do his weg wowk?" Tasted good.

"I'll see he gets a computer in that hospital room, a modem, a phone."

Mark nodded, chewed delicately. They both ate in silence. Ripley suppressed a grin. Hiding something. a game she got to play with Mark now and then. Mark waited. He enjoyed the game too. It was always worth it.

At last, she patted her lips, sucked on her teeth, and settled her elbows on the table, her chin on her folded hands, and grinned, exposing perfect, white teeth.

"The hotel idea was fun, Mark, wasn't it?"

"It couwd have been." Mark's stomach began to cramp. Again.

"The idea to call it Hell—that was fun, too?"

"Hiwawious." He'd eaten too much.

"All over now." She sighed theatrically. She should have been in the movies, Mark thought.

"Wooks wike." He rubbed his stomach. "Maybe it was a bad idea. Maybe I shouwd just go back to Saint Wouis. Joe doesn't need me hewe to hewp. Ow get in his way."

Ripley's patented Smile radiated warmth into the cool, air-conditioned room. Movie star.

"What?" Mark asked. He reached for the Tumeze in his pocket.

"Percy," she pronounced precisely, "Oswald."

"Pewcy Oswawd? What about—"

"Coming here."

"Oh? Oh!" Mark laughed. "Wiwwy? Coming *hewe*? When?"

"He heard about what happened. Called a press conference. He's on his way now. Be here by noon."

"Oh! Oh, this is wich!" Mark giggled, and Ripley laughed.

Mark swallowed a handful of Tumeze. He picked up his phone to make a few calls, waving a hand to Ripley as she left the suite, off to take care of business.

Letting him play.

Teresa Santiago

Like a magnet, Teresa drew street people to her. It had always been that way, all her life. Poor or destitute, down or out, broke or penniless, homeless or on the street, Teresa Santiago always had—it.

It. Charisma.

So, an impromptu, spontaneous meeting occurred minutes after she and Larry left the parking lot behind Hell, Dogless. It took place in the narrow alley behind the Sunset Bistro a block and a half away from Hell because that's where Teresa went after she left Hell. She went there because that's where she'd cached her scant property—a few changes of underwear, a Utah Jazz t-shirt, a sort-of dress, socks, and a paperback version of Mike Black's *Windy City Knights*—in a plastic bag behind a trash bin and because it was as good, or bad, as any other place. "Ain't no place home when you're homeless," Teresa often said. The meeting took place there because Teresa was there and wherever she was, street people gathered.

Besides, the police usually didn't bother the streeties in the alley behind the Sunset Bistro. Usually.

This had been an unusual night, with the earthquake at Hell, and Dog gone and all, so the meeting was unusual. It was morning, going to be another scorcher, and the "lay off" policy

Teresa had negotiated with The Man for the alley didn't seem to apply daytime hours. Besides, it wasn't an official policy and there seemed to be new faces in uniforms who hadn't gotten the word, or who didn't care. Or maybe The Man had changed the policy overnight. Teresa decided she'd have to look into it, but later. She had other steaks to fry, so to speak, now.

A cruiser would disrupt the gathering at one end of the alley and The Man would shoo them—"Move along, move along,"—and they'd shuffle to the other end of the alley, re-gather, resume their meeting, until another cruiser would stop and The Man would shoo them—"Move along, move along,"—and they'd shuffle back to where they'd been in the first place and regroup again.

Unusual meeting, but Teresa was good on her feet.

First things first. "Anybody seen Dog?"

No.

"Anybody hurt or busted? Except Booger."

"The New Kid from back East got run in," Tom-Tom said. "That's better than being run over, though. Jaywalking."

Teresa made a mental note. Two people to check up on at the jail later. Booger and The New Kid, whose name she still hadn't found out. Busy day.

"What happened?" She tilted her head toward Hell. "Anybody got a clue?"

Most in the crowd of eighteen or twenty streeties had heard something, some of their sources semi-reliable, and soon Teresa got the gist. No bomb—*thank Dog.* Maybe an earthquake, but likely some kind of sinkhole. Bad dirt under the place.

"Damn," Teresa said. "Some flunky engineer or paper-pusher is about to lose his suit, going to join us, couple of weeks."

Dirty, scruffy heads nodded in sympathy. A couple bottles of questionable content and vintage got passed around, tilted to lips in sympathetic toasts, and somebody lit a roach.

Teresa became convinced that Dog wasn't trapped inside Hell. He was somewhere else. He'd be back, when it damn well suited him to get back. Dog was okay, she became convinced. Probably.

Teach, unusually aggressive in her diminutive way, elbowed through the crowd of bodies standing close to Teresa. Teach stood at attention and tugged frantically on Teresa's sleeve. She raised her hand.

"Yes, Teach? You don't have to raise your hand."

Teach tucked her arms around her bony chest. "I watched TV at Whitmore's Appliance." She nodded east toward Houston Street, where the store displayed TV's in the window 24-hours a day.

"And?" Teresa coaxed, patient.

"Well, I *saw*." She anchored a fist on a hip, petulant.

"What did you see?" Patient.

"Oh. Uh, yes. I saw a news story on CNN. Guess who's coming to town?" She smiled, and looked around for an answer.

Just then a cruiser stopped and tooted its siren. "Move along, move along," and the group moved along.

Minutes later, at the other end of the alley, Captain Freddy said, "I give up. Who?"

Teach had forgotten the question in the change of venue, and it took a few minutes to regain the thread.

"Percy Oswald," she said at last. Glowing with triumph, she grinned, exposing a dentist's nightmare of troubled, misaligned teeth. "He was on CNN. He said that he's coming to do battle with the Devil. Because of Hell, the earthquake and all. He says he's going to destroy Hell."

Another contingent of the city's finest arrived during the uproar that followed and moved the discussion to the other end of the alley. By the time she got there, and the crowd re-gathered around her, Teresa had a plan.

"Listen up," she said. They did, mostly. "You all know Oswald is rich, right?"

"Right, and a good Christian," somebody said. Mutterings of agreement. Visions of sugarplums danced in a few heads.

"If you think Oswald'll rain his largesse on us poor folk, you got another think coming."

After a brief digression to explain to some of her company what "largesse" meant, Teresa got to the point.

"Percy Oswald claims to be a Christian, share the wealth, help the poor and all that, but I know. I've read about that man. Yeah, he's Christian and he's got enough to share but he ain't going to, not with us street folk, he ain't."

"Why the hell not?" Tom-Tom looked offended, belligerent.

"He don't like street folk. Thinks we're dirty. Hates dirty folk. It's such an obsession, he owns a soap factory."

"I'd be happy to shower with him," Mrs. Doran said. "Right now. Even use his soap." Lots of laughs.

"How come he hates street people?" Captain Freddy asked.

Teresa shook her head. "He had himself an experience. He wrote about it couple of times in his newspaper, *The Christian Conspirator*, and in his magazine, *Miracle Monitor*. Ever read his stuff? He met some bum back when he started his ministry. A scruffy dude dressed in rags, dirty, foul-mouthed. *You* know."

"He wrote a book about it, too," Teach said. "I forget what it was called. It was supposed to be fiction."

"*Cold Day In Hell*," Little Ricky said. "I read it. If he called the guy he met an angel—"

"True or fiction, it scrambled his eggs," Teresa said. "An angel being a homeless person. Or a homeless person being an angel. Cussing, stinky, raggedy. Angels ain't homeless." She twirled a finger at the side of her head. "Scrambled his eggs."

Teresa didn't say it maliciously because several people in her congregation suffered from scrambled eggs. They knew it, and some nodded in grim sympathy for fellow-afflictee Percy Oswald. In fact, she was well aware that most did, to varying degrees. *Me too, I guess. In my own damn way.*

"Okay," Captain Freddy said, "so we ain't going to panhandle from him while he's in Las Vegas protesting Hell. Well, what *are* we going to do? You got some sort of plan or something?"

"Mr. Oswald wants to protest Hell, make it go away. He'll get some help from the local church community, but it ain't going to be enough, is it? I mean, they ain't done shit so far, am I right?" The response was a bit listless because the crowd, now up to about thirty or more streeties, didn't know where Teresa was taking them. Yet.

They were attentive, curious.

"No, sir. Those churchies, they're pretty busy. Church work, jobs, errands, bingo. Families to visit. Yard work. Some of them are retired, can't get out much. It's hot, not healthy for old folk. It's Sunday, a day of rest, not supposed to demonstrate on Sunday. Oswald will need help."

Some of the smarter, more sober members of her congregation were beginning to catch on, and raised their voices in agreement.

"I don't see, um—" Teach looked perplexed.

"He's going to need help," Teresa said, "from *us*."

"Why?" Tom-Tom asked. "Why should we help him if he don't like us?"

Teresa shrugged. "Could be we have some fun. Besides, what else you got planned for today?"

More nods, mutterings, but still not as wildly enthusiastic as Teresa wanted.

Teresa put the clincher to the debate. "Maybe Dog shows up, gives us a hand."

That produced more approving mutters and nods. When Dog led a rally, or "street theater" as he called it, everybody had fun. What else did streeties have to do besides survive? They couldn't take a dip in the family pool to cool off. No trips to the Caribbean to relax. Couldn't relax much at the public library, even when it was open, what with "Move along, move along," even if a body could read. Couldn't even rent a goddamn video.

So, Teresa and Dog provided streeties with an outlet for pent-up aggressive, creative energy. Provided games for them.

Teach still looked perplexed. "I don't think Mr. Oswald will let us help."

"We'll just have to convince him otherwise," Teresa said. "It'll take work, planning. Organizing. It might be fun."

"Fun, sure," Captain Freddy said. "Especially if Dog shows up. C'mon. Tell us more about what you got in mind, okay? We'll help." He turned to his fellow conspirators. "Won't we?"

Shouts of agreement, raised fists, bottles, and joints.

Teresa told them. Something Dog had occasionally talked about. A story from his past, when he was a hippie on the East Coast, way back in 1967, October. What he and a few thousand rebel friends did to The Man, or tried to do, to stop the War.

"It almost worked," he'd said when he talked about it now and then, wistfully, about that long-ago effort to thwart the System, screw The Man. "The magic was almost there. Maybe someday it will be."

It had been the time of his life.

Now seemed the right time and place with the right people. "Could be fun. It'll take some planning. Organizing. Me and Dog, we're good at that. So what do you say?"

Teach finally caught on. She jumped up and down, giggling, mouth agape in snaggle-toothed excitement. "We're going to raise Hell," she squealed. "We're going to raise Hell."

She wet her pants.

Lois Ward

Joe was mostly unconscious, heavily sedated, when the ambulance arrived at Clark County General Hospital. Lois and Joe got separated immediately. Some doctor-types wheeled Joe off to treat him, and another doctor overrode her protests and insisted on looking at her.

She had to partially strip to let the doctor examine her. The doctor asked Lois questions, probed, poked. A smiley-faced psychologist, collegiate-looking, balding but with a ponytail. Traumatic experience and all. Couldn't be too sure. Some people Lost It, you know, but you're cool, man.

She was fine, except for a scraped knee. She just needed a shower. She showered and felt better.

When she got out of the shower, a nurse suggested she put on a spare suit of clothes she had handy and let them launder her mustardy and bloody uniform. Lois said okay, and took her own stuff, and the stuff she'd gotten from Joe in Hell, and put them in a paper shopping bag the nurse provided. "Scrubs," she called the pale green shirt and pants she gave Lois. They looked like the suits they wore on the doctor shows on TV. They almost fit, but unlike the hospital gowns they gave patients, they weren't open in the butt.

Which was good. The hospital was cold, the AC on high.

Lois went to find Joe. Took a while. The hospital was a

maze. Everybody seemed to be in a big hurry—there had been two shootings, three car accidents, and a food poisoning episode at a dentist's convention that night—and nobody had time to talk with her. When somebody did, they either didn't know where anything or anybody was, or their directions were all wrong. She discovered that, because she wore doctor duds, she could go where patients and visitors couldn't go and nobody questioned her.

She got lost twice.

She finally found Joe by accident as she walked into a room she mistook for another hallway. There he was, in bed, asleep, looking like a fat beached whale, flat on his back, slack-jawed.

No, Lois decided, he looked more like some Frankensteinian experiment, hooked up to a maze of tubes and wires. Machines beeped and clucked. IV bottles hung from a metal tree, bedside, dripping get-well juice. A bandage on his forehead. A doctor—or nurse, or whatever—had his back to her, as he tinkered with Joe's leg, which hung, cocooned in white plaster, above the bed in what looked like a torture device.

Joe was unconscious, drugged up, the doctor said, unnecessarily. Lois could see. He went about his work and Lois left. Nothing more to be done here.

Lois was shocked to discover that it was after six o'clock. More than three hours since the earthquake. How had *that* happened? Mary would be up soon, and Lois wanted to be home when her daughter awoke. Make pancakes for breakfast, help her get dressed. Chat. Play. Be a mom.

She should take Joe's stuff—the camera, video tape, tape recorder, the stuff he gave Lois—to his office. Check mail, answering machine, e-mail. There'd be calls. How's he doing? How can I help? Will he be able to finish the surveillance job I hired him for? What about payday?

Yeah, Joe. What about payday?

Later. Home first. She felt hungry but didn't want to eat

now, at the hospital. She'd eat with Mary.

Then she'd check in at Joe's office. After that, if it didn't take too long, maybe she'd spend the day with Mary in the park. Or maybe they'd go to the library and read if it was too hot. Maybe she could get on the Internet and follow up some leads about Steve at the library.

Sunday. The darn library is closed.

She gave up trying to retrieve her uniform from the laundry when she discovered that the pervasive bureaucratic fog that enshrouded the hospital—nobody knew anything—extended into the laundry room too. Which took too long to find anyway. She'd wear the scrubs home—she couldn't find the nurse who'd given them to her—and return them when she came back to check on Joe.

She had Joe's car keys. In a lucid moment in the ambulance, he'd said he was parked on Dallas Street, behind Hell. She'd get a ride to Hell and take Joe's car home. If it hadn't been towed.

Why was he there, in Hell, when the quake hit? Lois had asked in the ambulance and before, but he hadn't answered, and he was in such pain, she didn't press him. Did he know about the stolen steaks? Or was he checking up on another employee? Something about that video tape? She shook her head. Too much. Another mystery—maybe more than one—for another time.

It took a bit more time to catch a ride. She couldn't afford a taxi and she didn't want to wait for a bus.

She got clever, found the door between the nurse's lounge and the employee parking lot. There, she caught some nurse-types getting off shift, an older black man and two plumpish Hispanic women, and hitched a ride with them, going her way.

Sunday morning traffic was sparse and they dropped Lois on Dallas Street, next to Joe's car, before anybody could start up much of a conversation. Everybody was butt-draggy tired anyway.

Lois got out of the air-conditioned car into the rising morning heat, broke into an instant sweat, thanked her benefactors, and they took off.

The disaster scene regular crowd had thinned considerably from what she'd seen when the ambulance had pulled out of the backside parking lot hours earlier. The area had been cordoned off haphazardly with long webs of yellow tape, and clean-up worker bees were cleaning up. A few cops and suits with hard hats and clipboards puttered too. No flashing lights or squawking radios. Crisis over.

Lois took the parking ticket off the windshield, got in Joe's battered Dodge, and tossed the ticket into the glove compartment. She rolled down the windows—no AC, and the car was an oven. The interior smelled like scorched paper, leather, and rubber. Oily and stale. Lois adjusted mirrors and the seat, put on her seat belt, started the car, and drove home.

At a stoplight, she idly looked at a paper on the passenger seat. It looked and smelled like a scrap of butcher paper. Then she read the writing on it and her heart froze.

Joe knew.

A honk from behind startled her—she hadn't noticed the light had changed—and she drove on.

Joe knew about the theft.

Or maybe not. The paper might not be from those steaks she'd stolen days ago. No, too much of a coincidence. Joe there in Hell, by the freezer, unannounced, at night, sneaking around, by himself. Doing something with a videotape? And this piece of paper, looked like something from the Hell restaurant freezer, all right. In Joe's car. Too much of a coincidence.

Joe knew.

So—*now* what? Would Joe fire her? How could he? He didn't know for sure, did he? Had he been secretly running a video camera last week when she—but no. If he *had*, why hadn't he said anything sooner?

Maybe he suspected, wasn't sure who, and was going to ask her and the other guards about it. What would she do if—no, *when*, assume the worst—he asked?

Answer truthfully, that's what.

A Sunday school teacher told her *that* long ago: "Morality is doing right when nobody's looking."

She'd forgotten the night she'd snatched those steaks that helping poor people eat was right but stealing wasn't. *Hiding the truth from Joe wasn't right, either.* She knew it but she just hadn't gotten around to facing it, yet. She'd avoided those guilty eyes in the mirror. She was *going* to tell him, but—

She resolved, right then, to confess to Joe about the theft tomorrow, or later today, right after he wakes up. No, Mary first, then to the office to put away his stuff in his safe, then call him—no, drive to the hospital. Confess in person. It would be good for the soul to face the music. Pick up her uniform.

The resolution was like a load of fatigue had magically lifted from her shoulders and she felt instantly better. She knew she should be worried about money, about finding another job— which she might have to do soon since Laceby's didn't pay enough by itself and now that Joe was down and out for who knew how long, and they didn't need anybody to guard Hell anymore.

She should be worried about what she was going to do for a living next, but instead she felt good. Relieved.

Without thinking about it, Lois turned into the Square D Mart parking lot two blocks from her apartment. She stopped, turned off the car, and sat, sweating. She checked Mickey Mouse. Almost seven. If Lois didn't get home when Mary woke up, Roommate Annie said Mary often went back to sleep for another hour. It was a weekend so it was okay—she didn't have to get ready for school. It had happened two or three times, so it was okay if Lois took a little time—just a little time, why not?— to—

To look for Steve. Again. Or look for clues, rather.

Lois had pulled into the convenience store parking lot like she was on automatic pilot to the spot where Steve might or might not have been five months ago when he disappeared.

She'd parked here before, many times in the past five months. She'd parked here so often that the clerks and managers at the Square D knew her and had stopped hassling her about it. They knew why she was there. Looking for her lost husband. Again.

She got out and locked the car, put the paper bag of her and Joe's stuff in the trunk and locked it. She nodded a hello at the clerk on duty—another new guy. Mexican. Again. They went through a lot of employees at the Square D. Low wages. Many were Mexican.

The man of duty the night Steve left the apartment for the Square D to get her some Tumeze was Mexican. Lois preferred licorice flavored Tumeze, in the three-roll pack, but not too many places had them. The Square D kept a box behind the counter, special, for her. The Mexican clerk had left town two days later, alarmed when he was questioned about a disappearance, possible kidnapping, possible foul play. When Lois traced him to Mexico City, finally got an interview with him, he told her Steve had been in the store. At 10:15 p.m. The night he disappeared. He bought a package of Tumeze, licorice flavored, three-roll pack.

And a package of cigarettes, Winstons, filtered, box.

She hadn't said what brand of cigarettes Steve smoked. He'd offered the information, unaided. Credibility. Steve had been out of cigarettes that night.

She interviewed the man by phone through an interpreter with the man's court-appointed lawyer constantly intervening because the man was in jail. Drug charges. Authorities on both sides of the border told Lois that he was a notorious liar. They doubted his story, said it was only an attempt to curry favor from somebody who might help him keep out of prison. They had tried to discourage Lois from interviewing the man in the first place, but she had been persistent, and she'd learned a lot about how to get things done, how to navigate upstream past bureaucratic barriers.

She learned a lot in her so-far fruitless search for Steve. One day three months ago, and a month after she interviewed the clerk in Mexico City, she retraced, as she often did, one route Steve might have taken back from the store. This time, she found cigarette butts tucked against the foot of a fence post. She didn't recognize the brand, and it looked as if they had been there for weeks or months. Three well-hidden butts. Three butts meant that whoever smoked them did so *on this very spot* on different occasions, or had stood here for a long time once. But she— there was lipstick on each butt—hadn't been back to the spot for at least a few days, or weeks. Or months.

Maybe she'd seen something.

It was worth the effort to try to find out. Lois had tried everything else. She'd bugged the cops daily. Hospitals. Jails. Morgues. She'd interviewed every clerk, every passing motorist, jogger, panhandler, streetie, every employee of nearby businesses, every resident of the apartment complex she lived in and another one between her place and the Square D, delivery people, and every cab company in the city. She'd retraced every possible route until she could walk each one blindfolded. She'd searched Dumpsters, trash cans, gutters, and sewer drains. She'd even checked rooftops for discarded—whatever. Nothing, except for the drug dealer she tracked down in the Mexico City jail.

The cigarette was a Canadian brand, Coach's Menthol 101s. Sold in six locations in town. It took some finagling to get the names of five regular women customers from two stores, and to narrow that down to one woman, because she was the only one who wore the right brand and shade of lipstick—Lady Jayne's Luscious Lips Accent, Devil-May-Care Red. Finding out the lipstick brand on the ends of the butts was a piece of work.

Lois found the woman, who worked for an escort service. She told Lois on the phone that she was on the street the night

Steve disappeared because she met a client there. Yes, she would meet with Lois and talk about it. On the way to their rendezvous, minutes after they'd talked on the phone, the woman got hit by a taxi as she crossed the street. Killed instantly.

The next day, she went to the Trustworthy Vigilance Agency and begged Joe—he was *Mr. Foxworthy* then—to help find Steve. She couldn't pay him much from her wages at Laceby's, but she'd do payments, if that was okay. She told Joe about her attempts to find Steve, and Joe apparently became so impressed with her instincts and her skills, including computer research skills she'd gained at the library, that he hired her.

When she wasn't working for Joe, she used his computer and phone to hunt for Steve. She was still trying to find the john the woman had been with that night but the escort agency had closed, their owner had vanished, as had the other two girls in the agency. Nobody would talk, and she still couldn't find him.

She'd learned that no fact eluded the determined researcher forever. She'd find the john. Eventually. Maybe *he*'d seen something. She refused to think the john might be Steve.

The incident with the cigarette butts taught her that other clues, however obscure and small, might still exist. She just had to be persistent. Which is what she intended to do right now. She'd walk home, take her time. Look. Again.

She stood on the corner, arms and shoulders slack. Relaxed. She closed her eyes, breathed evenly, listened, smelled, tried to feel the very texture of the hot air on her skin. *These are the sounds and smells that Steve experienced, right here.* She concentrated on the sensations. The ubiquitous whine and swoosh of traffic, a far-away siren, the occasional toot of horns, the dings and clatter of somebody pumping gas a few feet behind her. The gut-rumble thump-thump-ka-thump of a car stereo. Two men talking in Spanish on the corner a few feet from her.

She smelled gasoline, burnt rubber, popcorn, dog poop, cologne from the men at the corner.

She smelled Steve.

That had to be her imagination, she thought. Mennen and sweat. That's what he'd smelled like.

She'd cooked dinner. She ate, Steve didn't, and Mary had gone to bed early with a cold, dinner untouched.

Lois got sick, probably Mary's cold. "Tumeze, pretty please," she said, mimicking the TV ad. They were out.

So Steve went out to the Square D to get her some Tumeze, licorice flavored, three-roll pack. And some cigarettes for him. Winstons, box. Filtered. He never came back.

Sweat dribbled down her chin. It was going to be a scorcher. She opened her eyes and looked around, trying to see the familiar sights with fresh eyes, looking for clues, however obscure.

She sighed. Nothing new came to her. She left the car and walked the few blocks home slowly, letting her weary feet, the flow of pedestrian traffic, and the color of the traffic lights dictate her path. She saw, heard, smelled, or felt nothing new.

Steve had vanished at night and this was morning. He'd vanished on a Tuesday, and this was Sunday.

Lois sighed and entered her apartment quietly. The AC was on, set for low, still a drain on the power bill, but necessary. Roommate Annie was asleep in her room, snoring softly, the door closed. Mary was asleep, too, in their big bed, and Lois felt suddenly, overwhelmingly, exhausted. She kicked off her shoes, lay down beside her lightly snoring daughter, and gazed fascinated at her little girl's pretty face, her long lashes, her pert lips slack, her light, reddish curls—daddy's hair, daddy's nose— draped over one rosy cheek.

Lois felt content in Mary's presence, despite the day she'd been through. She allowed herself another smile, a little one, a quiet one, as she pulled a corner of the blanket over her shoulders, and let sleep overtake her. Just for a few minutes. Until Mary woke up. Rest her eyes. Just a little.

*A*t first she thought the body was Steve's. In the other dreams—nightmares—it had been Steve's body. But this one was smaller. Shabby clothes. Hairier. She'd never really seen Steve's body in the other dreams. She'd just seen where the body was located. His grave, or the ground near it.

Each dream held the intense dread of death, a concrete emotional presence, a reality, like smoke in the air. In each dream, she felt—knew—that somebody was dead, very close by. It had always been Steve, dead, in each dream.

Not now. This was a different person, dead, curled up in a fetal position. She stood over him, wondering about the milky film coating the small body. Scruffy beard, long-haired. She couldn't see his face for the dark hair, stiff, covered with—

—frost. In the dream, Lois got the sudden distinct impression of intense cold. Not just coolness, as with an air conditioner, but bitter, bone-deep cold. She shivered, rubbed her arms, and smoke, frosty breath, came out of her mouth.

The man she stood over was dead. She knew that, because this was her dream, and she saw Steve in her dream all the time and Steve was dead. She knew Steve was dead in her dreams. This man was dead too, because he was in her dream. She knew that.

He had just died just now. That too was true, she knew—again, without knowing how she knew it.

She also knew who he was. And where he was.

Joseph Foxworthy

The nurse handed Joe the receiver. "It's for you." The nurse sounded peeved.

"Who else could it be for?" Joe wanted to say, but didn't. Why bother? He felt too woozy to be cranky, though this particular nurse was an officious pain in the ass. Long-faced and frowny. He reminded Joe of a female Ichabod Crane in Disney's "Sleepy Hollow."

Joe held the cold, plastic receiver awkwardly in his left hand as he tried to reach a glass of water on his bedside table with the other. Just out of reach. *Lois? Ripley? Erroll's doctor? It couldn't be good news.*

"Hel—" His throat felt like sandpaper and he grunted to the nurse. She interrupted her important task to push the table to within Joe's reach. Then she left the room.

"Hello?" He sipped cold, coppery water and put the cup down.

"Joe, awe you aww wight?"

"Broken leg." Joe sighed. "A bump on my head. They were worried for a while, but it's okay. But the leg. Jesus, I mangled it. These drugs. For pain. I think I'd rather endure the pain. I feel like crap."

"I'm sowwy. Wook, I don't know what covewage youw insuwance pwovides, but if it isn't enough, wiww you wet me hewp?"

"Well, Mark, you see . . ." Long pause. "I don't have any. Insurance, I mean. I was—"

"Uninsuwed? That's dweadfuw. How can you—"

"Well, I'm *between* insurance companies, actually. I had to switch. Long story."

"Weww, don't wowwy, Joe. I got it."

"Thank you, uh, Mark."

"My wesponsibility." Long pause. "Joe, I weawize how tiwed you must be wight now, but I have to ask. You undewstand. When you came to the westauwant wast night— heww, *wast night?* It's onwy been a coupwe houws. Uh, did you—wewe you—that is, did you come at such an odd houw because you have news about—"

"No, uh, Mark. I'm sorry. No. That last lead, the bearded lady who we'd heard about that may have seen your daughter? Finally traced her to Orlando. In a mental institution. Not all there. Hallucinates. Dead end. Sorry."

"Oh." Long pause. "Weww. I'm not discouwged. Maybe the beawded wady had wewatives? Maybe hew doctow—"

"I'm in contact with a colleague in Florida, but the trail's thin. She had a boyfriend—*apparently* she had no relatives— who visited her once. We don't have a name. Thin trail, but a clerk there talked with him. The clerk doesn't work there anymore. Thin trail, as I said."

"I appweciate youw effowts."

"Uh, Mark." Joe cleared his throat. "About my employees—"

"Yes. None of youw staff huwt in the quake, I heaw."

"Right. Only me, you, and Lois Ward in there. I hear. Uh—" Joe coughed and reached for the water cup. He sipped past a dry throat. *Maybe I should wait.* "About my employees—"

"Bad wuck fow them too, even if they wewen't in the buiwding when it cowwapsed? No paychecks, wight?"

"Uh, well, yeah—"

"I may have a sowution. That's wiwwy why I cawwed."

"Oh?"

"Joe, do you wemembew how we met?"

Joe barked a laugh at the memory. "How could I forget?" It hurt his head to laugh.

Joe had been a crime reporter with the *Contra Costa County News*, twenty years on the job, when he got a phone call from the eccentric, reclusive billionaire. Mark had been impressed with Joe's work on a story that helped police nab a gang of pick-pocketers who prayed on patrons of Mark's new fleet of riverboat carnivals plying the waters of the Sacramento River between Sacramento and San Francisco.

Joe had wanted an interview with Mark after he'd effectively busted the gang, but Ripley had defended against that intrusion deftly. Still, Mark was impressed with Joe's persistence—and with his sense of humor.

At about the same time, a Vice President In Charge Of Something Important in a Trane Enterprises subsidiary company—Rubber Poultry Stores, the novelty and party supply chain in the San Francisco Bay Area—had insulted Mark, mocking his speech impediment behind his back to a group of cronies. Mark had heard, though. Unseen, in the next room at the time. Mark resolved to fire the miscreant, but he discovered that, somehow, the man's contract was ironclad. Ripley had goofed, but that was another problem for another time, more easily solved. The bottom line was that Mark was powerless to punish him in a way that would—leave a mark, so to speak. The man could quit, of course, but Mark couldn't fire him.

But he could play with his head. Mind games. Mark's favorite sport. One night, while watching *The Godfather*, Mark got the idea for the perfect prank.

To pull it off, he needed help. He thought of Joe. A simple deal. Help pull off the joke and Mark would not only pay Joe handsomely, but also give him an exclusive interview. A big deal, because nobody interviewed Mark Trane.

The timing couldn't have been better. Joe's job at the

paper had turned stagnant, business politics rather than failed craft, and he was ready to change careers—to what, he hadn't been sure at the time.

Joe took the gig. A lark. And damn good money.

Mark had bought a major chunk of Wallyland Entertainment Corp, its properties, characters, and associated rights, the year before, so it became no problem to acquire the head of Wallyland's number one star character, Wacky Wabbit. Two weeks after Mark hired him, in the middle of the night, Joe put the famous cartoon character's head, soaked with raspberry Jell-O, at the foot of the offending VP's bed, planted an audio-video pick up, and left to record remote.

Message delivered.

The VP stormed into Mark's office the next morning, livid, threatening lawsuit. Mark showed him the videotape—at about the same hour Joe removed the video pickup from the VP's bedroom—including the part where the VP screamed and shit his pajamas when he woke up and saw the head.

"Thewe wiww be mowe," Mark promised, quietly. Ominously.

The offender quit before noon.

Joe's hunch had paid off and he'd found his niche. He didn't even bother with the interview. The newspaper business was suddenly history. He'd had so much fun doing the gig—the B&E, greased by large amounts of Trane bribe money to secretaries, butlers, security guards, and such, was especially fun—that he went to work for a detective agency part time within a month. He quit newspaper work a month later and became a full time PI; he opened his own agency two years after that.

"Yeah," Joe said. "I remember."

Nurse Ichabod appeared in the doorway, a cell phone in one hand. "It's for you," she said. Peeved expression.

"Awe you up to a simiwaw pwoject? Now?"

Mark waved the nurse away. Ichabod looked indignant and offered the phone again in an outstretched hand, from across the room, by the door. *What? I'm going to walk over there and get it?*

"Why not?" Joe didn't even bother to ask about payment. "It's not like I have a lot to do right now." It would be ample. "My last job sort of caved in on me."

The nurse ahemed, and rolled her eyes. Important work to do elsewhere. Mark pointed to the phone in his hand—*one phone call at a time is sufficient, thank you.*

Mark laughed. "I'm gwad to heaw you haven't wost youw sense of humow."

"One of your employees." Ichabod sighed, tapped her toe. "Urgent—she *says*."

"I guess I can work here, if I can get a phone—*my own phone*, I mean—and a little peace and quiet, and so on." *I can deal with billing later.* "A laptop, a modem." *It'll help keep up with Erroll's bills.*

Ichabod sighed again theatrically, crossed the room, and put the cell phone on the bedside table by the water pitcher. "None of my business," she muttered and left.

"Wipwey wiww send somebody to check on you, pwobabwy within the houw. She'ww pwovide whatevew you need."

"So, what's the gig?"

"Pewcy Oswawd is coming to Was Vegas. Now, this vewy mowning. He says he pwans to bwing down Heww."

At the door, Ichabod turned. "Louise Wardell," she said. "That's her name, the woman on the phone."

"You want to—"

"Said something about a dead man," Ichabod offered as the door closed. "Or a dog, or something."

"I'm pwanning a weception fow him. One he'ww—"

"What?" Joe dropped the phone and picked up the other one, the cell phone. "*What?*"

Lois Ward

Mary woke up when Lois jerked awake from her nightmare about Dog—*Dog this time, not Steve. What's happening?*—and Lois had hugged her so tightly, muttering, that it scared Mary.

Lois made French toast, Mary's favorite, which helped soothe both of them, but it soothed Mary more than it did Lois. Then Roommate Annie got up, seven and a half months plump, ill and achy, and waddled to the bathroom. It got complicated and busy in the too-small apartment. Typical morning.

Quickly showered and changed into jeans and a shirt, Lois grabbed her cell phone and a phone book while she dried her hair and ate. She tried to reach the police department first. It was hard to tell them what she wanted—"I think there may be a dead man in the walk-in freezer at Hell"—and not sound like a crank—"I saw the body in my dream. I think he's dead, but maybe not." She got bounced from desk to desk. By the time she got transferred back to the person she'd spoken to in the first place, she had her talk down well enough, but it had taken up a half-hour with nothing to show for it. She could have driven there in fifteen minutes.

"Well, maybe he's still alive in there," she told Roommate Annie, irritably, while she looked up the Fire Department number. Annie knew about the Steve dreams.

"So, if maybe Dog's alive," Roommate Annie said, sipping a glass of chocolate milk, "you think maybe Steve is, too?" It wasn't really a question. Junior college psychology. Roommate Annie tried to help. They were friends.

"Yeah, well—"

"Mom, can I have a glass of chocolate milk, too?"

"Fire Department. Is this an emergency?"

"Just maybe he *is*, you know?"

"Mom?"

"Hello? Ma'am?"

So it went. After the Fire Department, the Bureau of Civic Work's Building Inspection Office, the City-County Department of Disaster Aid and Management Public Relations Officer, and City Hall, she got transferred to the Police Department.

Desperate, at last she called Joe at the hospital. He'd know what to do, could get somebody to check it out. It took more time to get through to him because he was already on the phone when she called, but she badgered a cranky clerk into taking a cell phone to him anyway.

Lois had told Joe about her dreams. He'd seemed sympathetic without really believing that she'd seen the grave in the desert. They were just dreams, he said. They'd go away. More psychology.

"What?" Joe kept saying that. Lois was getting tired of it.

"This is *different*." She tried to keep the whine out of her voice. "Not just because it had Dog in the dream instead of Steve, but—Joe, what if I got the dream wrong? What if Dog is still *alive* in there?"

"Hm." Long pause. "Okay, let me make some calls. Say, you didn't talk to Stan Gomez, did you?"

"Do you think you can get him to check it out?"

A snort. "I might get lucky."

Or maybe not.

So Lois decided to go to Hell herself. She took Mary

with her. Roommate Annie needed the break and Lois needed time with Mary. But she needed to *do something* about this Dog dream or she'd bust. So she decided to go to Hell with Mary in Joe's car.

After, she'd go to Joe's office, drop off his stuff, check his mail, check to see if her car was done, then take Mary to lunch, then to the park. Or the library, if it was too hot.

No, it was Sunday. The library was closed. No mail either.

Joe's car wouldn't start and Lois spent minutes—*That man could be in there freezing to death right NOW!*—to get it jumped. But traffic was light.

She arrived on Dallas Street and parked across the street from Hell's back parking lot just before nine. It had been two hours since she'd had the dream. Six hours since the earthquake.

If he's in there, he'd be dead. No hurry, now.

Still, Lois hurried across the street, Mary's tiny hand firmly in hers, trotting along beside her.

The parking lot was almost empty. One police car, a fire department van, a few cars. A dump truck. A few hard-hatted clean up worker bees with brooms and shovels. A giant bureaucrat spider had spewed a web of plastic yellow Keep Out ribbon here and there, around the lot and near the door. The Trane company black van was gone.

"Lois?" Teresa Santiago called from behind her, across the street. "That you?"

Lois stopped on the broken and buckled sidewalk and waved. Teresa waddled quickly across Dallas and puffed up beside her. She smiled at Mary and bent down to shake her hand.

"You must be Mary, right?"

Mary looked at her mom, got an "it's okay" smile, and offered her hand solemnly. "My name is Mary Ward. What's your?"

"My name is Teresa Santiago." The big woman stood and lost her smile. "Lois, honey, have you seen Dog? You know, the hairy little fellow—"

Lois blanched. "Funny you should mention him."

"Why funny?"

Lois told her about the Dog dream. She had to start back at the Steve dream, and restart a few times, but her story got smoother with practice. Teresa understood dreams.

"I dig juju, honey," Teresa said. "I got it."

"Juju?"

"Never mind. Just tell your story. I'm listening."

Lois did.

"In the freezer, huh? Damn." She glanced at Mary, smiled. "Pardon my French." Then back to Lois: "He said something about getting some more steaks. Yesterday. I told him to hold off, that maybe it wasn't a good idea—"

"I know. I shouldn't have—"

"Mom?"

"Just never you mind guilt-tripping yourself, honey. I ain't seen that man since I told him to forget about them steaks, pushed it right out of my mind, figured he forgot about it too. But now . . ." She shook her head. "We got to find out."

"Mom?"

"What if he's still in there? Still alive."

Teresa eyed the yellow tape web and the bureaucrats milling around—The Man. "You got to go in there and find out. I can't."

"Mom?"

"I tried to call the police—"

"I know. You said. But we can't wait, not if . . ."

"Mom, I got to go to the bathroom."

"Lois Ward?" A male voice shouted to her from somewhere inside the parking lot. Lois spotted the man. Middle-aged, bald, potbelly, suit. Captain Stan Gomez waved to her from the far end of the lot next to his car.

"Can I see you for a minute?" He waved again as he slammed the car door, crossed the lot toward her, trotting fatly, ducking under strands of yellow tape.

"Yes," she shouted back. "Sir."

"Mom, I have—"

"Honey, there's a port-a-potty right over there. It'll have to do for now, but can you wait a minute?"

"I'll take her and stand guard," Teresa said. "And bring her right back. That's Gomez. He don't like me. Best you chat with him with me elsewhere."

Lois didn't remember if she'd told Teresa that she'd called Joe and that Joe had called Mr. Gomez. It didn't matter. If Joe *had*n't called—

"Miss Ward?" Gomez stopped ten yards away, on the other side of the rickety chain link fence. He stood, panting.

Mary looked from her mom to the big bag lady, who smiled toothsome. Lois nodded "it's okay," Mary returned Teresa's smile, took her hand, climbed through a wide gap in the fence, and headed toward the potty.

"I can't stay long," Teresa said over her shoulder to Lois as she walked away, Mary in tow. "I got a parade to plan."

"How come you smell funny?" Mary asked Teresa as they walked away. Teresa laughed and Lois didn't hear her answer. She climbed through the fence gap to join Gomez, who held it open for her.

"Parade?" Gomez asked Lois, wiping his forehead with a handkerchief. Lois shrugged, and Gomez waved a "never mind" as he repocketed the handkerchief.

"That was Teresa Santiago," he said, unnecessarily. He frowned, something she'd seen on Joe's face now and then. "What do you know about her?"

Lois gave the cop a defiant look. She'd had enough bureaucrats for one day. "She's helping my daughter go to the bathroom. That she's a nice lady and—"

"Sorry to bother you, Miss Ward—"

"Lois." She offered her hand. Yes, he reminded her of Joe. He'd had said they were friends.

"Yes." He took it. Beefy, sweaty, but firm and sincere. "Lois. I'm Stan Gomez."

"A friend of Joe's. He's mentioned you."

"Yeah, he's mentioned you, too. In fact, we were just talking. He told me a funny story." Gomez—*Stan*—didn't look like he thought the story was funny. They walked toward Hell's back door. "Want to hear it?"

"Okay." Ducking under and stepping over yellow tape.

"Me and Joe go way back, did you know that?"

"Sorry." A frowny man in a white jumpsuit and hardhat intercepted them in front of the door. "Can't go in there. Safety hazard." He nodded at the yellow tape maze as if that explained.

Stan nodded, muttered something about "official business," and waved a badge casually at the frowning official and kept walking, Lois in tow.

"Your funeral," the official muttered behind them.

"I was a deputy county sheriff," Stan said, "back when he was a reporter up in the Bay Area. Did he ever tell you about that?"

"Well, he said he knew you before he became a detective."

"There was a B&E up there, big mansion, big money. I investigated. He wrote a story. Our paths crossed. We liked each other right off. Reporter and a cop, we liked each other, imagine that. One night, we both had time off, drank a few beers, and he told me what really happened in that B&E." He laughed as he parted the yellow tape at the back door to let Lois duck under. "Nothing like what he wrote or what I investigated."

Stan ducked under the tape. "Seems like—you sure you haven't heard this story?"

Lois squinted in the dark hallway. "I don't know—" It seemed darker than it had been last night. A little more than six hours ago. Hot, too. Hotter than outdoors.

"Well, maybe *he* should tell you, not me." He took out a flashlight from a back pocket, turned it on, adjusted it. "His story. I don't know if it's really true. It's one hell of a story. Ask him about it."

He shined the light up the hallway where Joe had lain, and past, toward the kitchen doorway, where Lois had huddled during the earthquake. Debris still lay scattered all over, not much cleaned up from what she'd encountered earlier. Whoever was supposed to clean the place hadn't gotten the message. No, that wasn't it. Yellow Keep Out tape. Nobody was supposed to be in here for safety reasons. They'd clean up later, when they got the okay from the safety people.

Still, somebody had done a cursory job, mopping up broken glass and spilled mustard, and the metal shelf that had collapsed on Joe had been righted. It leaned against the outer wall. A stepladder lay propped against the shelf.

"Okay. I'll ask him. Now, will you—" Lois was about to ask why he'd brought her inside Hell, but she knew. Joe called him. Stan knew that she knew that he knew that—and so on. So no need to ask. "But—"

Oddly, Stan seemed to understand the unasked *other* question: what had Joe said to make Stan follow up on Lois' dream story?

"Well, your boss told me *another* funny story. A few minutes ago, he phoned. I was on my way to the office." He shined the light to the right, past debris littering the floor. "This one involves me, and you—" He barked a laugh that didn't seem to have much fun in it. "—and a man named Dog." The light reflected off a ghost-white rectangle. The walk-in freezer door.

"Did—did—" Lois swallowed past a paper-dry throat.

"I've been after Dog's sorry ass since he came to town." He walked slowly down the hallway, toward the freezer. "A real trouble-maker, that one." Lois followed, close. "Joe knows that I'd listen to anything I could use to bust him. I've tried to bust him three, four times." The light skittered about, probing among the spilled bottles, cans, canisters, jars, and stuff on the floor. "The shithead doesn't *stay* busted."

They hadn't cleaned up along here at all. Not even a token.

"So when Joe calls me and tells me this story—shit, maybe he should tell you this one, too. Maybe Joe should write for TV. Such an imagination. The way he can tell me this story so that I end up outright *squirmy* with curiosity—I can't put my finger on it. It's not like he confessed that he *knew* anything—or that *you* did. It was all so—so *hypothetical*, the *way* he told the story.

"I laughed, but not loud." They stepped over cardboard boxes. "Or too long. I got to wondering. The *way* he told it." Gingerly stepping over and around stuff. "I mean, what *if?*"

He sighed. "Besides, it's my goddamn job."

He shined his light on the door, the frame, the door handle, and the debris that had fallen in front of the door.

"Look here," he said, pointing with the light. "Sloppy plan, all this janitorial stuff right here beside the freezer. Lazy."

He tried to open the door. The handle came down, but the door didn't open.

"Jammed," he muttered. "These mops fell down—" He grabbed a buffer handle, put it on its side, in front of the door. "See how this is wedged—" He grunted. "Give me a hand—" He handed her the flashlight so he could use both hands to tug the handle up and away from the door.

It gave, and Stan set the machine aside. "You saw me remove that, right?" He puffed, wiping his hands.

"Yes, I—"

"Shit, I should have used a handkerchief. Could be prints." He took out his handkerchief and wiped his forehead as he talked. "Now, do you think that buffer fell down there, jammed this door *before* the quake—I mean, *because* of it—rather than *after*—I mean, *after* those yahoos said they searched down here?"

"I'm sure I—"

"Because if this door got jammed *before* those yahoos

searched—*allegedly* searched—down here, that means they didn't look in this freezer, right?"

"I—I guess—"

"If *that's* the case—and if we find what I, to tell the truth, hope we *don't* find behind this door, then a few heads will roll, don't you think?"

"I don't—"

"Or maybe not. If somebody asks me how I came to suspect there's a dead man here, what am I going to say? Tell them that some private eye doped up on painkillers told me a story—a goddamn *story*—and I *believed* him? I haven't figured it out yet. Maybe I got more to hide than those Fire Department people do. What do *you* think?"

"I think maybe—"

"They finally cut the electricity about a half-hour ago. Somebody else screwed up. This fridge has been on all night."

"Mr. Gomez—Stan—"

"Then again, there's—"

"I think we should just look." Lois' patience had worn thin in the heat of Stan's display of what seemed like anger—except he smiled, but it didn't seem a particularly *jolly* smile. It was dark, stuffy, and hot inside Hell.

And she wanted to *know*.

Stan sighed. His jaw muscles worked as if he was chewing a piece of gristle the size of casino dice. Lois suddenly realized Stan had been babbling because he was nervous. Or scared.

Then, hand wrapped in a handkerchief—so he wouldn't smudge possible fingerprints—he opened the walk-in freezer door.

A puff of white frigid air belched past them.

"Shitshitshitshit."

On the floor in front of them, lay Dog. Frozen stiff. Dead.

Percy Oswald

Percy grinned toothsomely into the bright Las Vegas morning as he stood in the doorway of his private jet and waved at the cameras. Theo stood behind him, her usual place, smiling, waving.

He felt exuberant, presidential, despite the straw hat and casual short-sleeved shirt, and for an instant, he fantasized about stepping off Air Force One, a military band playing "Hail to the Chief." A brief fantasy. He was a humble man, and a band would have been too much. The cameras were nice.

"Make a note of this, Theo," he said, stepping down from the plane. She followed, close. "Good turn out."

"I got it," she said. Theo knew. Those responsible for mustering this many reporters on such short notice would be rewarded. Good for staff morale.

"I plan to raise Hell, ladies and gentlemen," Percy told the reporters, and their tape recorders and cameras, and the hundreds of thousands of potential supporters—and contributors—beyond.

"When's liftoff?" a reporter asked.

"Five o'clock today." *Just in time to catch local and West Coast prime time news, live. Look at their eyes light up at that.*

Brief speech, quick Q&A, but good face time—leave

them a bit hungry, always best—then into a chauffeured rental van and away. Important Man, Important Things To Do. Stay Tuned. He left the gaggle of reporters while his smile still gleamed, before he wilted in the windless, cloudless desert air.

Nine-thirty. "We're making good time," he told Theo as he settled back, sipping bottled water.

"We'll make the noon news." She punched a number on her phone. "Local TV. CNN, the networks. Radio. Good coverage all over. A couple top anchors are coming in from the networks. This is too big for just local stringers." She patted him on the knee. "You make good copy, Oswald." Then she redirected her attention to the phone, talking with somebody up ahead. Tony O'Grady, local honcho for Oswald Publications. Organizing.

Percy smiled, closed his eyes, and tried to relax, take advantage of the lull, conserve his energy for the coming battle he'd lead. For the umpteenth time since the dream last night, he focused inward. He questioned that inner vision that directed him here. It remained clear, that vision, resisting his best efforts to be objective, to find fault. The feeling that all his life had brought him to this place and this time—the feeling of *rightness*—persisted.

Nothing else since that rainy October night in 1967 had seemed so clear, so *real*. A message. That night had been only the first part of the message. Last night had been the middle. This afternoon—he checked his watch again—will be the end.

"Chancy, striking so fast," Theo said. She held a hand over the phone and frowned at Percy.

"What?"

"You give up organization, preparedness—"

"Move fast, bulldoze obstacles, take the lead—"

"I know. Speed isn't always haste." She shrugged. "But."

"But?" He nodded toward the phone with his chin and sipped water. "What's up?"

"Talk to O'Grady." She handed him the phone.

"Tony? Thanks for that reception at the airport."

"Yeah, well. I know you counted on local church leaders to gather their flocks, but it won't happen."

"The churches won't cooperate? I thought—"

"Oh, I can muster a few hundred troops from the pews, but only a few hundred. Maybe a thousand."

"Why so few?"

"It's Sunday. Day of rest and all that. Besides, the locals aren't used to mobilizing so fast. There are other factors."

"Other factors?"

"They aren't *in charge*, the churchies. No clout, or not enough. A lot of them will find excuses to stay away, besides it being Sunday, because—well, they won't admit this—but some don't like the people who *are* in charge."

"Then who runs the show?"

"Woman named Teresa Santiago and a fellow named 'Dog.'"

As they drove through the glittering and gaudy Las Vegas streets, O'Grady gave Percy the rundown on the local scene, as he'd done with Theo a minute before. "It's a big group," O'Grady said, "bigger than you'd expect, and pretty well-organized for a bunch of derelicts. It's this Teresa Santiago, and Dog. Hippies. Old school liberal agitators. Save the trees, preserve the parks. Down with the capitalist pigs. Where they lead, people follow. The people we need. In a hurry, that is."

"Let me think."

"We could wait," Theo said. Percy handed her the phone and she got back on with O'Grady. Organizing.

Percy chewed a Tumeze.

He hated street people. Filthy, foul-mouthed, rotten lazy bums. Hated them all—well, most of them. Un-Christian attitude, but who's perfect? He knew his pathological antipathy to dirt related to that person—or angle, or demon—he'd met in the rain that night in 1967. He owned Oswald's Pure-As-Heaven Handsoap Company because of it.

It hurt him gut-deep when he had to "make nice" with poor people, put on a smile, shake their hands, even embrace them. For the cameras, and the collection plate. For the cause. He gave away a lot of soap. He showered a lot.

If he waited now, he'd be less likely to have to deal directly with this San Diego woman and her dog, let alone the great, unwashed hoards she apparently commanded. If he waited, he'd get more people on the street, have a better-organized performance for the media.

If he delayed, the loss of momentum would cost him. Local bureaucrats might have time to intervene. Opposition might arise, organize, interfere, or even stop him. Momentum counted.

He'd have to share the spotlight with local church and civic leaders.

That's what decided him. To wait felt inconsistent with his dream, his vision. He knew exactly what he needed to do— and it was his alone to do. No, he had to act fast.

"Act now."

Plus, O'Grady was right and neither wishful thinking nor fervent prayer would change the political climate. Expedience. Go with the flow. Know whose what to kiss and when. He'd have to be careful to stay out front, keep control.

"What did you say, dear?" Theo asked. The van had pulled over to the curb at some seedy side street.

He reached over and took the phone from Theo. "Tony, we go as planned, same time. Do what you can with the churches, but I'm in front, and I'll work with what I've got."

A mob of dirty, ill-clothed people milled about on the sidewalk inches from the van, some touching it, leaving greasy prints on the windows. Percy looked through the tinted glass, appalled. In the mob, cameras and reporters jostled.

What in God's name goes on here?

"That means you embrace the local culture. Okay. We got media. You'll meet with some homeless organizers at a place called Jesus' Bread Basket. It's a soup kitchen—"

"I know," Percy said, a quiver in his voice. He saw the sign above the crowd.

He took a few minutes to breathe, to prepare. To find his smile, adjust his face. When he was ready, he nodded to Theo, who opened the van door.

He stepped out, smiled and waved.

Cameras, reporters. Questions. Smiles. Be nice.

The crowd parted sluggishly, like oozing grease, to let Percy and Theo into the cramped storefront church-cum-soup kitchen.

He was introduced to a minister, whose name he immediately forgot. He made small talk with the minister and his lieutenants for a few minutes, smiled for cameras, did sound bites for the microphones. Hand-gripped with local tribal leaders. Photo op.

"Where's this Ms. Santo Domingo?" he asked the minister.

"Teresa Santiago." The tall minister shrugged bony shoulders and looked droopy. "We expected her a few minutes ago, but . . ."

He was comparatively clean, and dressed slightly better than his flock, but too many sheep crowded the small, windowless space, it was too hot, and they had no air conditioning. Two pathetic fans moved hot air around. Hot, smelly air.

"Maybe we could adjourn," Percy said, wiping his brow, a hint. "To someplace more comfortable?"

They ditched the media and Percy and Theo were herded into a back room where they met Santiago's lieutenants. A frail, twitchy woman called Teach. Some glinty-eyed psycho monster named Captain Freddy. A silent little rodent called Larry. A half dozen others. Santiago's right hand men.

Percy cleared his throat, began the delicate work of Taking Over. "Ladies and gentlemen, I want to—"

Somebody threw up in Larry's lap and Percy had to dig deep to maintain his dignity and composure. Compared to the others in the room, including Larry, he failed miserably. Nobody called him to task for it.

He chewed a Tumeze, and after a moment, reasserted his command. He outlined his plan. March over there and surround the place. Hold hands, everybody. Sing, pray. Then, at the right moment, at a signal from Percy—

A commotion outside, in the soup kitchen hall. *What now?*

"Teresa," he heard people say, streeties and reporters in the thick crowd. "Teresa Santiago." *They sound—reverent.*

An enormous Hispanic woman in a broad, faded skirt, a billowy blouse, a scarf over her helmet of short, gray hair, pushed her way into the room. She stood in the doorway. Monumental. A force to be reckoned with. Mount Rushmore on legs like pillars.

People hushed. They stared at Teresa, still. They sat forward, expectant.

Here's charisma. Lady, you are some piece of work.

Big fists anchored on big hips. Her face was broad, jowly, and Percy had no doubt that when she smiled, she radiated light and energy, just as now, frowning, she radiated dark despair. Such a look of sadness he'd never seen in his life. His heart went out to her in her grief—whatever it might be.

A jet whooshed overhead, and a horn honked somewhere. Somebody farted in the main room.

The bag lady named Teach raised a hand timorously. "What—"

"Dog," Teresa Santiago said. "Dead."

The silence stretched, shifted, became a stunned fog. A long moment passed before the sound of weeping entered. Larry. Teach. Captain Freddy. And others.

Lois Ward

Lois followed Captain Stan Gomez from the building as he called it in on his phone. He asked Lois a few questions as they stood outside in the parking lot, waiting for forensics, or the crime scene investigators, or the coroner, or whomever he'd called, to show. They didn't get far in their chat before Teresa returned Mary from the port-a-potty, and Teresa got the news about Dog.

The big woman took a step toward the building, but Stan moved into her path. "It's him," he said. "No shit."

Teresa hesitated, then accepted, and nodded, face ashen. She looked away, eyes bright, into the pale sky above the Strip, perhaps at some memory.

Stan apparently wanted to question Teresa about Dog right away, but something in her eyes made him back off. She looked dangerous, Lois decided. *Or lost.* Besides, Stan's phone rang just then. He muttered something about not leaving town to the big woman's back as she stalked off, her fists knotted like hammers, and took the call.

"Mom, I like Teresa." Mary smiled. "She smells funny, but she's nice."

"Yes, honey, she's nice."

"Did her dog get hurt?"

"It's okay, honey." Lois patted Mary's hair, distracted.

What do I do now? What do I say? If I hadn't taken that nap, maybe I would have seen him back there. Maybe—

"Hold on a second, sir," Stan said to his phone. He cupped it in his hand, gave Mary a quick smile, and spoke to Lois. "We'll have a few more questions for you, Ms. Ward."

He'll find out about the steaks; that's why Dog was there, I'll bet, to steal—

"Lois?"

He sounded kindly and Lois realized that she must look shocked, maybe ready to throw up. She felt dizzy. "I'll be tied up here a while," he said, gesturing at the phone. "Where can I reach you in, say an hour?"

"An hour?" Her throat felt like sandpaper.

"Or two." A tinny voice yelled on the phone.

She looked at Mary, who blinked back up at her, smiling. She didn't want to go back to the apartment. The park was out. Too hot. The library? It was Sunday.

She needed to call Joe. Needed his advice.

Maybe I need a lawyer.

"Um. How about Joe's office? I have—"

"Good. I know where it is. I'll drop by. Or call. Or send somebody. If you go somewhere else, please let me know right away." He gave her his business card and returned to the phone, turning away from her as he talked. *His boss on the phone?*

Lois and Mary left and went to Joe's office.

The office was an old, cramped affair in an industrial park west of the Strip. It hunkered, invisible from the seldom-used, pot-holey West Industrial Road, between and behind two shops. Gravel parking lot. On one side, Loren's Fast Times Auto Repair was always busy, engines revving, hammers banging, power tools chattering and hissing, loud country and western music blaring all day and into the night. Smelled like a gas station. Primer-painted junkers parked out front next to glittery sports cars and custom vans, a few hollowed out, among them Lois' car, Being Repaired. Joe's office shared a common cinder block wall with a small office and break room behind Loren's shop.

On the other side, also sharing a common cinder block wall, Quality Entertainment Services, Inc., a pinball and poker-game repair shop, made for quieter neighbors. There, shady characters that dressed and acted like hoods from a bad gangster movie, or like movie producers, and drove expensive cars, came and went at all hours. Nobody bothered Joe here, or his infrequent visitors, and Lois knew she and Mary were safer here than in many other places in the city.

Joe had two computers in his office, one an old Macintosh, the other a newer PC, both "in-kind" payoffs for services Joe had rendered their former owners. The Mac had games on it. Mary was okay there, kept herself busy. Lois had stocked books in a cabinet in case Mary got bored with the computer. There was a TV and a VCR.

A small fridge in the alcove just off the bathroom-shower had a few yogurts, pickle jars, peanut butter jars, burritos, and other stuff. A cabinet with crackers, coffee, and assorted mismatched knives, spoons, and more stuff. A microwave. A Coke machine and a candy machine in front of Loren's. If Mary got tired, she could nap on the sofa. Lois had slept there often, and Mary had, too, a couple of times.

Lois even had a change of clothes tucked away in the closet for Mary.

I'll call Joe first thing. Lois' stomach knotted with trepidation as she unlocked the door, disarmed the alarm, turned on the lights and air conditioner, and booted up the Mac for Mary at a small, battered desk across the room. She found a box of Tumeze in Joe's desk drawer as she waited for someone to answer the phone at the hospital. She chewed and waited.

Joe, she was told as she booted up his PC, could not be disturbed. It had taken extraordinary effort to get that cell phone to Joe an hour ago so she could tell him about her dream about seeing Dog in the freezer, and the man on the phone sounded like the same crabby-butt she'd badgered then. She left a message and hung up.

"Mom, can I have some pickles?"

"Sure, honey." Lois played back Joe's phone messages, notepad ready. Clients, employees, friends. A bill collector. The reporter from the *Clark County Chronicle-Progress*, Miles Doughton. A few people who didn't leave names or numbers, just cryptic, mysterious messages only Joe would be able to decipher. As she'd expected.

"Do you want one? There's a few left."

"No, thanks, honey."

A message from Erroll's doctor. Joe had left instructions that calls from Erroll's doctor were to be passed to him as soon as possible. She wrote down the message, set it aside to try to call Joe again in a half-hour.

The phone rang. Lois checked caller ID. The reporter. She let the answering machine take it.

Then Lois took out Joe's things and laid them on his desk in a neat row. Tape recorder. Camera. Videotape. Wallet.

She glanced through Joe's e-mail. Clients, employees, that reporter again. Bill collector. She saved the messages.

She straightened the things on Joe's desk again. She put his wallet in a drawer. Sharpened pencils. Checked her phone. The battery was low so she replaced it with one from Joe's stash of extra batteries.

Fidgeted, trying to avoid thinking.

In the ambulance, Joe had told her to take care of business. Lois had done secretarial work for Joe, transcribing notes and reports, doing phone interviews, setting up appointments and meetings, doing research, cataloging files.

Nothing left to do now but look for Steve.

Lois had found a missing person website, like "America's Most Wanted," but on the Internet, rather than TV. It was for missing people not necessarily connected with crimes, or maybe cases that weren't important enough to make the network

TV cut.

One part of the site was like the side of a milk carton. "Have You Seen Me?" Thousands of missing people. Updates and new reports added daily. Another part of the site had descriptions of bodies or parts of bodies found all over the country, and of people in mental institutions, and in hospitals in comas, who had no identity. Maybe somebody knows something. Worth a try. Success stories also got posted. She found lots of John and Jane Does in comas in hospitals all over the country. The site had so many links that Lois still hadn't explored them all.

She also had once checked a "Psychic Lost & Found" site. That got her on to UFO abduction and Satanic cult and "parallel dimension" sites and similar ilk. Desperation, she decided, prompted her to spend more time in those sites than she should have, hours wasted. Frauds. New Age whackos. Religious bullshit. A dead end. Her father had been a preacher. She understood, or thought she did, the limits of faith in a rational world, and she didn't believed in magic. Or prayer. Things happen for a reason.

She didn't believe in dreams, she told herself. Much.

She tracked news sites for Las Vegas, Clark County, southern Nevada, and Southern California, and police investigations of all kinds up to the state level. Terrorists. The drug war. Immigration from Mexico and Central America and elsewhere, legal and illegal. The homeless. Smuggling. A few others. She kept finding more sites. There was a woman in Pennsylvania who had a son last seen in Las Vegas about the same time that Steve disappeared. They corresponded.

She found it isn't just women who get randomly kidnapped, robbed, raped, and murdered. Men disappear too. Not as often as women disappear, but it did happen. She studied gangs and serial killers and perverts and pedophiles.

She'd learned more than she wanted to know about why people abandon their spouses. Those sites were more depressing than the serial killer sites.

She shook her head, decided to take care of Joe's business first, look for Steve later. It could get deep, she knew.

About Dog. *I've got to talk to Joe about the steak thing before Stan Gomez sends somebody.* Joe's business affairs. Mary. There was enough to keep her busy.

She sighed, picked up the tape recorder, rewound, hit play. Joe's voice. She took notes on a notepad as she listened. He described a woman, then a car, then read a license plate number. The tape ended and Lois rewound it and set it aside as she called Joe's contact in the Nevada Department of Motor Vehicles, License Plate Bureau. Run a check. That's what Joe would have wanted done, why he'd recorded the plate number. Lois had made calls for him before. The woman on the phone asked how Joe was. She'd heard. They chatted for a minute.

"It'll take about ten minutes," the woman finally said. "I'll call you back."

"Mom, we're out of pickles."

"We'll get some on the way home."

Lois flipped through the images on Joe's digital camera. Several views of a dimly lit car—probably white, Lois couldn't tell what model, but it looked new—in a dimly lit parking lot, and a close up of a license plate, the one she's just called in. Bad lighting. The images would have to be enhanced, if Joe wanted them. He had a contact that did that.

"Mom, can we go to the library today?"

Lois put the camera in the drawer with the tape recorder and wallet, popped the videotape into the VCR, and hit rewind.

"Not today, honey. It's Sunday. The library is closed."

On the TV screen atop a cabinet beside Joe's desk, a face moved, huge, distorted, inches from the lens. Lois hit freeze.

Joe.

The image was vague, the light source obviously behind the camera, dim, inadequate, but definitely Joe. She rewound more. Joe backed away from the camera, dropped from view, then reappeared and stepped backward amid vague geometric shapes, dark on dark, toward a knife-edge of bright light—*a doorway?*—into the light, and out of sight.

Lois let the tape run backward and thought. For a few seconds, she didn't get it. But only for a few seconds.

The hallway behind Hell's kitchen.

"I want you to read to me, Mom."

Lois gasped. "No, no—"

The camera that had taken the images had been high against the hallway wall, facing down the hall toward the casino, past the back door to the parking lot. The bright light was the door. She could see the ghostly pale oblong of the freezer door beyond the back door, but just barely.

"But, Mom—"

The camera that had taken the images flickering in quick-time reverse on the TV screen had been on the metal rack that had fallen and crushed Joe's leg in the earthquake.

"—you're just watching TV."

Joe had been there in Hell to retrieve the tape. He had been spying on her. He must have known about the steak theft and was trying to catch her in the act.

"I'm sorry, honey. We can't go there because it's—"

"Maybe we could check."

"It can't be." She continued to watch the tape run backward, aghast. *Am I on it?*

At the bottom of the screen, a vague woman-shape stalked backward through the back door light and backed to the dim freezer, her face hidden in deep shadow. Dark, yes, and Lois couldn't identify the woman, but she could see what she did. The woman-shape lifted an object that lay in front of the freezer—*a floor buffer?*—propped it against the wall beside the freezer, then stood at the freezer door, motionless for a long moment.

"There's a pickle store next to the library."

Then the woman removed something from the freezer door, a broom—Lois realized it was propped open with a broomstick—walked backward, and out the back door.

"Then we could check. When we go to get pickles, we could drive by and see if the library's open."

The buffer hadn't fallen because of the earthquake. The woman had—

"No, wait—"

On the screen, Dog propped the freezer door open with a broom. Then he exited the walk-in freezer door and walked backward out the back door.

The phone rang.

She'd put it there *before* the earthquake.

"Mom?"

If Joe had been spying on me, would he have asked me to take care of business? He knew I might look at the tape, or was he so out of it—

Lois checked the caller ID. Not Gomez or the reporter. DMV.

The woman had hesitated at the freezer door, as if to listen, before she took out the broom holding the door open and blocking it shut with the buffer.

"Mom?"

"Lois? That car you wanted?"

"Yes?"

She must have known. Must have.

"Mercedes. Registered to a Mrs. Samantha Gomez. Big shot, works for the city. You want an address? Phone number?"

On the tape, still playing in reverse, the mystery woman walked backward through the back door, down the hall, past and under the camera. Back into the hotel.

"Mom?"

Samantha Gomez

B obbie answered the phone before the second ring. "Sammy, honey," she said, "this is a bad time—"

"Did you *see?*" Samantha's voice cracked.

"What? See what?"

"On the TV." Samantha gestured impatiently at the TV across her office.

"Sammy, honey, please—"

"Don't give me any of that 'I'm too busy right now' caca, Bobbie. You wouldn't call me 'Sammy, honey' if you weren't alone. You wouldn't have answered the phone."

"All right, all *right*. What the hell are you talking about?"

"On the TV, darn it, on the *TV*."

"Wait—just *wait* a minute." Bobbie left the phone. Samantha paced, flipping between channels. Two local stations had the story, live, with reporters on the scene in front of Hell. Dog was homeless, a trouble-maker ne'er-do-well, but the media loved him. Another channel had reruns of Gilligan's Island. The other had a Taco Bell commercial. *Well, maybe not all that important.* CNN was on a Mexican family found dead of the heat, boiled to death in a broke-down water truck in the New Mexico desert—

"Oh, Jesus." Bobbie was back on the line. "That poor, poor man. How terrible."

"Bobbie, did you know him?"

"*Know* him?" She barked a laugh. "A hobo?"

"He's been on the news, you know, talking about, you know, 'up with the homeless,' and 'down with Hell,' and—"

"I've heard *of* him, if that's what you mean. A harmless hippie agitator, likes to get on TV—*liked* to, that is. A real pain in the ass, but harmless, mostly."

"Did you *see* him? I mean when we—*you* know."

"Did I see him in there when I came out to meet you? Sammy, honey, what—"

"Because if you did see him—"

"If I saw somebody go into our refrigerator, especially a dirty streetie, I'd report it to security, don't you think?"

"Well—"

"Well, what? Don't you believe me? Sammy, honey, what's this *really* about? I would have seen this or somebody would have called. Somebody will, I guess. Why did you call? Really?"

"I—I'm sorry, Bobbie." She sighed. "I didn't mean—we needed to talk, but we got interrupted. In the van, and then the earthquake. That's why I called. I saw on the TV about this Dog, and I needed to—"

"I understand." Bobbie's voice softened, and Samantha felt warm in all the right places. A long pause.

"I needed to talk to—"

Simultaneously: "I needed to talk to—"

They both laughed, tension released.

"How can we get together, Bobbie? We're so busy. Before, when your boss decided to name the place 'Hell,' I thought we were busy, but now—"

"Yes, now." Bobbie cleared her throat. "This man in the freezer, on top of the earthquake. Maybe it's a good thing."

"Good thing? A man is dead. Bobbie, maybe it's too late. The construction. The books. People will find out. There'll be an investigation. Not just the earthquake, but this dead man."

"It'll be okay, Sammy, honey."

"What? What are you—"

"Sammy, honey, sit down and listen."

Samantha sat, tapping a foot.

"It's what I wanted to tell you last night in the van. Before we got interrupted. By the earthquake—and other things." She giggled. "We can go, you know? Just *go*."

"Go? What do you mean?"

"I chartered a plane. That's what I wanted to tell you. We can go now, send for our stuff later, or just buy new stuff. I have a plane. Get it?"

"No, I don't—"

"It's *time*, Sammy, honey. Time to go away, you and me. Just the two of us. We can start over—"

"What? Bobbie, no, wait, I—" *I was going to tell you that we're quits unless you stop with cooking the books, the doctored manifests, the double billing, the kickbacks, whatever else—the whole illegal stew.* "I—I—"

"Oh, Sammy, honey, it doesn't matter about a dead hippie. We'll be on the beach at Rio before anybody even looks at the books. Believe me, I know how to handle this. We've talked about this before."

"Yes, we did." *This isn't right. I don't want to run away. I want you in public, free and open.* "But, Bobbie, my job. *Your* job. We can't just—"

"To hell with the goddamn job, Sammy, honey. I've socked enough away. We'll be okay."

"You'll be arrested."

In a Humphrey Bogart accent: "Trust me, sweetheart."

"Oh, Bobbie, I'm scared, so—"

Samantha's secretary opened to office door, peeked in and wagged a hand frantically. She cupped the phone. "What?"

"Percy Oswald is here. And—"

"Sammy, honey, I can send a car by. This minute."

"And?"

"It's what we've dreamed of, planned for."
"He's with Teresa Santiago. And—"
"It's not impulsive. I have it all planned out."
"And?"
"Us, Sammy, honey. This is all about *us*."
"Your husband's on line three."

Mark Trane

Mark answered the phone before the second ring. "Twane."

"Joe. Thought you might like a report."

"Awe you stiww in the hospitaw? How awe you?"

"Yeah, I'm still in bed. Recovering, they tell me. These painkillers—you don't want to know."

"How's Wois?" Mark stifled a cough, popped another handful of Tumeze, and chewed. Licorice flavored, his favorite.

"Uh, fine. I sent her home. She's okay."

"Good. Give hew my wegawds."

A pause. "Bummer about that earthquake."

"Ah." Mark waved a dismissive hand. "It was subsidence, I heaw, not an eawthquake." He tossed the empty Tumeze wrapper at a wastebasket. Missed. "Wike a pothowe in the woad undew the buiwding. They have them in Fwowida a wot."

"Did you hear about the man in the freezer?"

"Wipwey cawwed." *What's troubling Joe? Painkillers?* "I saw on TV. Sad."

A sigh. "Yeah, another bummer. Poor guy. It may cost us some time and finesse with this rally. There's an investigation. There'll be questions."

"It shouldn't take vewy much of youw time, wight?"

"No. We can talk about that later. I got your stuff after

you called. One of your people dropped by with a few cartons. I guess she talked with somebody here. I went right to work."

"So, what have you accompwished?"

"I got lucky and put one of my operatives in place right away. He just called in. Here's what I have on Oswald and Santiago as of about ten minutes ago." Joe briefed Mark on the meeting at Jesus' Bread Basket and the rally being organized.

"What a wadicaw pwan. Cweative. Oswawd moves fast."

"Yeah, with Santiago's help. That's in our favor. Oswald and Santiago won't have time to second guess us."

"Good job, Joe. I'm pweased."

A pause. "Mark, there's something I need to talk about—"

"Joe, don't *wowwy*." *He sounds dejected.* "It's okay. I *know*."

"Uh—what?"

"I know you've wooked. I know how hawd it is to find peopwe. Some peopwe awe hawdew to find than othews. You'we doing youw best, I know, and I appweciate it."

"Ah, about your daughter. Yes. I haven't—"

"Don't wowwy. I undewstand. Concentwate on this wawwy today. You can get back to my daughtew tomowwow."

"Yeah, but." A pause, then a sigh. "It's about my, uh, employees. The security at the hotel." *Really dejected.*

"Joe, I have an idea to keep them empwoyed."

"To keep them—uh, what?"

"Joe, when we'we done, wet me tawk to youw doctow about youw medication."

"I'm sorry, I—"

"Just take notes. I have a pwan that wiww wequiwe a few peopwe to impwement. Can you wecwuit a few peopwe who can be twusted to keep a secwet, to mobiwize on a moments notice, to do a job fow Foxwowthy Vigawance Agency?"

"You mean my, uh, security guards?"

"Them and whoevew ewse you have on youw paywoww,

ow can get. I need about two dozen, but as few as fifteen wiww do, I bewieve. Can you get the bodies? Today? Wight away?"

"Yes. I think so. Sure, yes."

"Good. Wet me teww you my pwan—" Mark outlined his plan.

"I can do it," Joe said at last, his mood brightened.

"I know you can, Joe. I twust you compwicitwy."

Silence.

"Joe? You okay?"

"I'll get on it. I'll get back to you—"

"No need. I'm watching devewopments on TV, and Wipwey has opened fow business just down the haww. Aww's weww, Joe."

They parted, and Mark had the feeling that Joe had left something unsaid. Mark wondered what it might be. He dismissed a few notions as petty and decided Joe would cough it up—so to speak—when he was ready.

He popped a handful of Tumeze, and chuckled as he chewed, a little boy with a secret. Some practical jokes were funny even in the planning stage.

He picked up the phone and called Ripley.

"Yes, uh, Mark."

She sounds as distracted as Joe. What's with everybody?

"How awe you—" He broke off to stifle a cough, and popped more Tumeze.

"I'm on it. It's a total loss. I don't have a real cost estimate yet. I have fifteen calls to return to insurance—"

"Wight. I'm suwe you'we on top of it. How up-to-date awe you on the Oswawd wawwy? What he and Santiago have pwanned?"

A pause, brief. Mark heard nails tap clickety-clickety. She's thinking: *His building collapses, people are hurt, one killed, and he plans a goddamn joke.*

"I sent a man to infiltrate. He's wired and I'm monitoring. It's like we're there in person."

"Good. Can you patch me in my office? I want to wisten too. Do you have video?"

"I'll send a tech over. It'll take a few minutes and you'll be live, audio and video. The video is shaky, but it's live."

"Good. Bwief me."

Ripley briefed Mark on what she's seen and heard from her wired spy, and Mark briefed her on what Joe was up to.

"Mark, do we need Foxworthy's inside man now?"

"Wedundant, I know, but don't wowwy about Joe. What about this poow man in the fweezew?"

"What about him?" *She sounds—weary? Nervous?*

"Joe says thewe'll be an investigation."

"Don't worry. I talked with a detective a few minutes ago. Accident, looks like. They may want to talk to you, but later. Routine. I'll be there just in case."

Yes, I've heard that hitch in her voice before, but I can't remember when.

"Can we do something fow the poow man's famiwy?"

"His—his *family?*"

"Yes. A gestuwe."

"Ah. Good PR. Right. A secret donation, but there'll be a leak. Make us look generous, concerned. Could sidestep a lawsuit, too. I'll look into it."

Is she going through menopause?

A young man with wire-rimmed glasses, a toolbox, and a pocket protector filled with pens and gadgets came into the office as Mark hung up. The tech tinkered with the wire worm's nest behind the bank of video monitors other technicians had installed in the last hour. Mark made calls while he waited to be connected to Ripley's inside man at Jesus' Bread Basket.

He called a caterer. And a local novelty and party supply wholesaler for one of his subsidiary companies. A costume shop.

Images came up on a monitor, shaky and distorted, as Mark worked the phones. The tech muttered and fidgeted with wires, knobs, and doohickeys. The image cleared and Mark looked over a hairy man's shoulder at a crowd of indigents pressed together in a small room.

Audio. Somebody wanted to get a local biker gang to participate in the rally. Game plans.

Mark didn't bother to take notes. Ripley was on it.

He thought about putting cameras outside the hotel. A dozen or so, located so he could see the action, real time, from the best angles. With audio, shotgun mikes. He knew some people.

Then, suddenly—inspiration.

He'd go down there, incognito, in the crowd, on the street, see it happen close up, first hand. Feel it, smell it. Live.

Nobody will know it's me. Won't that be fun?

Lois Ward

Lois didn't even try to call the hospital. She could drive there in Joe's car faster than she could get connected to Joe on the phone. This was too important to talk about over the phone. She wasn't about to take any excuses—if Joe was asleep, she'd wake him up, by gosh. This was darned important.

It was all just too complicated. She needed advice, she needed Joe's help with this.

No, actually, it wasn't even her tape. It was Joe's. His business. She was just an employee. Not her problem, but Joe needed to know about this, and fast.

She'd have to talk about the steaks. She didn't want to think about that. What could she say? No, she'd just tell Joe what she saw on the tape, what his DMV contact said about the car he saw, and let him take it from there. No, that wasn't right. She couldn't pretend that she didn't know—what she knew—about what she'd done, and hadn't done. She should confess, face the music, that's what. Right off the bat.

"Are you okay, Mom?"

"Yeah, honey, I'm okay." She popped a Tumeze, licorice-flavored, chewed, and put the package in her purse. "Let's go get you some pickles." There was a Safeway on the way.

"Then can we check the library?"

"Let's go visit Uncle Joe instead."

"In the hospital?" Had Lois told Mary about Joe? She must have. She felt twitchy. She hoped she could drive okay.

She locked the videotape and the digital camera and Joe's wallet in his safe, turned off the computers and lights, turned down the AC, patted her purse to make sure she had her cell phone, and locked the office.

Loren was working on her car as she came out. "Need a part," he said, grinning, wiping his hands on a grease rag, smelling of gasoline. "Sorry. It'll be Monday."

"Okay," Lois said. Joe's car wouldn't start again.

Loren put in a new battery. "No charge. I owe Joe a favor."

Lois tried not to fidget. Loren got Mary a Coke from his machine. Didn't take but five minutes and they were off.

A block away from the office, on West Industrial Road, they passed a patrol car going the other direction. Two officers she didn't recognize. Lois watched in the rearview mirror as the car slowed and turned down the street where they'd just been. A dozen businesses lined that side street, but Lois felt certain the cops were heading to the office to question her. She expected the phone to ring any second, but it didn't.

Lois considered taking Mary back to the apartment but decided against. Roommate Annie might not be there to tend Mary, it was out of the way, and despite the urgency of her present mission, she wanted to be with Mary. She reached across the seat and patted her daughter's bony ten-year-old knee. Mary giggled, a carefree little-girl lilt, and for a few seconds, Lois forgot about all the—*stuff*—going on.

It didn't last. On the radio, news about the investigation into the subsidence at Hell, a man named Dog found in the Hell freezer, a protest rally planned for the afternoon at Hell, some big shot TV preacher in town, some Mexicans found dead of the heat in the New Mexico desert, a big freeway accident north of town. It was darn hot, and open windows didn't help much.

What if the cops are with Joe right now? I won't get a chance to talk to him first, will I?

Lois was in a hurry, but Mary remembered the pickles, insistently, so they stopped at the Safeway on Orlando Street, quickly got a jar, and quickly got back underway. They got to the hospital with no further delays.

The hospital felt cool inside, icy.

The grumpy man she'd talked to on the phone earlier wasn't there. Instead, when she said she wanted to see Joe, people became very nice and a nurse escorted her and Mary to Joe's room.

Joe was on a phone, a laptop computer open in front of him. The room looked like a small radio or TV station. Monitors, keyboards, phones, gadgets, wires all over. High tech stuff, not just medical. He smiled when he saw Lois and Mary, eyes crinkled, teeth bright, closed the laptop, and ended his call.

An awkward semi-hug for Mary off the side of his bed, and small talk, little girl and favorite "uncle." Joe gave her a handful of quarters to distract her from a steady stream of questions about his plaster leg and sent her down the hall to the pop machine. "Coke for me, please, and for you if you want. And your mom. Get whatever candy you want."

When she left, he turned sober. "You look like you just killed the Pope."

Lois found a plastic chair and sat. She cleared her throat and Joe offered her a glass of water. She sipped. Tepid, metallic, but it wet her whistle.

"Maybe not the Pope." She avoided his eyes. "But maybe I—I killed that man."

"Oh? Tell me about it."

She looked at him and he gave her a nod. She felt relieved.

She took a big breath and told him about the steaks. Darn stupid. Then she told him about the nap. Also stupid. It only took a couple minutes. Joe listened, expressionless.

"There's more—"

Mary came back and they sat, the three of them, family-like, drinking Cokes, munching potato chips. Small talk.

"Mary," Joe finally said, "why don't you go on down to the waiting room—it's right by the Coke machine—"

"I know where it is."

"—and watch TV there. It's bigger than this TV."

"But—"

"Your mom and I need to talk detective talk."

"It'll only take a minute, honey. Later, we'll check to see if the library is open, okay?"

"Okay."

Mary left.

"Odd dream you had, about Dog." Joe smiled, sipped Coke. "I had to pull rabbits out of hats to get Stan to check it out."

"Stan Gomez. You didn't tell him—"

"I didn't tell him you see dead people in your dreams, no. Never mind that. Cops have been by to ask questions, but my doctor shooed them away. I can't keep them at bay for long. I expect Stan to pay a visit any minute. He called and I pleaded sick, but he'll be back. So, spill. What's on your mind?"

"I looked at the video." A gulp of Coke, a better dry-throat antidote than tepid water. "I checked that license plate."

Lois told him what she saw, and what the DMV told her.

"Damn," he said at last. "Did you put it all in the safe?"

"Uh huh."

"We'll have to get that tape enhanced. It might not be Ripley. You're sure she put that scrubber in front of the door?"

"That's what it looked like, but I didn't—"

"We'll check it." Long pause. "Damn." A phone rang somewhere down the hall, and a TV blared from an adjacent room. Some medical machine ticked and beeped behind Joe's raised bed. The air conditioner hummed. Lois sat silent. "Damn."

From down the hallway, Mary's crystalline giggle responded to a cartoon voice on the waiting room TV.

"Joe, if that woman killed that man—"

"Don't you worry about it, Lois." Joe stirred from some deep reverie. "I'll take it from here."

"About the steaks—"

"I said don't worry about it. It was stupid, but you did it for the right reasons. That don't make it right, but it helps. Hell, Lois, people make mistakes. Everybody. You can let it drive you nuts or—"

Joe's face suddenly sagged, deep lines forming in his cheeks. Lois had seen that look before, a few times, the sudden distraction. *Is he thinking about Erroll?*

"Joe?"

He blinked. "After I called Stan—after you called me about that dream—I wondered. Maybe I taped Dog going into that freezer." He grunted. "Then, when I heard, I *knew*. Damn."

"Uh, Joe, shouldn't we give the tape to Captain Gomez. It could be evidence—"

"Yeah, that and my pictures of Samantha Gomez's car at the scene. You do know that Samantha is Stan's wife? I wonder why she was there. Is there any connection between her and Ripley? Or Trane? That wasn't her on the tape, was it? Mrs. Gomez, I mean?"

"No, I don't think so. It looked like, um. Ms. Ripley."

Joe grunted. "Me and Stan go way back. We're connected. Me and Trane—well, I got to think this out."

Long pause. "I'm sorry about those steaks, Joe."

"We'll talk about steaks later. Don't worry about this tape. I'll take care of it."

"What do you want me to do?"

Joe gestured at the equipment around him like the gutted console of a jet airplane. "Trane has me on a project. I need people to help. Maybe you could—no. No, I want you to go back to the office. Wait. I'll call."

Lois stood. "Okay."

"Park inside Loren's garage, or behind the trash bin out back. Close the blinds, don't turn on any lights, and don't answer the phone. I don't want Stan or his people to know where you are. Not till I've thought this out. I'll call you."

"If you don't want me to answer the phone—"

"Oh, right. Give me your cell phone number again."

"Okay." She did. "What if Stan comes here—"

"I'll play sick. It won't be hard." He smiled and Lois saw real pain there.

She restrained the sudden urge to hug Joe—too awkward across the high rail of his hospital bed, and he did look like he was in pain, and besides, they weren't that close, really, so she restrained herself and started to leave.

"Wait," Joe said. She stood in the doorway. "Stan talked to you? At the scene, after you found the body?"

"Uh-huh."

"Did he—did he ask about, um, my other employees?"

"Other employees? He asked if I knew any of them, where they were, if anybody else was back there when the earthquake—or subsidence, I guess—hit. I told him no, I hadn't seen anybody—"

"Did he say he wanted to, uh, *talk* to—uh—?"

"To the other guards?"

Joe nodded.

"Uh-huh."

Joe's already pale face drained another shade of white and he looked as if he was going to be sick.

"Joe? It sounds like we're hiding. Is that right?"

"You just go on. To the office. Don't worry. Don't talk to anybody, except me. I'll be in touch."

Lois took Mary away from her cartoons, and left, puzzled at Joe's distraction. He was usually so sharp, especially when he had a detective puzzle. He enjoyed the challenge, often pacing and talking his thoughts out when they were together in his office. "Sound boarding," he called it, and Lois had learned a lot by being his soundboard.

"Something's not right," she muttered as she drove back toward Joe's office. *Something about his employees? He sure seemed concerned about them. Come to think of it—*

"Yeah," Mary said, whiney-voiced. "Not right and not fair." She pointed out the window. They were passing the library.

"What, honey?" She'd check at the office, to keep busy.

"The library's closed."

Stan Gomez

Stan sat in his unmarked patrol car, four blocks from Hell, stuck behind another damn fender-bender, this one with injury—*goddamn Sunday drivers*—AC on high, sweat-soaked shirt stuck to the leather seat, mouth tasting like an ashtray, gut growling. For some reason, he smelled like mustard.

Maybe he should pop his light and siren, move these people. No, the officers up front were doing their best to move bent metal and extricate some damn fool. The granny from Iowa in the Buick in front of him would have a heart attack if he hit the siren and he'd get bogged down even more.

It had seemed like a good idea at the time, to go to the hospital, question Joe there himself, since his calls to Joe didn't get through and the officer he'd sent got brushed off by some doctor. The crime scene people were still at it inside Hell and in the parking lot, and if they found anything he should know right away, they'd call. Nothing much for him to do at Hell. He'd been fidgety, so he decided to drive to the hospital, see Joe. See how he was doing, poor bastard.

At the time, though, he didn't expect to encounter a goddamn traffic accident in the middle of the goddamn block.

Maybe he could grab a bite to eat at the hospital.

What does Joe really know? What about this hunch he called me on? What was he doing in Hell at that time of night?

Stan hadn't had breakfast, and it looked like lunch was out of the question, what with this rally. And he'd barely started investigating the Dog death.

Poor bastard. What a way to go. At least it wasn't violent.

Dog had been a pain in the ass when he was alive but Stan didn't hate the little shit enough to wish him dead. But he was now and somebody would have to investigate, account to relatives, and in Dog's case, to a politically savvy constituency, namely the homeless and winos Dog befriended. And the media.

"Lucky me," Stan muttered.

He'd run out of Tumeze.

Why's that bastard Oswald in such a hurry? Can't he wait until tomorrow?

Stan had been on the phone with one of the rescuers who'd helped evacuate Joe—what did you see? Did you look down *that* direction, toward the freezer? Was there anybody else in there when you were there? Did you see anybody besides your own people? Then dispatch called him about the rally.

"Shitshitshitshit," he told dispatch. Then he mustered troops. Traffic control, crowd watch, undercover, and so on. It took longer than he'd expected. That big freeway accident south of town, people on vacation. Short-handed. He had his watch commander call people at home.

Then he'd called Samantha at her office—he knew she'd be there, but was surprised that his call got right through—to talk to her about it. But she was as busy and agitated as he was and the conversation was short, strained. No help there. He hadn't really expected any. Right to assemble and all that. Stan knew. Samantha knew. The call took only a minute.

The sheriff, on the phone again and again—didn't trust his own people, micromanaging, asshole—told Stan fifteen minutes ago that he was flying home from his vacation in Pocatello to "take charge" and would arrive—this part was hilarious—this evening, conveniently *after* the rally would be over, and there would be no *goddamn point* in him being there. Except to tell everybody in the department and the seven bureaus, starting with Stan, how they'd fucked up—he'd find *something* to bitch about—and how he would've done it better. Except to strut like General MacArthur before the TV cameras just in time for the ten o'clock news, tell everybody that he'd "taken charge," and had everything under control.

"Shitshitshitshit."

Where the hell is Lois Ward? What does she *really know?*

And no goddamn Tumeze.

He checked his phone again. He'd called Ward's apartment, but got no answer. Then he'd called Joe's office. The phone was busy, so he sent a patrol car—he couldn't go himself at the time. His officer had radioed in—she wasn't there.

"Shitshitshitshit," he told the officer, and sent her back on duty.

He should talk to Ward himself. *Maybe I should go over to Joe's office first, see for myself. Shit. All this fuss over a goddamn accident.*

He felt exhausted, yet less than three hours had passed since he'd found the body. It was almost noon.

Somebody had finally cut off the power to Hell. Why the hell it hadn't been cut off by the subsidence, and why the hell somebody told somebody to leave it on afterward—or turn it *back* on?—or somebody *thought* somebody told somebody to leave it on, or turn it back on, and who knew who told what to who—was somebody else's goddamn business. They finally turned it off.

Would it have saved Dog's life if the power had been turned off earlier? Joe didn't know. Again, somebody else's problem.

Nothing for him to do inside Hell but get in the way of the crime scene people, so he did some interviews outside, retreated to his air-conditioned car and did more interviews on the phone, sent an officer to take a statement elsewhere, and wished he could eat, shower, get some goddamn Tumeze.

The coroner had arrived, finally. Who knew why it had taken him so long. Maybe he worked for the same lard-ass screw-ups who'd left the power on. *Goddamn wimpy rat-faced little fucker.*

The coroner—Dick Graves, stupid name—had pointed out a contusion on Dog's head. "See that icy patch by the scuff marks?"

"Uh huh."

"I figure he slipped while trying to push the door open, bonked his head, froze to death while unconscious."

"Can a person freeze to death in—what? Six hours?"

"Depends." He ticked off points on his fingers as Dog got zippered into a body bag. "One, he was probably unconscious so he couldn't try to keep warm. Two, he's underweight, malnourished, and I'll guess he had no energy, hadn't eaten in a while. I'll check. Three, there isn't much air in here. He didn't suffocate, but that could contribute. Oxygen. Look at his clothes."

The white frost that covered Dog had melted considerably since he'd found the body, and more since they'd turned off the power, but much of the frost had lingered in the creases in his shirt and pants. "So?"

"Cotton. Holds moisture, not good to stay warm in if it gets wet. If he was outside, sweating—well, I'll check that too."

"So he got himself lathered up, came in here to steal something to eat, or to get cool, whatever, and the door gets jammed shut when the shit hits the fan, he panics, bangs on the door, slips, knocks his head—"

"And lays there till his heart stops. Maybe his heart stopped first, before he froze, or the knock on the head was fatal." He shrugged. "I'll know more once I get him on a table."

At that point, Stan realized that although Metro had arrested Dog twice, he couldn't remember his real name.

So, frustration piled upon frustration, he called the hospital again, got transferred to maternity, then decided to drive to—to this traffic jam.

Maybe I should—

Granny moved forward a few inches, and Stan made his break. He turned across the on-coming traffic lane, returned a raised middle finger at blaring horns, bumped up over the curb in front of a Taco Bell, crossed behind it to a side street, got back onto a main drag—*clear of traffic, this street, thank God—* and headed west, across the Strip, toward Joe's office. It was only six or eight blocks away.

As he pulled into the gravel parking lot in front of the Trustworthy Vigilance Agency office, he saw a tiny face peep out of the blinds at him. *Lois Ward's little girl, whatshername.*

He knocked on the door. "It's Stan Gomez, Ms. Ward."

The door opened. "Sorry." Lois Ward smiled, waved him in. "Mary has pickle juice on her hands," she said, as if that explained anything. He heard water running from the bathroom.

"Mommy, this soap is yucky."

"Ms. Ward, we—"

"How can I—"

They'd all spoken at the same time. Stan and Lois laughed.

"Just a minute, honey. Just a minute, Mr. Gomez."

Ward—*Lois*—went to the back room, and Stan sat at one end of the sofa. *I should call her Lois. It might help.*

She returned, buffing the little girl's hands with a small towel. Stan stood. The little girl—*Mary*—glared at him.

"Mommy, please don't tell me you have detective business again." She sat, pouting, before a Mac computer.

"Why not, honey?" Lois sat at the far end of the sofa, opposite Stan, crossed her knees, taping a foot.

"Because I won't get to play games."

"Well, honey—"

"Uh, that's no problem, Ms.—Lois. I won't take up much

of your time and I won't interrupt your game." He turned to Mary, tried his Father Knows Best smile. "Okay?" It felt flat.

"Okay."

Stan interviewed Lois Ward. It wasn't much of an interview.

Mary kept interrupting. Potty. Yogurt. How does this computer thingie work? Shoe untied. Too hot. Tummy ache. Deliberately being bratty, not caring that Stan knew it. Lois responded to each interruption.

Amazingly, the phone didn't ring once.

Lois twitched and fidgeted. Being alone with Stan didn't bother her. That wasn't it. Stan had smiled at the burly tattooed mechanic next door, who glared back at him, when he parked. Loren Something, Stan recalled. Busted on stolen goods a few years back. No conviction. There to protect Lois and Mary, his glare said. Stan didn't doubt.

He knew a few hundred-pound cops who could knock him on his back in a flash. Lois was tiny, but who knew what she knew, what Joe had taught her.

No, something else bothered her.

Slow to answer, evaded eye contact. Fidgeted. Sweated. She was so twitchy that Stan wouldn't have been surprised to find a dead body behind the sofa. He resisted the urge to look.

"Who else besides you watched that back door?"

"Uh, just me. I think. I don't know, really. That was my, uh, assignment."

"Uh huh."

"It was open, you know. Had that little plastic tape across it. Supposed to be open for safety, Joe said, so I had to check it. Don't know why they put that tape there. It's not like it would keep anybody out."

"Uh huh. How often did you check?"

"Well, *before*, I checked it every half hour, sometimes only every hour, checked the handle to see that it was locked, opened it up and looked outside—"

"What about *after*? Last night. When it wasn't locked."

"Well, Joe said they had to keep it open because of safety. It wouldn't close good, he said because the wall—"

"Uh huh."

"And he said I should check it more than usual, so I did."

"How often did you check it?"

"I was supposed to check it every half hour. Joe, he sort of left that to me. I do my rounds—the restaurant, the casino, and the hotel—but I don't go on the other floors where they keep the safes and all the gambling stuff."

"Uh huh."

"So I checked the back door every half hour."

"When was the last time you checked?"

"The back door?"

"Uh huh."

"Um. Let me think."

"Mommy, what's this on the screen?"

Lois had last checked the back door about a half-hour before the subsidence. She hadn't seen anything in front of the freezer door then, but she'd barely glanced at it. No, she didn't open the freezer and check inside. She never did. Why would she? It never occurred to her that somebody might be in there. She was on her way to check it, the back door, when the building fell apart. She didn't get that far.

"What about the other guards?"

"Other guards?"

"Yeah, the other night guards—"

"Oh, yeah, them." A shrug. She twirled a finger through her hair. "I didn't see them that night. I think we had different areas to patrol. Why overlap? And different hours. I did nights. Joe said—before, when the restaurant hadn't opened yet—that I had this specific territory I was supposed to walk up and down and check out. The restaurant, the kitchen—"

"Do you know any of the guards names? The other guards who worked for Joe?"

Another shrug. Twirl, twirl. "Gosh, I don't—you'd have to ask Joe. See, we never went out together for a beer after work or anything like that, socially." Shrug, twirl. "I mean, the hours. Some worked different hours. Who'd want to get a beer at eight in the morning? That's when I got off my shift, at eight. I always wanted to go home and go to bed. After seeing Mary off to school but school's out now so I don't have to hurry—"

"Uh huh. But at the office—"

"The office?"

"Uh huh."

"You mean *here*?"

"Uh huh. Did you ever meet any of Joe's—

"Mommy, can I have a Coke?"

So it went. Awkward. Ultimately useless.

A good half hour wasted, Joe got a Tumeze from Lois, bought a Coke, and left. Headed for the hospital. He called, and got through, but Joe's phone was busy. Or turned off.

Joe had told him that Lois was very smart, which is why—or one of the reasons, he said—that he'd taken her on when she'd asked for help in finding her husband. Joe had told Stan that she was the best detective he'd ever hired.

At the office—and, come to think of it, at Hell when he'd found that body—she'd acted like an airhead.

No, not dumb. Nervous.

Hiding something?

He'd have to ask Joe. After all, he reasoned as he drove—traffic, light on this stretch, at least for the moment, thank God—she had no reason to know how Joe staffed his assignments. Why would she, a mere employee, albeit a favored one, know such administrative details?

No, he had to talk to Joe about that. There was nothing more to be learned from Lois Ward. She probably hadn't seen anything, probably didn't know anything. End of discussion.

The nervousness had some mundane explanation. *Petty theft? Screwing on the job?*

Maybe one of Joe's other boys had been back there and had seen something. Not likely if the area was Lois's assignment, and assignments never overlapped, so Lois had said, but Stan would be thorough, check it all.

What was Joe doing at Hell that time of night?

He was at the intersection of Fremont and Paradise, heading east, waiting for the green. Over the soft whoosh of the AC set to high, and the engine's hum, Stan heard the distinctive slam of metal on metal. In the intersection in front of him an airport shuttle van had hit a Goodwill truck. Glass flew. Steam and fluids gushed. People swore. Horns honked.

"Shitshitshitshit."

Lois Ward

As Mr. Gomez pulled out of sight, Lois called Joe. The phone rang four times before Lois realized that maybe Joe didn't have caller ID, and might not want to answer, thinking it might be Mr. Gomez, or Metro, or some other flavor of trouble, and they hadn't worked out a code for her to call him, so she hung up, fidgeted, then called again. Two rings, then she hung up, waited, and called again. Joe answered before the first ring ended.

"It's me," Lois said. "Mr. Gomez was here."

"What?"

"He just left. He didn't say, but I'll bet he's heading for you right now."

"Damn."

"I did what you said, but I think he saw Mary in the window, or saw the car. I had to let him in."

"Okay, don't worry about it. What did you talk about?"

Lois replayed the conversation to the best of her recollection, prodded by Joe's questions. Joe kept going over and over the part about the guards.

"I didn't discuss my other gigs with you, did I?" he said.

"Yeah, I—"

"You never met any of the other guards, not at work of after? Not last night?"

"Yeah." *He's in his Perry Mason voice, cross-examining. Why?*

He sighed. "Okay. Okay." Pause. "Anybody else call?"

"No, it's—" The phone beeped. "There's a call right now."

"Don't answer the phone for anybody but me, okay?"

"Okay. You got my number?"

"Right. I'm working on something. It'll get us out of a few jams. I'll need a little more time to—"

"Joe, are you in some sort of trouble?"

"Me?" A snort. "Besides a broken leg, painkillers, a whacko assignment from Trane—but you don't need to know about that. And I got to think about this steak thing, too, don't I?"

"Oh, gee, Joe, I—"

"Wait, that was out of line. I didn't mean—well, what it sounded like I meant. I mean, I'm not concerned about the steak thing. I mean, I *am*, but don't *you* worry about it, okay?"

"Okay."

"I'll call you, in a few minutes, so you stick close by, okay? How's Mary?"

"Okay."

They hung up, and Lois sighed. *What's wrong with Joe?*

"Mom, is Uncle Joe okay?"

"I don't know." *It was more than the steak. Something else.*

Lois returned Mary's somber gaze, and it looked like her daughter knew she was distressed. More, it appeared that Mary sensed that it wasn't the time to interfere, just as, when the police detective was here a few minutes ago, Mary had sensed that her constant interference was welcomed. Lois smiled at Mary, and nodded. Mother and daughter communion. No words needed.

Mary returned the smile, and went back to her computer game, humming, kicking a leg back and forth under her chair to some internal music.

What could it be?

Lois replayed the conversation with Joe in her mind. Something to do with the other guards. She tried a few possibilities, sound boarding to herself, not as good as having somebody else to do it with, like Joe did with her. She broke off and decided to try it with Mary.

Lois poured out the problem to Mary after swearing her to the utmost, cross-your-heart, swear-to-die, stick-a-thousand-needles-in-your-eye secrecy.

She told Mary about the stolen steaks. Might as well start at the beginning, honesty and all that. She endured a reprimand from her ten-year-old partner for the petty crime and moved on to what she knew, or suspected, and what Joe had said about his other employees.

"Maybe you should ask one of those other guards," Mary said.

"I don't know who they are."

"Look it up." Mary pointed to Joe's PC.

So Lois did. It didn't take as long as she might have expected. She'd learned a lot about computers since she'd started working for Joe, and she knew his private filing and code system, so it didn't take long.

Payroll records, contact addresses, phone numbers, bills, job applications, background investigation information. Even notes on contacts and informants. Client billing, itemized, with separate explanatory notes, private notes. Client info, confidential. Easy to find.

It felt like spying, but Lois rationalized that Joe had told her to take care of his business. Besides, Joe was in some kind of trouble, so much so that he got nervous when he had to talk about it. As she looked through his computer files, she thought—hadn't he been spying on her?

No, that last thought came unbidden and unwelcome, and, she decided, Joe had reason to spy on her because she'd stolen from a client. She'd only done it once but that didn't make it right for her to spy back.

Then she found it. Billing to Trane Enterprises for services rendered. Hourly rates for four guards, various shifts. Surveillance equipment rental and maintenance.

Lois knew that Joe had no surveillance equipment installed anywhere in Hell, but he was billing Mr. Trane for audio and video equipment rental and maintenance.

"Double billing?" Was that the term? Anyway, it was illegal.

"What's that mean, Mom?" Mary came over and stood at Lois' elbow, watching the monitor over her shoulder, on tiptoes.

Payroll records for the four guards. Didn't match the billing to Mr. Trane.

"Did you find a crime, Mom?"

Then she found the checks to a clinic in San Francisco. Where Erroll was. She did the math.

"Some crimes, honey, are bigger than others."

Teresa Santiago

"Down with Hell! Down with Hell! Down with Hell!"
The unoriginal chant spread through the Hellward marching crowd from somewhere in the middle of the group strung out along blocks of sidewalk, back into the people-jammed parking lot of the First Christian Church of Zion, Southern Nevada, where the demonstrators had assembled, and forward to the front. The spontaneously created chant wasn't exactly the chant Teresa wanted, but it would do, and it was still early. The ragged chant helped keep cadence, keep spirits up for the march through the blast furnace mid-afternoon heat. The air smelled like brimstone and tasted like ash.

Volunteer marshals with red armbands tried to keep the crowd from spilling on to the street. They were mostly successful. So far. Police watched. Helicopters hovered overhead, TV and police. *We're not invisible, now.*

Most folks wore black armbands. For Dog.

Crude, hand-painted signs waved above bobbing heads. "Justice for the People." "Hell Hath No Fury Like the People Scorned." "No Way in Hell." "To Hell With Trane Ent." "Down With Hell." "We Demand Answers." "Who Killed Dog?" "Murderer."

"Down with Hell! Down with Hell! Down with Hell!"

"It's like in those movies," Santiago shouted above the

chant. Larry was right there as usual. Ditto Teach, Captain Freddy, Mrs. Doran, and others, beside and close behind her, as she marched along the not-quite-wide-enough sidewalk at the head of the army of homeless and churchies and hippies and bikers and reporters and a few ordinary citizens who refused to fit into neat categories.

"You know the kind of movies I'm talking about?"

So was Percy Oswald. Right there, up front, step for step with Teresa, awkward because she stood a head taller than him, elbow to sweaty elbow with her, smiling and waving for the cameras and tape recorders, reporters scampering and stumbling ahead to get shots and sound bites as the group marched past. Oswald deliberately placed himself on Teresa's left, nearest the street as they marched northward, Hellward. *Must be his good side.* And, she conceded, *better camera angle. Smart man.*

Oswald's wife, whatshername, marched two paces behind her husband. Smiling, ever supportive, she constantly had a phone to her ear, which she often passed to her husband.

"I don't see movies much," Oswald said through gleaming teeth, smiling. "Enlighten me."

"Down with Hell! Down with Hell! Down with Hell!"

The media had done its job, with help from Teresa's and Oswald's lieutenants, and what looked like a lot of genuine, unsolicited public interest in the cause at hand. Ordinary citizens, Teresa noticed, had joined the throng. Maybe curious, maybe supportive, she couldn't tell. She studied faces.

"So many movies are based on revenge," Teresa yelled over the tramping of feet, the shouting and chanting, sirens blaring, horns honking.

They numbered about five or six thousand strong, and growing, it seemed. People arrived by the busload, carload, and by foot and bicycle back at the assembly point. Even a taxi. Teresa foresaw a rash of stolen bicycle reports to keep The Man busy come Monday. Broken car windows. Stolen stereos. Busy times.

"We mustn't confuse vengeance with justice," Oswald said, smiling. He spoke clearly, loudly, into a camera thrust into his face at paparazzi range. "Judgment can wait for cooler times. Today, the Lord seeks—we *all* seek—answers." A ragged cheer erupted behind him, and the reporter left, satisfied, before he got trampled.

"The bad guys kill the hero's girl," Teresa continued, "or partner if it's a cop show, or they kidnap his kid, and then the good guy kicks righteous ass for two hours. Everybody in the audience thinks 'I know somebody whose ass I'd like to kick like that.' That's why they're so popular, those revenge movies."

"I'd mention the concept of forgiveness, Teresa," Oswald said quietly through his perpetual grin, no cameras too close at the moment, "for the sake of argument—I've written about this subject—but at what sacrifice to unity and harmony, right? In the face of the common enemy—unity. Am I right? And harmony."

"Harmony, Mr. Oswald—"

"Call me Percy, please."

"Harmony, Mr. Oswald, don't make for good movies. It don't make for good life neither, sometimes. Unless you think it harmonious and unifying the way rich people treat poor people."

"Point made, point made." His wife tapped him on the shoulder and he took the phone from her, chatting intently.

"Down with Hell! Down with Hell! Down with Hell!"

Who knew how many of this bunch would get arrested for drunkenness, possession, pick-pocketing, panhandling, public lewdness, loitering, trespassing, disorderly conduct, soliciting, resisting arrest, or just-plain-old Being Poor In Public. And the traffic—thick. There was no way—No Goddamn Way—this crowd could be confined to the sidewalk, marshals or no. Another logistics problem—would The Man give up the street, and inconvenience drivers, to avoid the problem? Or let the problem happen, and then freak out?

Teresa sighed as she walked, sweating in the blast

furnace mid-afternoon Las Vegas goddamn heat. Somebody had distributed a lot of umbrellas to people in the crowd and Larry carried one, held up high over Teresa's head, and she was thankful for the bit of shade it provided. Colorful umbrellas, red and white striped. *Dog would have thought of that. Where'd they come from? Stolen? So many?*

Nobody had fainted in the heat. So far.

"And sequels," she continued. "You hear an actor say 'This time, it's personal.' They pay somebody to write that crap. Do those damn Hollywood writers even know what 'personal' is?"

Teach raised a hand. "Personal m-means—"

"Damn right," Teresa said.

The march strung out on the sidewalk in a thick line along the six-block route between the church assembly point and Hell, bunching at the street lights, where horns blared, and people shouted, cursed, and chanted, and cops worked overtime. They controlled the lights by hand at each corner, letting a bunch of protesters cross, then letting a bunch of cars through. "Move along, move along."

The head of the march had reached the corner of Dallas Street and Paradise Drive where a small parking lot in front of an abandoned gas station faced Hell across the busy street. Teresa had been privy to some of the discussions with The Man about the set-up. The crowd would stay in the parking lot, demonstrate for two or three hours, hear a few speeches, then disperse. That was the plan. Somebody had built a small raw plywood platform backed against the sidewalk across the street from the Hell hotel front entrance. Microphones and loudspeakers had been mounted, chairs set up on the stage, and sawhorse barriers erected to keep the crowd off the street.

Lots of police on hand, Teresa noticed, to keep traffic flowing, keep people off private property. Keep folks moving along. Available to respond, if necessary, to whatever contingency required attention. Not quite in full riot gear, the cops—that would be pretentious, provocative, maybe dangerous.

Maybe it ain't a matter of good policy. Maybe it's because it's just too damn hot.

Larry helped Teresa climb crude stairs to the platform, where she stood, hands on hips, sweating like a prizefighter, panting. She surveyed the scene and knew it wouldn't work. Too many people, not enough space. Too hot. People were angry and would get angrier. She smelled a pre-riot calm in the air, precursor to the bitter stench of tear gas.

"This ain't going to work," she muttered. *Dog would have known how to handle this.*

"Pardon?" Oswald had mounted the platform behind her. He was on his phone with one of his lieutenants. He'd been on the phone every few minutes since they'd met back at Jesus' Bread Basket.

"I said, this ain't—"

A ripple of noise—"Look there." "What's that?"— surged through the crowd and heads turned toward the front of the Hell hotel across the street, people jostled, crowded to see, protest signs and umbrellas bobbing above them. Teresa turned to look. Four delivery trucks had pulled into the hotel driveway. A small army of young men and women unloaded them.

"What the hell?" she said.

They looked like huge ice cream trucks, painted a diagonal bright candy-stripe red and white. On the sides, in gaudy Barnum and Bailey circus letters: "Wholesale Entertainment Supply."

The young men and women unloading the peppermint-colored trucks all wore identical red short-sleeved shirts with a logo on the breast in white letters, too small for Teresa to read thirty yards away. They wore identical tan shorts, white socks, and black shoes. They all looked to be in their teens or early twenties, clean-cut, clean-shaven, and they all smiled. Identical, healthy, clean-cut, all-American smiles, as they unloaded the trucks.

They looked like some teen-age church group setting up a picnic for the needy, except they all had little red horns, like Halloween devil's horns, clipped to their heads.

Somebody told Teresa the logo on the shirts read "Trane Enterprises, Inc."

In a series of crisp movements, rapid but efficient, as if they'd rehearsed the exercise before, they unfolded and set up a long row of tables in front of the hotel and unloaded cartons onto the tables. Cartons of bottles.

A sign unfurled and fluttered down the side of one of the trucks. "Free Water."

A cheer arose from the demonstrators. "Down with Hell," died out and, quickly, in its place, "Water."

The crowd surged against police along the sidewalk like a water balloon about to burst.

Oswald tapped Teresa on the shoulder. She turned, annoyed.

"What?"

"We got the whole thing."

"We—what?"

The water balloon burst. With a triumphant, thirsty roar, the crowd surged across the street to line up for the water bottles being distributed free by Trane Enterprises employees, dressed in devil horns and casual yuppie attire.

"My God," Teresa cried out. The riot she feared had begun.

"It's all right," Oswald said. "We have the streets. I told you." He held up his phone as if that explained.

"What the hell?"

"I got it all worked out. Look." He pointed to the far end of the street, where cops moved sawhorse barricades back, into the intersection, and across it, blocking traffic on a length of street at the one side of Hell that they could see.

"Well, I'll be damned," Teresa muttered.

"You'll be *blessed*, Teresa. We have it all, all around the casino, all four blocks. All ours for the next couple of hours."

"All?"

"If Trane thinks this little stunt of his"—he pointed to the crowd milling around the water trucks, people pouring water on their heads, spraying each other, laughing, party-like—"will sidetrack our plan, he's mistaken."

"All?"

"Well, not the street itself, couldn't work that out, quite, but the far side of the street, the sidewalks, all around the block—all four blocks, and the intersections. More room that way. We'll get these people back in a minute, on this side of the street, back in order, you'll see."

"All?"

"Oh, Teresa, for Christ's sake, look." Now, Oswald pointed the other direction, toward Dallas Street, which fronted on the backside of Hell a block away. There, too, police moved barricades forward, and the crowd shifted, off the street to the far-side sidewalks. Traffic was being diverted around Hell, all the way around. The streets belonged to the people. Not *exactly* the streets. Metro officers were emptying the streets, neutral territory, a no-man's zone. The opposite sides of the streets around Hell, the sidewalks, belonged to the people.

"For a couple hours?" Teresa spoke over her shoulder. She couldn't take her eyes off the sight. People moved back off the street is a semi-orderly manner, their belligerent shouts of only a few minutes ago gone, *cooperating*, as it were, with the police, graciously, as if they *knew* they'd won a victory of sorts, even if they didn't know how they'd won it. A human chain formed by Trane's devil-horned yuppies passed water bottles across an intersection to the people. Orderliness spontaneously replaced near chaos.

Teresa turned to Oswald. "How the hell did you do that?"

"You're not the only one who wants to avoid a riot. My city contacts believe I can keep a lid on things. I promised."

The phone Oswald gestured with started ringing. "I'll

take it," Oswald's wife—*Theo, that's her name*—said, grabbing the phone from her husband's hand. "You better get started."

"Right," Oswald said. He moved toward the microphones and began to regain control of his army.

"It's a damn miracle," Teresa shouted to Larry. If Oswald's manipulations on the phone hadn't worked out, or had been delayed by a minute, the riot she's feared might have occurred anyway. Then, too, there was another miracle. So far, and as far as she knew, nobody in the crowd, a lot bigger than she'd expected and still growing, had succumbed to the heat or been hurt.

"Good luck, or miracle." She shook her head. Larry shook his head. "Who knows and who cares?"

Oswald's voice boomed over the loudspeakers. He had his work cut out for him, Teresa saw. The crowd was entranced by the prospect of getting a water bottle from one of the smiling, devil-horned Trane Enterprises employees. They milled up and down the sidewalk on the opposite side of the street from Hell, gradually surrounding the building outside the police barricade as the sawhorses moved into the street to push them back. Other trucks arrived in front of Hell. More demon chains passed boxes across the barricaded streets. Food.

Percy Oswald's international renown as a fiery orator came to the fore and heads began to turn toward him, people began gathering in front of the platform where he orated. For the first time in public, he outlined his plan to destroy Hell, and through that destruction, the administration of a righteous and just blow for all the indigent and down-trodden peoples, the poor and disadvantaged, the weak and disenfranchised, blah, blah, blah. People began to pay attention.

Teresa watched in amazement as he regained control of a crowd that, until he began to speak, Teresa would have bet nobody could have contained or controlled. *Maybe not even Dog.*

"Man," she muttered as Oswald weaved his magic, "you

are some piece of work." She'd lost control, never had it really, but Percy was *in charge*.

In minutes, she expected he'd have the mob mobilized, under his power, and he'd begin his real work, the true assault on Hell. The plan he'd told her about at Jesus' Bread Basket, the one that she'd also had—Dog's idea finally manifest. Oswald had had the same idea. *Damn if that wouldn't have made Dog laugh his britches off.*

More Trane trucks arrived, parked on the street; boxes of stuff got passed out to the crowd. Teresa smelled—*hotdogs*?

As people returned their attention to Oswald's preachment and fell under his hypnotic sway, Teresa noticed some of them looked odd, something wrong with their faces. Many in the crowd were eating. Some made a strange noise. Like ducks.

She craned her head to see what the newly arrived trucks parked in the street in front of Hell hotel were passing out. Difficult to see clearly what with all the people. In a moment, she had it.

Cartons of rubber Groucho fake nose and mustache glasses. Beanie propeller caps. Rubber chickens. Kazoos.

And what the people ate, the salty scent wafted through the air. Fresh baked pretzels. And smoked fish.

Joseph Foxworthy

Joe had largely conquered the pain, though it still came and went, unexpectedly, in sharp spasms. When it did hurt, it hurt like all hell. The break had been clean enough, his doctor said, routine. They'd had him on morphine at first, but that hadn't worked, who knew why, so they'd changed to a different painkiller. Joe didn't remember the name, but it worked, mostly, left him relatively pain-free and clear-headed. Mostly.

A good thing. He had a lot to do, including helping Trane organize his little practical joke for the demonstration. He would not have refused Trane, even if he'd been on his deathbed.

An enthusiastic and reliable contact at a fraternity house at the university did the trick, and Trane already had people waiting to load supplies at one of his company warehouses. Joe got that out of the way in jig time, leaving the details mostly up to his contact. He also hired and equipped photographers to record the event from different angles for Trane to enjoy later.

Then he focused his attention and energy on the Dog thing.

That tape. It was the key. He'd inadvertently videotaped a murder, it looked like. No accident. And Samantha Gomez? Why was she there at that hour?

Joe got on the phone and the computer to get more clues.

Clues he got, but not answers. For that, he'd need help.

There seemed to be a clock running—Ripley had made moves that seemed to indicate she might be thinking of skipping the country, and soon at that. So he had to work fast.

He couldn't afford to have Stan's investigation slow him down, not if he was to succeed.

He needed Lois to—

That's when he heard Stan come down the hall. "Gotta go," he said to the person on the phone, a contact at a travel agency. "Call me." He hung up.

Joe closed his laptop, lay back, went limp, his eyelids drooped, and he tried to drool. He moaned. Stan stood by his bedside. "Stan. Grab a needle. Great stuff."

Stan shuffled, shrugged, and scratched, like a reformed pickpocket who didn't know where to put his hands. He wrinkled his nose at some nasty hospital smell and tried to smile, tried to not look disgusted. Everything smelled like copper to Joe.

"Uh, no thanks," Stan said. He cleared his throat. "Listen, I need to wrap up, a few questions, this Dog thing—"

"How is that son-of-bitch?"

"Joe, you called, and I—me and Lois, we went into Hell—"

"Open for business, then? About time. How's the buffet? Wait a minute—didn't they close it down, the breakfast bar? Something about cracks in the wall, right? Yeah, I remember. Open, then close. Hell of a way to run a business."

Stan quickly gave up. He talked with a nurse who came in to check on Joe. "He isn't always out of it like this, is he?"

"No, sir," the nurse said. "He's usually pretty coherent. But the painkillers." She shrugged. "It works different for different people. We had him on morphine at first." Another shrug. "I'll talk to his doctor right away."

"All this equipment." Stan gestured. "What the hell?"

The nurse barked a laugh. "A half hour ago, he was on that cell phone, giving orders. None of my business. Some prissy little asshole came in here—sorry. About the language. Come in here with computer stuff, ordering us around, this morning. Some big shots are bigger than others, and all of a sudden Mr. Foxworthy is King La-de-damn-da. Sorry. About the language. Me, I just change sheets and bedpans, I don't ask questions—"

"Thanks. I appreciate your help."

"None of my business."

While Joe muttered to himself, drooled a bit, rolled his eyes, fluttered his hands limply, he listened as Stan put on the charm, securing a call from the nurse if—*when*—Joe became coherent enough to answer questions. Stan went a step further, charmed the nurse into promising to write down anything significant—"There's this investigation, may be a homicide, front page stuff, real serious business"—that Joe might say.

Joe wasn't sure but he thought he saw Stan slip the nurse a bill, maybe a twenty. *Stan wouldn't do that. Not that big a deal.*

Or maybe he was flirting with her. *Yeah, that's it.*

He left.

When he was certain Stan had left, Joe called Lois.

"Lois, Stan just left. We didn't talk. I was out of it at the time. Painkillers. Do I sound okay?"

"You sound a little groggy."

"Painkillers. You don't want to know. Anyway, I got a plan."

"A plan?"

"I did some digging. I have some contacts. I'll keep this short, don't know when I'll be interrupted again, and there's a lot you don't need to know, but there is this. I found out stuff about Trane Enterprises. About Roberta Ripley, Trane's right hand man, and what she's been doing for the past few months— well, since she got here in Las Vegas, maybe even before, I'm still looking at raw data, preliminary stuff, and there's more to come, but suffice to say I think maybe the lady has been ripping off her boss. Now, we can use that—"

"Ms. Ripley?"

"We can use that. With your help. To keep—well, to keep my ass out of jail, okay?" *And don't forget about Erroll.*

"Out of—" Long pause. *Is she thinking about herself now, and the steaks?* "Okay."

"I think that video relates. For some reason, Ripley decided to kill Dog, and that ties in with her ripping off Trane. It ties in with Samantha Gomez being at Hell at that hour. A meeting? Somehow they're related, but I don't know how, quite."

"How did you—"

"Twenty years, good contacts, good research, computer savvy. A good knack for hunches. Plus luck. And, well, I'm privy to knowledge that gives me an edge, you see."

"No, I—I don't see."

"You don't have to. All you have to do is follow instructions. We'll find out what's really going on, maybe deliver a murderer to Stan. That'll go a long way toward—well, it'll help."

"What about Ms. Ripley? We should tell Trane about her."

"We might."

"Might? Why would—"

"I said 'might.' There's stuff you don't know, Lois, and maybe you don't need to know. We've had this talk, remember?"

"Yes, I remember." A sigh. "What do you want me to do?"

"There's a good girl. Now listen carefully. Don't write it down. I'll want you to repeat back to me what I've told you until I'm sure you got it right."

"Okay. Shoot."

Joe shifted a pillow behind his back, tried to fluff it up. Sometimes the pain overshot the medication, he hurt like hell, and he couldn't get comfortable. Through gritted teeth, he told

Lois what he wanted her to do, and how he wanted her to do it. He went into as much detail as he could think of, "to make sure we've covered all the bases. Just In Case, right? Any questions?"

"Yeah."

Joe wiped sweat off his forehead. "Shoot." He felt dizzy.

A sigh. "Joe, I'm—I'm scared."

"Don't worry, Lois. Everybody gets scared." *I'm going to faint. I hurt like hell.* "It's okay. Even I get scared. We've had *this* conversation, too."

"Yeah. About Steve."

"Lois, you're stronger than you think." Joe buzzed the nurse. The pain was getting unbearable. "I've seen you work. With clients, on the phone, on the street. You're tough."

Sweat dripped onto the phone.

"Lois. Please." His voice cracked, and the room spun. *Where's the goddamn nurse?* "I need you for this. I really—"

"Okay. Okay."

"Okay." The nurse entered, frowning, concerned. "Go for it."

"Now? Right now?"

"Mr. Foxworthy," the nurse said. She sounded alarmed. She sounded fuzzy, far away.

"Now, Lois." He dropped the phone. Passed out.

Roberta Ripley

The phone conversation with Sammy disturbed Ripley at first, especially when Sammy practically hung up on her. *Why isn't she happy?* The answer came quickly enough. Sammy *was* happy with Ripley's decision to leave the country together—at long last, *together*—but she *was* busy, as Ripley was too, right now with this Hell mess, so Sammy's abruptness could be forgiven. It *was* a bit of a shock to tell her so suddenly, and on the phone, so impersonal—*but we'd talked about all this, before*—but with the Hell mess and all, she didn't really have much choice. Things were coming to a head, and she had to act fast.

An instant after Sammy hung up, Ripley found herself in six separate conversations—two on the phone, three in person in her office, her make-do, slapped-together office in the Buttes, and one via e-mail—at the same time.

Sammy's a fragile flower, not as hardy as I am.

She needed to get to Sammy in person, go to her office—*talk* to her, really talk, before she could call the charter plane company, get them on the runway. Things kept happening, four and five at a time, nonstop, not just one right after the other in quick succession, but multiple, simultaneous crises.

She felt like a mad juggler. Exhaustion would knock her to her knees the minute she dropped the ball. She gulped coffee to try to keep ahead. It worked, for now, but she knew the crash would come and when it did, it would be bad. If things went off the way she wanted, the way they were supposed to, she'd be in an airplane when it happened and she'd find herself asleep in Sammy's arms.

Maybe by tonight things will cool off enough.

The reporter, Miles Doughton, from the *Clark County Chronicle-Progress*, stood in front of her desk. He had a jillion questions, required spiffy quotes. Fortunately, he had a tape recorder so she didn't have to slow down for him. He brought no photographer with him so she didn't have to pose, worry about her messy hair, the salty scent of sweat over-riding her cologne, the stains under her armpits, the dark circles under her eyes, and the need to paste on The Smile. She gave him the quotes he wanted as she dealt with the others.

A man named Matthew O'Donnell, Vice President in charge of Something Important from Basalt Construction, Inc., the outfit serving Trane Enterprises after the primary construction company that had erected most of the building under the Yellowstone ownership fell to bankruptcy and multiple felony indictments, in company with a Doctor Jeffrey Somebody, attached to some city or county building permit or construction oversight agency, stood next to the reporter. One short, the other tall, one beefy, the other skinny. Both had prominent sideburns. Mutt and Dr. Jeff. They wanted access to "materials relevant to an investigation of structural damage to the building."

Humbly, Mutt and Dr. Jeff interjected their query as they could. They fidgeted, hats in hand, literally, waiting for her to finish with the current—for the next few seconds—phone conversation, and maybe the other one on line two, before they got their two cents in, and a useful answer.

They were easy to deal with, too, Ripley knew. Mutt and Dr. Jeff actually represented one conversation, not two, so she actually had only five going at once, not six.

They looked scared. Or confused. Ripley knew what scrunched their scrotums. If the building collapse involved construction, if the materials used, or the procedures used, were substandard, shoddy, or the least bit suspect, or if the government building inspectors had dropped the ball somehow—if the tees weren't dotted and the eyes not crossed Just So, heads would roll. These two looked like prime candidates but they were in a good position to shift the blame onto some unfortunate subordinate.

If. If they acted fast, got the data they wanted, called in debts from appropriate movers and shakers, dealers and wheelers, covered their own asses, and pointed at a patsy. So they'd be patient, Ripley knew, if they were led to believe their patience would be rewarded in a timely manner. She hinted at such, kept them on ice while she dealt with the phone.

Insurance. "We'd better deal with that in person, don't you think, Mr. Trout?" Fingernails: clickety-clickety-click. "Confidential. I'm sure you understand I can't promise—"

She listened a few seconds, answered a question from the reporter with a shake of her head, smiled at the phone, said "That'll be fine," told Mutt and Dr. Jeff: "I have your material, and I'm sure I can get it, with your help—" and took line two.

"A visitor," her secretary said. "Police investigator Freda Wiseman, to see you."

"Can *you* deal with it?" Ripley had been able to pawn a lot of calls onto her secretary, but the Las Vegas police department was different. She'd called in some debts among her few Metro contacts to keep the hounds at bay while she got work done. It had only been marginally successful. Metro, it seemed, functioned on an unusually high degree of integrity.

"She wants to talk to you. Routine, she says."

"Tell Officer Wiseman I'll be free in five minutes."

Ripley tapped a few keystrokes, clickey-click, hit send— e-mail reply to the freezer manufacturer—closed her laptop, and sighed as she returned her attention to Mutt and Dr. Jeff.

"You understand that, because of this subsidence problem, many of my files are not with me at present." She gave them The Smile, tried to pat a stray strand of hair back into place.

"You just said you have the files," Mutt said.

"Yes, but I—wait one." She turned to the reporter. "Mr. Doughton, could you please excuse us?"

"I just have a few more questions—"

"I'm sure. Wait in the outer office and I'll give you my undivided in ten minutes." The Smile. "Will that be okay?"

Doughton sighed, surrendered, and retreated into Ripley's outer office. He'd cooperate. She'd given him more than he had any right to expect.

"Take calls for ten, Dora," she called though the open door.

"Got it," the secretary replied from the noisy outer office.

Relative silence ensured inside when the door closed, and Ripley turned her undivided to Mutt and Dr. Jeff. "Both of you." The Smile. "Asses in a ringer, right?"

"Ms. Ripley," Mutt began, rubbing his sideburns nervously, "I don't know what—"

"Cut the shit. You know what's at stake here. So what is it? Padded billing? Materials under code? Inspectors paid off?"

Dr. Jeff blanched. "We don't have to stand here—"

"Shove it, clown. You do." The Smile. "Have to. I may be the only one that can save your asses, am I right? Hm? Am I right?"

"Please, Ms. Ripley," Mutt said, voice whiney. "We're only trying to do our jobs. These are unusual circumstances—"

"We're just trying to make sure," Dr. Jeff said, "that our people aren't unfairly, you know—"

"Any cooperation you could provide—"

The Smile fell abruptly and Mutt and Dr. Jeff shut up. "I," Ripley said. "Have. The. Files."

Mutt and Dr. Jeff exchanged sober looks. Mutt said: "We

also have information."

Dr. Jeff said: "We go down. . . ."

The gloves are off. Ripley tapped her nails. Clickety-clickety-clickety. "All right, here's what'll happen. I'll get you those files you want." She shrugged. "You understand. It'll take time. Like I said, I don't have them here—"

Sullen silence.

"They're in my other office, in Hell. I haven't had time yet to go back and—"

"You can't get in there now," Dr. Jeff said. "We've got it closed down. No entry. It's unsafe."

"And *you*," Ripley said, "can't get me in? Now?"

Mutt and Dr. Jeff exchanged sober looks.

"Make it happen," Ripley said, "and I can get you the files you want by dinnertime." Smile. "Within the hour, maybe."

"What's the catch?" Mutt asked.

"Give me forty-eight hours. Then do whatever you want."

"What about that demonstration?" Mutt. "The police—"

Ripley hadn't gotten where she was by being slow. "My escort is right outside," she said. "She doesn't know that. Yet."

"I'll need a phone," Dr. Jeff said. "A place to make, uh, confidential calls."

"See my secretary."

"We'll meet you at the hotel," Mutt said. They left.

Ripley shut down her desk, grabbed her purse and phone, and rose before they'd reached the door, walked out on their heels.

She dealt with Doughton in the outer office easily enough. She managed to let him overhear as he whispered to Dora that Mark Trane was on his way to the demonstration where he planned to sneak in among the crowd, incognito, to watch. She'd made it up on the spot—sometimes she amazed even herself, how quick she was—and the reporter fell for it. He apologized quickly and dashed from the hotel.

Ripley started out behind Doughton. When Ripley moved, like a supertanker at sea, she created a vacuum into which lesser beings fell. Sheer momentum. At a glance, Ripley got Officer Wiseman's number. A wimp. The smaller, frazzled—*weaker-willed*—officer fell into place, two steps behind Ripley.

"We'll talk in the car," Ripley told Officer Wiseman as they got in the elevator. "Do you have any eye-liner?"

Mutt said they'd meet me at Hell. Maybe I'll have to give them some files after all. We'll see. Some files. Not all, oh, no. Some got damaged in the subsidence, some got lost, so sorry. But not the really good stuff. That goes with me. Just In Case.

"Do, um, do you want some deodorant, too?" Officer Wiseman smiled apologetically.

Lois Ward

Lois hadn't discussed with Joe what to do with Mary when she went to confront Samantha Gomez, per his instructions, in Ms. Gomez's office at City Hall. Though he'd been thorough in his instructions, Joe had been in a hurry, and Lois had been a bit flustered, tired, and she admitted, a bit scared. She simply hadn't mentioned that Mary was with her.

She'd done it before, had Mary with her, once or twice, when it seemed all right—a supermarket stakeout, and those witness interviews at the playground—but she didn't want Mary with her on this assignment. If anything went wrong—and the more she thought about it, the more likely it seemed that something could go wrong—she didn't want to have to protect Mary while she protected herself. She might have to—what? Fight? Run? Whatever. No place for a child.

As she drove, she chewed her last Tumeze, crumpled the package, tossed it to the floorboard, and tried to remember if she'd ever seen a movie where the detective had a child with her when she confronted the bad guys in the warehouse for the final shootout. Or him. Most movie detectives were guys. There was one movie, Sylvester Stallone in it, about the cop with a mother—"Stop or My Mom Will Shoot." Was that it? Dumb movie.

That was a mom, not a daughter.

Her apartment was between Joe's office and City Hall, roughly, so Lois stopped to check. Joe had told her to hurry, but Lois told herself that it wouldn't take a minute.

Roommate Annie *should* be home. It *was* Sunday. *What if she isn't?* Before she spent much energy thinking about what she'd do in that case—grab some crayons and a coloring book and hope Mary would be all right alone in the lobby while she confronted a murder accessory suspect?—she got lucky. Roommate Annie was there, awake, in a good mood, watching cartoons.

"Baby-sit? Sure, why not?"

Mary was tired anyway.

Roommate Annie had laundered Lois' uniform. "Might as well've," Roommate Annie said. "I had stuff to do anyway, so."

There was no trace of mustard stain on the shirt, and Roommate Annie had put the earring back in the breast pocket. "Sorry," Roommate Annie said. "I didn't find the mate."

"Huh," Lois said. "I found it at Hell last night. I don't *think* it's mine."

She shrugged, changed into the uniform—*Who knows? It might help*—gave Mary a quick hug, popped a new package of Tumeze into her pocket, and left.

The plan was simple, so Joe had assured Lois. Samantha Gomez had been there, at Hell, as the photos and the DMV contact confirmed, and as Joe had seen for himself in the parking lot, although vaguely. Ms. Ripley had been there too, if the woman on the videotape was indeed Ms. Ripley. Somebody had gotten into the passenger side of the black van, Joe had seen, but he didn't know who, or who was in the drivers' seat. Both Roberta Ripley and Samantha Gomez were at Hell about the same time, so it looked like. What was the connection? It hardly seemed coincidental, but Joe couldn't otherwise connect the two women to each other, and he couldn't be sure—*absolutely* sure, and under the circumstances, he felt he had to be absolutely sure because a lawyer might make a problem with that videotape as well as his in-the-dark eyewitness account, and he'd find his own ass in a sling if he wasn't right, probably would anyway—that Ms. Ripley had actually, deliberately locked Dog in the freezer for—why?

Or had it been somebody else who locked Dog in the freezer? Had it been Samantha Gomez? Or somebody else?

Did these events relate to the collapse of Hell in the subsidence—or the sinkhole, as some experts on TV were saying?

If things went well, as Joe assured Lois they would, Samantha Gomez would not only reveal the connection between her and Ms. Ripley, but also reveal why Ms. Ripley propped that floor waxer handle in front of the freezer door, locking Dog inside. If that was really Ms. Ripley on the videotape. If that's what she'd really done. Did Ms. Ripley intend murder? If so—why? Did Samantha Gomez know about it? And what *else*?

A lot of "ifs," Joe admitted, but he gushed confidence, a counter to Lois' trepidation. A fishing expedition, yes, but necessary. His instincts told him so—and it would work. Maybe Samantha Gomez would get nervous, and let something useful slip. Lois was to watch her expression, remember what she said. It would become part of what Joe would deliver to Stan Gomez, poor bastard.

Lois said nothing about Joe's fraudulent billing of Trane Enterprises, and Joe said nothing about the steak thing. Lois sensed that Joe hoped to use this investigation to counter or soften the blow when Mr. Trane discovered Joe's fraud. She believed—chose to believe, and not look at it too closely—that somehow the deal would also keep her out of jail.

How all this would work out, she hadn't a clue, but Joe seemed confident, and she let his confidence propel her forward, like a dollar bill in a gust of hot air.

Joe drilled her on what she was to say and do until he seemed satisfied she got it.

The uniform, Lois quickly decided, reading Samantha Gomez's secretary's haughty expression, impressed nobody.

The customary formal exchange—"May I help you?" and "I'd like to see Ms. Samantha Gomez, please," and "Do you have an appointment?" and so on went quickly.

"Please tell Ms. Gomez that I have some videotape." Nervously, Lois had forgotten to hold it in reserve.

Open sesame.

As she passed the secretary, Lois felt pleased with herself. She felt—*tough*—until she got inside the office. Ms. Gomez was much more intimidating than her secretary. A lioness compared to a gazelle. When she walked into the office, Lois felt in the presence of—*power.*

"What do you want?" Samantha Gomez sat behind her desk, arms folded across her chest.

Without being invited, Lois fell, weak-kneed, into the chair in front of Ms. Gomez's desk. The office was air-conditioned, but Lois felt sweat trickle down her sides. She'd forgotten to use deodorant. *No, wait. Am I supposed to sit? Did Joe say?*

"Ms. Gomez, I have some—some—"

There was something odd about Samantha Gomez, but Lois couldn't quite put her finger on it. She looked frazzled. Angry. Eyes bloodshot, hair all over, makeup runny. But that wasn't it.

"Speak up, Ms. Wardell." She tugged impatiently on her ear. "As you can see, I'm busy."

"It's Ward, Lois Ward, and I—" *Something not right.*

"Who did you represent, Ms. Warden?"

"Ward. I—I'm with Trustworthy Vigilance—" *Wait a minute, I'm not supposed to say that, am I?* She smelled sweat. Her own. Her armpits tickled.

"If you're selling something, I'm not—"

"No, no, I have, um—" Suddenly, Lois lost her voice. She was going to faint. *Balls? Heck no. Nerves.*

Samantha Gomez smirked. "If you don't leave right now, Ms. Warner, I'm calling security." She reached for the phone.

Lois had blown it. She couldn't remember a word Joe had told her to say. *No, wait, I was supposed to say something about Joe's pictures. Of the car in the parking lot. Get her reaction.* She'd blown it. Ms. Gomez was beyond being buffaloed, if she had ever had been intimidatible, and now Lois was in deep doo-doo.

Her mind told her to run, but her legs turned to jelly and her stomach lurched. Dizzy. She felt like a deer caught in headlights. She fumbled for the Tumeze in her pocket.

Her fingers found the earring.

"Hello, security?"

Suddenly, Lois realized what was so peculiar about Ms. Gomez. She wore only one earring. On her right ear. The left earlobe was bare.

The one on Ms. Gomez's ear was an exact match for the one in Lois' pocket.

Lois drew the earring from her pocket, held it up to compare it with the one in Ms. Gomez's ear. They were the same.

"Gomez here. I have a—" Samantha Gomez saw the earring Lois held. Her face turned paper-white, her eyes bugged, her jaw dropped open and she dropped the phone.

The earring. *The* earring.

As Ms. Gomez unconsciously touched her empty left earlobe, Lois realized that Ms. Gomez knew—and Ms. Gomez knew that Lois knew—that the earring Lois held up to the light—*oops, stupid move*—the one she'd found in Hell's backside parking lot, matched the one in Ms. Gomez's ear. The pair, reunited.

Samantha Gomez rose. "Where did you—"

Lois regained her legs. Adrenaline flowed and she ran.

"Stop that woman," Samantha Gomez yelled behind her. "Security! Securi—"

Lois made for the nearest elevator, changed her mind, took the stairway—*much faster*—got to Joe's car and out of the parking lot without being stopped. As she drove off, two security officers burst out the front door of City Hall, looking for her.

She'd botched it badly. Still, she'd found out something significant. Ms. Gomez had acted guilty, couldn't disguise it.

Guilty of what? Theft? Of the earring?

The earring. Joe hadn't known about it. Lois had forgotten it, until she saw Ms. Gomez.

Still, she'd compromised the mission, upsetting Ms. Gomez so. This was only part one of Joe's plan. She was supposed to call Joe right after the meeting and Joe would guide her through the next step—confronting Ms. Ripley at Hell.

How can I do that, now?

She fumbled for her phone as she drove and called Joe. A nurse told her Joe was asleep, couldn't be disturbed. Something to do with the painkillers not working right, about his heart rate, blood pressure. Medical mumbo jumbo. He *had* seemed hyper when they'd talked a few minutes ago.

She asked the nurse to have him call her as soon as he could. Urgent.

Now what?

Samantha Gomez

Samantha stood at the floor to ceiling window behind her desk, looking out, pounding uselessly on the reinforced glass. The car left the parking lot, an old beaten-up Dodge, that prissy little rent-a-cop looking up through the windshield.

Her phone rang. Security, reporting what she already knew. She didn't scream at them.

"Now what?" she asked the walls.

She paced.

She'd forgotten about the earrings. Bobbie had given them to her as a For-the-Hell-of-it present last March. Some pricey little bauble she'd picked up in Seattle. Silver and turquoise. Largish but not too gaudy. Exquisite craftsmanship. Bobbie said it set off her eyes Just So. Of course, she put them on when she went to meet Bobbie last night.

Something had bothered her all day. Like she'd lost her keys or wallet, or there was an appointment she had to keep but had forgotten to write it down. She couldn't put her finger on it, quite. Being so busy since the "sinkhole episode," as some reporters called it, especially after they found that body in the freezer there, she hadn't spent much time or energy scratching that itch. It came and went, thinking about the missing *something*. She was busy, darn busy.

When that little cheerleader brought out her earring—*her*

earring—it all fell into place. What had been missing was the earring. Right off her own ear. She hadn't even noticed. Well, she *had* noticed *something* seemed different, but—

"Oh, what the heck." She sat at her desk, opened up a package of Tumeze, and chewed.

She called her secretary. "Donald, I'll need a little time here. Take calls."

Bobbie. She'd know what to do, wouldn't she?

Maybe not. Bobbie was—going crazy. This stuff about going to—where did she say?

Pacing aggravated a bruise on her hip, one she'd apparently gotten in the tumble in the van with Bobbie in Hell's parking lot. She'd wanted to talk to Bobbie about their relationship then. She had found that Bobbie had wanted to talk to her too. About—not quite the same, no, not quite.

Leave? Now? With Bobbie?

She thought how delicious that would be. Get away from Stan, with Bobbie.

But Bobbie was—is—clearly, absolutely—crazy.

"I guess I knew that." *Maybe I always knew it. Dangerous. Maybe that's part of what made her so attractive.*

The phone range. "I thought I told you—"

"Relax, honey, it's me." Bobbie. Samantha plopped down in her chair, weak-kneed. "Can we talk?"

"Uh, yeah, I guess so. Bobbie—"

"I got some last minute business. Details. Are you packed? Never mind. We'll go—"

"Wait, wait." She had to get control of this conversation, *tell her*. That was always tough to do with Bobbie.

"What is it, honey?" Concern in her voice.

"Remember those earrings you gave me? You got them in—"

"Oh, the darling silver and—"

"Yes, yes—those. *Listen*, Bobbie."

Bobbie listened. Samantha told her about the visit by the

rent-a-cop girl, the earring the girl had found in the Hell parking lot, and how Samantha had reacted—*not cool, not like Bobbie would have*—when the girl-cop had held out the earring.

"Maybe she found them elsewhere," Bobbie said.

"No, I'm sure of it now. After I got out of the van, I stumbled, remember?"

"Yes, I—"

"Something else I just remembered. What's the name of the private detective agency who does guard duty at Hell?"

"Trustworthy Vigilance Agency. What does that—"

"She said she worked for them, had a rent-a-cop uniform."

"Don't panic, honey. Now, *you* listen to *me*." Bobbie told her what she needed to do.

She made Samantha repeat her instructions back. "Okay," Bobbie said, satisfied at last.

"Oh, Bobbie, I don't—"

"No buts, honey. Take a deep breath. *Go*."

Samantha hung up, grabbed her purse and headed to the door. It wasn't until she had her hand on the knob that she remembered something else—important maybe—she'd forgotten to tell Bobbie.

She went back to her desk, and called. "I forgot to tell you. The cop-girl said she had a videotape. Do you think—"

"Oh, shit," Bobbie said and hung up.

Lois Ward

Traffic got thicker the closer Lois got to Hell. She switched to a side street to go around, but that didn't work. A fender-bender in the intersection ahead.

Again, she checked her phone, made sure it was on, the batteries charged. She could get lucky, Joe could call, any second, tell her what to do next.

Horns honked, engines roared and revved, a radio thumped a hip-hop bass beat somewhere. The smell of scorched asphalt, gasoline, her own body odor, and, for some odd reason, buttered popcorn, permeated Joe's car. All windows open, no AC, no wind, she dripped sticky sweat.

She called Mary. She was okay, watching TV. "Mom, can you bring home some pickles? We're out."

"Okay, honey."

She thought of calling the hospital again, but the last time she did, minutes ago, the nurse said he'd call her back the instant Joe was able to take calls, "unless you'd rather I call you every five minutes?" No point in annoying people at the hospital. Further. *Maybe they're afraid I'm a relative ready to sue them for fouling up his medication.*

She sighed. Joe was down and out in la-la-land and she didn't know when he'd come up.

She considered going to the hospital. "Fat chance."

What could she do back at the office? Or at home?

No, she had to carry through with the plan, botched though it was. Her meeting with Ms. Gomez had resolved nothing. She was guilty of something, but what? Murder? Something else?

Joe's plan involved a second confrontation, seeing Roberta Ripley right after Samantha Gomez, and using information—or clues, or suspicions, or suppositions—gathered in the first meet to gather more in the second, maybe even a confession. Dramatic. Joe liked that, the Perry Mason in his blood.

For it to work—the confrontation with Ms. Ripley—Joe had to know what happened in that first meeting with Ms. Gomez. Joe hadn't known when he sent Lois to Ms. Gomez that he'd be gaga when she met with Ms. Gomez and he wouldn't be up for a debriefing. Joe was Out Of It.

So—"So, I'm on my own." *What to do? What to do?*

Lois thought wistfully that this would be a good time to have Joe around to sound board the problem.

The driver behind Lois honked impatiently and waved his arms as if he could move the tons of metal, glass and rubber jammed in a long, neat row on the street out of his way with his clumsy, amateur magician's gesture. He was getting it wrong, couldn't conger up a waitress on a slow Sunday with that gesture.

"You dummy." Lois laughed. "Even Mary could—"

Mary.

She called. "Honey, I need to play that detective game with you again, okay?"

"Okay. Is Uncle Joe in trouble again?"

Not this time, honey, but your mom is. "This is pretend. Say there's this detective and she goes—"

"A girl detective, like you, huh?"

"Right, honey. Anyway, she confronts—we'll pretend she's me, okay?"

"Okay."

"I confront—"

"What's 'confront' mean?"

"Meet. Like a showdown, only no guns, not like in the movies, just talk. So, I confront the suspect. Call him Ringo."

As traffic inched forward, Lois sound-boarded the problem about the botched Ringo interview and yet-to-be Butch interview with Mary, the ten-year-old mystery fan. As they talked, Lois got lucky, found an alley, ducked into it, and got around the fender-bender up ahead.

"What'll Ringo do now?" Mary asked. She'd gotten into the game, even trying to sound like Humphrey Bogart. Or Peter Falk. "Will he call Butch?"

"Why would he do that?" Lois got only three blocks before traffic jammed up again. She parked Joe's Dodge four blocks from Hell, in the first space she found, in a little strip mall, in front of the Kwik-Kash Loan King Op n 24/D Y. Demonstrators had spilled haphazardly onto the street, snarling traffic even this far away from Hell. The police, those she could see, didn't try hard to control them. She walked.

"To warn him the lady detective is coming," Mary said.

Hundreds of strange people moved toward Hell. Many looked, dressed, and smelled a lot like Teresa Santiago— tasseled and scruffy. Smudgy too. A few looked better dressed, better fed, but they were a minority. Many carried candy-cane umbrellas, shade from the relentless heat, or hand-painted signs. "Down With Hell," some signs read. "Justice for Dog." Others.

"That's what he'll do," Lois said. She had to press the phone to her ear and block her other ear with her other hand because the crowd was chanting loudly in ragged unison. She couldn't make out the words because of a constant tinny buzz that went along with the chant.

"Butch will do something guilty-like."

Kazoos. People are blowing kazoos.

"I'll need to confront Butch, to catch him doing that

guilty something."

Many people in the crowd wore kid's propeller beanies. Some had fake Groucho glasses, with the big rubber nose, fuzzy eyebrows, and mustache. Many ate something that smelled fishy, and passed water bottles around. She saw paper-wrapped liquor bottles, and the air smelled heady with pot.

What are they chanting?

"This isn't just pretend." Mary's tone was accusing.

"I just thought of something," Lois said. "There's this videotape I told Ringo about."

"Videotape? Mom, what's that noise? I can barely hear you."

"Chanting, honey. Demonstrators." *Something to do with Hell, but what?* "Butch will want that tape, because she'll think there's evidence on it. Otherwise, why would I mention it to Ms. Gomez—I mean Ringo? The evidence is bad for her—him."

"This isn't pretend. Where's this videotape?"

"In Joe's safe. Butch doesn't know. Maybe she'll think I have it in my purse or that it's still in the camera."

"Butch and Ringo are girls?" That tone again. *Smart girl.*

"Um, yeah."

"What's that smell?" "Shut up, Hell?" "Down with Hell?"

"Girl bad guys? Mom, do you think she'll try to ambush you?"

"I don't know, honey." *No, it's not "Down with Hell."* "I don't remember exactly what I said to Ringo, not quite."

"No, wait, I got it. She'll be at the scene of the crime."

"What? Why?" *It would make sense, "Down with Hell" would, but that's not it.*

"Bad guys always return to the scene of the crime, Mom." Mary's exasperated sigh came through the phone tinny but clear. "She'll look for the camera—"

"If she don't find it, and I find her, I can make her think I got it in my purse—"

"Mom, this is dangerous. Maybe you should—"

"That reminds me. Uncle Joe might call. I have to go."

"Mom, be careful." *She sounds like Joe.*

Lois tried to run, but the crowd was too thick, thicker the closer she got to Hell. She jostled her way forward as fast as she could. Because—

—because if Samantha Gomez called Roberta Ripley, she'd do it right after I left, so Ms. Ripley's had—my gosh, almost 20 minutes—to be ready for—whatever. Or to be gone.

She was a half block from Dallas Street and the backside of Hell, passing in front of the Sunset Bistro, when it hit her fully, what Mary had said, how much danger she really faced. *Roberta Ripley could try to kill me.*

An idea. She called Mary back. "Honey, it's me."

"What? I can't hear you." The crowd roar amplified as it bounced between the Foxtrot and Hell's backside.

Lois rounded the corner onto Dallas Street, where the din grew even louder and the crowd surge changed directions, marching now sideways parallel to Hell, shoulder to shoulder down the sidewalk, chanting. *'Up with Hell'? Is that what they're saying?*

"Just a minute, honey."

The crowd pushed Lois along for a few yards before she ducked into an alcove, the recessed entryway to the staircase leading to a dentist's office above the Foxtrot XXX Bookstore. Not much quieter, but enough. Two bums stood there sharing a joint. They eyed her uniform for a second, then ignored her. She ignored them. "I said," she shouted, "I'm going to keep the phone on, in my purse when I confront Butch. Just in case."

"Will the batteries last?"

Smart girl. Lois checked. *Maybe. Maybe not.*

"I think so." The alcove smelled like piss and pot.

"I'll listen. If anything goes wrong, I'll call 9-1-1."

"Good girl." *"Up with Hell?" That doesn't make sense either, but that's what they're chanting.* "I'll call just before I see her, okay?"

"Okay. Be careful."

She dropped Mary into her purse and reentered the crowd.

She swam downstream and crosscurrent through the demonstrators until she crossed the sidewalk and stood with one foot in the gutter of Dallas Street directly in front of the Foxtrot front door and directly across from the Hell's backside parking lot and the kitchen back door. The chanters pressed by on the sidewalk behind her like an ocean tide. "Up with Hell! Up with Hell!" Louder.

They were all on *this* side of the street. Dallas Street, she could see now, was mostly empty, and the Hell parking lot—no people there. Wooden sawhorse police barricades lined the street along *this* side and dozens of police officers stood behind the barricades, facing the crowd. The demonstrators seemed to be circling Hell, marching *that* way around it, like Indians circling the wagon train, chanting "Up with Hell!," kazooing, waving umbrellas and signs, eating, drinking, smoking.

Lois took a deep breath and took one step further onto the street. She had no more than laid a hand on one end of a sawhorse, to ease through the narrow gap between it and the one next to it, when the nearest cop stepped deliberately in front of her. He held one hand out, waving her back. The gesture looked almost effeminate, but one look at the big man's stony frown and Lois knew he wouldn't let her get across.

Now what do I do? She looked around. Barricades and cops lined the street all the way around both corners. Hell was inaccessible. *How would Ms. Ripley get in? No, she wouldn't have any problem because she works here. All she'd have to do is—*

Suddenly, it hit her: *Ms. Ripley won't be here. The building is closed. Hell is surrounded by demonstrators and police. She's somewhere else. I've goofed.*

There had been a plan, something about confronting Ms.

Ripley. *In her office? In Hell? Where in Hell is her office?* She'd worked the plan out with Joe, and then with Mary. There *had* been a plan, but to save her life, she couldn't remember it.

The heat, the crowd, the noise. She was going to faint. She stumbled against the curb and almost fell to her knees.

A hand reached out, gripped her elbow, and saved her. A big man wore a propeller beanie and Groucho glasses. "Wois," the Good Samaritan said. "Awe you aww wight?"

Roberta Ripley

"Oh, shit," Ripley said. She hung up and stopped, legs rubbery, and leaned against the cool bare concrete wall.

"Are you okay, ma'am?" Her baby-faced police escort couldn't have been old enough to shave, but he was strong enough to climb with her up seven flights of stairs and carry two big boxes filled with files and disks down the dark staircase. He stopped as she spoke and looked back up at her from three steps below, arms around the bulky, heavy cardboard boxes, frowning genuine concern. There was enough light in the stairwell to see by and he'd tucked his flashlight into his pocket.

Officer Freda Wiseman had ridden with Ripley to Hell in Ripley's car, the black executive van—it was all she had on a moment's notice—asking questions and scribbling notes as Ripley gave crisp, rapid-fire answers, sounding helpful but not really, and deftly negotiated the busy streets. Four blocks from Hell, the streets became impassable, clogged with traffic and demonstrators, and Ripley abandoned the van in the first parking space she could find and talked Wiseman into commandeering a ride with a bus filled with Hellward bound officers.

Ripley stepped off the bus in front of Hell and immediately put her hands over her ears. The demonstrator's— the *mob's*—chanting reverberated off the walls, painful, rock-concert loud. *What in hell are they chanting?* The blast furnace heat drenched her instantly in a sweaty sheen. And the smell. Unwashed body, fish, marijuana, popcorn, beer.

Mutt and Dr. Jeff had come through, and Arrangements Had Been Made. Ironically, the Bull-Goose-Cop-In-Charge had been Sammy's husband, who sounded royally peeved at being ordered by somebody more powerful than he was to allow Ripley to enter the building. The man had smelled almost as foul as the mob. He dismissed Officer Wiseman, gave Ripley a curt nod, introduced her escort, Officer Avery Gordon, and gave Ripley and her new escort-officer instructions. She heard little of it. Didn't matter.

She had to put on a helmet that weighed a ton, looked silly, flattened and mussed her hair, and fell down over her eyes. No doubt, some of the TV cameras among the fragrant, loud mob saw her, recognized her, and taped her, but that couldn't be helped. In a few hours, it wouldn't matter anyway.

The mob's odor disappeared and the loud chant faded and it got cooler, as she and her escort entered the hotel lobby and climbed the dark staircase. She took off the helmet as soon as she got to the first landing and handed it to Officer Gordon. He frowned dutiful disapproval, but she gave him The Smile. He was a quick study. She had his number. He put away his flashlight—they could see enough. They climbed to her office.

"Ma'am?" Gordon took a step back up toward her.

"I'm fine," Ripley said. "I'm fine." She waved him away with her phone hand. He stood, frowning, irresolute.

She'd never been in the hotel stairwell before. She used the elevator, of course, but before, there'd been power. A half-inch wide crack meandered up the wall by her hand. *From the sinkhole?* The narrow, vertical stairwell felt tunnel-like, something Alice might chase a rabbit through. It smelled close, damp, pungent, like fresh paint. Dark. Cool.

People who work with their hands—worker bees—know about places like these. Carpenters, painters, welders, electricians.

The mob's distant chant echoed dimly, unintelligible. A tiny rivulet of dust cascaded down the wall by her hand.

"You shouldn't have come up all this way," Gordon said. Courteous, kind, brave, clean. A six-foot-four Boy Scout who didn't sweat, didn't seem to get out of breath. "I brought a water bottle—"

"I'm all right." She gestured again with the phone, remembered that she held it in her numb fingers, and dropped it back into her purse. "I'm all right." She tried The Smile, but it lacked wattage.

"Ma'am, I can set these boxes down, carry you down, and—"

"No, no, that won't be necessary." *Shut up, Dudley Doright. I have to think.* "Thank you."

They were just below the fourth floor landing. She'd managed her call to Samantha while she'd been in her office, boxing, collecting, purging, deleting. She'd sent the Boy Scout up one floor to check for a Very Important but non-existent box in Mark's apartment, gave him a set of keys to a cabinet, many keys, pointed out the wrong one. Kept him busy finding the right key and then the wrong box while she finished packing boxes, deleting files, and making arrangements with Sammy.

The plan was to hand the files and disks—*except for the two disks in my purse, my insurance policy*—to Mutt and Dr. Jeff outside Hell where they said they'd be waiting, if they showed up. With the demonstration, chances are, they wouldn't show. If they did, they might not be able to find Ripley in the chaos. If they didn't show, she'd instructed her secretary, Dora—her own Right Hand Man—to misdirect the boxes by U.S. Mail to the wrong Nevada State Bureau of Ass Coverage. After sufficient delay, the poor overworked and underpaid but ever-so nice, cooperative, cute-but-dingy Dora would discover the mistake in the tangled mess of notes on her desk—"It's been *so* busy lately and my horrid boss Ms. Ripley is such a can-I-share-this-with-you-boys?—*bitch*"—then she'd grovel before whoever required it, flirt and flatter as needed—she'd taken lessons from Ripley—apologize, and then get the boxes routed to the right place. By U.S. Mail.

Further delays would occur while Mutt and Dr. Jeff borrowed a computer nerd from another department to crack passwords to get to what they expected would be the Good Stuff. By then, Ripley and Sammy would be on some white-sandy beach, rubbing number ten sunscreen up over the smooth, hard hills and down into the soft, warm valleys of each other's torsos, sipping margaritas, and practicing Portuguese.

In either case, step two was to rendezvous with Sammy at a bar by the airport and drive to the hangar where a charter plane would be ready.

"Now this."

"Pardon, ma'am?"

"Nothing, Officer Do—uh, Gordon." Ripley took a breath, dusted off her hands, straightened her blouse, touched up her hair. Smiled. "Let's go, shall we?"

Officer Gordon looked relieved and started down again.

At the foot of the stairs, just inside the lobby, Ripley suddenly stopped and gasped. "I forgot something."

Officer Gordon put the boxes down. "Tell me what it is and I'll—"

"No, I'll get it."

"Ma'am, I'm not supposed to let you—"

"Officer Avery—*Avery*." Ripley stepped closer, put her hand gently on his biceps, and looked deep into his eyes. "This is important." She breathed. "I need *your* help."

"Ma'am, I—I—"

"Please." She stepped closer. "Avery." Breathed. "A little favor?" Touched. "For me?" Looked. "I'd be ever so grateful." Smiled. "Oh, my. Is this your flashlight?"

Precious seconds wasted away before Officer Gordon was prepared to run from the building stark naked with his hair on fire if Ripley had asked him to. Instead, she'd asked him to take the boxes outside and wait. He left, not thinking about the reprimand he'd likely get for abandoning his charge, walking awkwardly, trying to deal with a bulging flashlight while carrying two cardboard boxes. He grinned a stupid Boy Scout grin, but he left.

Ripley ran through the dark hallway between the hotel and the kitchen. *Damn, I should have asked for his flashlight.* The mob's chant faded as she left the lobby, and grew louder again as she got into the kitchen hallway, closer to the open back door. There, she stopped, by the door to the kitchen.

"Down with Hell?" Is that what they're chanting?

She was convinced the girl rent-a-cop wasn't bluffing. That Sammy was concerned—*terrified*—when Sammy had called Ripley back to tell her about the videotape was no indicator that the girl—Lisa Wardell, that was her name—wasn't kidding. No, that wasn't what convinced Ripley. She knew the girl, knew Warden—knew *of* her—through Ripley's periodic and routine dealings with Joseph Foxworthy, the girl's employer, the PI who managed security—*Ha!*—for Hell, and guessed the girl was too naïve to pull off a bluff. Ripley prided herself on her ability to read people, and this—this *little girl*— yes, she'd *seen* her once—didn't have the balls to bluff.

So there *was* a videotape. The little girl dreamed of a big score. Blackmail. Inept, but real.

Sammy hadn't been specific about what was on the tape. Maybe Warner hadn't been specific. Didn't matter. The tape was *not* of a rendezvous with Sammy, oh no. Ripley had been too cautious for that. Nothing anybody could have caught could be as awkward as tape of *that* place, *that* moment. Last night, right *here.*

Nothing else *counted.*

No, not "Down with Hell." Like it, but not quite.

And there was Foxworthy. Inside Hell when the sinkhole subsided. Broke his leg, poor unlucky bastard.

She knew, of course, that Foxworthy had padded his

invoices. Five, sometimes six, employees, 24 hours? More like one or two, and probably only at night. Electronic equipment, monitors, cameras, and so on? Ripley knew no such equipment existed. She wasn't about to blow the whistle on Foxworthy, involved as she was in her own little project. Didn't want anybody looking too closely at books. Not yet.

Knowing Foxworthy didn't have cameras inside Hell, or outside, made her meet with Sammy last night possible—and made the encounter with that dirty hippie easy to handle. Unobserved.

But Foxworthy *had* been in *this* place at *that* time—or close enough. Why? A connection? His employee *had* said something to Sammy about a videotape. Ripley didn't believe in coincidence.

She stood by the door to the kitchen, looking down the hallway, as she had last night, letting her eyes adjust.

Maybe the girl had it with her in her purse, or in her car. Maybe she had it at home, or at Foxworthy's office, or in a locker in the goddamn Greyhound Bus Depot. Maybe it was still in the camera, right here In Hell.

Ripley couldn't take the chance that it wasn't. It felt too untidy to leave a detail like that unattended to. She had to look, had to know. If it was—end of problem. If not—then, what?

Run.

That was already on the agenda, so no problem, really. A plane was waiting, and so was Sammy.

Still, while she was here, she had to look.

She moved forward slowly. The hallway behind the kitchen was dark, littered with debris. She could barely see the obstacles on the floor—boxes, burst cardboard cartons, cans, bottles—and again she regretted not having the flashlight.

"Mumble with Hell," the mob outside chanted. *Not as loud right here as out front.*

She slipped on a spill—it smelled like mustard—and fell on her butt.

She got up, wiped her hands on a towel, and decided to search between the back door to the parking lot and the kitchen door; the camera would be *somewhere in this area*. If she didn't find it in ten minutes then she'd go. Out the back door. Walk back to the van, or flag down a cab. Get Sammy. Go.

Light from the back door, behind her when she faced *this* way, helped her see better. She got down, used a towel to cushion her knees, and began to carefully sift through piles of towels, toilet paper, cloth napkins, jars, cans, boxes. And stuff.

In a few minutes, she found it. On the floor, buried under a pile of towels. A video camera.

She pulled the camera out, a bulky, old model, and held it up to a sliver of light spilling in through the Hell's kitchen back door behind her. She saw tape in a little compartment.

Over the mob's chant—*"Up with Hell!" That's what. Why are they*—a noise from the back door, and a shadow occluded the light. Somebody coming.

A voice, sharp and distinct over the mob's chant, and close, said: "Ow. Heww, that wiwwy huwt."

Teresa Santiago

Teresa shook her head, amazed, as Larry helped her climb the rickety steps back up onto the plywood speaker's platform. They'd finished marching around Hell twice but it felt like more. They'd walked eight blocks, total, between the white concrete anvil and the August sun hammer, cheek to jowl with ten thousand people, stinking of BO, fish, pot, and booze, all chanting, marching, waving signs and umbrellas, drinking, smoking, eating, kazooing.

Oswald had orchestrated the move, getting everybody—*everybody*—to move out of the street itself and occupy the sidewalk across the street from Hell rather than the sidewalks nearest. Maybe ten, fifteen thousand people. Teresa understood—the wider the circle, the more room for more people.

"Up with Hell! Up with Hell! Up with Hell!"

As far as Teresa knew, the heat hadn't killed anybody. So far. A miracle, that.

She thanked Larry with a nod, wiped sweat off her forehead with the back of her hand, and accepted a sip from his water bottle. Cool and sweet. She refrained from gulping it all down. Handed it back, nodded thanks, tried to catch her breath.

Larry stood on tiptoes to hold an umbrella over her. He wore a propeller beanie but no Groucho glasses. Teresa couldn't remember the last time she'd seen Larry so—so what? Not giddy-drunk happy, not ha-ha happy, not that, not so soon after Dog's death. Not sad or grim either, as he had been when he heard. Elated? Not quite. Triumphant? Exalted?

Amazing transformation from grief to—whatever it was, and not only Larry but Teach, Captain Freddy, Little Ricky, Tom-Tom and others. From her vantage on the platform, she looked out over the marcher's bobbing heads, mostly streeties but some townies, circling clockwise around Hell, and saw it in *all* their faces. The same look of—*what? What's going on here?*

"Up with Hell! Up with Hell! Up with Hell!"

Amazing, whatever it was. She'd had little to do with it. She'd lost control of the demonstration. Oswald had outmaneuvered her and her streetie comrades followed him.

She'd expected Oswald, the fiery TV preacher, to quote the Bible every third sentence—"Can I get an 'a-men,' brethren and cisterns?"—and her troops would only go along with that bullshit if they felt it might be fun and she said it was okay, wink-wink. Let him take care of the churchies, she'd rally the streeties.

He sounded like Dog, like a wild-eyed, hairy, commie street whacko, not a starch-collared, frowny-faced, churchy, Nazi whacko. He sounded like Dog. That stopped Teresa cold.

Oswald Took Over. He'd done it so fast, so subtly, but with such power and authority.

Dog would have admired it. But then, if Dog was here, it wouldn't have happened.

The demonstration would proceed as planned, Oswald told the teary crowd at Jesus' Bread Basket and the TV cameras after Teresa told them about Dog. Oswald gave a passionate speech, in Dog-like language, cadence and temper, bemoaning Dog's death, and somehow working it into his agenda, as if he'd come to Las Vegas to protest the death specifically, not just Hell. He Took Over.

Teresa was amazed, but not dismayed, really. "It's

okay," she said with a sigh. "Without Dog—"

"What?" Oswald had given his beanie and Groucho glasses to somebody, as she also had, and had preceded her to the platform, his wife right behind him. He stood close to her as he had all day, usurping her place in the sun, while supporting her, sympathetic to her loss. The perfect minister. It made good footage. Maybe he *was* sincere.

"What?" He cupped an ear, but Teresa waved "never mind" with a fat hand. Nobody could hear over the ten thousand-voice chant Oswald orchestrated. Didn't matter. Besides, Oswald's attention was elsewhere. He watched the crowd march past the platform, circling Hell.

"Up with Hell! Up with Hell! Up with Hell!"

They'd almost lost it minutes after the vanguard of the demonstrators arrived on the scene. The Caterer From Hell, literally, had almost turned the rally into a just-for-the-fun-of-it carnival, blunting the point. Mark Trane, the little boy trapped in a billionaire's body, wanted to play too.

The umbrellas, distributed early on, seemed a good idea, something somebody maybe in Oswald's organization—she was Very Impressed with his organization—might have thought of. So she didn't ask where they'd come from until after hundreds had been passed out, all with the Trane logo in tiny letters on them. Who could fault a rich person for donating water to a thirsty crowd on a hot day? That was generous, even if the motive was to distract attention and garner sympathy. Carping against the gesture would be petty. But the plastic devil horns on the "caterer's" heads, and the red shirts? Then the Groucho glasses, and the propeller beanies, and the kazoos?

The crowd began to turn irretrievably at that point, their chant of "Down with Hell! Down with Hell! Down with Hell!" dissipating into a chaotic, joyous roar, and Teresa was horrified, convinced that Trane had out-pranked them, had beaten them at their own game. He watched, she was sure, by TV camera, clapping his clean, lily-white hands, giggling.

It would have been over in a few minutes and the sardines and crackers seemed a cruel after-thought, a painful, graceless after-the-bell kick to the crotch when the loser was down and counted out. Funny but not funny.

They'd *almost* lost it, but they didn't.

Tears of mute frustration had welled up in Teresa's eyes and she didn't see Oswald stalk to the microphones, didn't hear the first few notes of his call to rally, re-taking the high ground.

Again, he invoked the spirit of Dog, the beloved Merry Prankster of Las Vegas, and danced and joked with the crowd, for the crowd, and for the microphones, and the TV cameras.

"Go with the flow," he said. And: "That's what Dog would have done." And: "Hell, we can use this."

The crowd slowly turned back to him. He cajoled, laughed, preached, begged, screamed, danced, joked. He put on a beanie and Groucho glasses and people laughed with him.

He got them back.

When he had them again, he *steered* them.

"The joke," he said, "is on *them!*" He pointed to Hell and the crowd roared. He told them what he had in mind. Chant *this*, he said. Go *this* way, he said. The crowd roared with laughter.

"Do you think we can do it?"

"Hell, yes," they roared back.

"Then let's do it!"

And they did.

"Up with Hell! Up with Hell! Up with Hell!"

My God, he's doing what I planned to do, what Dog dreamed about doing. Only he's really *doing it.*

Teresa was amazed, and realized she was out of her league, had met her match. Oswald was good, damn good. Dog might have matched him, but nobody else could. She couldn't, not alone, not without Dog. She was worthless without Dog.

Teresa watched Oswald as he strode to the microphones now. He gained their attention slowly, casually, not trying to interrupt the chant, the one he'd changed from "Down with

Hell!" to "Up with Hell!" Not quite. Yet. Soon, though, the chant began to falter as people slowed the cadence of their relentless march and focused their attention on him. The march sputtered to a ragged halt and people stood still. Oswald's voice echoed off the walls of Hell and the canyons of walls around Hell.

"Now what," Teresa said.

Larry shrugged. He didn't know either.

"There's this thing in movies," she lectured Larry, only half listening to Oswald. "In books, too, I think. You're only supposed to invoke one miracle per movie. Or book. When you do two, people start to question your credibility. They don't believe you anymore. It's too much. I don't remember where I read that, but it sounds right."

Larry tilted his head quizzically.

"I *mean*," Teresa said, exasperated, "that whatever he's got planned can't top what he's done so far. He set me aside and took over, Larry. *Then*, just when it looked like Trane had us by the balls for good, he got us back together. Two miracles, I say. Now what? Another one?" She shook her head. "I think I know what he's got up his sleeve, but I don't believe it. I don't know if the Universe can take another miracle."

Larry pointed emphatically at Oswald.

"Hmph," Teresa answered. "Says you." She folded her big arms, frowned, and listened.

When he had the crowd sufficiently under his sway again, only a faint ruffle of idle chatter and laughter here and there, Oswald directed them to turn as one inward toward the walls of Hell, and asked them to pray, silently.

"Now," he said, "I know some of you ain't religious. Hell, some of you are atheists, but that's okay. This'll work. This'll work whoever you are, however you pray, and whether you pray or not. It'll work because we are going to manifest through our combined energies—whatever you call it—spirit, the Holy Ghost, good vibes, whatever—*combined* energies—*our* will, *our* desires—Hell, our hopes, dreams, aspirations—*all* of that internal unscientifical stuff—our very *souls*, if you want, why the Hell not?—*against those walls.*" He pointed.

The crowd grew even quieter. All eyes on Oswald.

"If you can't buy the program—buy into the idea of a combined mind-thing—*all* of us together, *for* all, brothers and sisters, united—sounds kind of communist, I know, but bare with me. If you can't buy into this for everybody's sake, then I have a request. Listen. Please." Low, intent. "Listen."

A whisper. "Do. This. For. *Dog.*"

Silence, rapt and reverent, manifest in the crowd around Hell, all facing inward. No one spoke. A helicopter whop-whop-whopped overhead. A disembodied woman's voice chattered numbers tinnily on a police radio. A horn honked far away, and a distant siren wailed. Somebody farted on the platform but nobody laughed.

In the immense silence, a silence as profound and tangible as the chant had been deafening before, Oswald told them what all their focused energy could do. What he *expected* it to do.

Up with Hell.

Teresa almost guffawed.

Amazing. She saw not one person in that silent, focused, rapt multitude that she suspected *did not* believe Oswald. Even some of the police and reporters looked smitten. The chant had been fun, a tribute to Dog in its way, but this—this was—

Up with Hell.

Amazing. *Is this what Dog would have done?*

Teresa knew her streeties well, knew they fed on scant fare every day. Not just food, not just clothing or shelter or jobs, but spiritual fare. Few expected things to get better. Even those few rationed hope in frugal measure. Many had abandoned all hope long ago. Many had merely lost their minds.

Cynicism reigned.

But not these people, not now. Teresa tried to freeze the

scene in her mind. She wanted to remember this, because *something was going on*. Not just the prank Oswald perpetuated for the media, but something more.

These people weren't the ones who started the demonstration. They weren't her streeties anymore.

Teresa clucked her tongue in amazement as she looked around. Everybody had it, the look. She now understood.

They believe.

Maybe it had been a joke to begin with, maybe that's why they'd gone along, but it became Something Else. The entire mob had come to believe, had been convinced, by one man's oratory, that they could accomplish a miracle.

Up with Hell.

Teresa fancied herself a rational woman. She too measured hope in small doses. Her cynicism seemed a better defense against the slings and arrows of outrageous fortune. The balance—a dash of hope in a gallon of cynicism—worked. She won victories, small ones usually, but victories nonetheless. "Thus do I refute entropy," she'd say after some small victory— getting a drunk out of the tank, getting an immigrant a job, getting somebody to see a doctor or dentist, so on and on and on.

But this. This was too much. Too Much.

She stood on the platform, the only person in the entire Universe who understood that the fervently praying, polished, plastic-smile TV preacher, this, this—*thief*—was robbing these people—*my people*—of their dignity, perverting their hope, their strength, what little they had, and she knew they had precious little, for *profit*. It was all for the TV cameras. All for money.

No, this is not *as Dog would have wanted it.*

She was ready to step forward, to grab the sonofabitch by the throat and throttle him, call him for the fraud she knew he was, when she noticed Larry. His face. He too believed, and that, she now understood, was what she'd seen on his face earlier, the triumphant, ecstatic something she couldn't define earlier.

Larry believed.

For a second, in the face of her amazement, Teresa's cynicism faltered. She didn't believe, no. Not quite. For a second, she wondered. Just for a second. That was all.

But that was all it took.

In that second, something happened.

It began as a low, deep rumble.

Lois Ward

"Wois? Awe you aww wight?"

Lois barely heard Mr. Trane over the crowd. She didn't have the strength or the spit to shout a response, so she just nodded. She *did* feel woozy, though.

Mr. Trane offered her a sip from his water bottle. Cool and sweet. It helped. She nodded thanks and returned the bottle. He grinned and said something she didn't catch. The yellow plastic propeller on his beanie twirled as his head bobbed.

She wanted to ask him why he was here, among the people demonstrating against his hotel, but that seemed petty. Mr. Trane had his reasons, no doubt, and he *was* eccentric. He could do whatever he wanted.

Apparently, nobody recognized him. Few pictures of him existed, and he was disguised, like many others, as Groucho Marx. He was invisible. Not her business anyway.

What she really wanted to do—needed to do—was figure out what she was supposed to do now. *Find Ms. Ripley. Yes, that's why I'm here.*

A disembodied, amplified voice tried to override the chant echoing between the Foxtrot Bookstore walls and Hell's walls. A loudspeaker. Sounded like a preacher. Unintelligible.

She leaned in to shout into Mr. Trane's ear. "I'm looking for Ms. Ripley." She pointed toward Hell. He smelled like sweat, cologne, and fish. "I thought maybe she—"

"What?"

It took a few tries before Mr. Trane finally got it.

"No, we moved ouw office to The Buttes, just tempowawy. Because of the sinkhowe damage, you know. Unsafe, they say. Wipwey isn't at the Buttes. She's *hewe*." He pointed to Hell.

"What?"

The chanting had dropped a few decibels and Lois could hear the amplified preacher-like voice now, but she couldn't see the speaker or make out the words. She wasn't listening.

"I saw Wipwey go inside the fwont way, thwough the hotew wobby, a few minutes ago, on my wast wap awound Heww. She wowe this siwwy hewmet. Weawwy funny."

"I've got to get in there." *Maybe he can do something.*

Still loud, but a few people had stopped chanting, and a few had stopped marching and stood, listening to the preacher-voice.

"What?"

"I've got to see Ms. Ripley. It's very important."

"If you go awound out fwont and wait—"

"No, I've got to see her *now*—in there."

"Okay. Why?"

Lois tried to answer, but she couldn't, not coherently, and that frustrated her more. She gave it a couple of starts, getting more frustrated with each bumbling try.

Mr. Trane finally had mercy on her. He nodded, and motioned a "wait one," walked into the street, empty except for cops, police cars, and barricades. He approached an older cop who stood apart from the other cops, three yellow stripes on his sleeve, some kind of sergeant or supervisor, Lois guessed. Looking annoyed, the cop started to push Mr. Trane back to the sidewalk.

Mr. Trane shook his head, took off his Groucho glasses, and talked animatedly to the cop, pointing at himself, at Lois, then at Hell. They talked. Soon, the cop's demeanor softened and a smile replaced it. He laughed. The cop talked into a radio, cupping the other ear to hear better.

Mr. Trane returned to Lois, smiling. By now, most demonstrators had stopped marching and the chanting had died to where Lois could hear herself. Most people stood, listening to the invisible loudspeaker voice—maybe it came from around the block at the front of the hotel. She didn't listen.

Mr. Trane absently handed his Groucho glasses to a demonstrator and waved Lois past the barricade, onto the street. "If I buy you dinnew," he said, "wiww you expwain what this is aww about?"

"Okay."

In the street, Mr. Trane stopped in front of the supervisor cop—"Stern," his nametag read—and they talked again. Lois didn't hear them.

"Officer Hanson here will escort you," the cop said to Lois. Officer Stern nodded to another cop, who walked up to them. To Mr. Trane, he said: "And thank *you* very much, Mr. Trane, sir."

Lois and Mr. Trane followed Officer Hanson across the street. The noise volume dropped a few more decibels as they negotiated a wide gap in the rickety chain link fence on the Hellward side of Dallas Street and entered the parking lot.

"What was that all about," Lois asked Mr. Trane.

"I bwibed him."

"You *what?*"

"My wesponsibiwity." He giggled. "Besides, I donated to the Powiceman's Benevowence Association. They hewp kids."

Kids. Mary. I almost forgot. She pulled her phone from her purse, quickly punched the number.

"Hello, Mom?"

"It's showtime, honey."

"Okay. I'm scared."

She put the phone back into her purse.

They stopped at the foot of the steps up to the back door, and Officer Hanson turned to Lois. "Damn—I mean, darn," she said. The chant had almost entirely died away, only a few die-hards, or drunks, kept it up. Above it, the preacher-voice rose in crisp, bell-like tones. Lois paid no attention to him. "Sorry about the language, ma'am—"

"Lois Ward."

"Yeah, Ms. Ward. I forgot to get you a hardhat. I can't let you in there without a hardhat. Regulations—and my ass. Sorry."

"I don't know how much time I have—" Lois began. Delay nagged at her. She felt like she should be in a hurry. Just a feeling, but it persisted.

"Maybe Wois couwd weaw youw hawdhat, Officew Hanson."

"Sure, but then I'll need one. To escort her in. Wait here and I'll—"

"No," Lois grabbed her sleeve. "It's important—"

"Officew Hanson—"

The arguing added to Lois's anxiety, and the feeling of desperate need to get in there—*right now*—grew. She turned away abruptly and started up the steps.

"No, wait—" Officer Hanson began.

"No, wait—" Mr. Trane began.

Mr. Trane and Officer Hanson started after Lois at the same time. Whether Mr. Trane tripped on the bottom step, or on Officer Hanson's foot, or a piece of two-by-four, or whether he tripped on his own shoelaces, which had come untied, didn't matter. He did trip. He howled in pain as he twisted his ankle.

"Ow! That wiwwy huwts!"

Trane plopped down hard on the steps, rubbing his ankle, and Officer Hanson knelt beside him. Lois went inside Hell.

The chant had disappeared entirely now, replaced by the amplified, disembodied preacher-voice, echoing wall to wall. His voice level fell one step inside Hell. Two steps, it dropped further and the words melted together, indistinct and sing-songy.

Before she took her third step, Lois saw Ms. Ripley. She gasped, startled, and took a step backward.

Roberta Ripley stood down the dark hallway, ten paces away, where Lois had found Joe after the sinkhole sank. She stared back at Lois, hair a tangled mess, eyes bugged, mouth agape. Surprised. She clutched something to her chest.

The video camera.

"You," Ms. Ripley said. She spat the word, vicious, and if looks could kill, Lois would have dropped dead.

Lois swallowed past a suddenly dry throat. She tried to look confident. Joe told her to do that when she confronted first Ms. Gomez, and then Ms. Ripley. She'd failed with Ms. Gomez before she'd started. She failed now. She took another step backward.

"That tape—" She lost her voice again, spitless. End of hard-boiled detective showdown-in-the-warehouse scene. She'd forgotten her lines. No, she hadn't had any to begin with. She wondered if Ms. Ripley had a gun. She flinched. Woozy.

"*This* tape?" Ms. Ripley ejected the tape. She tossed the camera, clattering to the floor behind her. "This tape," she said as she jerked brown ribbon from the cartridge, bundling it in her fist, stretching it, ripping it, "is history."

"But that's, that's—"

"Yours? Your bosses?" Pull, stretch, rip, pull, stretch, rip. The Smile. "Oops. Broken."

So Samantha Gomez did call her. She thinks she has the tape. My gosh. I'm here with a murderer.

"Why—" Lois began. *Or is Ms. Gomez the murderer?*

"Why? *Why?*" Ripley anchored a fist against her cocked hip. Her face twisted into a frown. "Did you *see?*" Eyes blazing. "Did you see what that—that—*hippie*—did—" Indignation. "To." Anger. "My." *Hatred.* "*Car?*" She jammed the cartridge into her purse, broken tape dangling out like confetti. "Did you *see?*"

"What—"

Both noticed the silence. Total silence, vast, universal, like the desert. Under it, a low rumble rose.

The building started to shake.

It's going to collapse. While Lois stood frozen, Ms. Ripley had started to run, back toward the kitchen, or the hotel.

Wrong way. Lois' voice failed her again as Ms. Ripley disappeared down the dark hallway, and the rumbling grew louder and the shaking intensified.

Lois thought to dive through the back door and safety in the parking lot, but suddenly she realized she'd backed away from the door, down the hallway toward the casino. She'd been backing up, step by step, from Ms. Ripley, almost to the walk-in freezer. No way could she reach the back door before the ceiling came in.

Things fell. Eight steps to the back door, two to the freezer. She dived for the freezer doorway.

That's what you do in an earthquake. Get in a doorway. Duck and cover.

The building shook. Lois didn't hear herself scream.

She half-dived, half-fell toward the freezer. Something hit her on the head. Hard.

Hell fell.

Eight Days Later

Percy Oswald

At his big desk in his big office at his corporate headquarters outside Idaho Falls, Percy rewound the videotape again and moved it forward frame by frame.

"I did it, Theo," he said. "I levitated Hell."

He looked at each frame for a long time before moving to the next, as rapt now as he'd been the first time he'd seen them two days ago.

Fourteen frames. The most important film in human history. Maybe. Percy called them "The Jericho Tapes." Had a nice ring to it. There would be a book, a movie. The media would love it. If.

"You mean 'we,' don't you," Theo said without looking up. She'd seen the frames. She sat on the sofa across the large room, shoes off, feet up, skimming the latest summaries, minutes old. Teams of detectives, secretaries, scientists, and experts submitted reports every four hours, or sooner if they had critical can't-wait news relating to the job.

The job—confirm the miracle, with hard, indisputable, scientific evidence. Oswald felt a need to hurry. He wanted to get the Good News out, solid and unassailable, before the inevitable detractors mobilized.

"Yes, of course. 'We.'" He glanced up at the clock. Five minutes till the conference call with the detective. *What's that all about? Why the mystery?* Click. Next frame.

Theo looked up. "You're tired, Percy."

"Ha." He rubbed red, gritty eyes. "I want *news*." Click.

Hours after the incident, he flew home where he began an intensive, spare-no-expenses investigation. A massive job, unprecedented in scope. He supervised it personally.

"Twenty-hour days—"

"I know—"

"Catnapping at your desk, eating like—"

"I *know*." Click.

"When did you eat last?" She sat forward. "Percy, I'm worried. Dr. Heaston is worried."

A snappy comeback died in Percy's throat, replaced by a yawn. He put down the remote. "Give me the abstract, then I'll take five." He nodded at the clock. "After the con call."

"The detective? Percy, why don't you—"

"Theo—"

"You'll fall asleep."

"The report." He yawned again. "Give."

Theo read. "We have 1,955 eyewitnesses. The lot."

"Anything there?"

"It's being transcribed, collated, but—" she flipped pages. "Too early to tell, but there might be some good material."

"Good. I don't expect any one witness to stand out, but the cumulative effect, you know. We can make a map. Who was where when they saw what. Does it say when we can have something?"

"It'll be days, maybe weeks before—"

"Hire more people. What else?"

"Audio had 172 tape recordings, for fourteen hours, nine minutes and 22 seconds."

"Most of which is useless, of course."

"Twenty-nine tapes caught the event. Those and fifteen others caught people's voices right after."

"Good. The team is focusing on those seconds, right?"

"Um, yes."

"Fine. What else?"

"We have 8,712 still photos, black and white and color, mostly from private cameras. Quality is mixed—"

"Most are too early, too late, or too fuzzy."

"The team is trying to isolate relevant shots. A few dozen so far, but nothing we can use."

"Yet. Forensics?"

"Ah, the scientists." Theo squinted at her papers. "I wish they'd write English. This is *supposed* to be a summary."

"We'll get a translator on that team." He scribbled a note. "What can you make of it?"

"'Multiple and contradictory layers of government jurisdictional—blah, blah, blah.' We need to get legal to break up some of this red tape. The University gets in and we don't."

"Their professors don't get paid well. We'll help them. And our PR people—"

"The public wants to know, yesterday—"

"Maybe PR is the angle, not legal." Oswald made another note.

"Both. Percy, the budget. We've spent—"

"Hang the budget. This is the Holy Grail, Theo. What I've worked—what *we*'ve worked for—for years. Since, since—all our lives. If not this, what? Hang the budget."

"Okay."

"Video. People believe what they see. What's the latest?"

"Nothing more, looks like."

"Well, give me the numbers again."

Theo sighed. Oswald understood, but ignored the silent admonition. He wanted to know the numbers by heart so he could rattle them off like an expert. When the media got to him, he'd be ready. *Numbers. And video. The more the better.*

"One hundred and forty-nine video cameras," Theo recited. "We have tapes from twenty-two TV cameras, forty-seven private, including the Jericho Tape. Twenty-six tapes from five security agencies—and yes, we've completed the sweep of businesses around Hell and we got them all. Twenty-three federal, state, and local law enforcement and other government agencies we know about. We got copies of twenty of them, but the others—"

"The Lord will provide." Percy made a note to check on how much his bribes cost for the different bureaucrats. Another number, useful in the future.

"—and there's Mark Trane's tapes."

For which I paid nothing. I wonder what his game is.

"Three hundred and six hours and fifteen minutes of videotape. Still, so far, nothing like—" She nodded at the wall TV screen where frame number eight froze.

"Darn." The Jericho Tapes. All he had. So far.

Fourteen frames showed what looked like Hell lifting off its foundation for almost a full second. Up nine inches *there* at the wall where the hotel abutted the kitchen, and seven inches *over here* between the kitchen and the casino wall. That's what his video experts had said. Then Hell fell into the sinkhole.

"Darn." Percy reached for a package of Tumeze.

He'd seen it from the platform, but who'd believe him? He'd been looking for exactly what the Jericho Tape had recorded from a better vantage, facing Hell across Dallas Street. He'd seen it, but from a bad angle, the wrong side. People would say what he saw—thought he saw—had been a trick of the light, fatigue, heat, or his foggy vision. Or wishful thinking.

Others from various vantages said they saw Hell rise too, but too many of those accounts were unreliable. Many *wanted* to see what they later said they did see—true believers—and that made their testimony suspect. Subtract the drunks, potheads, and nut cases, and what's left?

"Just dreams," he muttered. "That's all."

He had to be certain—absolutely, one hundred percent, unassailably, undeniably certain, that a miracle had happened, defying the immutable laws of the Universe. If he couldn't prove it—*beyond a shadow of a doubt*—to all comers, however skeptical, then it may as well not have happened at all.

I know what I saw.

Which is why the Jericho Tape was so critical. In those frames, it looked as if one could see, through a long rent in the building, like a tear in stretched fabric, *people on the other side of the building.*

Or maybe not. Only fourteen frames, it happened so fast, and it wasn't clear, not quite. Maybe the camera shook at the vital instant, maybe what he saw in the rent in the side of Hell wasn't people on the other side, just an optical illusion.

I saw, darn it.

Experts would tear the Jericho Tape apart and critics and skeptics would have a field day. The circus had already started. Somebody insisted that the water distributed by Trane's people at the rally had been laced with LSD. A government plot. Terrorists. The Mafia. Aliens. Ridiculous, but all got time on CNN.

If those fourteen frames were all the real evidence that he could produce from the Las Vegas incident, then the matter would never be settled, really.

Percy needed to know.

"I need more tape, darn it."

"What you really need, dear—"

"Mr. Oswald," his secretary said through the intercom, "your conference call with Las Vegas is on two. You got some other calls."

"Thank you, Hanna."

Theo stood and put on her shoes. "Do you want me to stay? Or return those calls?"

"I'll record. You take care of these notes." He handed her

his notes. "I'll ignore these messages later."

"When your conference is over," Theo said over her shoulder as she left the office, "I'll have Hanna remind you to sleep. I'll see you're not disturbed for—"

"Yes, yes, dear." Percy opened line two. "Percy Oswald here. Ms. Ward? Trustworthy Vigilance Agency?"

"Lois Ward, yes, sir. Thank you for joining us."

"'Us'? Who else is 'us'?"

Mark Trane

"Pwop me up, pwease. A bit highew." The nurse raised the bed until Mark nodded "okay."

He looked out over the side of the Rubber Duckie, his yacht, across the brown Mississippi at the Kansas City skyline. The air tasted salty. It smelled damp and cool, a welcome relief from the dry, blast furnace Las Vegas heat. *Pretty town, pretty river.*

"Too bad," he muttered. "Too bad."

"Pardon, sir?" Nurse Bianchi, short, athletic, early thirties, cheery voice, puffy hair, starched white uniform, puttered with his IV. Another dose of painkiller.

"Nothing." He stifled a cough and reached for his Tumeze, a habit. Not there.

Mark had been lucky. Officer Hanson had shielded him from debris when Hell fell and he suffered only a broken leg and minor bruises. She was still in the hospital, serious but stable. Expected to recover, but it would be months. Concussion, broken back, broken ribs, internal injuries. She'd been the most seriously injured at the scene. A hero. He found ways to thank her, and the police department, subtly, anonymously.

"Evew been on one of my cawnivaw boats, Ms. Bianchi?"

"Many times. I take my kids, sometimes I go with

friends, or with my husband. I wish there were more."

"I'ww make a note." He did. *There will be at least one more.*

He checked his watch. Mickey's hands said five minutes till the conference started. He wished he could attend in person but his doctors said no. No travel. They'd wanted him in a hospital, but he'd persuaded them to let him stay on the Rubber Duckie—temporarily. But when it got worse—

It hurt, more than the broken leg and the bruises. Not the pain. The painkillers took care of that. But *knowing.* That hurt.

"Woww me inside, pwease." He felt woozy.

The nurse rolled the bed inside the yacht's spacious cabin and jockeyed it into position. Around Mark, in easy reach, monitors, keyboards, phones, scanners, printers. Stuff. His links to the world.

"Somebody ewse's pwaygwound soon."

"Pardon, sir?"

"Nothing." He punched a number on a keyboard. A phone rang hundreds of miles away.

"Hello, Mister Trane."

"Mawk. Tewesa, you must weawn to caww me Mawk."

"Okay. Checking up on me?"

"You *have* been wewuctant. Whewe awe you now?"

She laughed. "People own cell phones so they can ask people where they are. Haven't you ever wanted to be alone?"

"No."

"Mark, I'm *right here.* Where are you?"

"I'm wight hewe, too."

"See? We're both right here. Reminds me of *Buckaroo Bonzai.* Ever see it? The movie. 'Wherever you go, there you are.'"

Mark laughed. She was interesting and fun.

"Now," she said, "when are you going to tell me what this is *really* about? Not the conference. I mean—"

"Soon." *Too soon.* "Maybe aftew."

Santiago had at first refused to attend Lois' meeting, and Mark had to use considerable pressure to get her there. The donations to the Las Vegas shelters, to the free clinic, and the local pro bono lawyer's group hadn't swayed her. The promise of a park, a people's park, where the wreckage of Hell now stood, that did it. She didn't know, yet, but she'd supervise the project.

She's curious. She knows there's something else besides this meeting. Interesting, fun, curious. Smart.

"I'm in a cab right now. We just parked at Joe's office. Crummy neighborhood. Low rent."

"Tip weww, pwease." He'd sent her enough money.

"I got it. Uh, Mark, did she tell *you* what's it all about?"

"Wois? The confewence? No."

"I'll bet you didn't ask hard. You *like* surprise parties."

"Admit it, Tewesa—you do too."

A sigh. "Yeah." A pause. "Uh, Mark, you *are* going to attend? By phone?"

"Yes, I'ww be thewe."

Mark disconnected and activated his monitor and camera in Trustworthy Vigilance Agency's office. "Take a bweak, Ms. Bianchi, pwease. I'ww caww if I need you."

"I'll be right outside." She left.

Across the small office—*Joe needs real furniture, desperately*—he saw Lois go to the door, welcome Teresa with a handshake, and usher her in. He adjusted the sound pickup and panned the camera, saw Joe in a wheelchair behind his desk. *A new desk.* Another monitor on a table next to him. Oswald looked uncomfortable and impatient despite the ever-present smile.

Where are the others? Where's Stan Gomez? No Stan, no show.

Stan Gomez

The problem with Las Vegas traffic, Stan mused, is that you could learn where the jams happen and find side routes, but you still get stuck. Construction. Or accidents.

Ahead, in the intersection, another fender-bender.

"Shitshitshitshit."

Five minutes to showtime. He'd be late. He popped a Tumeze. Even that was awkward with his arm in a cast.

His phone rang. Another crisis needed attention. He'd had no rest in the past week—eight days, actually. After Hell fell, all hell broke loose. Twenty-hour days were common for everybody.

Several officers had been injured one way or another when Hell fell. Stan had a broken arm and bruises. Miraculously, nobody had been killed. The dense crowd around the building had been protected from flying debris by a good-enough distance from the building, by chain link fence, by parked police vehicles, by barricades and police bodies and umbrellas. Nine hundred and ten injuries. Two hundred and fifty-one had been his people. All minor—*thank God for hardhats*—except Officer Hanson.

And Ripley. Correction: one fatality.

"What, what?"

Just another crisis, like the others, an endless series. He listened, solved it, found a traffic gap, got around, and drove to the meeting. He'd be late.

His arm hurt.

Goddamn Joe's dramatics anyway. "And the name of the killer is . . ." Stan screamed a girlish scream. "Thunder thunders and lightning flashes, and the lights go out, and a shot rings out. 'Aha!' detective Foxworthy declares as the lights come back on, standing over the dead body of Chief Inspector LaStraud, or whatever the hell his name was. 'The killer is . . .'" He screamed again, but stopped as a bum on the sidewalk gave him a look.

"Get a job, buddy," he muttered. The phone rang again. He ignored it, busy driving one-handed.

He parked in front of Joe's office, shut off the phone— *give me one hour of relative peace and quiet, please*—saw the cab leave—*Who the hell was* that?—and his wife's car parked nearby.

"Shitshitshitshit."

Lois opened the door for him.

"This better be good," he said. "I've got a job."

Lois nodded, tried a strained smile. She ushered him in.

Two monitors sat on a big table, one had Oswald's face on it, and the other had Mark Trane's. Joe sat behind his desk in a wheelchair. *Ironsides, but no beard.* On Joe's beat-up sofa, Teresa Santiago sat. And his wife.

"Hi, Sam," he said.

"Hi, Stan," she said.

Teresa Santiago

Teresa almost rose to let Stan Gomez sit on the sofa by his wife, but she didn't. The glare between husband and wife, as husband entered, chilled the ACed room another ten degrees.

They didn't expect to see each other. Police investigator married to murder suspect, or accomplice. Awkward. Teresa had a hunch, just by the look of them, that the Gomez's relationship had been strained long before Hell fell on Roberta Ripley.

She eased her bulk back into the lumpy sofa and watched, curious and somewhat amused. Stan pulled out a folding chair, awkwardly flipped it open with his one good arm, turned it around, straddled it, and pointedly sat as far from his wife as the room would allow. He sat near the door, as if ready to escape fast, should the need arise. His foot twitched, antsy.

Samantha crossed her arms and legs, foot a-twitch like Stan's, rolled her eyes, heaved a bosomy sigh, and theatrically ignored her husband.

Both Gomez's gave Joe silent if-looks-could-kill looks.

Nobody in the room looked comfortable.

Joe scratched a spot under his leg cast with a long stick. He'd seen Hell fall on TV, from three miles away in his hospital bed, yet he was the most banged up in the room. He looked like a little boy outside the principal's office, trying to look more churchie than Tom Sawyerish. *Guilty of something.*

Oswald's smile beamed as luminescent as ever on his monitor, but Teresa had seen the real thing, saw it right after Hell fell, and this was the fake one, the for-the-media job. *What's he got to sweat about?*

Trane looked pale and tired. He tried to smile, but it kept falling off his face and he shook his head, woozy, Rocky trying to go the distance. *Hang in there, old man. We still got to talk.*

Lois tried to look competent and smooth, In Charge, but she failed miserably. *She's so tiny. Not getting enough to eat.* The yellow bruises around her big brown eyes, the one shaved eyebrow with the caterpillar stitches, and the bandage on her elbow made her look like the little match girl, except she dressed better. Nice blue suit. She looked like the maid.

Lucky she hadn't been killed.

Teresa admitted to herself as she studied the other people in the room—in the game—she'd been fooled. She assumed this was Joe's show—he'd invited everybody—but it was Lois'. Both her demeanor and Joe's, now, said so. Teresa wondered if she'd have been more anxious to come if she'd known in the first place that Lois, the rookie detective, ran the show and not Joe, the grizzled vet. Or less. She liked Lois, nice kid, but Joe packed authority, and Teresa fought back irritation with herself. Some Enemy of the State she was, still kowtowing to authority like a good little worker bee. Vestiges of the old Good Girl remained after all these years.

No—it had been Trane who'd convinced her to come, *bribed* her, and did so without compromising her Enemy of the State status, even in her own mind. *Worth it. Especially the park.*

She thought about Teach and Captain Freddy and Tom-Tom and Little Richard and Booger and The New Kid and Mrs. Doran and Larry and what they'd think if they knew about her deal. They *would* know, soon enough. How'd she tell them—that would be a challenge. If they weren't behind her, it wouldn't work. She reminded herself it was a monument to Dog. Strength in that.

Later. Now—

So itty-bitty Lois Ward is the detective running the scene where the suspects gather and the killer gets fingered. If Joe is going along with it than she must have something.

"Ahem," Joe said. "I think we're all here."

Samantha Gomez

S amantha hadn't expected to see Stan. She wasn't sure what she'd expected. Joe had been persuasive though mysterious on the phone with his hasty, last minute invitation. He'd sounded excited. He said there'd be others but he didn't say who. He hadn't mentioned Stan. She hadn't asked. She should have been more—what? Cautious? Apprehensive?

Joe *had* mentioned Bobbie. He'd been vague but it was enough. Samantha was curious. Lois Ward had been the last one to see Bobbie alive and Ward would be there, Joe had said. Samantha had no place to go.

This last week—eight days—she'd been constantly tired, but wound up too. On edge. Couldn't sleep. The medication didn't help. Nothing seemed right.

She thought she understood why Trane was here, but why Oswald? And that bag lady?

Then Officer Wrong walked in, superior smirk in place, as ever. It worried her that he was here. Annoyed her, of course, but worried her too. The investigation into Bobbie's death was still on. She thought she'd kept their relationship on the QT, but investigators had come up with enough ties to keep them suspicious. She'd answered a gazillion questions and it was wearing her down. How did she let herself get talked into coming here without her attorney?

She glared at Joe who ignored her, scratching himself.

As she looked around the filthy little room, she wondered if any of the others had retained a lawyer. No. Joe, Ward, Trane, and Oswald had committed no crimes, weren't suspected. *Why's the bag lady here? What's Oswald's interest? What's going on?*

She sighed. If it had to do with Bobbie, she'd play along. Had too. But Stan was here, and that felt *wrong*.

The wrongness began to outweigh her curiosity and she felt on the verge of panic, felt an urge to go, just go. She'd have to pass within feet of Stan to do so, but that couldn't be helped.

She decided. She grabbed her purse, ready to stand, to leave, when Joe ahemed.

Lois Ward

Joe's ahem drew everybody's attention. He didn't say more, just nodded to Lois. She leaned on his desk, feeling small and inadequate. She hid her shaky hands behind her back and tried on a smile. It didn't take. She wished Mary was with her, in body, not just in spirit, but she had school and a big test.

Big test. Me too. She took a Tumeze. Licorice flavored.

Lois ahemed in unconscious imitation of Joe, checked her notes again, all neatly arranged on Joe's desk, and the VCR. Files. Audio tape. CDs. All in place.

"Thank you for coming," she said. In brainstorming the session the day before with Mary at home and later with Joe in the office, she'd decided to speak formally, address everybody by last names. No appeal to friendship through familiarity. Straight up, honest. Lay it all out. Confession's good for the soul.

"I've got to start clean, or this won't work." She took a breath and dived right in. "On Wednesday night, three days before Hell fell, I stole a bunch of steaks from the Hell restaurant walk-in freezer. I gave the steaks to Ms. Santiago and her friends. I can't explain why I did it. I just did, is all. I—I apologize, Mr. Trane, for stealing from you, and to you, Mr. Foxworthy, for lying, and to you, Ms. Santiago. I'm responsible for Dog's death. If I hadn't—"

"Bullshit." Teresa leaned forward, chubby elbows on knees. The sofa creaked. "Mr. Trane, sir—*Mark*—if it's anybody's fault that this girl stole those steaks, it's mine. I talked her into it. She thinks it was her idea, but it wasn't. It was mine. I shouldn't have done it, but, well, I did. It's hard to explain. Then when Dog came back—" On the verge of tears, her voice cracked and her shoulders sagged. "Dog did that on his own. Nobody's fault what Dog done but his."

Teresa turned to Stan Gomez. "Mr. Gomez, sir, it was a petty theft, hardly worth—"

"Where's all this going?" Stan Gomez glared pointedly at his wife, who refused to glare back.

"The point," Joe said, "is that we know why Dog was in the freezer."

"What happened next?" Mr. Oswald asked. He looked antsy.

"I think maybe Dog got frustrated that I didn't bring out some steaks," Lois said. "I saw him out back, Thursday and Friday nights, but I don't think he saw me. Anyway, he finally goes in. That's three a.m. Sunday morning. Easy to get in because the door's open—for safety. They'd closed the restaurant because of some structural problem, I heard, and left the door open, but they put this yellow tape to keep people out." She shrugged. "I was supposed to watch the door. I did, every half-hour or so.

"Before that, before Dog shows up—" She started the VCR. "Well, this'll explain what happened better."

Dark geometric shapes flickered on the monitor, a band of light sliced angular darkness. Vague shapes. "This is the view from the video camera down the hallway," Lois said, "looking past the back door—that bright line here on the right," she pointed with a yardstick, "to the walk-in freezer—the white rectangle here—and the hallway to the back of the casino farther on.

"Mr. Foxworthy installed his video camera at about three

p.m. Wednesday. He hid it under some towels on the top of a metal shelf against the back wall thirty feet down the hallway from the back door toward the kitchen. He did it because he had evidence from an independent informant that steaks were being stolen from Hell. The camera was there to catch the culprit—me."

"Wait a minute," Stan Gomez cut in. "You mean he didn't have any cameras in there *before?* What kind of surveillance—"

"My turn to confess," Joe said. He turned toward Mr. Trane's monitor and Mr. Trane's camera swiveled, whirred, to look back, a single unblinking eye. Lois paused the VCR. She felt faint. She knew this had to happen, she'd discussed it with Joe, but Joe had said he'd handle it himself, and would discuss it no further.

"Mr. Trane, sir," Joe said, "I had no surveillance cameras installed anywhere inside Hell from the time you hired me to guard the place until it fell down. I also over-billed you for employee hours. I claimed I had more than—well, only Lois was on the payroll."

Silence.

Lois could hear the snaky hiss of a paint gun from Loren's shop, and a faint, unintelligible but distinctly broken-hearted twang of some country and western tune on KVEG. The office AC hummed. A siren moaned far away. Teresa shifted her weight and the sofa protested.

The office smelled of fresh paint from next door.

Stan Gomez looked at Joe, jaw slack. "Joe, you better watch it. We're talking fraud here."

"Weww, Mistew Gomez," Mr. Trane said, swiveling his electronic eye to Mr. Gomez as he spoke, "it wooks wike thewe's a wot of cwime, but some cwimes awe mowe impowtant than othews."

"What?" Stan Gomez looked insulted. "How can you say that? I don't get it."

"Wemembew that Mistew Foxwowthy wepowted to Wipwey, my wight hand man. Wipwey nevew wepowted the discwepancies to me and it's not wikewy that she didn't know."

"What are you saying." Samantha Gomez's face was red.

"I still don't get it," Stan Gomez said.

Teresa and Oswald also spoke at the same time, but Lois didn't hear them either. She'd lost control—already—and she needed to get it back. Now. Desperately: "Shut up and listen to me, darn it."

Silence, instant. *So, yelling helps sometimes, and rudeness. I'll remember that.*

"We can deal with other stuff later." She glanced at Samantha. "The real crime I called you here about is who killed Dog. And why. That's more important, isn't it?"

"Maybe," Stan said. He crossed his arms and glared at Joe. "Only one tape? We've talked about withholding evidence, haven't we, Joe?"

"We've given you everything—"

"We kept a copy of the tape," Lois said. "We're giving you the rest now. Any problem with that?"

Joe shrugged and looked between Joe and Lois. It looked like Joe had finally realized this was Lois' show, not Joe's. *He's slow, but persistent. Like a bulldog.*

Lois restarted the tape. After a moment: "Here we see a woman go out the restaurant back door. You can't tell who the woman is—it's too dark but we can see she came from inside the hotel. Now I'll fast forward here." A few seconds passed in silence. "Now you see Dog enter through the back door. You can't see him well enough to identify him—too dark, but when we found the body—well, it's Dog. He looks around, then goes to the freezer, opens it—see his face in the light as he looks around? He closes the door quickly—you can't see him well now, but—see there?—he does something next to the freezer— see that in his hand? It's a broom. He opens the door, goes in, props the broom in the doorway—see the handle in the light from inside the freezer? W figure he didn't trust the door to open from the inside, afraid of being locked in. Claustrophobic?"

"Yeah," Teresa said. "He liked to sleep outside."

"Now we wait thirty-seven seconds—" They waited. Nobody spoke. Conway Twitty twanged, Loren sprayed. AC, siren, sofa. A jet flew over. Nobody spoke. Or moved.

Suddenly. "There, in the back door, the shadow. Do you see her now? She comes in, turns toward the casino, the freezer, we just see her back. A woman, that much is clear, but that's all we can tell, but if you compare tape, you'll see she's the same one who walked out the back door a couple minutes before Dog walked in. She walks to the freezer. Hesitates, listens, looks around. Grabs something by the door—the same janitorial stuff that Dog looked through to find the broom still in the door. See, it's a floor buffer. She removes the broom from the freezer door fast—see the light go out? Now you can barely make out what she does here in the dark, but we know because we saw the result later. She puts that floor buffer down so that the handle blocks the door shut, jammed between the freezer door and the back of the metal shelves beside the door. The door won't give from the inside. Of course, when we found it, it looked like it fell there when Hell fell. Now we know different. Then she leaves. Head down, we still can't make out who it is, out the back door.

"Next image comes three minutes and fifteen seconds later when Joe shows up to collect the tape and put in a new one. It was a twelve-hour tape, you see, so he had to change it at three a.m. because he'd put it in at three p.m. Then Hell falls. I mean, the first time. No need to see that. It's an anticlimax anyway. The real show's over."

Lois put the yardstick down on Joe's desk and wiped her hands. Sweaty. She'd done it. She nodded to the video monitor. "There's your killer." She turned off the VCR.

"You didn't see her face," Samantha said, a defensive whine in her voice. "It could be anybody, it could have been some—"

"It wasn't you, we know," Lois said. "You were about to arrive in the back parking lot in your white Mercedes when this happened. Joe saw you arrive and took pictures of your car. Recorded the time on his tape recorder too. Match the timing between that and what we see on the tape and you're okay. Mr. Gomez has them, the pictures, and tape. The earring you dropped? In the parking lot? Remember when I showed you at your office, how you reacted? Mr. Gomez has it. Do you still have the mate?"

Samantha's turn to glare at Stan, but it was his turn to ignore the glare.

"There might be a phone record somewhere, Mr. Gomez," Lois said, "if you want."

Samantha pointed at the VCR. "You don't know who that is, really. It's too dark—"

"Mr. Trane," Lois said, "did Ms. Ripley ever wear earrings?"

"No, she nevew wowe jewewwy. She was an acwobat, you know, befowe she took up accounting."

"So what does that—" Samantha whined, indignant.

"You can't see her face," Lois interrupted, "but you can see enough to know the woman who locked Dog in the freezer isn't wearing earrings."

"So what?" Samantha said. "People lose earrings. I— I—"

"Why do you care?" Teresa turned to Samantha, brows furrowed. Lois couldn't put her finger on her tone. Compassionate? Yes. Teresa cared that Samantha seemed to be suffering. "Was there some—*relationship*—between you and—"

"I don't care what any of you think," Samantha screamed. "You're wrong—*wrong*." She stood, fists knotted, face lobster-red and contorted. "Bobbie wouldn't hurt anybody. She—she *loved* me. And I—" She bolted for the door, wiping away tears.

The group listened in silence as Samantha gunned her engine and sped out of the parking lot, spitting gravel.

"Maybe you should—" Joe began.

"Let her go," Stan said. He rose and softly closed the door Samantha had banged open in her haste. "She won't go far. She's not a bail-jumper, my Sam. Responsible. Married to her job." He chuckled and sat. "On her way to another fender-bender." The chuckle fell off his face revealing pain etched like graffiti in the bone underneath.

He looked at Joe and Lois, sudden realization. "You weren't sure, were you? That's why she was here, so you could see her reaction?"

Joe and Lois exchanged a sober, silent glance.

"We could rule out anybody else in Hell that night," Joe said, "besides Lois. Only Ripley had cause to be there. Mr. Trane couldn't fix the time when she left. Circumstantial, but—"

"Okay," Stan said. A shrug. "Well. She knew. Must have talked with Ripley before . . ." He took out a notebook and pen and scratched a note.

Joe ahemed and motioned Lois to hand him a thin file beyond his reach. He flipped it opened, glanced at it—he knew what was there—and talked slowly. "Mr. Trane, Lois and I found evidence that prompts us to believe your Ms. Ripley was preparing to leave the country with a lot of money. Your money. Possibly she was going to take Mrs. Gomez with her, or planned to. We haven't figured that part out. We think Mrs. Gomez can fill in a lot of details. Who-knew-what and when-did-they-know-it sort-of-thing." He glanced at Stan who looked lost in some reverie located beyond the battered, mismatched filing cabinets by the far wall.

"Anyway, we think she met with Mrs. Gomez that night relative to that. I think I saw Mrs. Gomez get into the company van—the big black executive van?—parked out back just before I went in, but I'm not positive." He shrugged. "It was dark."

"Copies for me?" Stan muttered, still lost somewhere.

"Yeah, Stan. Uh, you can take it from here. We just wanted to get it started." Joe cleared his throat and shifted in his wheelchair. "Anyway, Ms. Ripley knew there was no surveillance camera in Hell, because she knew I was filing invoices for, uh, nonexistent rented surveillance equipment. She didn't tell you, Mr. Trane, because she was picking your pocket herself. Had been doing so, we believe, for quite a while, we're not sure how long. She didn't want to tell you about my, um, indiscretion, because she didn't want you to know about hers."

"So thewe wewe no camewas and she knew it. So nobody would see when she wocked that poow man in. But what about the secuwity guawds? One of them—oh. Thewe was onwy one." He coughed lightly.

Trane looks so pale. Sick?

"Ms. Ripley knew that too. She felt safe enough, but she didn't know that somebody had stolen steaks from the freezer and that I found out about it and set up a camera to catch the steak thief. She walked into a trap I didn't know I'd set for her. Though, of course, I didn't know it was her until today."

"I still don't see why she did it," Oswald said.

"Simple," Lois said. "When I was in there with her, in the back hallway, just before Hell fell that afternoon eight days ago, when I caught her trying to destroy the tape—well, you all read that story in the newspapers—but I didn't tell anybody that I'd asked her why she did it. Killed Dog, I mean. Mr. Trane, correct me if I'm wrong, but Ms. Ripley was a tidy person. You might even say she was, um, fussy, right?"

"Yes."

"How do you think she'd react if somebody scrawled graffiti on her car? The company van, I mean?"

"She'd be fuwious. She'd—"

"Graffiti?" Stan looked skeptical.

"I asked why she killed Dog and she said: 'Because of what the sonofabitch did to my car.' Pardon the language, but she said it."

"Your daughter's tape," Stan said. "It isn't too clear. We're still analyzing it." Mary had been smart enough to tape record the phone tucked in Lois' purse, and she caught the brief, tantalizing but indistinct conversation between Lois and Ms. Ripley before Hell fell.

Lois held up a piece of paper with a squiggly design on it in crayon. Mary's artwork. "Ms. Santiago, do you recognize this?"

"Yeah. Dog's sign. Big fancy D, little bitty O, squiggly G, with a tail like a dog's. He did some Fuck-the-System graffiti, pardon my French, when he thought he could get away with it. So Dog signed Mr. Trane's big van?"

"Just before he went in to steal steaks. We think Ms. Ripley was in the van at the time. She got pretty mad and followed Dog inside the back door, and—I guess she punished him."

Lois turned to Stan. "I didn't say anything to the police before because we just confirmed that there was a sign like this on the van. It took a while to find the van because it wasn't in the obvious places. We found it, yesterday, in police impound. I thought it would be a good idea to get another sample from somewhere else before I said anything. I found this," she held up Mary's drawing, "yesterday, on a trash bin behind the Sunset Bistro, where Dog hung out."

"Yeah, he slept there a lot," Teresa said. "He, he—" She broke off, dusted her eyes.

"I'm trying to follow this," Oswald said. "Really."

"Okay," Joe said. "Sequence of events." He ticked the points off on his fingers. "Ripley calls Gomez to a late night meeting in Hell's backside parking lot. We don't really know why, for sure, but Gomez comes. Ripley leaves her office, goes out the back door to the van, waits to pick up Gomez. She's in the van when Dog comes by, scratches his sign on the door—he can't see she's in there because the windows are tinted. Then he goes inside Hell to steal steaks. She follows, locks him in the freezer, returns to the van to continue waiting for Gomez. Gomez arrives. I see her cross the parking lot and get into the van. The van leaves, heads around to the front. I go into Hell to get the tape, Hell falls. That's it."

"Ripley murdered Dog because he scratched her car," Stan muttered, as if the words gave him indigestion. "Road rage in a parking lot."

"Mr. Gomez," Teresa said, "maybe Ripley didn't really kill Dog."

"What?"

"Maybe she intended to let him out. Maybe she intended to call Lois, or the police, to go let him out after a few minutes. Or maybe Dog could have gotten out himself."

"Ha on that," Stan said. "You didn't see the autopsy. He slipped on an icy spot, fell, hit his head. Unconscious, soaked in his own sweat. Malnourished. Weighed no more than a wet mouse. He froze to death."

"Would Ripley have gone back for him if the sinkhole hadn't sunk just then? Or called for help?"

Stan shook his head. "You have a lot to learn about the law, Ms. Santiago. You don't have to pull the trigger, but if you're responsible for who did—"

"You still have an investigation to conduct," Joe said. "More than one. Lois for theft. Me for fraud. Ripley for murder. Mrs. Gomez for—what?"

"Maybe not." Trane said, softly. He stifled a cough.

"Maybe not *what*," Stan said.

"If I don't pwess chawges fow the theft of the steaks, ow the fwaud? Wouwd you stiww pwosecute?"

"Is there a lawyer in the house," Oswald said.

"He's right," Stan said. "I just investigate, I don't bargain. That's a different TV show." He stood, looking old.

"Goddamn job," he muttered. "The thing about the graffiti might not have held up in court, but who knows? Ripley's dead, so what's to prosecute? Paperwork, anyway.

Thanks for the dog and pony show, Ms. Ward. I trust you'll all cooperate? From now on? While I finish up?"

"All of which," Oswald said, heatedly. He hesitated until he got everybody's attention. "All of which has nothing to do with me. Why was I invited here? I have important things to do. Things that will shape the way mankind thinks and believes for—"

"Have you checked Discovery's orbit?" Lois said.

"What?"

"You'll know what to do."

Oswald had fingers in many business pies, including Discovery Company, a Las Vegas-based sand and gravel company that subcontracted for Mark Trane Enterprises, as Lois and Joe recently discovered. Another computer disk. Lois exchanged a heavy glance with Joe, and Stan showed interest too. Oswald looked more confused than concerned. Around the room, Significant Looks darted like subpoenas searching for defendants.

"So that's why Percy's here," Teresa said. "Everybody's guilty of something. Except Mark. How do you plead, Mr. Trane?"

"Guiwty as chawged. What's the chawge?" Nobody laughed.

Stan walked to Joe's desk and scooped up his files. Lois handed him the videotape, audiocassette, and computer disks. "If there's anything more—"

"We'll call," Joe and Lois said at the same time.

"Oh, my God," Teresa said. On Trane's monitor, his face turned blue, his pale, shuddery hands clutched his chest, his mouth gaped, and his eyes bugged. A white-clad figure moved between Trane and the camera. A woman shouted for a doctor.

Busy fighting to save his life, the doctors and nurses on Trane's yacht, The Rubber Duckie, anchored across the Mississippi River from downtown Kansas City, didn't pay attention to the camera and microphone linking him, live, at least for the moment, to the meeting in Las Vegas. Lois Ward, Joe Foxworthy, Stan Gomez, Teresa Santiago, and Percy Oswald watched Mark Trane die.

Five Months Later

Lois Ward

A sudden wind gust ripped dirt from the ground and dashed it into Lois' face.

"Doggone it." She gagged and spat grit. She'd gone into the desert now and then since Steve disappeared, when she had time. When she went into the desert, she came *here*, to this stretch of dunes loosely anchored here and there by giant scarecrow-like cactus, tangled sagebrush, and stiff, dead grassy clumps. A half-hour northwest of town an ill-maintained, unmarked gravel road ended abruptly, as if the county or rancher or whoever owned it ran out of money *right here*. The road became a faint pair of ruts in the soft, gritty earth and the merest hint of a jeep trail wound among the dunes, northwesterly. Here.

This was where her dreams sent her, the rutted tracks leading close to the grave she'd seen in her dreams. Steve's grave.

She knew about the sudden violent gusts and had come prepared. She took a pair of goggles from her bag now and put them on, spitting grit.

She rubbed her ears, surprised to find them icy. She pulled up the collar of her jacket and shivered. Not as bad as the blizzards back home in Rock Springs today, but cold enough.

She looked at the familiar landscape, shadowless, the sun a hazy blob behind leaden clouds. Rain coming. She could smell the dampness.

She'd walked a half-mile in from the end of the gravel road, where she'd parked her car. The twin ruts turned sharply westward two hundred yards ahead, but she wasn't going that far. A hundred and fifty yards ahead, to the right of the ruts, northeastward, a narrow packed-dirt trail, maybe a deer trail, spotted with animal turds and the occasional pile of rodent and other small critter bones, angled off. The faint trail, hard to spot unless you looked for it, meandered amid more sand dunes, a decrepit beach eons abandoned by a prehistoric ocean. Back among those dunes, not far, maybe seventy or eighty yards, prominent twin dunes, looking like ample breasts, straddled a longish, narrow hump of darker dirt, disturbed dirt.

A grave. Steve's grave.

Maybe.

Lois stopped in the rut at the base of the trail, suddenly immensely tired, and leaned against the long-handled shovel she'd brought with her this trip. Dizzy. She hadn't eaten breakfast.

"I miss Dad," Mary had said on Christmas morning, three and a half weeks before. Mary said it wistfully but not quite sadly, as if her Dad—you could her the capital "D" in her voice—was up in Carson City on business, and he'd be home soon, but was missing the present-opening ceremonies today. Too bad. Disappointing, but not catastrophic.

No tears. Why?

That's when Lois got it. She realized that she too hadn't cried since Steve disappeared. Hope? Denial? Grief locked up in a hardened, shock-proof heart? Growing up, she'd learned to avoid pain by not drawing attention to herself. She was smart, and went that survival tactic one better. She stopped feeling. She didn't have to hide emotions she didn't have. It worked, but at a price.

She couldn't remember when she'd cried *before* Steve left.

Lois shivered and took gloves from her bag and put them on, flexing stiff fingers.

She'd talked to a psychologist that Joe knew who didn't charge her—a favor owed to Joe—but mostly she read books and surfed the Internet. Tried to educate herself. The families of the World Trade Center, Oklahoma City, and others. How To Deal With Grief 101.

Bottling it up—becoming an emotionless zombie—didn't work.

Closure, they called it. People who lose somebody have to deal with it and move on. Bury the dead. Grieve, and move on.

Lois needed to deal with Steve's death, to move on, if not for herself, then for Mary's sake. Mary's grades were bad, and there'd been trouble at school. Was that incident with the fire in the girls' bathroom a cry for help?

She'd driven around in the desert before, in the weeks after he disappeared, to see if she could see—or feel, rather—where his body lay. It didn't take long before some internal compass steered her to the gravel road and the trail beyond. To this place. To Steve's grave. Down *that* way. Not far.

She sighed, hefted the shovel, and walked down the trail. She plodded on, head down, breathing as if she were climbing Mount Everest.

She stopped, at last. Instinct told her where she stood. She looked up.

There. As she'd dreamed it. The grave.

She'd gone to within thirty yards of the grave three times since Christmas, since she'd decided to face her demons. When she got to—*this point, yes, there're my tracks from last time*—she'd stopped and chickened out, turned back. Three times.

Not this time, she'd promised herself. That's why she'd

brought the shovel, this time.

Still she hesitated, knees weak, leaning on the shovel, stomach roiling. She had a package of Tumeze in her pocket, licorice flavored, but she knew it wouldn't do any good.

What if?

The questions rose again like a disturbed hornet's nest, circling and buzzing. Hornet-sized demons, buzzing.

What if he's here? What if he isn't?

"Either way," she muttered. She anchored the shovel in the sand, took out a water bottle from her bag, and sipped. Her hands shook. "Either way." Tepid, metallic, but wet. It didn't help.

If Steve's body was under that dirt mound, then Lois had to confront the reality of his death, the end of her search for him. She'd have to grieve.

What if she couldn't cry? What would that say about her?

She didn't know how to grieve. Maybe she did, once, but she'd forgotten. That was part of the price she'd paid to don her emotional armor. *Nothing gets in, but nothing gets out.*

Worse: If he was buried here then the dreams *meant something.* However bizarre and inexplicable, she had a gift. Or curse. She saw dead people, like that kid in the movie. Really.

But she didn't see dead people. She saw their graves. Steve's. Dog's. Ms. Ripley's.

She'd dreamed about seeing Steve's grave the night he disappeared and she'd dozed off waiting for him. She'd dreamed the same dream six times since. Four times before Hell fell that first time, twice after it fell the second time.

Then, she'd dreamed about Dog, the morning after Hell fell the first time. She saw, in her dream, the closed walk-in freezer door, knew Dog lay beyond that door, dead. Just as she'd seen Steve's grave, she knew Dog lay *right there*, dead.

Then Ms. Ripley.

That cinder block that hit her head as she ducked into the

shelter of the walk-in freezer door frame the second time Hell fell had knocked her out. Then, after she'd gone unconscious, she *saw* where Ms. Ripley lay in the rubble eighty feet down the hallway. Crushed. Dead. She'd *dreamed* it.

Enough people had seen her go into Hell's back door that a rescue effort got underway while the dust still flew and the ground still shook. Mary kept her head. Smart kid. She called 9-1-1 on a separate phone right away and told police that she had a cell phone connection with her mom, trapped in Hell.

"Over here! Over here!" Mary shouted over the phone in Lois' purse as rescuers tore through the debris. They reached her in minutes. Only minor cuts and bruises and a monster headache. She revived while they dug her out. Some said it was a miracle.

"I'm okay," she told Mary first thing.

Then she told the rescuers exactly where Ms. Ripley's body lay. "Four or five feet this side of the back door to the kitchen," she'd said. "In the middle of the hallway. She's dead."

"You saw her?"

"Uh-huh." She didn't say how she saw her. Then she'd passed out again.

Three people. She'd seen the graves of three people.

She'd tried to make sense of it, but had failed, utterly. All she could find in common with the three was that she knew each, they lived in Las Vegas, and that each had died.

Why hadn't she had dreams about Mr. Trane or Erroll? She'd expected to dream about Mr. Trane's grave after the funeral but it didn't happen. When Joe asked her to take over the office while he went to bury his brother, she knew she'd see Joe over a fresh grave that night, shoulders shaking with grief. She didn't.

She'd seen Steve's grave six times, and the other graves once each. What did that mean?

Touch? Steve, yes, and she didn't remember ever having touched Ms. Ripley, or Dog. She *had* touched the steaks Dog ate, and she *had* touched Samantha Gomez's earring, and maybe

Ms. Ripley had touched it too. So what?

Time of day? Weather? Diet? She carried a recorder to add to her list of possible connections. It was a long list.

Nothing she read from the library or on the Internet helped.

No use. If she was gifted or cursed with some X-Files ability, or disability, three samples weren't enough to tell her how the phenomenon worked or why. If she were ever to understand it, she'd have to experience it again. Maybe more than once.

She dreaded that. She darn well didn't *want* to see dead people's graves.

If he *wasn't* buried here? What did that do to the dreams but make them more maddeningly unexplainable?

Maybe he was still alive, Out There, somewhere. Did that mean that when he'd left to go to the Square D to get Tumeze for Lois, he'd made up his mind to not come back? Did he *willfully* abandon his wife and child?

What could drive a man to do such a cowardly, morally indefensible act like that?

Was it *her* fault? Had she driven him away?

Maybe he didn't love her, or Mary. She *had* been cold, aloof, sometimes. No—often. Moody.

"Either way." The hornet-demons buzzed and threatened to send her running back to her car. "Either way."

They won. She pulled the shovel from the ground and started back.

Her phone rang. She stopped, took off her gloves, tucked them under her arm, and took the phone from her bag.

"Lois, Joe here."

"I'm okay, Joe. I brought my phone, like you said."

"Yeah, I know. Look, the reason I called—" Pause.

"What, Joe?"

Lois had talked with Joe about going to the desert to face her demons. "Let it go, Lois," he'd said. This was after Erroll had died. Joe knew about letting go. "Believe me, it'll hurt."

Joe. Good friend. Wore armor too, but it had holes.

"There're some mysteries that aren't meant to be solved," he'd said, desperation in his voice. "It's not like TV."

Unsolved mysteries.

Like why Erroll chose to slowly kill himself with opiates and alcohol, a suicide that took thirty years. Could Joe have saved him? Like where Joe got the strength to stand with him, defend, and help him—even to steal from Mr. Trane to get the money to help—all those years.

And Stan Gomez, retired now, living in a modest apartment a block away from the mental institution where his wife now lived, if you could call it living. Aware that she didn't love him, didn't even like him—didn't like men—he stuck with her. Why? Could he keep it up for thirty years as Joe had with Erroll?

And Dog. Dropped out of UC Berkeley months short of a degree in economics with a minor in theater. No mystery about the name—Doyle Orville Gildersleeve, and his unique appearance—but why did he drop out? Why go onto the street, and why Las Vegas?

What about Ms. Ripley? Maybe she *was* insane, but why? Joe had fragmentary evidence that she started robbing Mr. Trane the day he announced the move to Las Vegas. What happened? What drove her to abandon her loyalty to Mr. Trane and steal from him?

Percy Oswald was busy with his own mystery. The media found out, the same time his tenuous corporate involvement with the shoddy construction of Hell became known, that he believed he'd levitated Hell before Hell fell. The world laughed at him, but Mr. Oswald remained steadfast, serious, spending millions looking for independent verifiable evidence, trying to get his name out of the *National Enquirer* and into *Scientific American*.

Lois didn't laugh. She had strange dreams so she

understood mysteries and the need to solve them, to put the demons to rest.

Why hadn't more people been injured—why had only Ms. Ripley been killed—when Hell fell? The walk-in freezer had saved Lois. "Well-built," the manufacturer said. "Luck," some called it, and "miracle," others said.

And Mr. Trane. Joe was stealing from him, and Ms. Ripley too, but he let them. Why?

Joe hadn't been able to figure out how long Mr. Trane knew he was dying of cancer, didn't know if that related to the Las Vegas move, or to his naming the place Hell.

Why had Mr. Trane given Teresa Santiago control of his empire in his will, told her to dispose of it, give it all to the poor, the homeless? Free rides, free shows, sleep in the parks, take one or two or as many as you want, everybody help yourself—no charge. Give it all away, dispose of it all, down to the bare walls, then give the walls away.

Lois understood why Teresa would supervise turning the site where Hell used to be into a "people's park," but the rest? She was a self-avowed Enemy of the State. Why did she accept the massive, practically impossible commission from The Man?

Joe had evidence—inconclusive, of course—that Mr. Trane had moved to Las Vegas not to find his daughter, but to "audition" Dog for the job he gave to Teresa. "Naming the place 'Hell,'" Joe said, "may have been to provoke Dog, to test him, see what he'd do."

"Or maybe he named it Hell because of the cancer," Lois said. "Knowing he was dying and all, like a last joke?"

Joe shrugged. Another unsolved mystery.

And the search for Mr. Trane's daughter Stacey? There had been no daughter. "Stacey died in a skiing accident in Park City ten years ago," Joe told Lois. "Poor little rich girl. I've known for two years."

"Why the search, then?" Lois asked. "Why did he hire you to look for her when he knew?"

"Not just me but other PI's. He deserted his wife and daughter long ago is why. Ran away." He shrugged. "That's not the story he told me—or himself, it looks like. When or why he started to feel guilty over it, I don't know. Another mystery. But his guilt ran deep."

Lois was tired of walking, thirsty, and it was cold. She was alone in the desert, nobody around for miles. Joe's long pause irritated her. "What, Joe?"

"Two jobs."

"Two jobs?" Roommate Annie had moved back to Fresno, to live with her parents, a few weeks after Hell fell, where she had a nice fat, healthy boy. Named him Donald. Lois had moved then, to a smaller place, cheaper. On their own, her and Mary. Belt tightened, but they'd be okay. "*Two* jobs?"

"Oswald's office called. He wants us to find a photographer who was at Hell when it fell. I'd like you to start on it as soon as you get back. When can you be back?"

"The second?"

"A contract from Trane's estate. A big check. Very big."

Long pause.

"Joe? Are you there?"

"Yeah. Lois, uh, Trane wants us—that is, his estate wants us, uh—to head up, Trustworthy Vigilance Agency, that is—to continue heading up—the, uh, investigation into the whereabouts of . . ." He coughed. "Of his, uh, missing daughter."

Long pause.

"We've been funded for a long time. A *long* time."

Long pause.

"Lois, I'd like you to head the investigation. I mean, would you be willing to—"

"There are some mysteries—" She stopped. Something on the ground caught her eye. A speck of whiteness.

"Lois? Are you—"

"I'm okay. I'll call you back."

But she wasn't okay.

She hung up and put the phone in her bag. She tossed the shovel aside, took off her goggles and her gloves, lay them on the ground, and knelt on her knees by the narrow deer trail that led to the grave-like mound thirty yards away that might or might not contain her husband's body. Wind had scooped dirt away to reveal a tiny, fingernail-sized pyramid of white cardboard.

Lois gazed at the buried fragment with a kind of awe, as though it were a holy relic.

Debris and garbage litters the desert around Las Vegas for miles in all directions. A zillion glass shards from broken beer and whiskey and wine and pop bottles glitter jewel-like from any angle, reflected in the sun or, at night, in the moon's glow and the starlight and the ubiquitous city lights on the horizon. Far from civilization's constrains, where you can howl at the moon if you damn well feel like it at the top of the your lungs, dance naked, piss *right here*, screw any takers, get shit-faced drunk and throw up anywhere you please, and toss your empties anydamnwhere you feel like, that's the desert. That's what the desert is *for*. In the desert, you'll find tons of broken glass as well as a zillion beer and pop cans, new and rusted, crushed and whole, and a million plastic bottles and cardboard boxes and Styrofoam cartons and hamburger wrappers and pizza boxes and toilet paper and .22 shells and shotgun shells and condoms and Playboy magazines and Bic lighters and other crap. Lois had seen a tire complete with rim and hubcap, a burned-out motorcycle, rusted box springs, and once, a kitchen sink.

But the stretch of desert where she now knelt seemed remarkably free of litter. The litter started petering out where the gravel road ended, got rarer as she walked along the rutted road and completely vanished as she took the side trail off the ruts toward the grave. An oasis. No bottles, no cans, no bullet cartridges, no condoms here.

But here, now, excavated by the wind, this tiny, white

cardboard pyramid lay.

Lois probed with her forefinger, gingerly, knowing what it was. Not knowing how she knew, but knowing anyway, and dreading the knowledge.

Tumeze. Box. Three-roll pack. Licorice flavored.

What Steve had gone out to get for her that night.

Lois wept.

She didn't know or care what started the weeping. The box, Joe's call, Mr. Trane's guilt-ridden obsession, her bone-deep weariness, all of it combined, or something else—another darn mystery and she didn't care to bother trying to solve it.

It was time. The dam burst. She just let go and wept.

She wept long and hard. Loud, convulsive sobs shook her body to the core, and it hurt. Her lungs ached, her face ached, her shaking arms ached. She ached down to her heart. She cried on and on and on, and when it started to rain, she cried more. She had no idea how long she cried, didn't care. The tears were the universe, and she let them own her.

She'd surrendered.

But she'd won.

The demons stopped buzzing. They fell like shot-down fighter planes in a video arcade game and crashed into muddy pools of tears and rain.

She'd won.

The tears cleansed her. The tears pushed her past her fear that Steve had left because she didn't deserve being loved. No more fear that she couldn't grieve, couldn't experience pain— and therefore couldn't experience love. She *could* love, because, now the tears told her, she could feel pain. One went with the other.

She wept on, grieving for her lost husband, the life they'd never know, expunging the pain. Killing her demons.

She thought about Dog, and Teresa Santiago, and Joe and Erroll, and Stan and Samantha Gomez, and Mark Trane and Percy Oswald and even Roberta Ripley. Demons plagued them all. Death ended the struggle for Mr. Trane and Dog and Ms. Ripley, but the others still suffered. There wasn't a darn—*no, damn. Not darn. There isn't a* damn *thing I can do for them.*

But for herself? She could weep. She did.

Some mysteries are best left unsolved. That was the secret. Let it go. Grieve. Move on.

Lois let the tears wash over and anoint her decision—unconscious, but as firm as deliberate choice nonetheless—to let the grave remain unopened, leave the mystery unsolved. She wouldn't even tell the police. If Steve was there or not, didn't matter. He was gone and Lois had found the strength to grieve and move on. She had a job and she was good at it. She had a daughter and she intended to be a good mom, the best she could be.

The dreams? Who said: "I wouldn't worry about it none. Those dreams are only in your head." Some singer. Wise advice.

To hell with the dreams.

In time—who knew how long—Lois realized her tears had dried and she sat in the desert mud wracked with silent, dry sobs. She slowly stopped crying, and kneaded her sore sides and cheeks. She gathered her gloves and goggles and put them in her bag. She stood, leaning on the shovel, falling down once, so weak-kneed had she become.

In her hand, the excavated Tumeze box. Licorice flavored. Three-roll pack. She didn't bother to look at the expiration date on it. She tossed it away, toward the grave, not watching where it went. She tossed the shovel aside. She wouldn't lean on it. She'd stand on her own feet.

It had stopped raining. She started walking.

Her phone rang.

"Mom, are you okay?" Mary. "When are you coming home?"

"In a few minutes."

"Will you get some pickles? We're all out."

"Okay."

About the Author

Ken Rand is the prolific and versatile author of more than a hundred short stories, two hundred humor columns, and a dozen books, including *The Ten Percent Solution: Self-editing for the Modern Writer* (Fairwood Press); *The Paradox Stone*; *Tales of the Lucky Nickel Saloon, Second Ave, Laramie, Wyoming, U S of A* (Yard Dog Press); and *Phoenix*. He's written thousands of articles, and does interviews for *Talebones Magazine*.

In 1992, after ending two-plus decades as a broadcast and print reporter and editor in Utah and then Wyoming, Ken Rand, moved back to West Jordan, Utah, remarried his ex-wife, and began his freelance writing career in earnest. In addition to numerous awards for his work as a reporter, Rand won 2nd place in the Writers of the Future contest, 3rd place in *Star Trek: Strange New Worlds,* volume 2, and has received four honorable mentions in Year's Best anthologies.

Rand has worked as a freelance writer, reporter, photographer, talkshow host and producer, editor, PR flack, furniture mover, temporary secretary, teacher, print and broadcast ad peddler, and announcer for sports events, daredevil shows, air shows, mudbogs, and stock car races.

He grew up in the little town of Port Chicago, Calif., which no longer exists; the Navy bought it because it was in the way of their ammo depot. A hippie before he lost his hair, he lived in San Francisco in the 1960s, where he attended the first Be-In. Rand makes kaleidoscopes just for the fun of it—he is the world's only humor kaleidoscopist. His writing and living philosophy is: "Lighten up."

Official website: http://www.sfwa.org/members/rand/

9 781934 648896